FRO

Born into a serv
Kilworth had att
schools by the ag
having played truant a lot, especially in Aden
where he spent most of his time fishing and
getting lost in the Hadhramaut desert.

He left school before his fifteenth birthday
with no qualifications and signed up with the
RAF. During this time, he started to write. In
1974 his winning of the Gollancz/Sunday
Times short story competition coincided with
his leaving of the RAF. He took an English
degree at King's College, London and began
to write seriously. He has now published
fourteen novels, over fifty short stories, several books for children and some poetry. He has
been married to Annette for twenty-eight
years, and has two grown-up children.

SCIENCE
FICTION
FANTASY

GARRY KILWORTH

Frost Dancers

HarperCollinsPublishers

HarperCollins Science Fiction & Fantasy
An Imprint of HarperCollins*Publishers*
77–85 Fulham Palace Road,
Hammersmith, London W6 8JB

This paperback edition 1993
1 3 5 7 9 8 6 4 2

First published in Great Britain by
HarperCollins*Publishers* 1992

ISBN 0 586 21463 1

Set in Palatino

Printed in Great Britain by
HarperCollinsManufacturing Glasgow

Contents

Author's Note

Remarkably, there seem to have been very few naturalist books written on the hare, so I am indebted to Henry Tegner's *Wild Hares* (John Baker Ltd, 1969) which appears to be the only work available dealing solely with this familiar creature of ancient lineage. Prior to Tegner's book, the last general work on hares was published in 1896, though there may have been one since which I have failed to uncover. In keeping with their private lives, hares have a low public profile. Up until 1910, hares were classified as rodents, which of course they resented, and then they were given their own order (*lagomorphs*) along with pikas and rabbits. The rabbits they reluctantly accepted, but when asked about pikas they simply looked mystified. Then only very recently the family name of brown hares became *lepus capensis*, where previously it was *lepus europaeus*. Some of the more staid amongst them still prefer their old title, feeling their national culture is being diluted by including them with Mediterranean and African species. Opinion varies on whether to call the female and male hares does and bucks, or jills and jacks. I have chosen the latter, to separate my hares more distinctly from rabbits, and, this being a work of fiction, 'jills and jacks' seem better suited to a lyrical fantasy. The story deals with two types of hares, the common brown (field) hare, and the blue (mountain) hare. The brown hare is larger and faster, but the blue hare more confident, with its own running tricks. The shallow home that the brown hare digs for itself, and the blue hare tunnels or finds in rocks, is called a form. Rabbits are newcomers to Britain, migrants come over with the Normans in the 11th Century, while hares have been native to the land since the dinosaurs went away. In certain remote enclaves of lagomorph society, the two species still retain a suspicion of one another, though happily in the main they are tolerant of each other's differences and live side by side as cousins.

GARRY KILWORTH, 1991.

This novel is for Sam Jones

'One June morning about four years ago I saw a sight that stopped me in my tracks. It was warm and sunny, about eight-thirty, and I saw a spiral cloud whirling in the dust around a cattle trough. I realised something was spinning round at great speed and was amazed to see it was a hare. It was whirling on its hind legs with its front paws out sideways and its ears down close to its head. It did not see me and I stood still to watch, the dust rose higher and higher, as it whirled faster and faster. Suddenly it dropped down and after sitting for about thirty seconds it went sedately off. I heard my father (a gamekeeper) say he had seen them dancing in the moonlight, but I always thought he was just kidding us . . .'

Letter to Henry Tegner, naturalist,
from Florence M. Lawes (1961).

PART ONE

*

Home is the Highlands

Chapter One

On this pale spring morning, a wet mist clung to the heather, and afforded some protection from birds of prey. There were still patches of hard snow, in the shadows, and cold pockets of air in the hollows. Skelter had woken with a start, having been dozing in his form. For a moment, he hunched himself inside the short burrow, unwilling to go out into the cold half-light. He twitched his nose and sniffed, scenting the damp heather.

'Oh well,' he said to himself by way of encouragement, 'got to go some time.'

Still he didn't move, and remained listening to the other blue mountain hares, feeding on the sedge outside. Finally, hunger got the better of him and shuddering he left his form to have a good stretch in the open air. Then he gazed about him at the rest of his clan. He realised he was one of the last to wake, but he refused to recognise getting up after sleep as a competition. There was more than enough food for the clan, so who cared who got up first?

Nearby a red stag, a knobber of under two years, was grazing, occasionally lifting its head to peer into the middle distance as if dreaming of a lost time. This creature need have no fear of eagles or wildcats, and could see a lot further than Skelter. However, it was coveted by hunters that would scorn wasting ammunition on a small mountain hare.

As he nibbled away at the sedges, his favourite food, Skelter's coat gathered the moisture from the grass and heather. Every so often he would stop and shake this unwanted liquid from his body, spraying other jacks and jills in the process, getting sprayed in return.

Mountain hares being gregarious creatures, Skelter did not move too far from his neighbour, a jill called Rushie. Occasionally they spoke between mouthfuls of food.

'I've just seen a click beetle in some fir clubmoss, that's a good omen, that is,' said Rushie.

'Everything's a good omen to you. Why should click beetles be lucky?'

'Well, they're not on their own, but they are if you see them in fir clubmoss.'

Skelter considered this and then dismissed it. Rushie was one of life's optimists.

He paused in his eating to scratch the side of his head with his hind leg.

Still, it *was* a fine day. There were a few high clouds about, but nothing that foretold of bad weather. The heather swept away on all sides, like a purple flood, to splash and swirl against rocky outcrops. Saxifrage formed colourful bands around isolated tors, as if the tall stones had been decorated with garlands. In the glen below, some peat hags showed rich-brown against a green backdrop, like great gutted beasts washed up on the shores of a lake. Nearer still, a busy noisome burn, swollen with recent meltwater, flailed its passage down a stony rut in the mountainside.

There was a bird of prey, a hen-harrier, wheeling over some stunted firs. Some small mammal, a mouse perhaps, had been pinpointed. The raptor dropped, snatched at the turf, came up with a limp form. It flew over Skelter's head, and eventually met its mate in the air, where an exchange took place. The female hen-harrier turned upside down in flight, and took the food from the claws of the male in its own talons.

'Did you see that?' he asked no one in particular, and his question drifted away without receiving a reply.

Skelter gave himself another scratch.

The red knobber had moved a little closer to the patch of hares now and was gently nibbling at the grasses. Suddenly his head came up, sharply, and a ripple went through him. One or two of the hares caught it too: something in the air. For a moment the whole mountainside froze. Rushie, close to Skelter's rear, was still as a blue stone, the mist curling about her face. Only a ptarmigan, rustling amongst some sheep's fescue, seemed oblivious of the atmosphere.

Skelter's heart was pattering, not at all close to panic, but ready to pump faster if necessary.

The scene remained frozen for quite some time, until gradually a thawing took place. Hares were the first to begin eating again, though still primed for instant flight. The ptarmigan muttered to herself, not really a part of the scene, but aware just the same. The knobber was slower to melt, its big brown eyes wide, its tense body on taut strings. A ringlet butterfly played around its head, as if taunting the timid creature. Then by degrees a change came over the deer, and it too resumed feeding on the grasses.

Skelter was not ready for the thundercrack at all, and when it came, he jumped his own height off the ground.

The deer staggered forward a few paces, a raw wound under its nearside foreleg. It let out a sound of despair that tore at the roots of Skelter's fear. One rear leg went from under it, so that it collapsed on that corner. It regained its feet again, only to have another leg buckle. It managed to stagger a few rickety paces forward, its eyes wide with pain, before collapsing completely onto its face, sending puffs of mist up from the heather.

Its fall triggered instant movement amongst the other creatures on the mountainside. Hares began hurling themselves in all directions, looking for their forms. Muscled fur flew, and white tails flashed panic. There was much whistling and grinding of teeth. True to their habits the hares had wandered all over the place. They were now between each other and their forms. One or two sensible ones used the nearest form, but were soon butted out into the open again by the true owners, once the latter reached them.

Skelter telemarked around Rushie, skated near another hare, and then curved in an arc through the heather. He found his form between the two rocks. It was shaped like a short tunnel with both ends open, and when he was crouched inside, he was hidden, just. He smalled himself as much as he could, wondering why his heart didn't burst, it felt so swollen with fear.

There was the sickly smell of warm blood in the air, mingled with a harsher odour. Skelter's flattened ears picked up the sounds of men as they crashed through the heather. They were growling at each other, the tones full of triumph.

A click beetle crawled around the entrance to the form, but Skelter ignored it. He was listening intently, trying to make out from the sounds the men were making, whether or not they

15

intended to stay or roam further afield. The little knobber was dead, Skelter was sure of that, but would that satisfy them?

After a while, the beetle went away.

One thing all the creatures of glen would agree upon was that those outside its craggy walls were not to be envied. The tumbledown landscape, draped in the colours of heather, alpine lady's mantle, gentian and purple saxifrage, was a home that they all held close to their souls. The dotterels who lived at the top and looked down on the rest of the glen were satisfied that here was the heart of the world. The deer would have no other grazing ground. Ptarmigan knew that their camouflage fitted the glen so accurately they might have been fashioned from its very rocks. The stoats and wildcats had no arguments over the lack of game. The hare clans would have preferred a glen without predators, but it would have had to look exactly like the one they knew and loved, down to the last burn, outcrop, peat hag, stunted pine and hidey hollow.

No one knew, or could divulge, what the resident eagle thought about the glen that was daily mirrored in the curve of his golden eye. This fearsome raptor that circled the glen, worrying the land beneath with his sweeping shadow, was only available for opinion at mealtimes, and those that joined him in these repasts were in no position afterwards to pass on any information they had gleaned. The rest of the creatures could only guess that since his terrible beak and talons were ever present, the eagle had no quarrel with those who extolled the virtues of his home.

No matter which way Skelter chose to look, the horizon curved upwards towards the clouds. Not that hares bother very much with such distances, but he thought it as well to glance around the sky occasionally for signs of eagles. Even so, this was considered by some to be a futile precaution, a waste of effort and certainly trying on the nerves. The saying was that you never saw the eagle that took you.

Rushie said once, 'Hares are very silly creatures a lot of the time. They show off too much.'

Skelter agreed with this, for he himself was an exhibitionist, who would just as soon clown his way to the attention of others, as do something clever or dextrous. There were days when he felt strong enough to brook an eagle, and days when he would run from a wasp. There were dusks when he was full of good sense, and dawns when he was giddy and wild. He was much the same as other hares in that opposites lived comfortably within his soul, and he did not give a hare-blown whistle for critics or censors.

Skelter was slightly more level headed than most hares, which meant that he at least recognised the weaknesses of his kind, though like the others, he could do little to improve upon the situation.

Chapter Two

Skelter had been born in one of the last litters of the previous mating season and was just under a year old at the time of the knobber's death. His father was Dasher, a fine frost dancer who had attracted a jill called Fleetie, and the pair of them had three litters of leverets together. Thus Skelter had several brothers and sisters and many cousins to share his highland home with him.

Growing up had been a hazardous business, with predators around every rock, behind every cloud, but having made it this far, Skelter had gathered together a number of tricks to enable him to stay alive a little longer.

In the highlands, man was not the most dangerous of the hare enemies. For one thing the mountains did not attract vast numbers of humans: they were the last stronghold of the wilderness. For another the jacks and jills of the heather did not destroy man's crops nor bother his chickens and ducks, so they were not hunted down as pests. Any deaths from men were likely to be from lone hunters taking potshots, but without any serious intention to destroy the clans. A far worse enemy was the stoat, that wily small-eyed killer that crept up on forms and stole the leverets. Then there were eagles, foxes and the occasional wildcat.

Skelter had grown up in the highlands, never straying far from the original form where he was born. His status amongst his kind was not yet established, as he had yet had no opportunity to box. His clan, the Screesiders, like other hare clans in the district, had no permanent hierarchy. Out of the mating season they were considerably unorganised, there being no real need for any kind of due order amongst them, with ranks and positions. They were not a fighting force, out to conquer, nor was there any need for government. In the mating season, or the frost dancing as they called it, things were different. The jacks all wanted the same jills and had to box each other to sort out a pecking order, but once all that was over, the system collapsed again.

Not that there was an absence of bullies or rough hares around. There were plenty of bad-tempered toughies who would butt you, kick you sideways, or bite you if they wanted your patch to feed on. They tended to be loners though, not interested in taking over the clan. Their power was used purely to satisfy their personal needs, not because they wanted to rule. Who would want to be a leader anyway? All it seemed to bring those who tried it – the stag monarchs for example – was a lot of responsibility, and heartache when things went wrong.

In any case, the jills were bigger than the jacks, and if a jack's ego got too big for him, some jill would be sure to knock him down to size. The mountain hare jills certainly didn't care to take on the leadership of the clan. They were too busy with their families in the mating season, and quite uninterested in organising anyone else when out of it. It was known that some of the lowland brown hares had matriarchs who set themselves up as leaders, but the blue hares of the highlands wanted none of it.

There was one particular jack in the Screesider clan, just over two years old, who others kept away from as much as possible. His name was Bucker, and it was said he could kick a rock to sand if he put his mind to it. He was a big handsome male, who had won the frost dancing for the last two years, and was beloved of many jills. Fortunately for Skelter, Bucker had taken a shine to the youngster, and often paused to give him advice.

'Whatever anyone tells you,' Bucker had told Skelter, 'the best defence is camouflage. When danger's in the air, or on the ground, *freeze*. Only at the last resort do you run. There are those who will tell you they can outrun a wildcat, or confuse an eagle – that's a load of nonsense, and well they know it. Beware of braggarts, for they've been the downfall of many a sensible hare. Remember too, one very important thing that I've learned for myself. *It's not always the fastest runner that escapes the predator.*'

'What do you mean by that?' asked Skelter.

'I mean, sometimes, in certain situations, it's wiser to run at a speed which will confuse your enemy, and this is not necessarily the top speed of which you are capable.'

Skelter still did not understand. Surely, you should always run as fast as you could?

'I can't see what you mean.'

He honestly *wanted* to comprehend Bucker's strategy, but it wouldn't come right in his head.

'I can't explain it, because it depends on the situation at the time. All I'm asking you to do, is remember what I said, for there will come a time when you'll need to think beyond the simple freeze or run policy.'

Skelter thought Bucker one of the *greatest* hares of all time, but this sort of favouritism earned him the animosity of other jealous males and consequently Bucker's patronage was almost a bigger curse than it was a blessing. Skelter knew that if anything was to happen to Bucker, then he – Skelter – had best run along the wind's back and join another clan.

Since birth, Skelter and Rushie had been inseparable friends. They were close to each other in ages, though Rushie had been born at the beginning of the previous season. They remained near to each other at feeding time so that they could talk between mouthfuls, and their forms were adjacent. During the winter gathering, when hares meet in large numbers, they had remained in one another's company, exchanging views on the hares of other clans. They were like brother and sister.

One evening they were out together on the slopes near the scree, nibbling this or that as it took their fancy, when a third hare came by. Skelter recognised him as the two-year-old jack, Swifter. One of Swifter's hind legs had been damaged in a rock fall, for which he compensated with a kind of lilt to his run, but he had more than usually powerful shoulders. Swifter had once boxed himself to second place in the frost dancing, behind Bucker. He was a rough, a hare who was crazier than most, denounced by some as a rogue male with no scruples.

Swifter stopped in front of the two younger hares. Ignoring Skelter, the older jack bit the head off an alpine gentian and sat staring at Rushie as he chewed.

Finally Swifter swallowed the flower, his throat pulsing, and he nodded.

'I shall dance in the frosts for you,' he said.

20

Then, with no more ado, the bigger hare turned and skidded down a slope of grass, into the heather below.

Skelter was quite affronted for his friend.

'Who does he think he is?' said the young jack. 'Just to walk up to you like that and make a claim on you. What an offensive hare . . .'

Rushie nibbled at some heather.

'Oh, I don't know,' she said.

Skelter looked at her, astonished.

'You mean, you aren't scandalised at Swifter's behaviour?'

Rushie lifted her head, to stare Skelter in the eyes.

'No, no I'm not. Why should I be? He's a very fine jack hare, with a lot of strength. His injury was caused by a fall, not by any problems before birth. I quite like the way he paid me that compliment.'

There was confusion raging in Skelter's head. He felt sure that Rushie would be, or *should* be, offended by the blatant proposal. Surely that was not the way things were done? A male must first establish his position in the mating field for that particular season, before daring to show any preferences for a female.

'I still think it's disgraceful,' said Skelter, grinding his teeth in annoyance at both Swifter *and* Rushie now.

Rushie said, 'You wouldn't be jealous of him, I suppose?'

Once again, Skelter was nonplussed.

'Jealous? Why on earth would I be *jealous*? An old hare with a limp? Certainly not.'

'I mean, jealous because he has shown favour to me, rather than any other female. Please don't think that because we are together so often, Skelter, you and I are a *natural* mating pair. I mean, it's possible we could be, because we've always been such good friends, but . . .'

'Nothing was further from my mind,' interrupted Skelter, haughtily. 'I have no interest in you as a female, whatsoever, I swear. You're good company, the *best* of company. I prefer to be with you more than anyone else,' he was anxious to get in his denial of baser intentions, 'but not for one second have I thought of you as a potential mate.'

Now it was Rushie's turn to grind her teeth, though for what Skelter could not imagine. He had behaved perfectly in his view, not pressing any claims on her, not saying anything untoward. What was she angry about? He simply could not understand why she seemed furious at him, while the real villain Swifter, with his loose talk, was exonerated from all blameful behaviour by her. It didn't make any sense.

'So, you don't admire me?' said Rushie.

'Of course I admire you, but as a hare, not as a female for mating with. Why, you're one of the most interesting . . .'

He stopped abruptly, as Rushie butted him in the flank, sending him tumbling over the edge of a small cliff. He landed with a thump on a soft verge.

Now what was the matter with her?

When he reached the scree slope again, Rushie had gone.

Miserably, Skelter began to chew at the grasses again. Then he stopped to stare out over the mountainous landscape bloodied by a dying sun. There was a flock of birds in the sky, too distant for identification. They swept away, brushing the silent peaks that had now purpled. The next moment they were gone, down behind the high jagged horizon.

I wish I was with them, thought Skelter. I want to get away from this place, with its Swifters and Rushies. There must be other places, where a jack hare can be himself, and not have to think around corners before he says something. If I was a bird I could go where I wished, talk to whom I pleased, and when things got awkward or boring I could wing away into the clouds, find another landscape where the grass is lush and the heather just as tasty.

As these thoughts tumbled through his head, the darkness came down like fine dust, to settle on the highlands. It thickened the shadows in the dark holes and cracks of the earth, and turned familiar rocks and trees to sinister strangers. Finally, the insipid moon that had been creeping timidly up the edges of the sky, encroaching secretly on the sun's hours, was able to deepen its colour. The sun had gone and the moon was no longer afraid of comparisons with its more charismatic sibling.

Skelter dozed, falling into a half-dream state. Suddenly, down below Skelter, a ghost-hare appeared, running zig-zag in field hare fashion between and around the rocks, its pale form barely visible amongst the dark heather. It seemed to glide, rather than run, over

22

the uneven ground. Skelter was alarmed that he had been making wishes, some of which he really did not want to come true, with his ghost-hare in the vicinity. If the sacred hare had heard his thoughts it might decide to grant those wishes.

The ghost-hare stopped at the top of rise, stood on its hind legs for a moment as if surveying the land ahead, then disappeared below the crown of the hill.

Skelter was not surprised at witnessing the ghost-hare's run. Every living hare had a ghost-hare to watch over it, though since ghost-hares were few, and the living many, the spirits of the sacred hares were guardians to more than one. It was fortunate that being supernatural, the ghost-hares could be in several different places at once and thus able to take care personally of each of its charges.

The last occasion Skelter had dreamed of his ghost-hare was as a leveret, just three weeks of age, and it was a pleasant memory. Ghost-hares sometimes appeared before in the dreams of the living hares as a portent, though whether one of doom or great fortune, no hare ever found out until whatever it was actually happened. It could mean something good was coming, or something very bad, or nothing at all.

Unfortunately, ghost-hares are known to be fickle: often there's no pattern nor reason behind the dreams. They might just be lonely for contact with the quick, or fed up with the prattle of the dead. Then again, they are hares, albeit sacred and profound, and thus enjoy a joke as much as the next. Just because they're insubstantial wisps of mist flying through the heather does not mean they're made of nothing but seriousness, or are devoid of a sense of humour.

Skelter knew from the oral tales that ghost-hares are not the spirits of ordinary hares, but are most of them close to two thousand winters old. They are the souls of hares who have at one time been worshipped by humans, and are thus sacred, having been deified into immortality. Since they have roamed the earth for such a long time, and are connected with the Otherworld, they know all things. They have run the ice of new-born glaciers in ancient blizzards; between their claws are the archaic snows of yesterwinters; they have danced in the frosts of antiquity.

Ghost-hares even know some of the horrors of the Ifurin, that place which tempts hares on their way to heaven, with false trails.

23

The journey to the Otherworld, after death, is short but difficult, through thicket-covered terrain with many tracks and highways. There are strange lagomorph phantoms that whisper from the tangled briars, to come and join them in feasts and frolicking. The dead hare must beware of straying from the path, must resist the sirens of the bracken, for they are only the images of hares, fashioned by dead stoats and weasels. They lead those tempted into a place called the Perfect Here, the heaven of predators, and the souls of these unfortunate hares are forever used to feed the spirits of their old enemy.

Ghost-hares also know that the time of the living hare is relatively short. They remember the highlands when men first came from their rock burrows into the light of day, out of the depths of the earth to hunt the hare for its flesh and pelt.

But if men hunted hares, rabbits were in even greater danger, for they were slower and were easily winkled from their holes. There was a strong belief amongst hares that rabbits were the result of man's poor attempt at copying hares. Why, rabbits did not even have hair on their pads! When men had tried to copy the magnificent hare, with its lithe muscled body and powerful hind legs, they had failed miserably. Hares said they didn't mind rabbits being around, but the creatures should know their place.

When the ghost-hare had run through Skelter's dreams and disappeared, he suddenly woke and found the darkness around him. He made his way to his form, reflecting on what his dreams might mean, if anything at all.

Chapter Three

The hares were gathered in the evening hills. Delicate smoke drifted from a distant crofter's hut, curling upwards towards reddening cirrus like claw scratches in the high heavens. In and around the crags, the silver snow became pink and warm-looking. Below was a loch like a fallen moon, silent and still, shining. A tumbling burn smoothed the edges of the uncut garnets collected on its narrow bed.

It was the best time of day, when danger was at its least. The light being poor the eagles had ceased to circle and it was too early for serious concern over foxes and wildcats, who preferred the darkness. The storytelling was about to begin. Nothing was real. All had become dreamlike, a fantasy wafting before restful eyes. A time of peace. If you stared at something long enough, a piece of bracken or a flower, it melted into a haze before your eyes and eventually disappeared.

'When the world was winters young,' began the storyteller, 'there appeared on the earth a mighty lagomorph: the magnificent Kicker, whose body flowed with long lean muscle, whose ears were like tall pines, whose hind legs were two mighty rivers of strength. There also came into the landscape at the same time a creature known as the Wind.

'At that time the Wind had a shape and a form, though nobody knows today what it looked like, and it claimed to be the fastest creature on the earth. Seeing the great Kicker, the Wind issued a challenge. It cried in that wailing voice we all know so well that it wanted to race the hare, for it boasted that it would surely win.

'Kicker was intent at that period in history on creating his own kind to populate the world, but the Wind would not allow him to rest, wailing and moaning in all the hollows and valleys, and calling Kicker a coward . . .' (Skelter and the other hares gasped at this) '. . . and a loser. Until Kicker finally agreed to race the Wind.

'The Wind told Kicker that the course would be a great circle around the earth, beginning at a small island most of us hares know well. Kicker agreed to this, but stipulated that there should be no start and finish: the competitors had to run until they were so exhausted they could run no further. Thus it would be a test of stamina, as well as speed.

'Agreeing to this the Wind set off immediately and had done at least three circuits of the world before Kicker had passed the island once. The speed of the Wind was so great it tore the skin from its own back, but when it passed Kicker, the great hare shouted, "Can't you go any faster than that? I'm just warming up, but I'm wondering whether it's worth the effort. I don't want to flash past you so fast it makes you look foolish."

'The Wind screamed at this remark, and increased its speed, flattening forests, raising waves to the height of mountains, and creating dust storms on the deserts. As it did this, its flesh began to tear away in large pieces, which were devoured by the cats and dogs in its wake.

'"Really," Kicker told the Wind, as it sped by him for the seventh time, "this is going to be too easy. Having seen the best you can do, I hesitate to actually start my run, because I don't want to humiliate you."

'The Wind howled at these words, and went even faster, scattering its bones over the world in the process. They sank in the seas, were buried in the mud or frozen in blocks of ice. Once the Wind's body was gone, with nothing to contain its spirit it began to break up into smaller hurricanes and cyclones, typhoons and tornadoes, which scattered in all directions. Many of these greater parts of itself broke up into even smaller winds and breezes, right down to the tiny draughts that slide into our forms when we are resting.

'The magnificent Kicker had counted how many times the Wind had circled the earth, and taking his time he did exactly one more circuit than this number, before claiming victory over his opponent. The Wind was angry of course, but was now without shape or form, and could only rush around in its disparate parts blowing things down until it ran out of energy.

'So it was that Kicker dealt with his greatest rival, the Wind, which to this day has never recovered its physical shape, and is still scattered over the face of the earth.'

Like the other hares, Skelter listened to the recounting of the legend with pride in his ancestor, recalling the day's events in the lull that followed the tale.

It had been a typical spring day for Skelter.

He had awoken before the light, to leave his short-tunnelled form so that he could feed on the heather while the dew was fresh on its flowers. Rushie, whom he had now forgiven for acting so peculiarly over Swifter, joined him shortly afterwards, and the pair hunched amongst the grasses and sedge and bit and jerked at any piece of greenery that took their fancy.

Rushie would not sleep in a form in the shape of a tunnel, which she said was too rabbity, but preferred instead to nestle between two rocks, her back bared to the night airs. She often told Skelter she enjoyed the sensation when the stars dripped dew onto her head and woke her before the dawn.

Gradually other grey shapes appeared around them, all silent save for the nibbling and munching sounds. No one bothered anybody else. There were no battles over prime patches of grass, nor confrontations over heather. Territories were not defined, yet somehow no one encroached on the food of another. They moved around in the otherwise stillness with nary a brush of coats, intent on the feeding, yet content with what they found, the heather as large as bushes and shrubs are to a human, their fine brown eyes covering a wide angle of vision around them.

Other creatures began appearing. Some ptarmigan rattled through the scree. A stoat was spotted down by the burn, but it followed the wind in a direction away from the clan. A quarrelsome savage little shrew, uncaring of the greater size of the hares, prowled and twitched between them, muttering and grumbling to itself, tearing earthworms from their holes, attacking beetles, chewing up caterpillars, spiders and woodlice, but in such a bothersome and noisy way that other creatures moved from the vicinity, whether they were large or small. If the shrew was challenged at all, it let out a high-pitched stream of vile invective, fortunately not usually understood by the recipient unless it happened to be another shrew, and showed itself ready to take on all comers at the drop of a straw by curling back its lips to reveal its incisors, and making hostile darts at its opponent.

Hares have often remarked that if shrews were just that little bit bigger, they could have been used by the other creatures of field and sky to drive man from the face of the earth.

Skelter thought about his ghost-hare appearing in his dreams, and since nothing had happened, neither good nor bad, he mentally shrugged at the fickleness of the fantastic. You couldn't trust it, he told himself. You couldn't trust it even to *happen*. What was the point in having dreams, if they didn't tell you anything? Everyone told each other their dreams, elevating the contents to an importance they did not deserve, for nothing ever happened.

Bucker stopped by him on his way to a meeting with the elders of the clan. The big hare looked strong and self-confident, and Skelter longed for the day when he was as self-assured and respected as Bucker. Rushie would have to take more notice of him then.

'Have you seen the golden eagles this morning?' asked Bucker.

Skelter said no, he hadn't.

'Well keep a wary eye out for them. The air will be as clear as burn water today. It's a cloudless sky. The raptors will be able to cruise at a much higher level, and still pinpoint their targets. Don't just glance around the edges of the sky. Look directly up, away from the sun, and watch for that tell-tale shape drifting around up there.'

'Yes, Bucker, thanks, Bucker.'

The big hare left them to carry on feeding.

After a few seconds, Rushie mimicked, 'Yes, Bucker, of course, Bucker.'

'What's that supposed to mean?' said Skelter, looking up at his friend. 'Are you insinuating something?'

Rushie looked at him with innocent eyes.

'Of course not, Skelter.'

'Then why are you repeating . . . why are you using that funny voice?'

'Was I using a funny voice?'

'Yes, you were.'

'Oh, well I'm sorry. How's this voice, that I'm using now? Does it suit you?'

Skelter refrained from answering. Sometimes Rushie could be

28

the most infuriating creature on the mountainside. He didn't understand her, that was the trouble. There were times when he was so fond of her he felt like bursting. Then she would go and do a thing like this, making out he was some sort of crawler, kowtowing to the more important hares in the clan. Bucker was his *friend*, didn't she understand that? It was no good trying to explain such things to females, they didn't have the same kind of thoughts on such subjects. He went back to tearing at the plants around him, taking his frustration out on his breakfast.

Gradually the dawn crept down from the high peaks and crags like a grey mist, gently nosing the darkness down into the gullies, through the glens, and over the edge of the world. There the blackness stayed, in deep chasms and cracks in the earth, to rest for the day.

Shortly after a weak sun had arisen, all eating stopped and heads went up as a wailing sound came winding through the hills from a far distant human warren. There was a moment of alarmed thoughtfulness, then back to the eating. It was only some man, blowing wind from a bag of pipes, such as they did from time to time. Humans were noise-makers, with their bangings and blastings, their boomings and blarings. They put on their coloured cloth and went crashing and crying about the countryside, causing rabbits to start from their hiding places, and ducks to fly up from the lowland flumes. No hare could fathom why, and had long since given up trying.

The feeding continued well into the morning, though there were some pauses for play. Rushie and Skelter went cavorting through the rocks at one point, earning the displeasure of certain matronly jills who thought such behaviour unseemly. The pair were amused at the starchiness of elderly mountain hares.

'There's no fun in them,' said Rushie. 'They've forgotten what it's like to be young.'

While play was in progress, the morning began to cloud over, with cumulus clouds growing dark tall columns above the peaks. Heavy mists came crawling out of the heather, looking for hollows in which to brood. The rocks shone with cold sweat, as if they were emerging from a fever. Chilled alpine plants tightened their flowers into small fists.

At noon the rain fell: a hard stinging rain that soaked the fur

29

through to the bone. Hares crouched in their forms, miserably awaiting the passing of the day-darkness. The noise of the rain was uncompassionate. Hares talked to one another, over the din, keeping contact for reasons of comfort, their vision limited to a body length.

When the downpour was over, the hares emerged looking bedraggled and half their normal size. There was much shaking and fluffing of the fur, each hare taking the soaking personally, as if the sky ought to be taught a lesson one day. Other creatures, the more dainty insects and one or two small mammals, had not fared well during the storm. There were drowned forms hanging on the grasses: a butterfly like a scrap of wet tissue; a spider torn from its web and swept away; a baby bird washed from a crag.

Gradually, the world righted itself, though the rain clouds continued to threaten the earth. Perhaps it was because of them that the eagle was not seen before it struck. A dark bird coming out of a dark sky, following a rainstorm – the hares might be forgiven for their lack of vigilance. A leveret was hopping around its form, calling to its mother, near to where Skelter sat shaking his coat.

'Don't go too far from your rocks,' warned Skelter. 'Your mother won't be happy with you if you do.'

The leveret scowled at him, suggesting he mind his own business.

'Well,' shrugged Skelter, 'I'm only telling you for your own good.'

The leveret hopped on, ignoring him.

A few moments later there was a rush of wind, a flurry. Skelter's heart stopped for a second, as the panic of some strange event passed through him. A huge shadow swept over the landscape: the shadow of death. Swiftly. A living cross with a seven-foot wingspan. There was a spread of feathers, covering the sky for a moment, then a short harsh cry of triumph as claws snatched up the quarry. One brief glimpse of dark red eyes as hard as garnets – and the leveret was gone.

When Skelter looked up, the infant was a dot in the sky, a hare no longer. No doubt already dead from shock, it was something else: a piece of meat to be torn apart by raptors in an eyrie perched atop a dizzying spire of rock. Great wings flapped slowly, carrying the golden bird into the fairytale realms of the unfathomable sky.

Birds of prey were not born, like earthly creatures. There were man-demons up there, living in the clouds, that fashioned these terrible feather-and-claw slayers out of the shards of thunder and lightning.

Only two or three hares had been aware of the attack: most were going about their preening or feeding oblivious of what had happened. The mother of the leveret had her back to the spot where the incident had taken place, and was feeding on some heather. Skelter was still petrified when she turned and looked for her young, began calling, at first in a puzzled way, then plaintively.

'Gone,' one of the other witnesses finally managed to tell her. 'Taken away . . .'

The mother ran in circles, distracted, failing to comprehend or believe what was being told to her. Skelter moved away from the spot, feeling both distraught and terrified at his near brush, a feather's brush, with death. One moment the world had been quite ordinary, the next, a place of carnage. It changed as quickly as a flipped pebble changes sides. Such sudden death was part of every day, but it never failed to shake the near victims to the centre of their being.

Rushie came to him.

'What's the matter? What's happened?'

'An eagle,' said Skelter. He became irrationally angry, not with Rushie, nor even with himself, but at what seemed to him some unreasonable aspect of the natural world. 'You can watch for them, day in, day out – you post sentries, keep your wits primed every moment of the daylight, and nothing happens. The eagles stay away, circle some distant peak or glen. Then you relax, just for a moment, forgetting them, and they're *there*, a bolt out of nowhere . . .'

Rushie sympathised, told him she was pleased it had not been him. Yes, it was sad about the leveret, but they were in the most danger, the young ones who knew no better. The mortality rate amongst the infants was very high, even in a place where man seldom trod.

By mid-afternoon, the incident was behind them, almost forgotten. The mother had ceased grieving, was fussing over the rest of her brood. Bereavement for hares is a short-term sorrow, and only the ghost-hares keep a tally of the living and the dead, it being important in their between-world existence to know the balance of the natural state of things. The souls of hares become flowers on the death of the body – the spirits of mountain hares appearing as purple saxifrage, and those of field hares as harebells. One set a cluster, the other solitary. It was necessary to manage such comings and goings, to ensure that there were spiritual homes for the dying and no soul was left to wander, lost and pitiful, the mountains or the flatlands of the Otherworld.

There were no more incidents or accidents that day. Serious mists began to descend around the mountains, which offered protection for the hares, until the evening came around. Then the phantom shapes of the mountains re-emerged, and a fine evening surprised all as it came in on the back of a fresh wind.

Once the storyteller had allowed a suitable period of time for reverence, following the tale, he rose and left. This was the signal for the hares to go to their forms, for a short rest before emerging for the night feeding.

Early the following morning, the eagle attack of yesterday being now a distant memory in Skelter's young mind, the jack went on an expedition down into the glen. The moon was full and there was a gentle light which softened the crags and liquified the shadows. The landscape had a golden haze on its tumbling slopes, and dips and hollows, which opened the world and made it looked inviting. It was a magical morning, ready for investigation, ready to reveal its secrets to brave young hares. Skelter felt an unusual urge to see what the world was like, outside the slope on which the Screesiders lived. He told no one he was going, in case he was dissuaded from his intentions, for it was considered stupid to wander far from the protection of the clan's forms. He simply began to feed further and further away from Rushie and the others, until he found himself near a narrow gully which wound its way gently down the side of the mountain. There was a certain amount of fear accompanying his curiosity, which bordered on panic at times, but some inner compulsion pushed him onwards.

He took a natural path, descending to the green lushness of the glen below. There were sheep down there, big quiet animals that stumbled around, kicking loose rocks. Such creatures never bothered hares and Skelter was not in the least afraid of them. A man wandered out of a stone hut to water a bush, but he was not dangerous either. Just a shepherd who had had a late evening drink, and could not wait until the morning to go to the toilet. He was too sleepy to notice Skelter and was soon gone, back inside his overnight shelter.

Skelter continued down the slopes, more gentle now, towards the loch at the foot of the mountain. This wonderful disc of water sometimes blinded the hares on the mountainside when it mirrored the sun.

Skelter next came across a stretch of woodland, a dark forbidding place of tightly planted sitka spruce trees, set out in rows. Underfoot was nothing but pine needles. Within the trees there was a stagnant darkness that never changed. The ebb and flow of night and day did not penetrate this unnatural woodland as it did the clumps of gnarled and crooked Scots pine, and the darkness had a musty staleness to it. It was heavy, still and unsavoury, and Skelter was glad to be out on the other side. No creatures lived in that poisonous darkness: it was a dead place, without movement, without sound.

Suddenly, a fox appeared, but with an unrecognisable creature between its jaws. Skelter froze, thanking his ghost-hare that the fox was upwind. It passed by, either unheeding or unaware of the hare. Soon it had merged with the rocks and stones, and was gone.

Skelter continued his journey towards the loch, until he came to the roadway that skirted the stretch of water. He rested on the edge of this black strip, nibbling at grasses that tasted and smelled faintly of the oil that sometimes floated on the surface of peat-bog pools. While he was chewing a bright light suddenly appeared and came straight for him, blinding him, then swung away at the last minute taking a roar of noise with it.

Skelter's pattering heart soon settled down again. It had been nothing but a vehicle: the machines that men went inside. Skelter had been told about them often, and had seen them from the heights, like black beetles winding around the loch. They were much bigger down here, and their eyes much brighter, but he knew that they never left that strip of black and as long as he stayed on the grass, he was safe.

What a monster though! he thought to himself. The cars and trucks could take on golden eagles, and eat them alive, if they were not so rigid in their movements. Of course, they were fashioned of metal, the same stuff men made their guns and wire fences and gin-traps from. Metal had a cold hard smell about it and hares were mistrustful of anything that was made of metal.

Eventually the dawn came, like a fine mist of light through the gaps in the mountains. The golden haze drifted away, to be replaced by a harsher light. Still, Skelter saw no reason to rush back to the clan. He was learning things down here in the glen. More vehicles had swept past him, and he was becoming used to them. He had seen an owl, sitting on the overhead wires that ran alongside the road. It seemed to be doing nothing, looking at something far away, beyond the ken of lowly hares.

A man came, walking his dog, so Skelter skipped into the rocks and hid there while the border collie sniffed along at the edge of the road, destroying his sensitive nostrils with the residue fumes of the vehicles. It failed to pick up even the strongest of animal scents, let alone the nuances that a fox would recognise immediately. Soon the pair were gone, and Skelter felt free to wander once more.

As the morning grew, Skelter became lonely, and decided to go back to his clan. He took the same route, up the mountain path, thinking that the world outside was a tame place really, almost as safe as his mountain home.

When he got back, Rushie asked him where he had been.

'Oh, I've been to look at the world,' he replied nonchalantly.

She stared at him for a moment.

'You left the clan? Are you mad?'

He was stung by this criticism, knowing it had some foundation. It had been a very silly thing for a yearling to do, but how could you explain a strong feeling to anyone? *I just felt I had to go.* Rushie would sniff at that explanation without a doubt. So he just hunched his shoulders and said, 'Not really.'

'Not really,' she repeated, in that funny tone she used when she did not understand something. 'Not really.'

She shook her head and began nibbling some sedge, but after a while he felt her eyes on him, and he looked up enquiringly.

'Yes?' he said.

'I was just wondering,' she asked, 'what it was like? The outside world I mean.'

'Oh,' he replied. 'Nothing to shout about.'

Chapter Four

One morning Skelter's life took a dramatic turn.

The Screesider clan were out feeding, as usual, just before the dawn. Other clans around the mountains and glens were doing just the same thing. If anyone believed that danger was in the air, they thought it was from foxes, rather than any other predator. No wildcats had been seen in a long time, and the visibility was too poor for the eagles.

A grey light reluctantly crept into the sky. The slopes were peaceful. The peaks were hidden in low cloud.

Suddenly, from above the scree, came the most terrifying sound the hares had ever heard. A hundred stoats, a thousand weasels could not have made such a noise. There were high-pitched whistles, screams, clashing sounds. The hares were petrified. Then came the smell of men and dogs.

Still the hares did not run. They were frozen into immobility, their best defence. Hearts were pattering against ribcages. Eyes were round with unknown fear. Legs were on taut springs, ready for flight.

The noise came nearer, and then out of the mists came a long line, a crescent of men, some being pulled along by dogs on leashes. There were sticks in human hands and they were beating the heather. There were round metal lids in the fists of others, which were clashed together. Horns were being blown, no longer muted by the thick vapours of the peaks. They blared panic into hare hearts. Whistles sounded, shrill and threatening, piercing hare eardrums like thin needles.

The figures were dark and sinister, as if they had come straight from the earth, had emerged from rock and mud. It was a hellish sight, accompanied by a hellish sound. What was going on? Who had done what to deserve this concentrated attack from mankind? What were they going to do?

The first hare bolted. Then another, then another, split seconds apart. Finally the whole hillside erupted with starting hares as they fled from the noise, not waiting to find out the answers to these questions. The humans were after *them*, of this they were almost sure, and they weren't going to wait around to be fully convinced.

His eyes bulging, his blood screaming, Skelter ran in a wide arc down the mountainside, away from the line of beaters. His mind was a haze of panic. He did not know where he was going, nor why, he just went. Rocks, shrubs, tufts flashed by him, moving the other way. There were hares whistling now, a note of desperation, which added to the confusion. The landscape was a whirlwind of grey shapes.

Twice Skelter lost his legs and went tumbling over, only to retrieve his feet without even breaking his stride. His fear would not allow him to think and he plunged across a burn and headed towards a cliff. At the last moment something made him swerve: it might have been a cry from another hare that went over the edge. He found himself racing along the rim of the cliff, then down into the glen as the slope fell away to the side.

In a narrow gully, the natural funnel for the hares coming from the slopes of scree, he considered he was close to safety. The beaters were a long way up the hillside now and advancing only very slowly. The sides of the gully were deep enough to hide his racing form, as he careered along its bottom. They could not see him and the dogs did not follow. He could smell the water of the loch below and was intent on reaching it, knowing that around its edge were tall grasses in which he could hide.

Suddenly he hit an impassable elastic barrier. He went into a ball as the barrier whipped round him, jerking him to a painful halt. It held him tightly enmeshed. He kicked and struggled with his bonds, but only succeeded in becoming more entangled. Finally, when he stopped thrashing, he found himself wrapped in a net. There were other hares with him. He could hear Rushie nearby, grinding her teeth, and whistling. Every so often the net would jerk as some other unfortunate victim was brought to an elasticated halt.

After a few moments, rough fingers grasped Skelter firmly by the ears. The indignation which might have been felt over such handling was swamped by the fear in his breast. Never in his life before had he been held captive, not even by another hare. It was a horrifying experience, and every vestige of confidence left his body. He knew he was going to die.

The net was peeled away and fine string was retrieved from between his toes, from the angles created by his hind legs. Finally he was held aloft, his body like a plumb bob above the earth, his back legs kicking futilely down at air. He could smell burnt foliage on the man's breath, and fermented food. There were other odours, from his clothes, and unpleasant, though sweeter, scents from his skin. Skelter was held up at eye level and was stared into, as if he were a vessel, his inmost thoughts exposed to the bright eyes of his captor.

The man let out a roar, his teeth rattling in his mouth, his face creased. It was a ghastly sight, a terrible sound, which had Skelter squealing for mercy. The man was surely going to eat him *alive*. The horrible mouth was open, slavering, and the stinking breath was foul in Skelter's nostrils. Yes, his head would be bitten clean off, swallowed, his body left to kick out the last of his miserable life. The terror was at its highest pitch.

Then Skelter was swung through the air, released, and he landed on something hard. He was in an enclosed wooden space, and he scrabbled to get out immediately. Something stopped him, even though the front of the container seemed open to the air. Every time he threw himself against it, he rebounded back into the wooden interior. Then, when his terror would let him see straight, he realised that the front of the cage was covered with a stiff net of metal. He was still trapped.

He found a corner of the cage, and hunched there, defecating in his fright. There was some hay on the bottom of his prison and he tried to hide his head beneath it, to escape the glare of his captor. Soon the man left him, presumably to deal with other captive hares.

The cage was eventually lifted up and carried down the hillside, to the roadway at the bottom, where large vehicles waited. Into these the hares were stacked, then the back of the vehicle was closed, and suddenly it was night. There was no evening, no fading of the light: darkness fell, deeper than any night known before. Shortly after this a growling noise filled the blackness, there were vibrations shaking the world, and then the feeling of motion. Skelter gripped the wooden floor of his cage with his claws, thinking he was going to slide into some great pit without a bottom, and fall forever downwards.

Skelter could not see any of his clan in the darkness of course, but he could smell and hear them.

'Who's there?' he whispered. 'This is Skelter.'

'Bucker.'

'Swifter.'

'Rushie!'

There were other names.

'What's happening to us?' asked Skelter. 'Bucker, you know things. What's happening?'

Bucker said, 'I don't know. I really don't know,' and Skelter could hear the suppressed panic in his voice.

If the great Bucker was afraid, what chance did the rest of them stand. However, a jill by the name of Sprintie, came in straight afterwards with some ideas. She did not sound as terrified as Bucker seemed to be.

'I expect we're being taken away to be killed and eaten,' she said. 'If they had killed us on the mountain, our carcasses would not last long before rotting. I think they want to keep us fresh.'

'What's wrong with rotten meat?' asked Skelter. 'Hawks eat it all the time.'

'Some carnivores get sick when they eat tainted food,' came the reply.

Rushie asked Sprintie, 'Aren't you afraid, if they're going to kill us?'

'It won't be now, and when it does come, it'll be quick. We'll never see our mountain again, that's for sure. I'd rather die anyway than live the rest of my life in a cage. Yes, I'm a little scared, but what can the worst be? A knock on the head, and you wake up as a flower.'

'You think so?' said Skelter.

'I'm certain of it,' replied Sprintie.

So the hares settled down despondently, ready for the worst, it being only death after all. Skelter wished the motion would end, as he was feeling giddy and ill, with the smell of oil, the fumes and the rocking.

Finally, the motion ceased, but outside the vehicle were sounds which could only have been created by men. There were mechanical things all around, and the barking of humans, and other unidentifiable noises. The night into which they had suddenly been plunged remained with them. None of the hares went to sleep for a long long time, and then when they did drop off, it was a light sleep, interrupted by many awakenings.

Daylight came as suddenly as night had fallen, and they were given food and water. The food was not fresh, but it was edible. The water smelled and tasted foul, as if it had been treated with some hillside minerals. Bucker said he thought it was poisoned, and though they all drank it because they were desperately thirsty, they lay there afterwards expecting to keel over and die with stomach cramps.

During that day, they were allowed to remain in the light. They were disconsolate and morose, lying on the bottom of their cages, only occasionally communicating. Once, one of them began thumping on the drum-like wood of her cage and the others followed suit until a heavy banging on the side of the metal box, accompanied by a loud human roar, stopped even that harmless pastime. Towards evening the whole place began to smell badly, of urine and faeces, and damp wood and hay where water had been spilled. The atmosphere became unpleasant and it was difficult to sleep. Cabbage stalks were left, and the odour from these was an additional irritant to the hares, who longed for the scent of growing heather. Bucker tried to kick his way out of the back of his cage, but it was a hopeless attempt at the impossible.

There came another night, and a day, with more of the same, then they were handled again. The cages were taken out of the back of the metal box and put in another one: part of a long line of trucks standing on metal rails. Doors were closed, the darkness came, but not as deep as before. Motion. Motion. Motion. A rhythmic rattling sound accompanied their passage into the unknown which hypnotised them into drowsiness.

Then the cages began to disappear as they stopped at places on their journey. First one, then another, then two or three at once, until only Rushie and Skelter remained to wonder what was going to happen to them.

For all they knew, the others had been killed and eaten by the time they were eventually lifted out of the truck, and placed on the concrete ready for collection by some human with a fierce hunger. When the vehicle in which they had been brought began moving again and disappeared into the distance, they could see the shining rails in either direction, going on forever. The landscape around the tracks was flat and dismal-looking, with not even a knoll, let alone a mountain, to break the monotony. There were buildings everywhere: not just a house here, a house there, like in the highlands, but masses and masses of them, stretching out in ugly array on all sides. Oil and smoke and fumes choked the air, and they found it difficult to breathe without feeling sick. There was a tremendous amount of noise too, of metal against metal, rubber against rock.

Human legs went by them, at a fast pace, their feet encased in polished hide. Once or twice a face came down to peer inside the cage, and teeth were bared on both sides of the wire. Skelter could not sense or smell any anger when these humans revealed their fangs, only a kind of amusement, as if the hares were things to be dallied with, as a twig or a root is played with by a leveret.

The cages were eventually placed on a trolley and rolled the length of the platform. Both hares were by this time resigned to their fate, and hardly even spoke to one another. They simply waited for death.

They were taken in yet another vehicle, out to a place which smelled not of oil and other man odours, but of rotting vegetation and confined animals. It was, they realised, a farm – similar to those in the highlands. There were the smells and sounds of domestic beasts: of cattle and horses, chickens, rabbits, ducks . . . and horror, of *dogs*. There was mud there, though, which was preferable to concrete, and grass and other familiar scents. Skelter told Rushie that if he was going to die, it was better here, than in some place of concrete and metal.

The cages were carried and put inside a large shed, where other animals were in captivity. A dog prowled around the floor, glanced up at them, yawned, but seemed totally uninterested in the hares. In fact chickens ran by the dog without fear. Unlike the dogs that accompanied walkers in the highlands which went berserk at the sight of any creature of the wild, especially hares and rabbits, this hound was so used to chickens, rabbits, ducks and other small livestock, it paid no attention to them whatsoever.

There was a kind of lethargy about all the animals and birds on the farm, each of whom knew that their next meal was coming at an appropriate time, that they would not have to hunt or forage for their sustenance, so they had lost much of their instinctive edge. They were timid domestic creatures, who had been de-wilded over generations, until they were pale shadows of their former savage ancestors.

When the hares had been there a short while, they realised they were in the same shed as a white rabbit. The tame animal had not taken the initiative, but now Skelter spoke to it.

'Hey, you. How long have you been here?'

The rabbit looked up from munching a carrot and stared at Skelter with soft brown eyes.

'Are you talking to me?'

'Yes, of course,' replied Skelter, surprised.

'In that case, you address me as Snowy, and treat me with a little more respect. I've been here two years, which means I have seniority over you in all things.'

Rushie chipped in.

'Seniority for *what*? We're all locked in cages.'

'You might be, but I'm let out occasionally, to run around the yard. I'm trusted not to run away, which they will never do with you wild creatures.'

Skelter said, 'Doesn't the dog bother you? Or the cat?'

Snowy twitched his nose.

'The cats – there are two of them, a big ginger tom by the name of Skeets, and Blackie, a spayed female – they can be a bit of a nuisance sometimes, but I just need to butt them, and they soon disappear. The dog, Rascal, he's no trouble. He's a border collie, a bit soft in the head.'

Skelter was astonished.

'You know the names of these carnivores?'

The rabbit explained, in bored tones, that there was a common language amongst domestic livestock, called Farmyardese, through which they all communicated. Certain creatures, like himself, retained the old family language out of a sense of pride, but others, like the cows, had been in captivity for so long they knew only Farmyardese.

'They are no longer what they were, but a separate species altogether now. The domestic cow – I mean, is there any other kind?'

Rushie wanted to know what would happen to them, the hares.

'Will we be kept as pets, like you?'

'No. They'll eventually come to take you away.'

Skelter asked, 'Where to?' but the rabbit would not answer.

'It's not up to me to tell you that. I know, of course, because the dog who goes everywhere with the master, has told me – but I don't think you want to know. It would scare you too much and I hate to see frightened hares.'

Skelter thought that perhaps the rabbit was just showing off, and trying to worry them for some amusement of its own. After all, the creature must have been bored out of its mind, sitting in a cage for the whole of its life. So it got out once in a while, to roam the farmyard? There was about as much excitement in that, as there was in being confined to a cage.

That night, the highland hare thought about his adventures, and the fact that he was still alive. He was missing his mountains and glens, the scent of the bee-humming heather, the smell of rain on the grasses, the deer gathering on the slopes – their antlers tangled with the mist, the wild peaks and crags battling with the clouds, the rushy burns and placid lochs full of sweet clear water, the salmon silver-leaping falls, even the wildcats and eagles – he missed even these old enemies – at least they were not like this lot around him, stuffed creatures with lack-lustre eyes and slack mouths, waiting out their whole lives for the excitement of death.

'I miss the highlands,' he said softly to Rushie, who was in the cage below him. 'I miss them badly.'

'So do I,' came the mournful reply.

There was nothing the pair of them could do about it but commiserate with one another. It seemed Sprintie was right, they would never see their old home again. How would they find their way back there, even if they escaped? There were stories of cats and dogs who found their old homes, after being taken away from them and dumped in a strange place, but they were creatures who wandered over the landscape anyway. They were not like hares, who did not venture too far from home, once home was established.

Night on the farm was a quiet time, with just the shuffling of the cows and the occasional snorting of the pigs to break the silence. The dog got up and wandered around occasionally, his chain clinking, but nothing spectacular happened. With the dawn – actually quite a long time before it – the cock began crowing and the pigs started squealing and becoming restive. When grey light appeared at the shed window, they could hear humans tramping over the yard, and the sound of buckets.

Then the pigs really began to let loose, as if they were having a battle over the slops they were being fed, shrieking at each other in the most obscene way. It alarmed both Rushie and Skelter for a while, until they got used to it, and Snowy told them it happened at every meal.

'Pigs are such pigs,' he told them. 'They always want what the other one is eating . . .'

The cows were led out to pasture, the tractor was started and went off into the morning, the dog barked at visitors, the cats went looking for rats in the barn, the hens were continually harassed by the rooster, and there were enough noises to keep any hare primed and ready for flight. These sounds later became merely interesting, and finally, as their time at the farm wore on, actually quite boring.

44

Chapter Five

The days on the farm were well spent, for Skelter learned more during that period, about humans and all those connected with them, than he would in a thousand years on the mountains. He sometimes wondered, at the end of two weeks, whether he might not know more than the ghost-hares who rode with a warrior queen in those far-off days of legend, when hares were deities and worshipped by men. He mentioned this to Rushie, who rebuked him sharply for his blasphemy.

In the evenings, a man came with food and water and grumbled at all the animals in turn. There was no coherence in this primitive attempt at speech, and like most wild animals, Skelter was convinced that humans communicated by gesticulation and motion, because the moans and coughs they produced could surely have no meaning in themselves. On the other side, they waved their arms continually, showed the palms of their hands, blinked their eyes and blew their noses, shrugged their shoulders, bared their teeth, furrowed their brows, and performed all manner of bodily movements. These gestures and physical demonstrations simply had to be the signs that carried the information, and the grunts and groans were just superficial accompaniment. Skelter was of the belief that most of the time the humans remained unaware of the noises they were making: that it was a subconscious act.

In the early morning, just after the light, the men would be around in the yard. Sometimes the shed door was left open and the hares could see the ungainly humans blowing steam from their mouths, clapping their chapped hands together and stamping their feet. It was a ritual, carried out every day, before the men did things with all sorts of metal containers and machines. They played all day with these contraptions, making noises, churning up things, providing fodder for the animals.

In the dawn too, the milk was stolen from the cows, none of whom were pregnant anyway, and the eggs taken from the chickens, none of which were fertilised either. It was a strange business. The humans did not drink the milk, nor eat the eggs: there was too much, too many, of both. They put them in containers which were collected by other men.

One thing was certain, everyone was well fed, well looked after, and not an animal was forgotten. Snowy had been there two years, without being eaten, though he told them that chickens, piglets and other creatures disappeared from time to time. There were sheep too, said Snowy, out in the fields. Skelter knew about sheep, from the mountains, where some of them roamed free. Free that is, until the shepherd came to round them up, and they went stupidly with him to lose their coats or their heads.

For most of the time though, the hares were bored. They felt that some kind of threat hung over their heads (which Snowy refused to go into), but terror loses its edge when it is ever present, especially as an unknown quantity.

'Have you ever tried to escape?' Rushie asked Snowy.

The fat white rabbit said that he had, and what was more, had been successful.

'I run away for a while every spring,' he said, 'when I can smell the sweet scent of something, I don't know, *enticing*, in the air. It never gets me anywhere, perhaps because I don't really know what I'm looking for, but at least there's a sense of freedom for a while. Not that I want to be free *permanently*, of course – I'd have to feed myself, and all that sort of thing.'

The two hares decided that Snowy was a pretty hopeless case. He had been born, like his parents and grandparents before him, in captivity. It would take a major upheaval in the animal world to prise him away from his soft way of life.

There was a small human who came into the shed every so often, took Snowy out of his cage, and cradled the rabbit in its arms. Hands would stroke the white fur lovingly, and noises like the cooing of pigeons came from the youngster's mouth. Skelter and Rushie shuddered at the idea of being held, and when the young human came to the front of their cages, they cowered in the corners, scrabbling to get out when the youngster made sudden moves, as humans were wont to do.

'He just wants to stroke you,' said Snowy, encouragingly.

'Not interested,' snapped Skelter. 'I'll bite the first finger that touches my fur.'

Snowy shook his head sadly.

'You'll never get anywhere like that. If you make friends with the boy, he'll start to cry when they come to take you away, and then they'll have to let you stay. The boy is very important around here, more important than the men. You get into his heart, and there's no end to the treats you get. On the other hand, he's in thick with the ginger tom, and if you upset him he's likely to leave your cage open, the shed door shut, and the big cat on the inside – if you see what I mean.'

'I'll take my chances,' muttered Skelter, but he resolved not to bite the finger that was constantly poked through the holes in the wire, just in case the story about the cat was true. Neither Rushie nor he wanted any doings with the mighty Skeets, whose dour expression and belligerent eye had already been turned in their direction.

The tom had prowled the interior of the shed, stopping to stare at the newcomers, while Snowy chattered away in Farmyardese. The cat, though he must have been listening, did not bother to answer the rabbit once. Then the feline monster, with one piece of his ear missing and a deep scratchmark on his nose, blinked slowly and left the vicinity. There was no mistaking the malevolence of his gaze. It burned a deep impression in Skelter's brain.

The boy and the cat were not the only dangers. There was also one of the men, who came in nightly to stare at Rushie, who was slightly larger and meatier than Skelter. There was no mistaking the look in the man's eyes, which was that of a predator viewing a possible meal.

'What's he doing?' whispered Rushie to Snowy, when the man was present one evening. 'Why's he looking at me like that?'

'He's wondering whether to risk stealing you or not. He's one of the farmhands, and he likes jugged hare. He's wondering to himself whether he can get away with grabbing you now, breaking your neck, and taking you home to hang on his back door. He's wondering whether he can do it, leave your cage door open, and hope that the farmer thinks you've escaped.'

'Jugged hare?' said Rushie in a small voice, not taking her eyes from the human face, with its grizzled chin and dull eyes. The man's teeth were stained brown from inhaling smoke and the gums were retracting to reveal the roots. Rushie could think of nothing worse than being torn apart by such ugly teeth.

'Jugged hare is where they kill you, hang you up until the flesh is rotten, then cook you inside a jug standing in a saucepan. Hares are too tough to eat even boiled or roasted when they're first caught. They have to let you soften a bit first.'

The man reached forward, as if going for the cage door catch.

Rushie jumped, and began thumping the back of the box with her hind legs, setting up an awful din. The man bit his lip and looked towards the shed door. Then his hand dropped to his side and he hurried away.

'That was a close one,' said Skelter. 'He was really going to do it, wasn't he?'

'Bet your life on it,' replied Snowy, 'and he'll be back.'

'Is that really true about jugged hare? How do you know all these things? You can't talk to humans.'

Snowy gave an impatient sigh.

'The dog – he sees everything – an observer. He's got eyes in his head. He watches what happens to dead hares in the house. They get hung on a nail on the back of the door until they smell high, then they're jugged and put in boiling water.'

'Disgusting,' said Skelter, vehemently.

'Depends whether you're a man or a hare – or even a rabbit,' said Snowy, matter-of-factly.

Two days later Skelter woke in the middle of the night with a start, and thought he caught a movement, a shadow flitting through the strips of moonlight coming through the gaps in the shed walls. In his old home it might have been an owl passing across the face of the moon, or a fish sliding its back above the surface of the loch, but he was not in the mountains, he was confined within one of man's prisons. Skelter was immediately on the alert, staring round the shed, finding nothing. Only the spiders whispering in the corners of their webs, and the mice muttering in the jungle of pots and boxes, were awake. Eventually he called out to Rushie, and got no reply from the jill. At this he became thoroughly frightened and shouted to Snowy, waking the rabbit from a deep sleep.

'Where's Rushie? You can see into her cage from where you are? What's happened to her? Is she ill?'

'Gone,' Snowy said, peering across the shed.

'What do you mean *gone*?' cried Skelter. 'Gone where? She can't have just . . . gone.'

'I didn't see it, but I think she's been taken. Her cage door is open, and there's no one inside.'

'We would have heard. *I* would have heard. She's just escaped that's all. She's got out herself.'

Snowy's coat glistened like white dust in the glittering changes of the moon. His eyes showed red. They looked misty in the light that fell across his face in golden stripes.

'The robber is a very stealthy man. He would have had her cage open and chopped her neck with his hand, before she even realised what was happening. I expect she never even woke up. Best forget her, and thank the stars that you're a rangy-looking hare, all string and muscle.'

Forget her! How could he forget her? It just could not be possible that someone could sneak in like that, in the quiet of the night, and kill Rushie without anyone hearing. That was beyond understanding.

'You don't know what you're saying,' he told Snowy.

Snowy shook his floppy ears.

'You think you will remember forever, but you won't. I've seen them come and go. I know about these feelings. You'll be worried about your own hide, soon enough, and then the sadness will leave you as quick as a ghost departing at cock crow.'

Skelter denied this, vehemently.

If Skelter had been unhappy before, it was nothing compared with the misery he felt now. It was as if a big chasm had opened inside him, and his heart had dropped into it, lost forever. He was alone. Whatever dire experience lay before him, that Snowy preferred to keep to himself, it was to be faced without Rushie by his side. Somehow all dangers had seemed less threatening when she had been there with him. He could not have felt more wretched were the hare thief to come into the shed right at that moment and take him away for the pot too.

The rest of that day he lay in melancholy silence, while Snowy chattered on about himself and things that concerned tame white rabbits. His inane monologues might have driven another hare mad, but Skelter was lost within himself, out of the reach of ordinary beings, even halfwits like Snowy. There was darkness in there, and loneliness, and deep despair. In the last few days he had lost everything and everyone he had known since he was a leveret. His beloved mountain home, his friends and relations, his prospects of mating with his jill. Nothing remained. There would be no miraculous escape, no wonderful rescue, no new beginning. It all went with Rushie.

Skelter only saw the man who liked jugged hare once more: he came into the shed and glanced around at the cages. The man's nose was swathed in pink-and-white pads. He stared at Skelter, gave a shudder, and left.

'What was that on his nose?' Skelter asked of the pet rabbit.

'Things for injuries,' replied Snowy. 'When they cut themselves they cover the wound with sticky pieces of cloth.'

'Oh,' replied Skelter, not really any wiser, 'strange habit.'

Day followed night, and night followed day, and nothing changed radically around the farm. Skelter thought idly that they must have forgotten why they had brought him to the farm, though it was possible that the young human had pleaded for his life, and had his request granted. Who could tell? There was no fathoming human behaviour.

Every day too, came new pain, as Rushie was missed. There was no one to talk to now, about the heather and the lochs, the burns and breeze, the tall pines. Through the shed door Skelter could see a dirty pond where ducks squabbled and played in the murky waters. This was the replacement for his loch. A tap by the farmhouse dribbled constantly, forming a stream in the mud which ran by the chicken coop. This was his burn. Not far away was the orchard, the plum trees just beginning to show blossoms, and in the far distance, an oak and an elm stood near enough together to be regarded as combatants for air space and water. Skelter could imagine the struggle going on between their roots, grappling with each other beneath the surface of the soil. These were his pines.

As for the mountains, there were none. Not a bump showed above the flat and level landscape, which gave hope for anything like a hill, let alone a ben. Without mountains there could be no glens. Without glens, there was no music for the soul, no spirit of landscape. Who in their right mind could grow fond of these flatlands, surrounded by marsh, with their ugly stunted alders and green scummy ponds? What was out there to get the heart singing, to get the spirit soaring? Bleak, dismal landscape that it was.

On a fine day, when the doors were wide open, Skelter could see a machine moving up and down the fields, with a regularity and precision he had never seen before. It left furrows behind it: long and straight.

'What's that out there?' he asked of Snowy. 'That machine thing?'

'That? Haven't you seen one of those before? I thought you had farms up there in those highlands you keep mooning over. That's the tractor we hear being started in the mornings. It's for pulling things. Ploughs, harrows, that sort of thing. So that crops can be planted, harvests harvested, and fat white rabbits can be fed. That's what that is.'

The fact was, Skelter's highland farms had bred sheep and only grew vegetables in small patches, outside the crofts. There was no place for these tractor things where he came from. Still, it looked a contented machine as it puffed and chugged its way over the rich chocolate-coloured earth. He liked it better than any machine he had yet seen.

He was interested too, to see the birds following it. Seagulls they were, for the most part, and rooks and crows. The occasional pigeon. They seemed to favour this machine.

Finally, there came the day when the farmer entered the shed and made purposefully for Skelter's cage. He was lifted up and carried out into the fresh air. There he was placed inside a vehicle and driven from the farm, which he was never to see again. Snowy hardly looked up, as he was whisked away, intent instead on a carrot. The white rabbit had seen too many prisoners led away to their execution. He could not afford to become sentimental or even emotional about it any more. It was a fact of life, from which he personally was exempt, and he had become inured over the seasons.

Skelter felt the return of motion sickness and buried himself beneath his straw. He was suddenly very frightened. As Snowy

51

had predicted, the sadness fled from him, to be replaced by a cold terror. Skelter's survival instinct was strong, and he could no longer afford to pine over the highlands and his lost friend. He had to be primed ready for escape, for he was surely going to a fate most horrible. Even Snowy had been reluctant to talk about it, and when that loquacious rabbit did not want to speak, it meant something really ugly, something too awful to think about was behind it.

They seemed to drive for a long way. When the vehicle stopped, he was taken out and placed on the ground next to a row of other cages. He could hear dogs barking, in the background, and there was the smell of men, the sound of men, gathered in large groups. For a while Skelter stared wild-eyed at the open field before his cage. Once, he threw himself against the wire, which was a painful experience he did not repeat. Gradually he began to calm down and concentrated on the sounds nearest to him, instead of those of men and dogs.

From the next cage to him, came a snuffling sound.

'Who's that?' he asked. 'Is that a hare?'

The reply came in a strange accent, though undoubtedly that of another hare.

'Ay, it is that. What's thy name? Where're thee from?'

'I'm a mountain hare, a blue hare from the highlands. Skelter, they call me Skelter.'

'I'm a jack – name's Trickster. I'm a brown field hare – from the dales. This is a forsaken countryside, what do you say?'

'It is indeed. I hate it. Tell me, why are we here? Are they going to shoot us, or what?'

The brown hare from the dales gave a low snort.

'Shoot us? Thou should be so lucky. We're here for a hare coursing. They open our cages, one by one, and let us run – only when we've gone eighty or so lengths they let the dogs go. Greyhounds. Thee has to outrun them, Skelter, or they tear thee to pieces.'

Skelter's heart pounded in his chest. The terror was already in his throat, threatening to choke him. Dogs! What fiendish game was this they had devised? Where did humans find these terrible ideas?

'Is it possible,' he asked, 'to outrun the dogs?'

'Aye, it's possible. Done it myself, once before, but thee has to be quick. How's thy zig-zag?'

'Zig-zag? What zig-zag?'

'When thee runs.'

Skelter said, 'I don't – we don't do that, in the highlands.'

There was a sharp intake of breath from his neighbour.

'In that case, thou'd better learn fast, for those hounds can run a straight line fleeter than a deer. It's the twisting and turning that confuses them. Good luck.'

'And to you,' whispered Skelter.

And another nightmare began.

Chapter Six

Since the cages were all lined up, facing the field, it was possible for Skelter to watch the proceedings.

The field itself was a meadow with rough turf, the grass too short to hide a hare. Fences had been set up on either side to form a wide channel down the field which led to a hedge at the far end. There were humans in boots and hats, some carrying canes, standing in small groups and yapping at each other. Skelter could not see the hounds at this point, for they were held behind the line of hares.

A little later the dogs were paraded up and down, and Skelter was able to get his first view of a greyhound. They had narrow heads, and necks belonging to drakes. Their flanks were lean and smooth, like that of a bream, and their legs looked long and fast. At the base of their spines were tails that would not have looked out of place on rats. Their mean tight eyes held no compassion. Skelter could see in the arrogant, aristocratic air of the greyhounds, a cruel streak that had no doubt been bred into them by their human masters. It was in their gait, in their demeanour, in their expressions. Skelter could smell the aggressiveness of the dogs from where he lay, crouched at the bottom of his cage. It was a stink that pervaded the whole atmosphere of the scene.

The entire circus was presided over by a man on horseback, who kept barking orders at other men. Mounted men always seemed to act in a superior manner to those on foot. This fact puzzled even the horses themselves, who could not account for it.

Some of the hares were drumming in fear with their hind legs on the backs of their cages. Others had been frightened into rigidity and were crouched in a corner of their cages. A kind of shuddering was passing back and forth, along the cages, which were touching all along the line.

A few hares were calling out in strained voices:

'Anyone done this before? Please, has anybody done this before? I want to know what to do. Answer me!'

'My legs! My legs won't move. How can I run if my legs won't move?'

'Is my jill here? She was caught along with me. Solo, are you here? Where are you, Solo? Solo?'

'Leave me alone. Just leave me alone.'

'I want to go back to my field. Why am I here? What have I done?'

The tension amongst them was incredible. They were about to make a short run for their lives, and any unfit or unwell ones among them would go down under the savage jaws of those sleek hounds. Skelter was not drumming, but he was trembling violently and wished the whole thing were over. He was glad now that Rushie was not here to smell his fear. Perhaps she had been the most fortunate of the pair of them, having gone swiftly with one blow, rather than having to anticipate being torn apart by sharp teeth.

Skelter was fifth in the line, and he watched with horror as the first hare was taken in its cage and placed a few feet in front of the others. Apart from this he knew that something was about to happen, because the dogs began to get excited, calling to each other in their own language. Their leashes were removed and they were held by their collars, at which point they strained against their masters' arms, wanting to be the first to streak off the line. Despite it all, Skelter could not help but admire their smooth lean fit bodies. They seemed fashioned to swim through the air, rather than run along the ground.

The hare was released.

It was a jill and she came out of the cage like a bullet, punching holes in the wind, and immediately started zig-zagging across the open meadow.

A strange silence ruled the morning at first. Not a whisper was heard from the dogs, not a grunt from the men. The hares were quiet too. All eyes were on the jill, as she darted, tacking back and forth, towards the far side of the field. Overhead, in the stillness, a flock of birds wheeled lazily, seemingly oblivious of the drama going on below them.

When she had gone about a hundred and twenty lengths, the dogs were let loose, and with them, all hell.

There was a startling roar from the humans, and they began barking and shrieking at the tops of their voices. There were twelve greyhounds all together, and they ran with tremendous speed. There was no talking amongst them: they were intent on seizing the quarry before it escaped. It seemed they were in competition, overtaking each other, and nudging, in their efforts to reach the hare. Skelter's heart was in his throat as he watched the jill telemarking over the frost-hardened turf, skidding occasionally. *Keep going!* he thought. *Don't look back.* It seemed the jill knew what she was doing, for she did not pause an instant, but made straight for the hedge on the far side of the meadow.

The lead hound came up to her tail when she was about ten lengths from the ditch running below the hedge, but she avoided the snap of his jaws, breaking left. The dog swerved, and a second hound was alongside her, driving her towards the previous leader. She did a skip and a jump, over the nose of the second hound, and reached the thick hedge. Unhesitatingly, she flung herself at the hawthorn. Her long muscled body curved through the air, forepaws touching, hind legs trailing. It was a slow graceful leap, as if she knew it might be her last and she wanted to go out with dignity.

Miraculously, it seemed to those watching from the far side of the conflict that she had managed to find a weakness in the foliage, and was away on the other side. The dogs all piled up against the side of ditch, milling around, shouting now, calling after the prey, no doubt telling her they would have caught her if this had happened, or that had not occurred.

Shortly afterwards the second hare was prepared.

The first two hares made it safely through the hedge, and Skelter was beginning to feel some hope. It seemed that the handicap the dogs were given was just enough to allow a healthy hare to outrun them. It did not seem important to the men that the dogs caught the hares, though of course the hounds themselves did not feel the same way about it.

So far Skelter had seen no mountain hares in the event, only field hares, so he would be the first of his kind to run that day. Skelter knew he was not as fast as a field hare, and this of course worried him a great deal. He would have to rely on tricks, yet the terror had erased all he knew from his mind. It was a blank. He *had* to calm down, get some sort of hold over himself, before the run.

However, before him it was the turn of the hare from the dales, who had already been through this horrifying circus once before in his life.

From the moment Trickster's cage was sprung and he left the starting line, Skelter could see the dale hare was in trouble. His telemarks were too acute, the angles too sharp, and he was wasting energy before the hounds had even been slipped. When the dogs were loose Skelter could tell from the urgency of their running that they knew, they just *knew*, they were going to catch their quarry.

They went as a body, hurtling across the field, the wind streamlining their coats. This time they did not bother to jostle or concern themselves with winning. They simply went straight for the kill.

Trickster might have made it.

At the last moment, when the dogs were up alongside him and he only had six lengths to go, he seemed to panic and doubled-back on himself, turning into the field instead of going for the hedge.

No! thought Skelter. *The other way!*

It was only a matter of time after that, with the hare desperately jumping this way and that amongst the dogs. Skelter could hear the jaws snapping viciously together. *Snap! Snap! Snap!* A piece of tail came away and Trickster rolled sideways. A hound took him by the back, flipped him high in the air. Trickster's scream, like that of a human baby in intense pain, pierced the air. Skelter and the other hares went into a frenzy of terror, running round their cages, drumming, biting the wire, scratching at the floor of the cage trying to dig their way out.

Trickster landed in the middle of the dogs and then disappeared, still screaming, under a melee of savage mouths. The greyhounds tore at the dying hare, ripping away pieces of skin and flesh, running around and worrying the bits they had in their mouths as if the leg or the ear was a toy.

There is a creed which governs the moral code of predators, whether they be wildcats, eagles or men. The creed runs: *The true hunter is one who hunts out of necessity, not out of the pleasure of killing*. This creed is not set down anywhere, nor repeated from mouth to mouth in plain words. It is a knowledge that is intrinsic to all creatures who hunt: deep within their souls they know they should heed the code. Those who are concerned with their morals, concerned with the purity of spirit, do not hunt out of the pleasure of killing. There are many men who observe the code of the hunter, but there were none present at the death of Trickster.

Trickster's screams had stopped, but the bloodlust of the greyhounds was high. They shouted to one another, in their own language, and the sounds were of fevered triumph. They ran and cavorted, evading attempts to restrain them. The humans now tried to get some order back into the beasts they had unleashed on the unfortunate hare, but it took quite some time before any sort of calm was restored.

There was a different look in the eyes of the greyhounds now. The heat of the kill was high. They were frantic to get at the next hare. They had tasted blood, and they wanted more.

The next hare was Skelter.

By now Skelter had come to recognise the procedure of events from the activity amongst the men and dogs. Once the confusion of the recent kill had settled down, there was an air of speculation amongst the humans. They moved amongst each other, making earnest noises, making gestures. Then a single bark would go up, and all noise ceased. The hounds at this point became attentive and began to get restless. Finally, there would be utter silence, a moment in which the whole world stopped, before the cage was sprung. Most hares believed that this suspended moment was the point at which they should sprint, run for their lives, until their lungs were bursting . . . except that Skelter, though he would not have thought it of himself, was an exceptional hare. He was actually capable of thinking ahead, making a *plan*, instead of carrying out one of the two traditional alternatives for escape – freeze, or run.

If the hare froze, of course, the men would just make noises and prod it with sticks, until it *did* run. So Skelter saw that there was really only one result, with no real alternative. Skelter had also noticed that none of the hares so far, even the experienced Trickster, tried to double back immediately on leaving the cage, and run to the rear. That must have meant there was a barrier of some kind, preventing the hare from running the other way. The barrier had to be arranged to funnel the hare out onto the open field, towards the far hedge.

However, there was one aspect of it all that Skelter realised had not been exploited, probably because the running hare was so terrified, it simply did what it had been traditionally taught to do: race away from the predator as fast as possible, using one or two unpredictable moves during the flight, like zig-zagging and leaping. Show your enemy your backside, and run! The white bobbing tail, especially if there were many of them, was supposed to confuse the hunter.

Skelter now remembered Bucker's words – those he had not understood at the time Bucker was advising him. He knew what they meant now. *It's not always the fastest runner that escapes the predator!*

Outside the cage the animation amongst the men had stopped, the dogs began to strain on their leashes, an air of expectancy fell upon the scene.

Then came the suspended moment.

Skelter's heart was thumping in his chest.

The cage was sprung.

He shot out into the open field, but only at half-speed, knowing that the hounds would not be released until he was a certain distance from them. There had been no deviations to this rule of the proceedings. Every hare that had been sprung had been allowed one hundred and twenty lengths, before the dogs were allowed to follow. Skelter gambled that even if he hopped and skipped casually over the field, eating daisies on the way, he would still be permitted his hundred and twenty lengths.

When he had gone a certain distance, he knew he was right. He could hear the hounds shouting and the men baying, as he made a line for the corner of the field, but at a much slower pace than his top speed. In this way he conserved his energy for the final dash for freedom, wasting little on his precious head start.

The far hedge seemed an infinity away, and he had to keep his panic in check, to stop himself from bolting too early. He even noticed a pigeon flying nonchalantly overhead, and it seemed incongruous that this bird should be so free and easy, while a life and death drama went on just a short distance away.

Halfway across the field, the shouting amongst the dogs suddenly stopped, and Skelter knew the race was on. He immediately kicked up into top speed. Had he been a field hare, he might have wasted even more ground space by zig-zagging and increasing the distance he had to run. But he was a mountain creature, a blue hare, and he did not zig-zag in flight. Instead he curved outwards, away from the pursuing hounds, in a wide graceful arc. It was not the shortest distance between two points, but it gave the dogs an extra piece of ground to cover, and it was certainly shorter than weaving or tacking.

The space between Skelter and the hedge seemed to close so very slowly in his own mind, but in fact it was only seconds between his spurt and the point at which he reached the hedge. He had left most of the dogs behind him, though one was gaining rapidly. Then, *consternation*, there seemed to be no break in the hawthorn hedge, through which he could fling himself.

He darted sideways, running along the side of the ditch, desperately seeking a gap. A brown hare, which lives in the fields and knows the hedges like he knows his own paws, would recognise weak places in the high hedge of hawthorn that Skelter would fail to identify.

There was a shout amongst the hounds, as they realised their prey had not yet escaped, even though he had tricked them with his fancy running. There was a renewed vigour amongst them, as they worked their tired muscles to greater efforts, and tried to be the first to clamp jaws on the small hare who was giving them so much trouble.

The lead hound came up within a length of Skelter's tail, preparing for the kill. Skelter could feel and smell the dog's hot musty breath on his body, knew the slavering mouth was fractions away from a strike. There seemed to be no escape. Skelter skipped desperately as the jaws snapped, taking a few hairs from his rump. There was a shout of triumph from the hound. Two more dogs came up alongside now, and cut off Skelter's retreat. They closed in.

Suddenly, a miracle appeared in the side of the ditch, a dark round thing which Skelter instantly recognised. A field hare, never having been underground, might have instinctively avoided the hole, and run on, no doubt to his death. Skelter had lived in tunnels all his life, although his form was much shorter in length.

It was a rabbit warren's bolt hole. He shot in, past a chamber occupied by a startled doe and her kittens, and out of the main entrance. Looking around he realised that he was now on the other side of the hawthorn hedge. The hounds were scrabbling around the bolt hole on the other side, terrifying the rabbits in their galleries below.

Skelter's heart was still battering his ribs, and his legs would not stop running. He crossed one field, then another, then another, before he finally came to a halt, exhausted. He lay on the cold ground and got his breath back, before surveying the countryside around him.

He was free! He had outsmarted them, for all their sleek and cunning ways, their narrow heads and bodies, their long legs. A whole pack of greyhounds! And a little mountain hare had shown them its heels. That was *something*. That was really something. He wished his clan had been there to see him. He hoped his ghost-hare had been watching from the Otherworld.

The cold air bit into his lungs as he gulped it down into his breast. His legs were still trembling with the fright and his muscles still twitching with the effort. He tried to get his bearings in this foreign land, where the mists snaked over the flats, and the sky was an enormous dome with horizons all around. Stark trees stood on the skyline, too few to interrupt his vision of the long flow of the level landscape to distant lines where earth met sky. The light here was murkier – not so much *softer*, but a kind of dirty yellow with more density, as bog waters were to the clear burns. It was a mysterious land, that held a sense not so much of *evil*, as dark secrets and ancient laws. Skelter felt he had taken a step back into antiquity, and that he would have to rethink his knowledge of the landscape, and remodel his expectations from it.

In enclaves between the ploughed fields were places of stagnant ponds, of small forgotten thickets green-barked by time and grown into themselves, of lone creatures not in their right heads, of eremites and inbred suspicions and distrustful eyes.

There was no evidence of any mountains around. On the cultivated land, which constituted most of what was visible to him, the occasional tree in the corner of a field could be seen above the hedgerows, but for the most part it was tilled earth, ditch and hedge, whichever way he looked. The hedges themselves were squared, neatly-trimmed and straight. Everything appeared very uniform, unwild, open.

There was absolutely no cover from eagles.

Chapter Seven

Skelter's prime concern was with eagles, and the fact that there were no rocks and gullies, no tufts of grass, no hillocks or hummocks, behind which to take cover. Although the hedges prevented him from seeing a great distance, he had come far enough in this alien land to know that it changed very little from one field to the next. Mostly they were fields of young vegetables, corn, rape seed, and other crops. There were also fields that had been tilled, but were not showing any green. Finally, there was pastureland, but not a great deal of that.

The sky was vast here: a huge area that frightened him with its openness. From that wide expanse at any time might come an attack from an eagle, dropping out of the dinginess with lightning speed. No longer did his horizons curve up around him, containing his world.

He had seen no other hares around, and could only assume they had all been killed off or moved out of this vulnerable place. It did occur to him that because the coursing was taking place nearby, the neighbouring hares had vacated the vicinity, and would return at a later time. The thing to do was to keep his wits about him, and try to cover that vast swathe of sky occasionally with a quick all-round survey.

Every so often his heart would patter, as a shadow swept across the land, and it only settled to a regular smooth rhythm when he looked up to see a magpie cruising like a hawk, or a pigeon playing on the air currents. Once, there was the familiar sight of a shadow that went in lazy circles, and Skelter looked up expecting to see an eagle winding up the world, only to find a heron turning above a small pond.

One thing he was relieved about was the fact that though there was little cover for him, there was even less for wildcats, who liked to sneak between rocks and outcrops. In that respect, and with no fear of being ambushed by foxes, he was able to travel in relative safety.

He satisfied his hunger with some corn shoots, that were still green and succulent. Then he set about investigating his new home. Skelter realised that it would take a miracle to return him to his beloved highlands, and he had already used a couple of those in surviving. He had a stoical disposition, and he came very early to the conclusion that he had to make the best of his new situation.

He found a field where a huge oak overshadowed the corner, and he fashioned his form under one of the great roots of this monster. Once or twice during the day he caught sight of a brown hare, way in the distance, but he was not yet in a mood to approach any of his cousins. He thought perhaps that this might be yet another of the escapees from the hare coursing, and that they might get together some time to pool their resources of knowledge. A field hare would know better than he what was the situation regarding eagles in the vicinity

Sighting the brown hare reminded him of his recent conversation with the hare from the dales, Trickster. It had been a terrible experience, watching him torn apart by the hounds. Skelter had seen hares shot, carried off by raptors, snatched up by wildcats, but he had never before witnessed the complete ripping apart of a body, so that the limbs, head and torso were separated from one another in two minutes.

Trickster had not been a small hare, either. Most brown field hares were at least two pawlengths longer than blue mountain hares. Their ears were taller, too. They seemed more sturdy, more muscled. What chance would Skelter have stood in the jaws of those vicious greyhounds?

That night he settled down in his new form, protected from above by the ancient root. The wind was chill, but bearable. The night sky was at first covered by a rash of stars, but later the clouds came over in sheets.

He heard a fox barking in a nearby field, but it was not close enough for him to worry.

There was a barn owl in the oak above for part of the night, but it had already had a successful hunt, for it disgorged a paw-sized pellet of undigested fur and bones which landed near Skelter's form: the remains of some small creature that it had killed and eaten. The owl gave out some shrill *kwick-kwick-kwick* sounds occasionally, then flew off, presumably in search of the secretive voles and dormice, of which there were many busy in the grasses around the ditch. Not that a barn owl would attack a fully-grown hare in any case, but it was as well to be wary of all predators. Who knew whether owls and eagles were not in league, one pointing out meals of interest to the other? You couldn't trust carnivores of any kind, even the shrew would exchange its own young for a choice worm or slug.

With the dawn came a sky streaked with yellow. There were many birds about which indicated a coastline nearby. Oyster-catchers and knots flew over in tight little flocks that twisted and turned instantly to unheard commands. There were also seagulls of course, but these birds reach many miles inland, and their name is misleading since they rarely go out to sea. They are more birds of the shore and field, attending the ploughing and seeding of the land. Still there was no sign of eagles, and Skelter emerged and began nibbling at the grassy edges of the ditch, and amongst the fresh barley. He found some succulent bark, and wonder of wonders, some hawksbeard which were delicious.

After he had been feeding for some time, he noticed that the hare he had seen the previous day had come closer, nibbling his way through the field. Skelter made a mental note of the hare's position, and promised himself that he would speak to the creature later.

However, Skelter did not get the chance of a peaceful approach. While he was busy with some bark, a heavy blow suddenly struck him on the flank. He went rolling into the icy ditch. Jumping to his feet, he looked up to see a large brown hare glaring down at him.

'What was that for?' he asked.

'*My* field,' snapped the other hare. 'Who do you think you are? *What* do you think you are? You look like a runt to me, with your short body and little ears. Keep off my territory, jack, or there'll be big trouble.'

Skelter was affronted.

'Territory? I don't know what you're talking about.'

The brown hare, a big jill, glowered at him.

65

'You know very well what I'm talking about. This is my field. You want to eat in this field, you come and see me first, and I'll tell you no.'

'A *whole* field? You want all of it?'

The jill shook her head as if exasperated.

'Where are you from, stranger? You have a funny way of talking. No, don't tell me, I don't really want to know,' she said wearily. 'Listen, you're obviously not acquainted with the rules around here. We stick to our own piece of ground, and we don't blatantly invade another hare's territory, not unless someone's looking for a fight. Let me give you a little word of advice. You're small, even for a jack. If you're going to insist on invading the property belonging to others, then you'd better be prepared to collect a few scars.'

Skelter climbed out of the ditch and backed away from the jill. She was indeed a formidable creature, with strong back legs and enormous shoulders. The way she ground her teeth at him made him sure she meant business. He knew he would have more than a tough fight on his hands if he tried to take her on. There was nothing for it but to try to make a dignified retreat without too much loss of face.

He said haughtily, 'I have no intention of breaking any rules. I escaped from a hare coursing yesterday, and I was just making my way across country . . .'

'I could have told you that,' she replied contemptuously. 'You think you're the first hare to come through my land? I get them all the time. They hold those meetings regularly, always in the same place, and I get the dregs of the earth wandering through my field. I'm sick to death of refugees stealing my crops. Now on your way.'

'Have you no charity?' asked Skelter.

'None whatsoever. If I did, I would have a tribe of you hares, all eating away at my larder. I can't afford you.'

Skelter began to hop away, but he turned for one last conversation.

'Listen, surely you're not the only hare around here, are you? Where's the rest of your clan? Taken by eagles, or what?'

The jill kicked a sod of earth impatiently with one of her hind legs.

'Eagles? Clans? Get out of here with your gibberish, before I lose my patience completely.'

This encounter did nothing to help Skelter's confidence. If he was going to meet with aggression from hares, what were the rest of the mammals going to be like? He was used to living side by side with many hares, sharing feeding grounds, acting as a group. Here was a hare that lived like a hermit, completely on her own. What was more this hare eremite did not *want* any other hares to share her field, and talked about being threatened by their presence. It was a strange new world that Skelter had entered here.

He left the jill's field, making his way through the hedge, and across a pastureland. Even before he was halfway across, he noticed yet another hare, staring at him with hostile eyes from behind a cowpat. It was obvious that he had gone from one occupied territory immediately into another. If this was going to be the pattern it was possible that he could travel forever and not find an empty space for himself.

He continued his journey, the smell of salt air becoming stronger all the time. Eventually he came to a road, which he decided not to cross, but to follow for a while. Staying a few lengths inside the field, he travelled in a westerly direction. On his journey he passed one or two humans who were using the road. One was on foot, another on a bicycle. Skelter was not concerned by the presence of humans, so long as they were not carrying guns and were not accompanied by dogs. If they tried to chase him, he could outrun them every time, and what was more important, they knew it too. His recent experience notwithstanding, Skelter knew that most humans were harmless enough beasts.

To Skelter's surprise the further he went the more the ground began to undulate. There was now a sparsity of hedges, and those that there were had been left to grow ragged and unkempt. They were thorns of a sort, shaped by an offshore wind into a sweptback position.

Marram grass began to appear on sandy patches of soil, and spiky gorse shrubs with small yellow blooms patterned the area in maze-like clusters. There was a sense of wildness about the place which Skelter found heartening.

Finally, he came to a line of sand dunes, tufted with marram, which he climbed. Once on the peak of the dune, he found himself looking out over an astounding stretch of water so vast that it took his breath away. It went out to the edge of the world, where it dropped away, presumably as a giant waterfall. The surface of the water was spattered with cuckoo spit and its whole scape was in a state of continuous flux. There was a roaring and booming from the surf around the ocean's mouth, as it continually bit at pebbly sands and dragged rattling shingle down its throat.

Skelter had never seen the ocean before, though he had heard a great deal about it from others. One clan was in contact with the next clan, all across the highlands, and they passed on their observations to their neighbours. Hare lore too, had many stories of the sea, and rabbits claimed they had crossed it over a thousand winters ago, coming from a distant land.

It was an impressive sight and one which had Skelter trembling from ear-tips to tail. There was something about its emptiness that frightened him. If the fields of the flatlands were stark and bare, they were nothing compared with the ocean. At least there were hedges in and around the fields, to break up the awful monotony, but the sea had nothing except itself, which admittedly it continually tried to gather up to form hedges. These simply collapsed or ran away from the great body of the water to peter into nothingness.

A blunt-nosed boat was crashing through the seas, dipping and rising, its funnel emitting an almost horizontal trail of black smoke as if it were trying to draw a line across the surface of the ocean. It looked squat and solid, made for rough channel waters, for barging the waves aside and bulldozing a passage through them.

When Skelter tired of staring at the expanse of dark green water, he began to make his way along the dunes. He went over the crest of one, and was about to descend, when he stopped dead in his tracks. There in the dip between the two dunes was a fox, staring back at him. He could see the creature's brown eyes, the sharp white teeth, the sensitive nose. It was the first time he had come face to face with one of these predators, though he had seen them at a distance, and for a moment he remained frozen.

The fox had a seagull hanging loosely from its jaws, its wings drooping, its tail feathers torn. There were other feathers scattered about the sands, and it was obvious that the fox had killed more than one of the gulls, and that she was in the process of caching this

68

bird. The vixen let the dead gull drop to the ground, but otherwise remained still.

Predator and prey rarely, if ever, speak to one another in the animal world. The languages differ so much that there is a vocal difficulty: foxes and their ilk speak with a low, even, mellow tone, while herbivore languages tend to favour a kind of sharp sing-song rhythmic sound. The cultural gulf between the two kinds of creature does not encourage social intercourse, even if there were no carnal needs to take into consideration: the predator's whole existence is inextricably enmeshed with the skills of hunting, stalking, and killing, while the herbivore's existence is concerned only with fresh vegetation and staying one jump ahead of the hunters. Finally, and most importantly, carnivores consider it unethical to converse with their prey, though the quarry often attempts persuasion or cries for mercy when all other forms of defence have failed. It is difficult to kill and consume a creature with whom you have just passed the time of day without a feeling of having transgressed some moral code or other.

So neither Skelter nor the vixen attempted any kind of vocal communication. There were other signs, which could be read fairly accurately however, and Skelter soon recognised that the fox had eaten her fill and was not inclined to chase him. If he walked into her jaws, it was doubtful she would refrain from closing them, but like many predators foxes are fairly lazy creatures and do not like to work unnecessarily.

The vixen's eyes said, Get Out Of Here Fast, and Skelter intended to do precisely that. He skipped around the edge of the dune and continued his trek along the high tide mark of the beach.

There were aerobatic terns dipping and diving over the shallows on the shoreline, and the inevitable heavy-eyed seagulls argued viciously amongst each other, pirating what they had not fished themselves, and generally behaving in a thuggish manner. The worst were the great black-backed gulls, larger in body length than Skelter himself, and ready to attack anything that moved if it meant food. When they weren't robbing the nests of cliffside birds, they were snatching fish out of each other's beaks.

One or two of these, accompanied by herring gulls, dive-bombed Skelter as he ran along the shoreline, carking harsh obscenities at the furry intruder. The attacks were not serious, the gulls had merely decided to mob a passing stranger for fun, but they were nonetheless worrying to a lone member of the *lepus timidis* family.

There was no cover from the creatures and Skelter ran full pelt down the smooth wet sands, scattering dunlin in his path, and gaining a little satisfaction from that. On reaching the point at the far end, he found the road again, which used a narrow man-made isthmus, a causeway, to reach a large flat island. Skelter could see farmlands on the island, with one or two buildings and houses, but no great conglomeration of human dwellings. However, at that time the wind was high and the waves were breaking over the roadway from either side of the spit, and it would have been suicide to attempt to reach the place. A creature his size would be washed away within a short time.

Instead, he turned inland again, and before very long came to a copse of deciduous trees. He made his way into the interior, under the brambles and briars, until the uncomfortable darkness of the woodland closed around him. There he began to feed on fungi. He felt contained for a while, in the dark green bosom of the thicket.

It was not in his culture to like the humid and succulent heart of a spinney, with its smells of mushrooms and toadstools, wet green vines, spongy moss and rotting vegetation. This was a place full of suspicion and dark thoughts, where weasels gathered to hold conferences and corruption could be found behind every ancient trunk. It was a secretive world, full of whispering wood mice, clicking beetles and meaningful silences.

He felt a thousand eyes following his every pawstep. A green woodpecker significantly ceased drilling for insects to watch him go beneath its tree.

He found, near the centre of the spinney, a rabbit warren. The day was coming to an end and he was desperate to find a safe place for the night. He decided to enter the main entrance and ask for sanctuary. Whether the rabbits would allow him to stay, was another matter, but he was determined to try. Anything was better than risking another night in the open country, where the cover was non-existent.

He moved cautiously down the hole.

Chapter Eight

Skelter entered the darkness of the warren, letting his eyes get used to the lack of light, moving slowly so as not to alarm any occupants. The tunnels were tight and airless to a hare, and he had the sense that his body was expanding and would become jammed. Overcoming his claustrophobia, he continued along the dark shaft, trying to keep his panic in check, for if he gave way to it now, and tried to scramble out backwards, there was a serious risk of becoming lodged. Still, he found it hard to breathe, and his chest felt constricted. Once or twice he stopped, his fear of the tight space making him regret he had ever entered, but after a while he managed to beat the terror down and continue the nightmarish journey.

At first he hoped that perhaps the warren was empty, that it had been abandoned, but it soon became obvious from the smell that it was inhabited. Then he began to hear the twitterings of kittens, and the murmurs of does. When he reached the first gallery, he peered inside. It was pitch dark of course, but he formed mental images from his other senses, especially from his sense of smell.

There was a doe in there, and she seemed alarmed.

It appeared as though she was about to squeal for help, so Skelter said, 'Don't worry, I mean no harm. I just want shelter for a night or two, until I . . .'

The doe shrieked, piercingly.

In a few seconds the tunnel was crammed with four or five other rabbits, mostly bucks. Their eyes gleamed red in the darkness. They looked angry.

'I didn't touch her,' Skelter told them.

A buck hopped forward a pace. He was not as long-bodied as Skelter, but he had a lot of meat on him. The buck also had right on his side, which is a formidable weapon, and this obviously gave him courage. The rabbits were on their own territory, which gave the buck another advantage. Skelter had to keep reminding himself that he was a hare, and hares are stronger, faster and meaner in battle than rabbits.

'What do you want here?' asked the buck. 'This is a warren. Go back to your field or your form, whatever you call it. We don't like strangers in here.'

'I don't have a form at the moment,' answered Skelter. 'I merely want some safe place for the night.'

The buck sneered.

'Don't give me that. All you need to do is scrape out a hollow. *That's* your form, for you.'

He hopped another pace forward, but Skelter ground his teeth in annoyance. Humans could root him out of his home, and carry him off to far lands, he knew that. Dogs could chase him across meadows, and he had to accept that. Foxes could stare him out in the dunes, and send him packing, and he had to take it on the chin. Perhaps other hares, whose territory was guarded jealously, might suggest he go on his way. But a *rabbit* telling him what he could or could not do? This was too much. He ground his nibblers again.

'You grind your teeth at me?' questioned the rabbit. 'This is my home, not yours.'

'Look,' said Skelter. 'If you want a fight, I'll give you one. I'll take you all on. Maybe you'll bite a few chunks out of me, but let me tell you I've had enough of being pushed around. I'll rip off an ear or two before I'm finished with you.

'On the other hand, we don't have to hurt each other. All I need is a hole to rest in. I don't know what you mean about a scraping in a field, but I'm not a brown hare, I'm a blue mountain hare. I'm used to hiding in the rocks, or in a short burrow. Open fields make me nervous. There's no cover from the raptors. Do you understand?'

The rabbit fluffed himself up, but seemed a little unsure of his ground now. He turned and glanced into the eyes of the doe behind him, who seemed to say, don't look at me, I didn't ask him to come here.

'Are you the chief here?' asked Skelter.

'I'm the biggest buck in the warren,' replied the rabbit, 'which means I have the biggest say in what goes on around here. Is that what you mean?'

72

'More or less. So if you say I can stay, no one will argue?'

'They can argue, but it won't get them anywhere.'

Skelter nodded.

'In that case, what do you say? I won't bother anyone, I promise. Do you have a spare side gallery, that you're not using at the moment? I'll try to pay my keep, by bringing in some food tonight.'

The rabbit still seemed unsure.

'It's not very usual,' he said.

'I'm aware of that, which is why I'll appreciate it all the more. I should be grateful for any help. I was taken from my homeland by men, forced to run a course chased by greyhounds, and now I'm down on my luck. It's not very usual to find one of my kind in these parts either. It's not a normal situation.'

The buck made up his mind.

'Oh, why not. It's not as if you're a fox or something. Come on then. My name's L'herbe.'

'I'm called Skelter.'

'Strange name,' said the buck.

'So's yours,' answered Skelter, beginning to bristle again.

'No, no, don't take on,' said L'herbe, soothingly. 'I didn't mean anything by it. Just that I've never heard a name like that before, even amongst the hares around here. But of course, you're not from around here, are you?'

The other rabbits were still clustered in the tunnel, a silent audience during this exchange between stranger and homesteader. Now that it was settled that the hare was going to stay, and there was to be no fight, they could relax and watch what happened without worrying. Rabbits are terrible worriers, obsessive creatures, and fret over the most trivial and commonplace things, like when they last used the south exit, or whether they have eaten the right food for a balanced diet. There were some rabbits that kept small pebbles in their nests, to turn or rub with their paw, in order to relieve them of some of their nervous energy.

'No, not from around here,' replied Skelter, 'but where does *your* name come from?'

'It's an old family name,' said the buck, 'which came over the seas with my ancestors.'

73

Skelter nodded, and said, 'Oh,' but his expression obviously gave him away.

'You don't believe me, do you?' sighed L'herbe. 'You believe in all that rubbish about us being invented by man. Let me tell you something, hare, before you get yourself into trouble down here. Men can only invent mechanical devices: things without real life in them. They may *look* alive, some of men's innovations, like the tractor, but in fact it's the men who make the parts move. A tractor can't move itself.'

'How do you know that?'

'Observation. Simple observation. Have you ever seen a tractor moving without a man in it? A tractor always *stops* before the man gets out.'

'But it sometimes keeps on breathing,' argued Skelter.

'Yes, it does that, I'll grant you,' said L'herbe, 'it keeps on breathing – but then men can stop it breathing, when they feel like it. You see, men *control* the things they invent. Do they control rabbits? If they did, they wouldn't have to hunt us with dogs and ferrets, would they? They'd just turn off our breathing, pick us up and pop us in their bags. You see what I mean? You've got to use your eyes a bit.'

Skelter was a little confused by the onslaught of these new ideas, but he was willing to accept that perhaps he was *slightly* mistaken about the rabbits. Perhaps the original rabbits were invented by men, but some had escaped and were now breeding amongst themselves, independent of man? He didn't say this of course, because he knew it would upset L'herbe, who he was sure actually believed he was a real animal. Rabbits like L'herbe had obviously been wild for so long, they had convinced themselves they had a past history, a glorious history, that began in another land beyond the sea.

'Well, you must know where you come from,' said Skelter. 'I won't argue any further.'

'But you're still not convinced?'

'Yes, a little.'

L'herbe seemed mollified.

'Perhaps we'll manage to convince you completely, by the time you leave us. Meanwhile, I'll show you to your gallery, which is right at the east end of the warren. Follow me,' he turned, then

74

yelled, 'clear out of the way you lot! Haven't you seen a mountain hare before?'

'No,' said one doe, truthfully, but she backed into a side gallery and let them pass.

'Getting impertinent, some of these does,' complained L'herbe. 'I expect it happens amongst hares too?'

Skelter followed him closely, realising the rabbit still wanted to chat.

'Not really,' he replied. 'You see, the jills are bigger than the jacks, so it's we who get impertinent, if anybody.'

'Really?' said L'herbe. 'I hadn't noticed. But then I don't go out and study hares, not as such. Jills bigger than the jacks? There's a thing. It wouldn't work around here, of course. You wouldn't catch the bucks following the orders of a female.'

'Well, we don't do that, exactly. Nobody orders anyone around. But I wouldn't talk to one of our jills the way you spoke to that doe. She'd knock my head off.'

They left that conversation there, both of them a little amazed at the difference in their two cultures. L'herbe said it just went to show that you could live next door to another creature, and not know it at all.

They finally came to an area where there were no rabbits, just a strong musty odour which offended Skelter's nostrils.

'What's that smell?' he asked L'herbe.

'That? Oh, you'll have to put up with it. That's why there's no rabbits at this end of the warren. It's the badgers. They live down there,' and L'herbe indicated a tunnel off to the side, larger than the burrows Skelter had come through to reach the place.

Skelter began to feel alarmed.

'Badgers? They're rather large creatures, aren't they?'

'Oh, yes,' said L'herbe candidly. 'Large omnivores. Black and white fellows, with fierce tempers on them. You never meet one that isn't in a rage or choleric about something. Creatures of bad humour, that's badgers. Now look,' said the buck, becoming practical, 'this isn't the best gallery in the warren, but you won't be disturbed here, and there's a bolt hole nearby, so you won't need to bother any of the other does or bucks by creeping past their burrows. You can come and go as you please. How does that sound?'

'Fine, fine,' said Skelter, anxiously, 'but the badgers . . . ?'

'Oh, you won't need to bother them, either.'

'I wasn't thinking about that, so much as them bothering *me*,' said Skelter, honestly.

'Oh, they won't bother you either. What makes you think they will?'

'Well, if they're predators . . .'

'Omnivores. Different thing. Eat just about everything that grows or moves. Blackberries, worms, mice, apples, you name it.'

'Yes, but don't they eat rabbits and hares?'

'Not if they live with them. At least, not those in the same warren, which they call a *sett* by the way. It annoys them if you say warren or burrow. If you should happen to meet one in the dark, make sure you say *sett*.'

'I'm not planning to meet one in the dark,' answered Skelter. 'I'm not keen on meeting one at all, in fact. Look, how – how will they know I'm from this warren? They might think I'm an intruder. After all, my scent is different from yours, and when it comes down to it, I'm a *hare*.'

L'herbe nodded.

'Quite right. Hadn't thought of that. I'd better tell them you're here, otherwise they might come in while you're sleeping and gobble you up before you can say *gwai chun*, sorry, that's ancient rabbit for "ghost feet" – it's what we call hares sometimes – because of your hairy pads, you know. You don't leave definite prints in mud or snow, do you? Now, what were we talking about?'

Skelter realised that L'herbe was getting his own back, for the 'man invented rabbits' argument.

'You were saying that you would have to tell them I'm here, so they don't attack me.'

'Right, well let's do it now, rather than later, shall we, or there might be a nasty accident. Now, when I yell, there's going to be some pretty ugly language coming back. I told you they don't like to be disturbed. It always brings out the worst in them, since they've got those foul tempers I told you about. Here goes nothing.'

The rabbit bellowed down the next tunnel.

'*Hēr-inne is hara.*' Then to Skelter, he said quietly, 'I've told them a hare is in here.'

There was a rustling from the neighbouring sett, then a harsh voice cried, '*Hwæt is? Ēow friþes healdan!*'

L'herbe shrugged. 'They're telling me to keep quiet,' he said.

'Maybe we should,' answered Skelter, nervously. He had been startled by the guttural power behind the voice down the tunnel.

L'herbe shook his head and then shouted, '*Gehyrst þu, þis folc hēr-inne is hara!*'

There was a grumbling sound, a movement, and then a big nose appeared at the end of the tunnel. Skelter was disturbed by the size of the face, and the large glittering eyes. He had never been this close to such a monster.

The badger, sour-faced, stared at Skelter for a while. Then he opened his mouth and yawned, revealing a set of sharp teeth that sent a shudder through Skelter. After this the creature waddled back from whence he came. A final shout echoed down the tunnel.

'*Friþ, hara.*'

'What did he say?' asked Skelter, anxiously.

'It seems to be all right. He said "peace, hare" but I'm not sure whether that means he doesn't want to fight with you, or you have to keep quiet while you're here.'

Skelter said, 'I rather think it's the latter, don't you?'

'You're probably right, anyway, I'm going to leave you to it. Just call if you get into any trouble. You only have to speak sharply to them, remind them that this is your home too, and they'll see reason. But I shouldn't think they'll bother you. Do you speak any *Mustelidae*?'

'What's that?'

'The language of badgers, stoats, weasels, otters and a few others. They're all of the same family, though you'd never guess it. I mean, a badger and an otter? But there you have it . . .'

'No,' replied Skelter bluntly.

Skelter could not imagine himself speaking sharply to the creature he had seen at the end of the tunnel. He determined to keep quiet at all costs, and settled down for a sleep.

The badgers, however, did not seem to heed their own advice, and were forever rasping something at one another. To Skelter it was a demonic language, and he wanted nothing to do with it. No self-respecting hare would use that tongue.

Chapter Nine

Skelter found that rabbits, like hares, preferred to feed mainly at night and rest up during the daylight hours. Though again, like his own kind they were not strictly nocturnal, and tended to do much as their fancy took them, generally drifting out in the early hours for their main meal. The first thing they did when they got outside, was sit in a hunched position on the grass, and worry about the weather.

When they had finished worrying about the weather, they began to fret about the shadows.

When they had conquered their fear of shadow and shade, of cloudy climes and starless skies, they expressed concern about being out of the warren too long. They became paranoid about what was going on below in the burrows, thinking that perhaps a fox or weasel found its way in without being seen, and was eating their babies.

This had to be checked and double-checked, before the bucks and does were satisfied.

When all this worrying, fretting and anxiousness was at last laid to rest, they became convinced that there was not enough time left to eat their fill, and immediately executed a nervous attack on the greenery of the woodland floor.

Skelter turned out with the rest of them, and found feeding amongst a group of nibbling furry forms a bit like being back in his mountains, except of course there were no mountains. He still had terrible bouts of homesickness at times when he just lay miserably dreaming of his highlands, and often made resolutions to get back there again, though he knew in his heart that such a journey was impossible, for which way would he go?

Still, the trees were better than the open fields. The only thing was, whereas in the fields Skelter had been overawed and a little frightened of the massive sky, in the wood he felt hemmed in, enclosed, and he began to suffer from a tightness of the throat and a feeling of panic occasionally, as if he were being held down by strong hands.

This feeling was especially strong in the warren, below the ground, where the air was a little stale and no matter what position you put yourself in, there was an earth wall facing you, an earth floor beneath you, and an earth ceiling above. Such an environment tended to constrict his skull. He had dreams about getting stuck in one of the passages, and being abandoned by the rabbits.

So, he tended to go for the widest clearings in the wood, until a rabbit called L'arbre suggested that these spaces were very vulnerable.

'You have to watch out for weasels and stoats, and of course, foxes. If you stay amongst the trees, they stand less chance of catching you.'

This did not make a great deal of sense, for amongst the trees Skelter could not see what was creeping up on him. He tended to jump at every flickering shadow, until the rabbits were viewing him with amusement. Some of the youngsters deliberately sneaked out from behind the trees. They pretended they had been eating bracket fungus. As expected Skelter jumped, on seeing them, and they apologised with, 'Oh, sorry, hare – didn't mean to startle you,' though of course that had been the intention.

Not that he, as an adult hare, need worry too much about weasels, but foxes were another matter. Foxes were as fast as hares, especially in tight places like the spinney in which Skelter found himself.

When the shafts of daylight came through the woodland in dazzling bars, the rabbits began to drift back down to the inner darkness of the warren. Some would come out again, during the day. There were always insomniacs, who could not sleep whatever time of day it was. Like hares, rabbits were not strictly nocturnal.

Skelter followed the rabbits down the hole. Having been made the brunt of a few jokes, he was like one of the family now, and the rabbits began to treat him in a more friendly fashion.

L'arbre asked him, 'What's it like, sleeping near the badgers? Bit disconcerting, eh?'

'You can say that again,' remarked Skelter. 'I keep thinking one of them is going to tear my throat out. What happens when the weather gets bad and the hunting is poor? Don't they ever attack you?'

'Never known it to happen yet. Badgers can always find food somewhere. I've seen them go out into the fields and eat turnips. They're not fussy in that way. They'll take a rabbit from another warren too, if they can dig it out. Weird, when you think about it. I suppose we're lucky, really, having them here. I mean, it keeps other badgers away – and foxes. They occasionally live with foxes, but they won't allow a stranger to come in, and badgers are pretty fierce when roused.'

'They're pretty fierce when *not* roused,' said Skelter. 'Even when they're just talking to one another, they sound as if they're going to rip each other apart any second. That language of theirs . . .'

L'arbre nodded.

'Ah, yes, the ancient tongue. *Mustelidae*. Bit different from our *Leporidae*, eh? You see, ours has changed a lot over the years. I like to think of it as a dynamic language: it's grown out of the languages of two main animal groups, one of which is *Mustelidae*, with some *Corvidae* at its roots. The other is *Felidae*. Don't ask me how our paths crossed with cats and crows, but it must have done at one time. Maybe all the animals spoke one language in seasons out of time. Anyway, we sort of take the words and make them our own, growing others out of the earlier roots.

'But badgers, weasels, otters and their ilk insist on keeping their language pure. That's what they say, anyway, though what a "pure" language is, I have no idea. I suppose most of us used to speak the way they do today, once upon a time.'

'It's a very harsh sounding tongue,' said Skelter. 'Rasping. You'd think they all had sore throats. It sounds threatening and aggressive too.'

'Well, that's badgers for you. Old fashioned, bad tempered and guttural. We've still got remnants of that language used by our foreparents you know – a tongue they spoke when they lived in the middle of a great continent, where the winters were very cold and the summers hot and humid.'

'That sounds like here.'

'No,' L'arbre said, 'not at all like here. I mean *really* cold – six months of ice and snow, and then the opposite. The humans were a bit different there too. Smaller, all with dark hair, and so many of them. A sea of humans.'

'What happened? Did they drive you out?'

'No, not really. It's where we started, and you know how we breed. Our numbers got too large for the interior, so hordes of us made our way to the west. We kept stopping of course, but then the population would build to a point where some of us had to move on, and we would still be getting pressure from the large numbers in the interior. Finally, we reached the coast, and settled there. That's where we got our names, from that coastal region.'

'Then you swam across the water to this land.'

L'arbre tutted in impatience.

'I can see you're still sceptical. No, we didn't swim. It's too far, and well you know it. We were brought here by some conquering humans who had the same problems as us with their population. They wanted new lands too. So we came to this island some thousand winters ago. That's our history, and you can't take it away from us, just because you were here before us. It doesn't work like that.'

L'herbe had joined them now, with another rabbit, a doe named La framboise, and this female of the warren viewed the hare with hostility.

'Why bother with him?' she said, 'he's so prejudiced he's blind to any argument. I always said that hares were narrow-minded bigoted creatures. You'll never convince them, no matter how hard you try.'

'Now wait a bit,' protested Skelter. 'I've never really spoken with rabbits before now. I'm willing to keep an open mind on the subject. It's just that I was brought up to see things differently from you.'

'You were brought up,' said La framboise, 'on a pack of vicious lies, designed to make hares look like superior beings to rabbits, which they're not.'

'We don't get the watery-eye disease,' snapped Skelter, stung by this attack.

'If you mean myxomatosis,' sneered La framboise, 'then say

81

so. That was a man-brought illness, made specially to kill us off because we were a threat to humans.'

'You know this for certain?'

L'herbe interrupted to cool the conversation down.

'Not for certain, no Skelter, but we're pretty sure man either brought it here, or somehow introduced it into the rabbit population. It suddenly appeared, without it ever being in existence before, and it was very bad. We went down like wheat under a harvester. Why would a new disease suddenly come up from nowhere? It's our old trouble you see,' he said with a sigh, 'we will *breed*.'

'I have heard,' confided La framboise, in a more reasonable tone than she had been using, 'that there's a kind of rodent or something that breeds faster than we do. You know what the rodents are like. They've never managed to migrate like us, so every time their numbers build up to bursting point, and they attempt to spread, they end up falling into the sea in their thousands.'

Skelter thought that sounded like a story, but he didn't say so, because he seemed to be on a better footing with the doe now, and he did not want the conversation to degenerate into another row. He could hear the badgers grouching away next door, and he didn't want to be left alone with just their voices for company.

He said to L'herbe, 'When you came across the sea with the humans, why did they let you go?'

'They didn't let us go. Some of us escaped, started breeding, and became wild rabbits again. We were never really *tame* rabbits, not like those you see in cages today . . .' Skelter remembered Snowy, and nodded encouragingly, '. . . if they escaped they would be feral animals, because they've been bred into something different from us wild rabbits. No, we were truly wild, having come straight from the fields of the continent, and brought over here.'

'So,' said Skelter, 'a thousand years ago some of your kind escaped, and began to spread out, over the countryside.'

L'herbe rolled his eyes.

'I can tell you of epic journeys that would make your pupils start from their sockets – journeys full of danger, of cunning, of strength of spirit. Some of them not that long ago either. Quests for new homes, when the old ones were destroyed or became too

82

dangerous. Why, in recent history there was one such odyssey, led by a famous rabbit called Le noisetier, who was advised and accompanied by the great prophet, Le cinquième.'

'Great prophet?'

'We have had many prophets – when you live under the ground as we do, not only close to the earth, but in its very womb, there are influences on the mind that make certain rabbits special. Mystical influences. Le cinquième was one such rabbit. He had visions and dreams, which he related to his warren, and these became truths.'

Skelter was impressed.

'Do you have prophets in here, in this warren?'

'We have Le septième.'

La framboise shuffled her feet, and L'arbre looked away, which made Skelter think that something was not quite right.

'And this Le septième, does he see visions?'

'Well, he once saw a fairy flitting about in the moonlight. Several fairies, in fact.'

'Fairies?'

'Small human-like creatures with wings. A bit like bumble bees, only sort of delicate, and they do magic.'

'And your prophet saw these, and foretold some terrible disaster that was about to engulf the warren?'

L'herbe looked down at his paws.

'Well, no, not exactly. It turned out to be the result of eating deceiver fungus and wood blewitt toadstools, but that doesn't mean he might not be useful one day. Just because you have one mistaken mystical experience, doesn't necessarily mean that all his powers are false, does it?'

L'herbe seemed to be asking for Skelter's reassurance on this point, so he gave it willingly.

'No, of course not. I expect your prophet's quite mystical really. He just hasn't had a chance to prove it properly yet. No doubt the day will come.'

'That's what I say,' L'arbre said, and his two rabbit companions nodded solemnly. It seemed to Skelter that they needed to believe in this prophet of theirs, in order to enhance the status of their warren, so what was the harm in allowing them their delusions? They had been kind to him, and who was he, a hare from the highlands, to pass judgement on this Le septième creature who might one day see skies running with blood and darkness sweeping over the land?

That night, when they were out feeding, L'herbe identified their prophet, by nodding in the creature's direction. Skelter stared at the skinny little rabbit for some time, looking for something special in him, but nothing emerged. He looked like any ordinary rabbit, though a bit undernourished. No wonder Le septième had taken to eating magic mushrooms – the poor fellow looked half-starved.

Thus the days passed in relative peace, until one dawn when some of the rabbits were out feeding, the most common predator in the land appeared amongst them.

Skelter was on the periphery of the group of five rabbits, tugging away at some dandelions, when there was a commotion, a disturbance on the far side of the glade in which they were feeding. Skelter saw a shape flow over the roots of a beech, and then rise up onto its hind legs before the rabbit that was closest to it – L'arbre!

It was a stoat.

The creature seemed to sway gently in the silver shafts of twilight illuminated from the heavens. The rabbit was completely paralysed. In fact, all the rabbits had frozen, as if hypnotised by the antics of this lean willowy predator dancing slowly before them. Skelter was petrified by fear himself. He wanted to shout a warning, tell L'arbre to run, but the cry stuck in his throat. Instead his legs remained on taut springs, ready to give him flight, if he were to need it. While the rabbits might glance towards the bolt holes, his instinct was to look for open ground, and an area in which to run.

The stoat seemed to glow with sinister light. Its tiny eyes were fixed on L'arbre and its parted mouth showed small white needles in a bed of red flesh.

The whole world appeared to have stopped in time. Nothing moved in the spinney, nothing could be heard. There were no insects buzzing, no birds twittering, no beasts breathing. The whole scene seemed preserved for eternity in the amber light from the risen sun. Skelter could not even detect the beating of his own heart and was certain that the end of the world had come.

Then as if nature found this situation unacceptable, and wanted to shatter the spell, a jay landed in the middle of the deadly arena, and hopped around picking at worms on the bare patches where the rabbits had been feeding. It seemed oblivious of the electric situation, muttering to itself *'Ja, ja, ist gut, ist gut. Viel Wurm. Schmackhaft Wurm. Guten Appetit, Vogel, guten Appetit . . .'* The colourful pink-and-buff bird, with its blue edged wings, went rooting in the soft moss, muttering about worms, and wishing itself good eating, without the least concern for the life-or-death predicament of L'arbre.

Not one of the rabbits or the stoat took any notice of this interruption. The tableau remained as if carved out of stone, the only movements those of the distracted jay, hopping over the ground, unaware of the drama, too interested in his tasty worms to notice that a death was about to occur.

The stoat stopped swaying, curled down onto all fours, and back arched, darted forward. It struck! The movement was alarmingly swift, like the strike of a snake, and all that registered in Skelter's eyes was a blur. The jay took off instantly.

L'arbre fell to the ground screaming, a sound that was quickly staunched by the stoat, who clung to the rabbit's throat. Blood spurted. There was a convulsive kicking from the victim, and then it was all over.

The scream broke the spell the stoat had passed over the forest glade, and rabbits began to bolt in all directions.

Skelter remained staring at the stoat, frozen by his fascination of the horrible scene. It was like a nightmare being performed live before his eyes, and the panic in him was paralysing his limbs. The stoat went up on its hind legs again, its keen gaze cutting through the shafts of light across the glade. Its tiny eyes glittered like polished garnets. Scarlet dripped from its mouth, from its ivory teeth, and ran down its white bib. There was bloodlust evident in its expression, in its stance. It was not necessarily satisfied with one victim. Skelter found some energy, and took off, but instead of following his instinct and heading towards a nearby field of mangolds, he ran towards the warren. He was down his hole in a flash and in his gallery a moment later. His heart was hammering in his chest. If the trees protected the rabbits from eagles, they encouraged other dangers, like allowing stoats to sneak up without being noticed.

Fear spread throughout the warren like a foul marsh gas, and rabbits lay in their burrows, waiting for the worst. It came. The stoat, obviously not content with a single kill, had followed Skelter back to the hole. Skelter could hear it at the entrance, snuffling and poking around with its nose. The stench of the creature made the hare dizzy with terror. There was the sickly smell of blood in the air too.

Then came the unmistakable sounds of tiny clawed feet descending cautiously down the tunnel from above. The stoat had decided to enter the warren. Skelter almost choked, not knowing whether to bolt, or to stay and hope the stoat passed him by or went in a different direction.

The odour of blood and stoat became stronger, and finally, the worst happened. He could see the small red eyes staring down the short tunnel to his gallery. The head moved back and forth, swaying a little, as if the stoat were getting used to the darkness. Skelter knew he could be scented if not seen, and now there was no escape except past the predator.

The stoat began to waddle slowly forward, its tiny eyes fixed on Skelter's throat. Skelter began to drum the hard earth in fear with his hind legs. The noise reverberated down the tunnels and some of the rabbits took up the same action, thumping the ground with their hind legs.

'Go away!' shouted Skelter in a high penetrating voice.

The stoat's answer was to bare its fangs, its top lip curling up. It blew hot air through its small nostrils and continued to advance. Skelter squealed in terror and began digging furiously, attempting the impossible – to tunnel himself out of danger.

Suddenly, just when it seemed that the stoat was going make its move, a badger appeared just off the main tunnel, obviously come to see what the noise was about. It stared around it with an annoyed expression, then on seeing the stoat, spoke in a harsh voice.

'Æt-brēgdan hēre!'

The stoat stopped, turned slightly, and Skelter knew it had understood what sounded like a strong command to remove itself from the vicinity immediately. Skelter had learned enough *Mustelidae* as a near neighbour of the badgers, to recognise that the stoat was being told to get out.

The stoat began to argue, but the force of the next torrent of words from the great badger drowned his protest. The slim predator took one last look at Skelter, then reluctantly swaggered away, up through the bolt hole. You did not question a badger's authority a second time, even if he was a cousin – not if you wanted to stay alive.

Here was a badger, come to the rescue of a hare, and Skelter almost bleated out his gratitude, but the badger took no notice of his attempts to thank him in *Mustelidae* and ambled away into the darkness of its sett, leaving Skelter limp with relief.

Chapter Ten

There were three days of heavy rain, during which time the warren became flooded in parts, and life became a dreary miserable burden. While he was out feeding, Skelter found himself dreading returning to the wet burrows, and the damp gallery which had softened to sloppy mud. This, coupled with the episode of the stoat, made him decide he was not designed to be a rabbit after all. For a start he was not obsessive enough to really get into their culture. He wasn't a worrier by nature, though if he stayed in the warren much longer, he might actually become a ganglion of insecurities.

Skelter informed L'herbe of his decision, and that able rabbit expressed sorrow at his leaving.

'We'll miss your funny ways,' said L'herbe, as a kind of compliment. 'You've made us laugh with your peculiar antics. I always thought hares were lunatics: now I know for sure.'

'Kind of you to say so,' remarked Skelter drily, knowing that these southern rabbits were as rude to each other as they were to any newcomer. It was nothing to do with species prejudice. It was just that they lacked any tact. He himself could have made some acid remarks about neurotic rabbits, but he suffered under the disadvantage of having been raised to be polite to his host.

'Where will you go? What will you do?'

'I'm not sure, L'herbe, but I think I shall cross to that island – at least, it's not really an island, because there's a causeway, but you know where I mean?'

L'herbe shook his head.

'You must be careful over there. Perhaps you should think again? I have heard tell that the island is terrorised by a giant flying creature with a tufted head. A mottled-grey fiend. A great monster, silent in flight, that sweeps in during dusk and dawn and snatches hares from their forms.'

This sounded like a golden eagle, but it could not have been, for golden eagles were not known to hunt especially at twilight – in fact they preferred good light. Nor were they dark grey, though these two details may have been rabbit invention. Skelter had noticed a tendency for the bucks and does to elaborate: their tales were rewrought each time they were told. With every new telling, there were fresh curlicues, creative centripetals added to the original. They could make ordinary blackberries sound like fruits of gods, when they were out of season.

'What does this bird look like? Is this some part of your mythology? You haven't been eating funny mushrooms, have you? This countryside is new to me, but I haven't seen anything of any size in the sky. Where I come from . . .'

L'herbe looked hurt.

'I know, I know, the golden eagles. Well, you've described them to me in detail, and I have to say that *this* creature, bird or flying mammal, is larger and fiercer. Don't look at me like that. This is not fabrication. I realise we have a reputation as story tellers, but this time I'm only passing on what I've been told. No one has seen the creature properly and lived, though there are those who claim to have caught a silhouette against the evening or early morning sky. It hides in a church tower during the day, and only emerges under cover of darkness. Some say it's a flying badger, with a weasel for a tail. The wings of a buzzard sprout from its shoulders when it wants to fly.'

'It couldn't be an owl or a bat I suppose?'

'I told you, it has a body as long as a badger. How many owls or bats do you know, that can take a rabbit or a hare?'

Certainly there were no owls that Skelter was aware of, with a body length to match a badger. Perhaps the rabbits were right? Perhaps it was some unique monster, a fantasy invented by rabbits to keep their young in check. Whatever it was, it was no use worrying about it, like a rabbit. You had to accept the world for what it was, and do your best to live in it, without fussing overmuch.

He said his farewells to L'herbe and the rest of the warren, some of whom he had become rather fond, especially the matronly La framboise. She reminded him of some of the older female hares in his own clan, and the memory was bitter-sweet.

The rabbits expressed sorrow at his departing, but he knew that within a short time most of them would have forgotten him. He was just an itinerant stranger, passing through a community that had been established generations ago. In any case, he was a hare, and despite the physical resemblances, a hare is not a rabbit.

As a farewell gift, he was allowed to leave by the main exit, which he did with pride.

Once outside the trees of the spinney Skelter felt as if he were several pounds lighter. The claustrophobia he had experienced in the warren had been more oppressive than he had previously realised, and it was only now that he was in the open air that he knew just how much he had missed having the sky above him, and the wind on his fur. There was a youthful exuberance in him. He bubbled inside. For a while he even entertained the idea of striking north, in search of his highlands, but when he looked out over the immensity of the flatlands, he knew this was not a journey he would ever complete. Better, he thought to himself, to set his mind on a life here, than to wander the flatlands forever.

Once again he was drawn to the seashore and that intriguing island beyond the narrow, artificial isthmus. Conversely, now that his horizons no longer curved upwards at the edges, and his world was open to infinity on all sides, he yearned for a contained area with definite natural borders. Not an airless rabbit warren in a tight little wood: something wide and open, but with edges to it. He was not used to limitless space, and never would be. If he could not have mountains to encircle his enclosure, why not the sea?

Ever wary of eagles, he made his way to the roadway which formed the causeway to the island. When he reached it he saw that the ocean was not quite as rough as it had been on his earlier visit. The waves were no longer breaking over the asphalt, but contented themselves with hissing around the rocky fringes of the narrow isthmus.

After the days of rain, there was a clear sky, full of birds. While his courage was high, he ventured out onto the causeway, running down the centre of the road, hoping that no men or their vehicles would come while he was crossing. Seagulls watched him pass, from their perches on the roadside rocks, their eyes inscrutable. Once again he realised how much he disliked the creatures. They were alien to him.

90

When he was halfway to his destination, a heavy vehicle came thundering down the tarmac. He first felt the vibrations, and skipped into the rocks, to nestle there until the truck had passed by. It seemed the right thing to do, though he hoped he had not picked up any rabbit thoughts, rabbit habits, without realising it.

When the vehicle had thundered by, leaving a cloud of blue smoke that filled Skelter's lungs and caused him to splutter and sneeze, the hare continued his journey, reaching the far side without further incident.

He turned off onto a beach where masked crabs lurked amongst the rocks, watching him with stalk eyes as he passed, and green crabs scuttled rapidly sideways down the rocks. There were keyhole depressions which held razorshell molluscs and bubbles on the incoming tide marking the places where sandhoppers were hidden. Like the hedgerow, the shoreline is a marginal strip, turbulent with life. It is the meeting place of two giants, the sea and the land; for where two worlds come together the activity intensifies, as the water-margin creatures trade between wet and dry, eking out a life in this narrow region.

Down below the splash zone, where the lichens flourished, was a wetland of snakelock anemones, parchment worms, heart urchins and tellin shells. Skelter nosed around the rock pools, nibbled at some bladderwrack, which he found bitter, watched some prawns darting, and came to a quick conclusion that the water margin was not a place for a hare, despite the wonderful variety of rocks that were to be found there. They were not the rocks of his homeland, in any case, being smooth and glib. He preferred his rugged and more complicated highland outcrops. When he tried to climb one of the sloping slabs its slippery surface caused him to perform an unintentional glissade down to the stony beach, an accident that resulted in a sore rump.

Some way along the shoreline, he struck out for open farmland, and once again found himself amongst neatly-hedged fields with parallel furrows and ridges, trees dotting the countryside and drainage ditches cutting every edge.

Once more he had near horizons, of squared hawthorn, blackthorn and hazel, their crests crowned by *hethers* which prevented the growing wood from springing upright. Under these natural barriers grew lush grasses and herbaceous plants – rye grass and red campion – and the climbing briars and brambles, and lolling ferns like hartstongue. In amongst these were wrens and chaffinches, flitting from dog rose to dog rose, hiding amongst the garlic mustard plants. This was more to his liking than the coastal strip.

In the short time that he had been in the flat country, Skelter had come to regard the hedgerow as a place of activity, swarming with red soldier beetles, brass moths, ants and ladybirds. On these insects fed the troublesome shrew, whom bank voles and woodmice avoided almost as assiduously as they did hawks and falcons. Skelter also found comfort in the hedge. It afforded him some cover from eagles, and he liked the busyness of the place better than the relatively empty ploughed or planted fields.

Although the rabbits had assured him that there were no golden eagles in the region, he still could not quite believe it. His mind and body were tuned to the fact of eagles, and it was going to take more than a few reassuring words from rabbits to convince him thoroughly that no golden killers inhabited the skies over the flatlands. There was also this strange aerial creature to consider.

It could be that this was a local story, which they invented to make fools of strangers. The highlands had its share of those tales, though of course the local population didn't take them seriously. It could be that this flying assassin was nothing more than a product of over-active imaginations. Rabbits, hares, vanish without a trace, taken by foxes or snared by men, and those left behind begin inventing exotic reasons for the disappearances.

'You see that mist-shrouded island? It's a place of terror, for there are headless hares there, that haunt the marshes and frighten wandering souls to death! Why only last season a hare was found stiff as stone, its eyes starting from its skull, and no reason for it . . .'

He was new to this region, and he could not just dismiss things out of hand before he had heard from others, especially hares. If the hares on this island said the same things, and made precautions against the creature, then Skelter would have to take seriously the idea that there was a large flying predator in the area. But as for *magic*, well that was so much damp hay as far as he was concerned.

From the shadow of the hedge, he made forays out into the

fields, for his meals. The land was a rich brown colour: good arable earth. It stretched gently away on all sides, combed or full of crops, further away from the sky than any he had seen before, but closer to heaven. Fertile loam beyond a highland hare's imagination. The soil covering his northern mountains had been sparse, allowing the growth of heather and sage, but little else. The peat hags had been covered with grass and weeds, but this flatland earth contained succulent treasures, one or two of them vegetables for which he had no names. Skelter ate his fill, thinking that at last he had found the garden of his soul, where he could indulge his palate forever.

In these fields he found vegetables of the same varieties as those which surrounded the rabbits' wood, such as alsike clover, lucerne, sainfoin and black medick, all grown by the farmers for the sake of the rabbits and hares, or so it seemed. There was also fodder cabbage and buckwheat, parsnips and swedes, field beans and white mustard, the names of which he had learned from his good friends the rabbits. He ate his fill, glancing up occasionally to see if he was being observed by friend or foe, ever wary in this place which was so very different from the land of his birth.

PART TWO

*

Lord of the Flatlands

Chapter Eleven

Bubba lived in the belfry of the island's village church tower, beside the great bell that never sounded, the rope having been rotten and unusable since mid-winter. Bubba had arrived in the tower shortly afterwards, and had used it as his roost ever since. He liked the tower. It understood Bubba.

It was true that Bubba had large sharp, diamond eyes and a tufted crown. If the rabbits or hares he had killed and eaten had ever asked him what he was, he would not have been able to give them a proper answer. His mother had been a man and it was Bubba's belief that he himself was partly human with extraordinary powers: the power of flight, of keen-sight, of silent movement in the dusk and dawn.

It was not natural for Bubba to fly in the twilights of dawn and dusk, but his mother had only taken him out at those times, and had been very secretive with him. It was as if mother had been afraid someone would see them, and so used the gloaming to cloak their excursions. Bubba's habits were not easily broken, and he had somehow caught the feeling from mother, that if he was seen by other people something terrible would happen. So Bubba continued the habit of hunting in half-light, when he could still see the prey himself, but was less likely to be noticed by other men. Twilight is a time of half-shadows, when shapes are not easy to define, and size difficult to judge, especially regarding creatures in flight.

He spoke no language known to animals or birds, so was unable to communicate, except with the church tower, and this he spoke to not with words, but with his head.

—Tower, you are my only friend. You keep me hidden from my enemies within your breast. Your old grey stones have seen much history, but have you ever seen a creature like me before?

—*No Bubba, you are unique, but that does not mean you are a freak, for you have perfection of form. You are invincible among all creatures, except man.*

—I am misunderstood.

—*Great beings are often misunderstood, unappreciated for their true worth.*

—Only you understand me, Tower.

Bubba then, was self-sufficient, needed only his own company, and missed only the mother who fed and raised him as his own. When mother had taken him out, Bubba had seen falcons and hawks and knew he was not one of them. He was unique, brought by his mother from a far off place of swamps and jungles, a place of rainforests and giant brown rivers.

Mother had transported him secretly to the big dark mansion on the edge of the marshes, with its great timbers and many rooms. Whereas Bubba was part human, mother had been part bird, controlling a flying machine. Mother had carried packages of white powder from the jungles to colder lands in his great rigid bird of metal, and sometimes Bubba had been allowed to go with him. Once or twice, Bubba had to protect his mother, by attacking people and tearing their faces with his talons and beak. Many humans were afraid of Bubba.

That Bubba was some other kind of bird was not possible, for they were all far smaller than he was, and were worthy of nothing but contempt. Bubba could bite the head from a tawny owl, bring down and kill a deer on the run, break the back of a hare.

When mother had died, the night the olive-skinned men had come bringing their small guns with them, Bubba had been locked in another room. He heard the plopping noises first, then the crashing and smashing, as furniture was turned over and drawers were pulled out, and pictures were torn down, and carpets were ripped up. Even then he knew that mother was dead.

When they opened the door and pointed their guns into the room, he flew at their faces, clawing and jabbing with his terrible hooked beak. They ran away screaming, clutching their eyes. Bubba found mother in a pool of blood, and had left him there. The men had left the way open for him to leave the house. So Bubba flew away from the mansion, out into the wild country. There he found he could hunt down quarry unprepared for a part-human with wings, and so each night Bubba feasted.

When the people wailed below the tower, every seven days, Bubba would croon along with them, remembering how his mother used to make noises for him, and Bubba used to make them back. Bubba was sad without mother, but the murmuring mortals in their stone-and-wood nest helped to soothe away Bubba's spiritual pain.

Yesterday evening Bubba had taken a rabbit on the run: had snatched it from the ground with only a whisper of wind. The other rabbits had not even missed their companion: had seen nothing, heard nothing, knew nothing. Bubba was the shadow of death. Bubba was the red slayer, whose secret turns and passes instilled doubt in the undoubtful, implanted fear in the fearless. Bubba came in with the darkness as darkness himself, his mighty shape with its terrible armoury of sharpened steel, ready to slash arteries and sever heads from bodies.

—Tower, I have a voracious appetite.

—*You are predator, you have to kill, it's in your nature.*

—That's not what I said, tower.

—*It's not what you say, Bubba, but what you mean.*

Bubba had no compassion for the dying, no emotion for those in pain. He had eyes colder than the stone from which the tower was built: a heart as dry as the mortar that held his nest together. Bubba felt he was ancient, a Dark Age creature, with a mind thrown backwards into a winter of nights. He was fashioned of mystical matter from the hands of the magician who was his mother. He was brute and brick, ire and iron. In his head were wildernesses that spread inwards to infinity; were pits that dropped to the centre of the sky; were heights that fell deep into the earth.

—Tower, am I wise, or am I mad?

—*You are both wise and mad, for the two are inexplicably interwoven in you.*

—What has made me mad, tower?

—*Time and loneliness have darkened part of your mind, Bubba, but this darkness makes the wisdom shine through more brightly.*

Inside Bubba's belfry were littered the skulls of now unnameable creatures, bones scattered like white twigs over the floorboards. There were spiders and insects in every corner, and birds used to come to this place before Bubba arrived, for there were droppings and hard white splashes of calcium on wood and brick. Once upon a time there had been bats and mice too, but Bubba had eaten all these: mere titbits snatched between proper meals.

Outside and all around the tower was his domain, as far as he could see, which was a land surrounded by ocean. He was the lord of the flatlands. He terrorised the countryside with his presence, swooping out of the sky like a winged demon, and carrying off which ever quarry he pleased.

—Tower, do I rule my kingdom well, or am I a tyrant?
—*Not all tyrants are despots, Bubba.*
—Is that my answer, tower?
—*Yes.*

Evening crept across the land, enveloping all with a faint blush, and filling holes with shade. Bubba stood on the spar which held the great bell, like a man would stand, a cloak of black feathers around his shoulders. When dusk thickened Bubba took to the air, flying out through the belfry window.

His wings were silent as he cruised above the land. He watched the quilted flatlands sweeping below him, eyes alert for movement amongst the deepening shadows. His eyes were so sensitive he could detect a gnat twitching.

He found a tall tree, an elm, and alighted on one of the uppermost branches. All around him were the end of day activities: the starlings gathering in a single tree, all talking at once; the twittering bats emerging from their hollows; the ducks settling; the weasels and stoats coming out after prey. Bubba's eyes lit upon a domestic creature, a small terrier that was hurrying along the bottom of a ditch to a good sporting ground it knew lay at the end.

Bubba shuffled on the branch, readying himself for the launch, while the unsuspecting dog scrambled up the side of the ditch and into the long grass. Bubba waited. Eventually the dog left the tall grass and began walking along a furrow, towards a rabbit warren in the corner of the field. Some way along the furrow shallowed out, the side ridges almost disappearing. When the terrier reached this point, Bubba took off, falling in a dipping arc.

There was an exhilarating rush of wind around his head. He came up behind the terrier, who was intent on reaching his own goal: a place where he could run out and surprise some rabbits and chase them all over the field.

At the last moment some instinct made the terrier look over his shoulder, but instead of glancing upwards, its gaze was directed down the channel formed by the furrow. The dog's head was still in that position when Bubba struck, the talons sinking into the back and side of the terrier's neck.

However, a terrier is not a rabbit or hare, and the dog was quicker than Bubba expected. It twisted violently. Bubba's talons were partly impeded by a thick leather collar with brass studs, that the terrier had round its neck, and amazingly Bubba lost his grip. The dog dropped to the ground, wounded but still alive. It dashed into some woods that abutted the ploughed field.

This had never happened to Bubba before in his life. That quarry should escape was unthinkable. His talons had been in the creature. It should be broken, dead!

Bubba wheeled away from the edge of the wood, then turned about. The terrier no doubt thought it was free from harm inside the forest. It was to learn that nowhere was a safe haven, where Bubba was concerned.

The giant bird flew straight into the line of trees, and weaved in and around the trunks, as easily and skilfully as a goshawk. Bubba was more at home amongst the trees, than he was in the open sky, despite his great size. He followed the terrier, as it desperately tried to throw off its hunter, running into thickets and briar patches, around large boles, under bramble bushes. Bubba sometimes landed in the trees, launching himself from a thick bough once he had the measure of his prey again.

The dog's whimpering could be heard over the whole woodland, and other creatures, badgers, rabbits, stoats, weasels, all found themselves holes and disappeared inside them. The smell of blood was in the air and terror went swimming through the green darkness beneath the canopy. It caught hold of the throats of young and old, and held them still.

Bubba was relentless, indefatigable, and tracked the dog in a circular route around the woods. Finally, he cornered the terrier in a glade. Bubba's diamond eyes flashed in triumph. Nothing escaped those claws, the size of a man's hand. Nothing escaped that huge hooked mouth.

He fell on the unfortunate dog like a rock. There was a choked-off yelp, a thrashing, and then Bubba's beak ripped open the dog's throat and let the gore out.

The blood tasted good. Bubba pecked through the eye-sockets to get at the sweet brains, still warm, inside the skull. When he had fed on these, he took the carcass in his claws and rose up into the purple-black sky.

Bubba was majestic in flight, and any who saw him from below would have gasped at his size, at his shape. Here, Bubba was unique. Here he was some dark savage god, omnipotent amongst the beasts of the field and the birds of the air. Nothing could withstand him except man, and man was not aware of his presence.

He carried the body of the small terrier to his nest and there he picked and tore at the meat with his beak and claws, until bits of flesh lay all around him, and the floor was speckled with gore. As he stripped the bones of hide, the flaps of skin and hair were scraped and then pushed aside. The offal was dispensed with very quickly, the soft warm meats going down into his gullet with speed: liver, kidneys, entrails.

In a day or so, the skull would join the other white sightless headbones that decorated the belfry. What had been a boy's pet, loved and cherished just a sunset ago was now the pitiful remains of a feast.

Bubba felt a little overfull from gorging.

—I have eaten, tower.

—*Your will be done.*

Chapter Twelve

There was one creature who was not afraid of the lord of the flatlands, or any other fiend for that matter. Her name was Jittie, and she was a predator herself, living on a tasty diet of snails, slugs and worms. She wasn't a large creature, certainly not as big as a rabbit or a hare, and though she had a vast array of weapons they would have been no defence against the mighty Bubba. That monstrous killer, now brooding away the daylight hours in his dark tower, could have snatched little Jittie from the ground, slit her belly open with one stroke, and swallowed what was inside in three gulps.

No, Jittie's strength of spirit lay in her attitude towards life. She was not naturally aggressive, like the shrew, though she would occasionally attack mice, rats, frogs, and even larger creatures than those. She certainly did not acknowledge any other creature as her superior. She was introverted, interested in what went on around her even when it concerned her only indirectly, and was rarely ruffled by anything. It would not occur to her to be frightened of another creature, even the badger, who was her only natural enemy.

Jittie was a hedgehog.

A badger was in fact the only indigenous predator who could have forced his snout between Jittie's spines to reach her vulnerable stomach. Even a fox could not do this, though foxes have been known to roll a balled hedgehog into water and wait for it to uncurl or drown before making a meal of it. Jittie's greatest danger was in being squashed on the highways and byways of man by one of his machines, since whenever she felt danger approaching she rolled into her protective ball and remained motionless.

The fact was, Jittie really didn't care about very much at all, except enjoying life in her quiet, simple way. She cracked open the shells of snails with her sharp incisors, pulled elasticated worms from their wormeries, and snatched slugs from the leaves of plants. She made herself a nest lined with leaves and pieces of moss to sleep out the winter, and one of dry grass in which to raise her young, if any, in the summer. If death came, on feet or wings, so be it: Jittie was a fatalist. If the worst came to the worst, the Elysian Fields of hedgehog heaven awaited her.

Her current summer nest was in a disused rabbit hole beneath a hawthorn hedge. She had seen the funny-looking new hare arrive the evening before and wondered why it stayed so close to the ditch, when all the hares she knew preferred the open field. Still, as she said to a neighbouring hedgehog, it was none of her business really. If the hare wanted to act in a peculiar manner, that was really up to itself, and was nothing to do with her. Unpredictable creatures, hares. Full of their own importance, always posturing, quite unreliable. Still, you had to admit it wasn't *natural*.

Not natural at *all*, said her neighbour. Then again, those madcaps were capable of anything, rushing around as if the world was coming to an end one minute, and standing stark staring still the next. Who could fathom hares? Other creatures moved around at a reasonable pace, getting things done methodically, correctly, efficiently, while hares . . . Why they jumped and jerked, danced around on their hind legs, boxed each other for goodness knows *what* reason, and generally put the jitters into anyone that came into contact with them. If they did anything useful at all, it was always a botched job, though they were either too lazy, or more likely too impatient, even to make a proper home for themselves, and lived in those little ruts that took about two minutes to scrape out. You would think they were nomads or something, the way they seemed happy with the minimum of comfort, but oh no, they lived in their shallow scrapings their whole lives, never going anywhere further than a quick run would take them.

Both hedgehogs nodded their heads, sagely, completely in agreement.

Still, said Jittie, they were all part of nature's varied world, and whoever had made them all had obviously seen a purpose for hares, though heaven knew what it was. Perhaps they had been put on the earth to counterbalance all the sanity, to stop the world from becoming too boring, to add a bit of spontaneity?

104

They were handsome looking creatures, everyone was agreed on that, but their brains had been put in backwards or upside down or *some*thing.

The neighbour clucked, pulling a worm out of the ground which didn't want to be eaten, and clung to its hole until the last moment.

That's a fact, the neighbour told her (crunching away). Their brains were in their feet, though sometimes their feet were in their heads.

Well, this one is a *bit* different, acknowledged Jittie, because he digs himself a little hole, like a rabbit. He definitely *wasn't* a rabbit, though he was smallish for a hare, and the tunnel he dug was only short, with an opening at both ends, like a flattened U shape. Maybe he was a runt, or something, abandoned by his parents at birth? Maybe he actually *thought* he was some kind of rabbit, and didn't associate with hares at all?

The neighbour suggested that perhaps Jittie ought to put him straight on exactly what he was, though she was sure she'd get no thanks for it, for when did a hare wait around long enough for niceties and polite talk?

No social graces, remarked Jittie.

Oh, you can say that again.

Jittie left her neighbour to wander along the ditch in search of breakfast. She found some juicy larvae under a dock leaf and ended their mortal torment of having to feed on second-rate vegetable fare, while two fields away – a journey beyond their capability – was a sea of young lettuces, food for the gods. She felt she was doing them a favour.

When she got back to the nest, the new hare was sitting looking at the world with sad eyes. He seemed a bit bewildered and not at all in his right mind.

'Hello,' said Jittie, in her best *Leporidae*, 'what's the matter with you? Lost?'

The hare blinked at her.

'You could say that, though I don't think I'm ever going to find my way back to where I came from. I've got to make the best of this dismal place I suppose.'

Jittie felt her spines tingle, and for once was aware of the fleas busy amongst the forest on her back. Like most animals, she was proud of her homeland, for although she knew the wetlands were a little dreary and flat, they had a mystique, she felt, and were not altogether without their attractions.

'I can say that, but not you!' she snapped, showing she was put out. 'We like it bleak around here. Gives the place an air of mystery and magic. Why, you of all creatures – a hare! – you should find this place *sacred*. This is where the human hare-worshippers lived: the warrior-queen and her tribe. This is where your ghost-hares first appeared, though *I've* never seen one, and wouldn't want to.'

The hare blinked again, an annoying habit.

'Oh, sure, sorry. I didn't mean to put the place down, only I come from the mountains, which for me has more interest, if you see what I mean.'

'Mountains,' nodded Jittie. 'They go up one side and down the other. So what? Does that make them interesting? Do the mountains have any marshes? No. Do they have any saltings? No. Do they have any hedgerows, ploughed fields, gates or stiles? No.'

The hare began to get sniffy.

'Don't really want any of those things. How come you speak such good hare anyway?'

'I speak seven languages fluently,' said Jittie, 'and can pass the time of day in four others. I'm a creature of intellect. I don't waste my days punching holes in the wind with my head, or showing off by dancing on my back legs, or doing somersaults like a clown. I employ my time usefully, listening, learning, utilising.'

'Clever snout,' muttered the hare, and dashed away, out into the field, to nibble sulkily at some cabbage stalks.

Jittie watched him go, decided he was not as fleet of foot as the local hares, but that his run was so peculiar he would probably surprise the foxes with it and survive that way. She could see he was miserable. Hares would be, away from home. If they ever made any journeys at all, which they did sometimes in the autumn, migrating to higher ground before the winter set in, it was only a short distance. Hedgehogs on the other hand, didn't care where they wandered, so long as there was food and and a place to rest.

She shook her head, and muttered an old saying. Then she made her way across the field to a rich bottomland meadow, with a river at the foot of its slope fringed by broad-leafed goat willows. When she reached it, after shuffling through the thick hedge, she found it was a sea of wild flowers. Buttercups blazed like yellow fire across the dipping slope, and the scent of the meadowsweet's feathery flowers filled the air. The delicate mauve-pinks of valerians were scattered through the bright raging suncolours of the buttercups, dandelions, meadow vetchling and tansy herbs. Butterflies, blues and fritillaries mostly, were like coloured dust settling on the field.

Jittie was moved by the beauty of the meadow.

Mountains indeed! Had he seen this? Did you get this in the mountains?

She grumbled away to herself, disappearing into the tall wild flowers and following the slope down to the river. Inside the meadowland were all manner of creatures, from mice to moles, but Jittie was given a wide berth as she waddled through this fairytale cloak of grasses and herbs.

When she reached the river, she dipped her head and drank down the cool, muddy water until she had quenched her thirst. There had been water in her ditch, but nothing tasted so good as the river.

Some distance down the bank coypu were busy doing something, but what took her attention was a local hare crossing over from one bank to another further upstream. It was probably coming to get at the meadowgrass. The hare was a strong swimmer, as most brown hares tend to be, and forged the current without too much difficulty, though by the time it scrambled up the bank it had been taken at an angle and landed right where Jittie was drinking. The hare, a jill, shook herself, wetting Jittie.

'Hey,' cried Jittie, 'watch it!'

The hare sat up and stared.

'Sorry,' said the jill, 'didn't realise you were there.'

'Do you ever?' grumbled Jittie. 'You hares! What's your name?'

'Why do you want to know?'

Jittie huffed in impatience.

'Why? Because there's a new hare arrived, from the mountains, and I thought if I gave him your name he might come looking for you, and you can help him adjust to the flatlands. He's going to get himself into trouble, otherwise. There's a fox highway not far from where I live, and if no one takes responsibility for him, he'll blunder into one of them and get eaten.'

The jill began to eat the wild flowers, annoying the bees that were homing in on the nectar. 'What's it to me?' she said.

Jittie stared at the hare, half up on its hind legs and chewing delicately, wondering how such a noble-looking creature could be so indifferent to the plight of others, especially her own kind. The local hares were renowned for being selfish, however, and Jittie did not like to see them get away with it. She persisted.

'I asked you your name,' she snapped.

The hare shrugged.

'Speedwell,' she replied.

'Good. Now that we know who you are, I can pass on the information to ... I don't even know *his* name. You hares are such secretive creatures. Anyway, this mountain hare will probably come looking for you, so treat him kindly, or I'll put a hex on you.'

The jill stopped chewing and stared.

'You wouldn't.'

'I would, as soon as look at you,' snapped Jittie, knowing that the local hares were amongst the most superstitious creatures on the earth. They had all sorts of talismans and symbols to ward off evil, though Jittie couldn't be bothered to learn what they were. The fallen twigs of the wych elm were important, she knew that much. 'I'll find a wych elm and work a spell with it that'll make your feet rot,' she said, enjoying herself a little, 'unless you agree to look out for this young jack and treat him well.'

'Not my *feet*,' pleaded Speedwell.

'First your feet, then your ears. They'll rot at the roots and drop off. Fine sight you'll make *then*.'

'You leave me no choice,' said the jill. 'Tell him where to find us, and we'll straighten him out – kindly.'

'Good, that's all he needs I think. He seems a sensible creature – for a hare.'

With that, Jittie walked away, up the meadow. She followed a ridge that was part of an ancient ruined fort built by humans who came to the land some two thousand summers ago: humans whose weaponheads still littered the meadowground. There had been a ferocious battle here, between the local humans and these metalclad newcomers from a distant country. Bronze and iron blades corroded amongst the roots of the daisies and buttercups, where leather garments had melted into the soil and provided the wild flowers with extra nourishment. Here, down amongst the worms, was the shape of a spoked chariot wheel, its royal tribal carvings imprinted on the clay. A standard, the emblem of which would be recognised by Skelter as the dreaded eagle, had all but dissolved in a vein of lime. There were bones there, iron bolts embedded in them, sundered from their sockets. More than that, the soil reeked with the spirits of warrior women and men waiting to be reawakened on the earth's final day. The outlanders amongst them had called upon gods of superhuman form, while the rebellious locals had looked to the divine hare to give them inspired victory. That victory had indeed been granted, as the charred remains of foreign corpses attested.

Soon Jittie's hedge came in sight, and she waddled towards it, looking forward to a long rest.

Chapter Thirteen

After his squabble with the hedgehog, Skelter felt affronted, and went out into the field to chew on cabbages. The trouble with the local animals, he thought, was they didn't understand what it was like to be a mountain hare. How could anyone compare these dismal surroundings with his beautiful highland home? The suggestion was ludicrous: the idea was pathetic. Mountain scenery was the most magnificent nature had to offer: it lifted your heart and made it soar. How *dare* this hedgehog say that the flatlands had a beauty to compare with what he had lost.

Wondering why he could never find any heather in the flatlands, Skelter tore angrily at the cabbages at first then gradually became depressed and miserable. A creature had offered him her friendship, in this forsaken land and what had he done? Rejected it. Instead of relaxing and getting to know the hedgehog, he had waded in with his criticisms of the local habitat, damning the whole landscape, extolling the virtues of his highlands. Of course that was going to upset someone who was born in the flatlands.

He saw himself through her eyes now: tactless, whining, parochial. The exile with the chip on his shoulder.

Skelter decided to apologise to the hedgehog, and returned to the ditch, but the spiny creature was nowhere to be found. He discovered her nest in the rabbit hole, but she had gone off somewhere.

He went back to the roots of the tree and pondered on what he ought to do next. Should he stay here, make his home in the corner of the field, or move on? This was not exactly heaven on earth, but then, what did he intend to find elsewhere? There were no mountains to be had. One field was much like the rest. What he was doing was moving around for the sake of it, to keep his mind busy. Well that wouldn't do. It was possible he might suddenly come upon a field of heather, or vegetation similar to what he was used to, but there had been no evidence so far to prove this probable. So, not only was he going to have to live without his mountains, but also his heather. The water here had a funny taste to it, too, not at all like the sweet water of the burns and loch of his homeland. It was too bad, he thought. Just *too* bad.

The sun was in evidence today and he settled down, letting it warm through his fur. He fell into a doze, from which he kept waking with a start, then settling back down again. By the time noon came round he was fast asleep.

It was a crow's call that woke him, and he jumped up with a start.

Something moved very quickly before his eyes.

Skelter jumped back against the tree.

It was a creature the badgers call a *noedre*, mountain hares call a viper, and flatlanders call an adder: the only indigenous poisonous snake in the land. Skelter had startled and annoyed the creature into rearing. He could see the snake was angry with him and it looked as if it were about to strike.

Skelter remained absolutely still, hoping the creature would go on its way. The trouble with adders was that they were unpredictable. Skelter couldn't be sure that the snake would bite him, but then again, it might.

The adder spat some strange sounds at him but since he understood not a word of the language used by the creature Skelter could do nothing but reply in his own tongue.

'Get away from me!' cried Skelter frantically.

This shrill appeal from the hare seemed to enrage the sun-coloured serpent with its dark zigzag markings even further. Its V-marked head swayed from side to side as it prepared to stab the hare with its fangs.

This was the scene that Jittie saw as she walked through her hole in the hedge. She was totally unprepared for such a sight and for a moment she too froze in her tracks. Then, realising the situation was a desperate one for the hare, she made a sound to distract the snake. The adder turned quickly. Jittie dashed forward, clicking her teeth aggressively.

* * *

111

Skelter had been so transfixed by the adder that at first he did not realise that it was no longer a threat to him. Then he saw the hedgehog, rolled into a ball, within easy range of the adder's strike. The snake's head flashed forward, as it bit the hedgehog several times.

Skelter was horrified. He skipped to the side, away from the tree, and dashed to a safe distance before looking back. The adder's vicious attacks continued, striking repeatedly at the defenceless little ball in front of it. The hedgehog could not escape the bites, as they came in lightning jabs, one after the other, the fangs finding a mark every time.

There was a feeling of anger in Skelter's breast now, towards the adder, but he knew he could do nothing to save the hedgehog that had intervened on his behalf. She would be dead within a short time. Her little body had been penetrated in over a dozen places, and still the snake struck, time and time again, completely devoid of any mercy.

'Leave her alone!' he shouted. 'Isn't that enough?'

The adder paused to look at the hare, its eyes yellow with contempt.

At that moment Jittie began to uncurl. First a nose came out, then a whole face, until she was standing on four legs before the adder.

Amazingly, she did not appear sick: in fact, she looked defiant. Jittie darted forward with surprising speed and sank her teeth into the adder's throat. The snake began to writhe, its coils winding around its adversary, but Jittie was not about to let go her grip. The coils twisted and turned, tying knots around its enemy.

Skelter watched the combat on the scruffy piece of turf below the elm with his heart in his mouth. Was it possible that the hedgehog could triumph, even as she was dying herself? She seemed determined to take the adder with her, to wherever it was that hedgehogs went after death. He marvelled at her strength of will, her stamina, her fighting spirit.

The snake uncurled itself, trying to slither backwards, out of Jittie's grip, but its small spiny antagonist chose this moment to renew her hold, and her sharp incisors bore even deeper into the adder's throat. The snake began to go limp, its struggles growing weaker and weaker, until it could hardly move. Then Jittie began to do the same to the adder as it had done to her, attacking it repeatedly with savage bites.

Finally, the adder lay still in the dust, as dead as a fallen branch.

Skelter let out the breath that he had been holding for some time, and ran over to the hedgehog.

'You gave up your life for me,' he said quickly, in case she should die before he had time to thank her. 'You are the most unselfish creature I have ever met. I am forever indebted to you. Do you have any last wishes? Have you any messages you would like passed on to your kin? I don't even know your name. Mine is Skelter.'

The hedgehog looked at him with a funny expression.

She said, 'I'm known as Jittie, but you can save your breath, because I'm not going to die.' She stared at the body of the snake, lying in the sun with its belly exposed to the sky. It was like a piece of discarded rope now: torn and frayed around the head. 'I warned him, several times. He stole two of my babies last year. I said I would get him, and I have. That thing there in the dust is called Stememna, and his mate will no doubt come looking for him at some time. She would be wise to stay away from me, though I've no quarrel with her at the moment.'

Skelter shook his head to clear it of the jumble.

'You're not going to die?' he repeated.

Jittie stared at him and shook her own head in impatience.

'You don't know very much about hedgehogs, do you? Neither did he, though I warned him often enough. Hedgehogs, my hare-brained friend, are immune to adders' venom. For some reason, adders can't get this fact into their heads. They are so used to everyone being terrified of them they think they're invulnerable. All I had to do was roll myself into a ball and wait until he had exhausted his venom, then attack and kill him. Well, it's over now, and I'm afraid he deserved what he got, that baby-killer.'

Skelter was still immensely impressed. 'I'm glad you're not going to die,' he said, 'because we can be friends now. Whatever you like to say, you saved my life. Unfortunately mountain hares are *not* immune to snake's venom, and if that viper had struck just once, I would have been a goner. That's what we call them by the way – vipers.'

'I know *that*,' sniffed Jittie. 'Well, *I'm* glad you've come out of the sulks, because they were doing you no good whatsoever. I'm happy to tell you I've had a word with a jill called Speedwell, who lives about two or three fields away, and I've told her you're here. She's a bit unreliable, hares – that is, local hares – always are, but at least she'll spread the word and they'll know you're around.'

It is not often in the animal world that two creatures from different species become firm friends. There are usually language difficulties, cultural problems and natural preferences and dislikes to overcome, and these are usually enough to put off any developing relationship. Most animals would shrug their shoulders and say, 'Why bother?'

In this case however, the hare and the hedgehog had seen something deeper and more interesting in each other, than is normally evident between species. For her part, Jittie admired the fortitude and strength of spirit showed by the hare, who had been torn from his homeland, transported to a foreign land where he was pursued by dogs, then left to wander without family or friend to whom he could turn in times of stress. Yet still he had maintained his will to survive. She had a profound respect for such mettle.

On his part, Skelter had seen a smaller creature than himself take on a formidable opponent, and come through victorious. She had gone into battle on his behalf, even though she maintained she had had old scores to settle, and his gratitude was substantial. He saw in the little hedgehog a force to be reckoned with, and was glad that foxes did not have the spirit of hedgehogs within them, or the red devils would be invincible.

Thus began a firm friendship, which was to last until one of them left for the Otherworld of hares or hedgehogs.

That evening the pair of them lay in their individual homes, the hedgehog on her nest and the hare in his form, and were able to converse without raising their voices too much. Skelter told Jittie about famous hare races that had been run and Jittie talked about foxes that had been fooled, and dogs that had been duped.

'Hedgehogs have no *glorious* history to tell,' she said, 'we've just been here, for a long time. We *last*. There are all sorts of stories

114

about us and humans, but we have none about hedgehogs and hedgehogs. I don't know why that should be, but it is. Now you hares, you have all sorts of tales to tell, only a fraction of which are true.'

'Truth isn't the object, in our stories,' explained Skelter. 'You have to look for other things, like symbols and images, and morals, stuff like that. The tales are there to enhance the real world, to mirror certain fundamental truths, though the stories themselves are made up.'

Jittie shrugged.

'Let's hear one then. I can see you're dying to tell me something.'

'Right, yes well, this was told to me by our storyteller, up in the highlands . . .'

'Get *on* with it.'

'It's about a mountain hare on the sun,' said Skelter, 'and another on the moon. It's a very strange tale: a love story with a sad ending. Way back in the misty past, when hares were gods, there was a jack and a jill who were very attracted to each other. The jack's name was Thunderfeet and the jill was called Lightninglegs. They were from different clans, but that was not the barrier to their union, for hares often mate between clans.

'No, what stopped them from getting together were the oaths they had made before they had met each other. Thunderfeet claimed he was the fastest hare that had ever lived, and that no other hare could beat him on the flat or over the glens, and he would only mate with the jill who could best him in a race. Unfortunately, this was the very same vow that Lightninglegs made in relation to herself: she promised the jacks who boxed for her favours that she would only mate with the male hare that could outrun her. So proud were these two hares, that they were willing to live a life of abstinence rather than mate with a hare of inferior ability.

'"I want my leverets to be the fastest creatures on four feet," proclaimed Lightninglegs.

'Thunderfeet announced that his leverets, ". . . will outrun the deer, the greyhound, the fleetest horse!"

'One fine spring day, Lightninglegs was feeding on the heather, when she saw a hare streaking through the glen, and she knew she

115

had found a potential mate. She raced at right angles to his run, and flashed across Thunderfeet's nose, making him skid to a halt and stare after her disappearing tail. *That's the jill for me, thought the jack*.'

Jittie interrupted the monologue with an impatient, 'But why didn't they agree between themselves, without telling any other soul, that one of them would win, and one lose?'

'Because *both* had sworn to mate only with the hare that could run faster. If Thunderfeet won, then Lightninglegs would have gone to him, but he could not have accepted her, because he had pledged his form to the hare that was faster than himself – and vice versa. Their own earlier declarations were the unsurmountable blocks to what would have been an ideal union, between the two fastest hares on the face of the earth. Their leverets would have been magnificent runners, and perhaps the fathers and mothers of a new superspecies of hare.

'Even a draw was no good – they had both said that their potential mate had to *win*. They were too afraid to race each other, because whatever the outcome, there could be no happy ending to such a contest.

'The pair of thwarted lovers spent a painful spring, watching each other from a distance, feeding from the grasses on either side of a burn, a desperate yearning in their breasts. Thunderfeet was so on fire within, he thought he would burst into flame, and Lightinglegs had a hunger inside that could never be satisfied by heather and sedge. The fact that they were each unobtainable fuelled their desire until they were both so miserable without each other they thought they would die.

'Finally, winter came around, and they met by chance one day in the snows by a frozen loch.

'"This is terrible," said Thunderfeet, "I can't go to sleep without seeing your eyes."

'"And I," replied Lightninglegs, "see your shape in every cloud, in every shadow."

'They agreed then, that something had to be done, and they decided to visit a wise old hare called Thinker, who lived with the dotterels high up on the mountainside.

'Together they climbed higher than most hares would ever go, to see the eremite whose form never completely thawed even in the summer, and found him counting snowflakes as they fell, to find how many it took to fill a square harelength. They told him their problem and asked him if he had any solution he could offer them.

'"Why of course," Thinker replied, irritated at having been interrupted in his important task. "It's easy to see that your skills are purely physical – you haven't enough brains between you to fill a paw-print. What you have to do is run *two* races, naturally – one of you wins the first, and the other, the second race. That way you will have both outrun the other, and can mate in the knowledge that you have both fulfilled your vows. Now leave me in peace, I was just up to one million and seven, and I've got to start again . . ."

'So the two hares went away joyful, and arranged the first of their two races. It was to be up a high mountain, starting at the foot, and finishing on the peak. Both Thunderfeet and Lightninglegs were very excited and changed their minds half-a-dozen times about who was to win the first race, and who the second.

'The race was started by a tortoise, who happened to be passing at the time. This slow reptile had no other part in the race, and subsequent retellings of this tale by creatures other than hares have become a little confused, giving the tortoise an active role in the running. It is of course absurd to imagine a tortoise racing, and winning, against a hare . . .'

'That's the way I heard it,' said Jittie, quietly.

'Well, it's totally untrue,' Skelter cried, 'because, as I say, the tortoise was simply asked to start them. That other story was put about by some rabbit I expect, envious of the running abilities of hares. It's complete fabrication. It's slanderous, it's propaganda, it's . . .'

'All right, all right,' grumbled Jittie, 'get on with the tale.'

'Right then, the tortoise was supposed to start the race. This it did, and the hares went racing off, up the steep incline, towards the summit of the mountain. Unfortunately, Thinker was right about these two particular hares, they did not have enough brains between them to fill a paw-print.

'They ran faster than the wind, both of them, and were neck-and-neck all the way up. When they neared the peak of the mountain, they both began to accelerate, because, to tell the truth, they had changed their minds about who was supposed to win the first race so many times, that Thunderfeet thought it was him who was supposed to be in front, and Lightninglegs believed she was expected to reach the top first.

'The closer they came to the peak, the more desperate each of them was to get ahead, failing to understand why the other one would not fall back. When they finally reached the summit, they were still neck-and-neck, but they were going so fast now that their shapes were a blur to the onlookers, and sadly they could not stop. They both shot off the top of the curved mountain peak, and out into space, one heading towards the sun, the other shooting towards the moon.

'And this is where they are today. Lightninglegs sits on the surface dust of the moon, mourning her lover, who has been parted from her forever. Thunderfeet runs around the sun, bemoaning his fate, his heart still full to overflowing. Sometimes, on a clear summer evening, they catch a quick glimpse of each other in passing, as the sun goes down, and the moon rises, and their ears prick up and their feet drum forlorn messages of love to one another.'

Skelter could hear no sound from Jittie's hole.

'What do you think of that then?' he asked.

Still no answer.

Skelter thought that perhaps Jittie was so overcome by the tragedy he had just related, that the hedgehog could not speak. Perhaps Jittie was choked with emotion at the thought of the two wonderful hares being forever doomed to remain on two separate worlds? It was after all a very sad story, and no doubt Skelter should have warned his new friend that the tale had an unhappy ending. He decided to go and comfort her.

He left his form and crept over to the burrow where her nest was situated.

'It's all right,' Skelter said softly, 'they may get back together some day . . .'

He waited for a response, and when he listened hard, he finally understood why she had not answered before.

From the depths of the rabbit hole there came the sounds of gentle snoring.

Chapter Fourteen

It was nearing dusk, and fantastical shapes began to form from ordinary objects. Winged shadows with no substantial form were gliding over the land. The spirits of the trees emerged from their hosts and wove new contours into the trunks and branches. Out of the earth came wraiths in their thousands, to chase away the last of the light.

Some twenty or so hares gathered in Booker's Field and awaited the twilight with a spiralling fear in their breasts. They watched the light creeping away, sliding into the ditches, up into the leafy regions of the trees, down behind the hedgerows. From out of the secret cracks in the earth the darkness was seeping, soon to flood the land and sky. The hares wished the light would go with a *snick* and the darkness come with a *snack*, for it was only during the gloaming that the flogre ventured out from his foul nest to prey upon the beasts of the field.

It was Highstepper who had given the monster its name: a welding of the words *flying ogre*. The other hares had gradually accepted this term for the giant creature that had been terrorising them since the new year stepped onto the flatlands, and now it had spread even beyond the colony, to rabbit warren and rookery. The crested grebes, the shelducks, shovellers and smews, the scaups and scoters, the widgeons, woodcocks and phalaropes, far and wide, had adopted the nickname of the *flogre* for this demon that had invaded their skies.

The hares were still together as a group, the mating season being not quite over, though soon they would disperse to their traditional fields to live their solitary late-summer, autumn and early-winter lives. It would be better then, and worse. Better because they would be scattered over a larger area and the flogre would need to search them out, and worse because they wouldn't have the colony to comfort them. A few of them, those who hated to be alone, would remain in pairs, but most of them would return to their chosen hermitage of six or seven hectares without a partner.

Dusk and dawn were dreaded by the hares. Other creatures too, were afraid, but many had hiding places. The rabbits, for the most part, remained in their warrens. The weasels and stoats found holes in the ditches. The rooks took to their rookery high in the elms, and the crow's nest was so secret only she knew where to find it. Only the hares had no hiding place, for they are creatures of the open, their homes an exposed shallow scraping of the surface soil. They did not know how to hide from creatures of the sky, for they had never been taught. They were entirely vulnerable to the flogre and were ever at his mercy – and since he knew no mercy, no compassion, no feelings of remorse, they were doomed to extinction.

Before the monster came, there was never a need to worry about what was going on overhead. There had always been hawks and falcons of course, but they never took a fully-grown jack or jill, and the leverets could be protected by the bodies of the adults.

Now it was different. There was a giant in the land: a giant with wings. Seven hares and several leverets had been taken by the monster, who required a sacrifice every dusk and dawn, though not always from the hares. Sometimes the flogre did not come, having found his victim before reaching the hares, but they would not know this until the darkness fell deep and strong. So they would lie in their forms and tremble, waiting for the mottled shape to swing silently out of the dark-grey evening, and snatch one of them away to oblivion.

'I don't mind dying,' said Longrunner, 'in the normal way, but this is like an execution. Every evening and every morning, we have to wait for the flogre to take his sacrifice, so that the rest of us can go on living out a normal life.'

Speedwell said, 'I know what you mean. Stoats and foxes are part of life's normal hazards, but this monster is too greedy. We shall be wiped out before the winter comes around again. All those who can get away, have gone – like the ducks and large waders. That narrows down the flogre's larder.'

The gloom settled around them, and they could see each others' eyes in the murk: frightened eyes that stared out into the gloaming.

Booker's field had a covering of shoots which rippled gently in the breeze like the surface of a lake, the green momentarily turning to silver as a flush of blades revealed their lighter sides. The humped shapes of the hares, visible above the short corn, showed dark and solid against this gentle landscape.

In the centre of Booker's Field was the stark stump of an ancient tree, its bark gone, the wood beneath as hard as stone, bleached white and toughened by the sun and rain. It stood about the height of a tall man, and one single bone-white bough spoiled its symmetry, projecting from the broken bole like an arm petrified in the act of waving to the scarecrow three fields away. No one knew what kind of tree it had been when it was alive, if indeed it had ever been such, for crows maintained it was the ossified soul of a man struck by lightning on his way to church.

Around this alabaster figure were the randomly-scattered forms of the hares. The dead tree was the colony's totem, meant to ward off evil, though in truth it acted more like a beacon guiding any flying predator to the right place in the right field. The farmer had given up trying to remove the stump, and the furrows from his plough rippled around its roots like the flow of fast water round a river rock. On hot summer days, the hares used its trunk to cool their coats, and on cold autumn evenings it retained the heat and was used to drive away bodily chills. The stump was a sacred object, but hare reverence did not extend to holding things so holy that you couldn't use them to warm your feet.

Highstepper said, 'I still say we should put a leveret out, where the flogre can see it, and let him take that. The young don't care about death like we do. They haven't learned how horrible it is. This is what should happen when monsters threaten a community – you offer sacrifices.'

The leverets snuggled closer to their mothers on hearing these words, the horror rushing to their brains and planting future nightmares there as thick as dry-tongued thistles.

Followme, the moonhare, leader of the colony, snorted her contempt.

'It's easy to see you're not a mother, you oaf. The young might not care so much about dying themselves, but *we* care about them. A mother would rather die herself than sacrifice her young.'

'Well, there's another good idea,' muttered Highstepper under his breath.

Reacher, the sunhare and Followme's mate, said in gruff undertones, 'I heard that, and if you don't keep your barbaric thoughts to yourself, one of us will come over there and box your face for you – and I don't mean with forepaws.'

'Well I'm scared,' said Highstepper.

'We're all scared,' replied the sunhare, 'but we're not going to start to sacrifice each other just so the selfish ones can stay alive. This is a trial in our history and we must see it through together. I've been helping Headinthemist to collect more lucky charms lately and place them around the field. They should help ward off the monster.'

Bittersweetinspring, the colony's most handsome jill, said, 'We've gathered just about every lucky charm the countryside has to offer, and still the flogre comes.'

They all fell into gloomy silence after this remark.

Speedwell changed the subject.

'I met that hare-speaking hedgehog today, down by the river, do you know the one I mean? Jetsam or something.'

Followme nodded.

'Well, it stopped me and told me that there was a new hare in the region – a mountain hare of all things, a jack. Said if we didn't treat this newcomer right she'd put a hex on me and rot my feet. Of course I told her where to go.'

'Of course you did,' said Followme in a sarcastic tone of voice, 'you're not frightened of being hexed are you, Speedwell? It doesn't bother you that hedgehogs have got a reputation as sorcerers and magicians, and have been known to magic the eyes out of a hare's head at a distance of two fields. That wouldn't bother you, would it?'

Speedwell shuffled in her form.

'Well, I must admit, moonhare, she did have me a *little* worried, so I thought I'd tell you anyway.'

'You did the right thing,' replied Followme, 'though I really can't see what the hedgehog wants from us. We don't need yet another hare around here, and certainly not some blue hare that hasn't the foggiest notion how to behave in the company of brown hares. I for one have never met a blue hare, has anyone else?'

It appeared that no one had. Their knowledge of blue hares was confined to field hare history, on which mountain hares had very little influence. The colony knew of the existence of such creatures, through word of mouth, but as to what they did and how they did it, no such information was available. Mountain hares lived a long way off, had their heads in the clouds, and were certainly not expected to come down to the flatlands and take up space that would be useful for field hares. It stood to reason that savages who liked to live on a lump of rock which turned to ice in the winter, and chewed on sedges and other unpalatable fare, would not like to live in a civilised society amongst those who were aware of the good things in life.

'So,' said the moonhare, 'if I have no idea what goes on in the mountains, why should a blue hare know what goes on in the fields? It stands to reason,' said the great matriarch of the herd, 'that if we are each ignorant of one another's culture, there would be no point in living together. Mountain hares being rough uncouth creatures, almost primitive so to speak, this jack would be uncomfortable in our company. He would not know how to act in a proper manner, would make mistakes and be miserable because of them. Of course, it is not their fault they are ignorant creatures, for they need to be surly aggressive characters in order to survive on the rugged peaks they seem to favour, but their lack of decorum would be a handicap to them amongst us more refined creatures.

'So, my judgement is that if this mountain hare ventures near Booker's Field, he is to be chased away.'

There was a murmur of approval from amongst the other hares, and Reacher, her faithful sunhare, drummed the earth with his hind leg to register his own agreement. It was not often that any of the colony disagreed with Followme: she was a very *large* hare, with broad hind legs, and strong claws. Those powerful weapons had raked many an upstart in their time. Reacher himself bore a few scars as a result of some earlier disagreements with his beloved moonhare and was usually the first to approve of her judgements.

There was a short period of silence, before Speedwell cleared her throat and spoke again.

'Of course, I wouldn't question your authority on *anything*, Followme, but there is the *hexing* to be considered.'

123

The moonhare gave out a surprised whistle and then said, 'Didn't you say that the hedgehog threatened to rot *your* feet off?'

'Yes,' said Speedwell.

'There you are then, the rest of us are safe, aren't we?'

Nothing more, except for a low whining sound once or twice, was heard from Speedwell for the rest of the evening.

The hares fell to silence again after this exchange and waited. As the dusk deepened, the wind changed and salt air blew in from the sea, refreshing and heady, and cleared the minds of the frightened creatures of the fields. A fox was scented to the east, but though it caused a slight flutter of panic amongst the leverets, the adults hushed them and said that the fox was too far away to be a nuisance to them. It was probably heading towards the farmyard, hoping to find the chicken coop unlatched and the farmer deep into his dinner.

Night began to move in with a serious determination now, mopping up the last of the light. The hares began to relax as another day came to its end. Soon they would be able to go out and feed under cover of darkness. The flogre was not known to hunt in pitch black, but always in that dreaded half-light that formed a flimsy meeting between night and day.

'Nearly there,' reassured the moonhare, 'courage everyone!'

There were murmurs of relief and one or two hares stirred in their forms, anxious to be at the greenest shoots before their neighbours.

Highstepper was the first out of his form.

He stood, stretched, and then rubbed his flank on the totem.

'All right, feeding . . .'

The sentence was never finished, though some of them swore they heard a shout of fear drifting down from a long way above the fields. They heard no sound come out of the stillness, prior to Highstepper's last words, though at least two hares felt the wind of the swooping flogre on their faces, and one said later that he caught a glimpse of a giant flying creature climbing the steps of the sky in the last of the light.

Once the drama was over and the hearts had stopped beating triple-time, the cadence of the evening returned to normal. The hares went out to feed, their minds numbed by yet another

124

encounter with the flogre. They called to the rabbits who were emerging from their burrows: 'Have you heard? Another one of our hares has been taken by the monster! Terrible isn't it? What? You lost a rabbit this morning? Le chou? Wasn't he the rabbit who was fond of cabbages? That's awful. We don't know what to do about it. Every dawn and dusk. At least you've got your warrens to go to. We're stuck out in the open. Yes, I know we *could* use an empty warren, but you know, we *are* hares. It would be unnatural, wouldn't it, to go underground. We'd go mad.'

Thus they gained some comfort from talking about it, sharing their grief with their manmade cousins, the rabbits.

The night passed, mostly in feasting. There were sentries posted at various times, but these hares rarely took their duties seriously, even though there were the normal dangers still to beware of, such as the other predators.

They played too, as hares are wont to do, racing each other over the meadows, down by the river. One or two swam across, to get at the grass on the far bank, then came back again.

They were in the middle of a game, when Reacher suddenly lifted his head and looked to the east. A dim, grim greyness was beginning to appear in the sky.

'Back to your forms!' he cried, and they scampered over the fields, through the hedges, and gathered around the totem once again, to face a dread new dawn, out of which might come the rapacious carnivore that was depleting their numbers, one by one, in order to satisfy its insatiable appetite for flesh.

Chapter Fifteen

In the dimness of his tower home, Bubba brooded on his life. Sometimes he was lost so deeply in himself he went into a trance. He was usually thinking about how much other creatures had, especially men, while he had to be content with living in a stone tower and eating fare that he had hunted down and killed himself. It was not that he disliked hunting, but that it was necessary to do it so often. Every dawn and dusk, unless he caught some large creature like the dog, he had to leave the tower and find running or flying meat.

He remembered that the man who had been his mother never used to have to hunt, but had his provisions brought to him by others.

—Tower, men have rejected me.

—*Perhaps they have their reasons, Bubba?*

—But I am of their kind.

—*Only in thought, word and deed.*

—You mean, tower, that though I think like a man and act like a man, they still do not like me?

—*Men do not like themselves very much, Bubba.*

Since Bubba was a very superior part-man, one with wings and able to fly, he believed he should be treated with far more reverence than ordinary men. They should hold him in awe, and bow down to him, like they did that figure on a cross in the church below. Surely Bubba was more important than a wooden man on a wooden cross? Mother had never gone to church, and now that Bubba lived in one, he could see why. Church was full of ordinary people, whereas mother had been larger-than-life, full of noise, especially when he had been sucking at bottles. Mother liked to hit things with his fist, mostly other men, whereas those people in church spoke and wailed softly and never used their hands against each other.

When Bubba's mother had been alive he only had to make a certain sound and food would be made available. They had hunted for sport, not out of need. Now this sound was ignored, as were all his sounds. Bubba was left to mewl and screech without any hope of anyone coming to see what was the matter or offering comforting sounds.

Bubba knew he was physically different from other men, and he guessed that this was what they disliked in him. Men were inclined to be suspicious of all those who did not match their physical and mental likenesses, even other men. The tower was right. The truth was, Bubba knew, that men were afraid, especially of themselves.

It was because of this rejection, that Bubba had decided to lift his own restriction on himself regarding preying on domestic creatures. Next spring, after the lambing, Bubba intended to feed on the soft flesh of the young of sheep, because he knew it would anger the men who looked after these creatures. He wanted to rouse a resentment in them, so that they knew who they were dealing with, for he was a creature who wanted his presence to be felt on the world.

If stealing lambs did not get him the satisfaction he desired, then he would do something worse – something far worse. The dark thought at the back of his mind had to do with stealing new-born babies left in wheeled boxes in gardens, or even more heinous, the beloved kittens and puppies that ordinary men doted on. Bubba knew where to hit his enemies. He had already taken a small dog, and he would do so again, if the opportunity arose. Nothing was sacred to him any more, now that mother had died. The world would recognise his existence, or pay the price with their precious ones.

—I will take their loved ones, tower.

—*You have the power.*

—Am I a man, tower?

—*You are as much of a man as you can be.*

—Then I can do anything I like.

Bubba shuffled amongst the skulls and bones of his victims, then down below, in the church, the music started – long deep notes overlaid with short high ones, like stardust settling on a dark field. Bubba swayed in time with the rhythm, and when the

127

voices broke into song below, he made noises in the back of his throat, the way he used to do to please mother.

Mother had never come to the church though. Mother used to to keep his hairy burly body covered with sheets and blankets while other humans went to the church. Mother got out of the nest of blankets at noon and growled and grunted at Bubba in a coarse tongue, while his big rough hands stroked Bubba's head. Bubba liked the petting from the hand, with its cracked and dirty nails. Then mother would fry some soft livers, giving Bubba raw titbits while he cooked, and then when mother was ready to eat he would fetch a small chicken from outside and break its neck, before throwing it to Bubba. Thus the two of them would feast together.

There were dreams in Bubba's head, when he tried to think back too far, of being in another world where there were more people like Bubba. There were strange memory-glimpses of another Bubba, a huge Bubba, that stared down from a great height at little Bubba. The look, though terrifying, was kindly. Then the big Bubba's face changed, to that of mother's, and there were vague recollections of sleepless times, of hungry times, until one day Bubba woke up on mother's wrist, and was being fed giblets from mother's fingers. These dreams were incomprehensible, but certain feelings went with them: milkwarm feelings that softened the edges of Bubba's soul.

After the singing and murmuring below Bubba's nest had stopped, and the gravel had ceased to crunch with human feet, Bubba decided to go out into the air. He went to the window with the point on top, and stood on the stone sill. In the distance he could see the river, winding like a long silver worm over the flatlands. There were clumps of trees, here and there, tufts on the landscape, and a shallow valley fell away from the rise on which the church stood.

The sky was full of birds: magpies, rooks, seagulls, sparrows, starlings, many others.

Bubba took to the air and cruised high over the fields, looking down on the patchwork quilt of farms. In flight he felt at his most powerful. There was a road running through the valley which carried the occasional box on wheels, and this went across a causeway to the mainland. Bubba swept down to have a look at how it crossed the sea, and found it rested on rocks against which the waves pounded.

Bubba found a telegraph pole and perched on its top, watching all that went on below him. A man came along peddling a machine, his legs going in circles, his head down. On his back was a sack. Then some small humans, with sticks. One of these looked up and saw Bubba, pointed, and made a noise. The small humans bent down and picked up stones, which they threw towards Bubba, but their aim was poor and they lacked the strength to throw high enough. Bubba stared at them in contempt, until they finally ran away.

He took to the airways again, sliding on the wind towards the seashore, seeing the creatures of the strand scuttling this way and that, doing small-creature things. Then he veered away from the sea into the centre of the large island, where there was a cluster of greystone houses. He wheeled over these, watching the humans put out their loose, removable skins on lines of rope. There were wheeled boxes down there, with babies inside them, but Bubba was prepared to wait. In any case, he had not long eaten, and would not be hungry until dusk.

When he flew over the church again, there was a group of humans putting a dead man into an oblong hole in the ground, lowering him in a wooden box. Bubba knew there was a body in the box, because that was where they put mother when he died. Mother was down there, under the ground. Bubba had tried to scratch him up again, once, but mother was too deep.

Bubba landed on his sill, and stayed there for a while, letting the sun warm his head and back. While he was there, dozing a little, a pigeon fluttered in, failing to notice Bubba against the dark interior. At the last minute, the pigeon realised its mistake, and veered off, sharply – but Bubba pecked at the bird savagely, stabbing a hole in its head.

The pigeon flew a short distance, then dropped like a soft brick, and fell with a thump on the death-box below, its wings fluttering. There were screeches from the humans, who looked up, into the sky, seeing nothing. Bubba melted back into his tower, happy to have disrupted the ceremony below. These people took themselves too seriously, entombing their dead in wood, earth and stone. Once dead, you were but a carcass, and fit only to be carrion.

If he had not had thoughts of escape and had stayed near his mother's body after he had died, he might have eaten mother, so that the pair of them could have been together for all eternity.

—Tower, I am lonely.

—*We are both lonely, Bubba.*

—We have each other, I suppose?

—*We are both lonely, together.*

Bubba settled on his bell-perch, waiting for the dusk to come around, when he could go out again and search for quarry on the fields, in the ditches, by the hedgerows.

PART THREE

*

Sunhare, Moonhare

Chapter Sixteen

By the time morning came Jittie and Skelter were fast asleep, after being up most of the night foraging for food. It was near noon before Skelter emerged from his form and shook himself. Today was the day when he was going out to meet the other hares in the district. Jittie had told him about a jill hare called Speedwell, who would help him become familiar with the locals.

Without waking Jittie, Skelter set out over the fields, in the direction the hedgehog had indicated during the night. He was to look for the white skeleton of a tree, standing in the middle of a cornfield, and this was where he would find the brown hares gathered.

It was a longer journey than he anticipated, during which he frequently if instinctively scoured the sky for eagles, and it was quite a while before he sighted the tall blanched stump. As he approached it, he saw several flattened humps on the ground, which he recognised as the field hares. One of them, a large jill, came out to meet him. Skelter was a little taken aback by her size: she looked formidable with her long, powerful legs. He noted the yellowish-brown pelage and black-topped tail which separated her kind from mountain hares like himself.

'Hello,' he said as she approached, 'my name's Skelter.'

'I am the moonhare, Followme. You're not welcome here, mountain hare. We have enough problems without having to worry about a lost soul. I'm sorry for your plight – I understand you escaped at a hare coursing – but we are under siege at the moment from a monster called the flogre and we have no refuge to offer you from this beast. You just wouldn't be happy with us, not at this time, so I suggest you move on.'

Skelter could sense the fear amongst the hares. They appeared to be in a state of shock and it seemed that this flying creature that had them battened down was the one the rabbits had warned him about.

'Look,' he said, 'I don't wish to intrude where I'm not wanted, but all I need is company of my own kind. I don't want you to feel responsible for me: I'm quite capable of looking after myself. All I want is to find a home. Don't you have a spare place for me? I won't be any bother.'

A jill called out, 'Why not let him stay, Followme? *Please?* I don't want to lose my feet.'

The moonhare looked distracted, glanced back at the author of this statement, then shook her head. 'Can't you see we're not in any state to take you in. You're better off on your own . . .'

Another hare had approached them now: a jack almost as large as the moonhare. He hopped up alongside the jill and sat up on his hindquarters, studying Skelter's face. Finally he spoke.

'Not very big, is he?'

'I was just explaining,' said Followme, 'that we can't take him in, much as we'd like to. We have our own problems at the moment.'

'That's true enough,' said the jack.

'Are you a moonhare too?' asked Skelter.

The jack looked puzzled, then said, 'I'm Reacher, the sunhare. Only females can be moonhares, and there is only one of those to every colony.'

'I see – moonhare and sunhare. Is there a starhare?'

'Are you trying to be funny?' snapped Followme.

Skelter hastily assured her he wasn't.

'No, no, I'm just interested in your culture. Why do you call yourselves a colony? Why not a clan? Or a husk? That's what we're usually called – a husk of hares.'

'Because,' replied Reacher, 'we're not a husk, not in the true sense. Unlike you mountain hares, we only get together during the mating season, from mid-winter to early summer, then we break up. So we call ourselves a colony.'

'Well, I *really* would like to stay and join your colony. I have nowhere else to go.'

'Impossible,' Followme replied, but Reacher's expression had softened. 'Oh, I don't know, where's the harm, moonhare?' he asked. 'I mean, this hare is homeless and we've lost so many lately he could fill one of the empty areas, stop them being taken over by the northern colony. You know they're always trying to extend their territory. If we're not careful, they'll have the whole island to themselves before long.'

This made sense to Skelter, and he could see that the sunhare's words had had an impact on the moonhare. She looked at her jack thoughtfully, while twitching her nose.

'You do have a point there, though we may have more leverets next spring than we have land to give them.'

Reacher nodded.

'But that's next spring. We could all be dead by then.'

'We probably shall be,' she sighed. 'Oh, all right then, come on. I'll introduce you to the rest of the colony. I hope you learn our ways quickly, because I'm not at all a patient or very tolerant leader. You must understand that, before we start.'

Skelter was ecstatic. At last he had found a home. It wasn't what he was used to, nor what he would have preferred, but it was better than being a stray, a maverick with no place to call his own, and no hares with whom to share his life. The field they were in was large, a sea of light green, and bordered by well-clipped hedges with trees locking them together. There was a five-barred gate like a window in the longest hedge, behind which a tractor could be heard chugging away. Beyond those borders were more fields and more hedges, in dreary succession, but if he closed one eye and studied it with a certain part of his brain, he could come to accept his new environment without too much heartache.

'What do you do about eagles?' asked Skelter, hopping alongside the moonhare, as they went to join the others.

'Eagles?'

Skelter looked up at the marbled louring sky. A high sheet wind was playing havoc amongst the grey swirling clouds. He could see crows being thrown around up there, but no eagles.

'Yes, you know – eagles.'

Followme shook her head as if it contained a wasp which she wanted to get out by way of her ear.

'I told you we shouldn't have him,' she complained to Reacher. 'Already he's prattling on about silly things.'

'What's silly about eagles?' asked Skelter.

Reacher replied, 'We don't know. What are they?'

Skelter was astonished.

'Why, they're – they're *eagles*, golden eagles. Like falcons only a lot bigger. Like buzzards, only more streamlined, larger, and swifter. They come out of the sky like lightning, and snatch a hare from the ground quick as quick. They circle, stoop, and *wham*, no hare.'

'Only one thing around here can take a fully-grown hare,' said Reacher, 'and that's a fox. He's the only creature, apart from the flogre of course, big enough and fast enough to catch us.'

'What about badgers?'

'Not quick enough.'

'No wildcats?'

'Wildcats,' said Reacher in flat tones.

'Yes, cryptic creatures with banded tails, bigger than a domestic, savage as anything. If you had wildcats, you'd know about it. They claw the bark off trees.'

The moonhare stopped in her tracks and said, 'Let's get this over with all at once. Are there any more animals or birds you want to talk about?'

'Pine martens?'

'Heard about them, but never seen one,' replied Reacher.

'Weasels and stoats?'

'Got them,' cried Reacher, almost triumphantly.

'So,' the moonhare said, 'we have established that there are no eagles or wildcats around here, that pine martens are scarce, that weasels and stoats have to be watched for, especially with regard to the leverets, and that foxes are the main enemy. In the meantime, our numbers are being depleted by a monster against which we have no defence, and who is far more important at the moment than any fox, stoat, wildcat, marten, weasel, or . . .' She paused, then said, 'This eagle bird. It snatches hares from the ground like a hawk takes mice?'

'Correct,' said Skelter.

'What time of day does it hunt?'

'Anytime, so long as the weather is clear. It has to be able to see us, before it can catch us.'

'Not at dusk and dawn?'

Skelter shook his head.

'Doubtful. I mean, maybe early evening when the light's still

136

good, or once the sun is well on its way up the sky, but mostly they need good light.'

'You wouldn't get one of these eagles who *only* hunted at dusk and dawn?'

'Not in the history of the mountain hare.'

Followme sighed.

'Ah well, it was just a thought. If we knew what it was, perhaps we could have found a way of dealing with it, but it seems the flogre is destined to remain a mystery.'

'I heard a silly story from the rabbits. Something about it being some kind of mythical creature, a badger that could fly, with a weasel for a tail,' said Skelter.

Reacher corrected him.

'*Stoat* for a tail. Well, that's what they say, though I've never seen it properly. No one has. It comes out of nowhere at dusk and dawn, and snatches hares away as if they were mice. It's slowly depleting the colony. We're not equipped to deal with this magical creature, whatever it is.'

Skelter did not feel this was the time for him to start pooh-poohing mysticism and magic, so he kept his scepticism to himself.

When they reached the tree stump, Reacher explained, 'This is our totem, Skelter, it helps protect us from predators.'

'How?' asked Skelter.

Several heads turned in his direction, but there was no immediate answer forthcoming. Finally, a hare called Fleetofoot, a yearling jill, answered him.

'Why, it's a good luck charm of course. It protects us with unseen magic. Have you never heard of a totem before? What did your colony protect itself with?'

She sounded defensive, but there was a lot of aggression and resentment in her tone too, which made Skelter feel uneasy.

'Actually, no, we don't have totems where I come from. There are lucky sights, like beetles on particular plants, but they're not taken all that seriously. They're more for the entertainment of leverets than anything else. Well . . .' he was getting some peculiar looks '. . . the young have imaginations, which we feed with games and things, like lucky beetles. If you see what I mean?'

'Not really,' said Fleetofoot. 'Are you trying to tell us that lucky

137

charms don't really work? That they're for the amusement of simpletons?'

At that moment, the moonhare came up to him, saying, 'Our augur, Headinthemist, has been looking at the omens, and it appears that all is well.'

'The omens?' asked Skelter.

'Yes, Headinthemist can divine the future from wych elm twigs, their position and direction when blown from the tree, and her prophecy is that your presence amongst us is acceptable.'

'I'm glad about that,' said Skelter, 'the trees like me, eh? Isn't this all a bit, well, you know, daft?'

Skelter saw that he was not making a good impression on his hosts, and he tried to retrieve the situation before it got any worse. The trouble was, he was unused to meeting other hares and couldn't seem to control his tongue. Up in the highlands you said what you meant, and you meant what you said. There was no need for diplomacy of any kind. In the highlands it was best to be blunt and forthright, not dance around the heather using flowery phrases.

'No, no, I don't mean *daft*, exactly. It's just that mountain hares tend to be a bit more pragmatic. We're suspicious of mystical things. I mean, I have dreams like everyone else, about ghost-hares. But I've never seen one in real life. The hare clans of the highlands tend to be a bit more down to earth, that's all.'

'The hare clans of the highlands,' repeated Fleetofoot in a sing-song voice. 'How quaint.'

The moonhare stepped in and rescued him. 'This is Skelter, everyone. Sunhare and I have decided that he may stay on a trial basis . . .' There had been nothing mentioned about a *trial*, but Skelter let it go '. . . and we want to make him as welcome as possible. Of course, he is a mountain hare, and there will be cultural differences to overcome, but I'm sure you will help to educate him in our ways. He seems a reasonably intelligent hare, so he should learn quite quickly.'

So, there it was, no question that he had anything to offer *them*. He was going to be civilised, whether he liked it or not, and they were going to civilise him. Skelter did not argue. He was the newcomer and as had been seen already, it would be best to keep his silence until he got to know them better.

'Thank you everyone,' he said, 'for letting me into your, um, colony, on um, a trial basis. I'll do my best to fit in. I expect you know my story, and where I come from, since news travels fast over the flatlands, but perhaps I'd better fill you in on some details. I lived in the mountains, of course, amongst the crags and heather . . .'

But the other hares had turned away now and were chattering to each other, not paying attention to a word he was saying. Skelter thought this was the height of rudeness, but he realised something now that hadn't occurred to him before.

This community of animals, on the almost-island, had remained quite remote from the landmass over the centuries. Only the birds of the air, who rarely spoke with the beasts of the field, would have any links with those on the mainland. The mammals here were highly suspicious of strangers, and a long way behind the rest of the modern world in their ways. Everyone knew there was a certain amount of magic in the world, for who could explain a *soul* or account for dreams of ghost-hares, but to overlay the whole of one's lifestyle with such dark forces was going too far.

These hares were highly superstitious creatures, with minds that shot out in the direction of fantastical thoughts. All very well for the art of storytelling, but not much good for practical purposes.

So, Skelter forgave them their rudeness.

Dusk began to move across the land, the shadows melting into greyness. Skelter noticed a marked change coming over the hares. They began to get nervous, nestling down in their forms, speaking in whispers. Frightened eyes glanced up at the sky. Some of the young were whimpering. The atmosphere was pensive and intense.

Skelter quickly dug himself a short tunnel form and slipped down inside it. He was quite tired, so he dozed for a while, unaware of the increased agitation that was going on amongst the colony. Some of them were staring at the spot where he had dug his form with horrified expressions, looking at one another as if to say, can you believe this?

Eventually, Skelter was woken by the moonhare.

It was dark, and he crawled out of his form and stretched himself before saying, 'Yes, what is it?'

'You have to leave,' said Followme, firmly.

Skelter felt utterly at a loss.

'Leave, what on earth for? What have I done wrong?'

Followme glanced down at his form.

Skelter followed her eyes, and then something occurred to him. 'Is this someone else's spot? I didn't know. I'll dig my form over there, if you like. Anywhere. I wish you would let me stay, that's all.'

'You don't get it, do you?' said another hare. 'We don't want you, because you've got rabbity ways. Headinthemist has studied the wych elms twigs again and they point to you as being a bad influence. You could be a spy for someone, maybe the flogre. Why didn't it come tonight? Because you were here? To give you a chance to settle in, before you began spying on us?'

'Why should I be a spy? You don't make any sense.'

'Look, no one's ever heard of a hare that burrows in the ground like a rabbit, and how do we know you're a hare anyway? You look a bit like one, but there's marked differences . . .'

'Because I'm a *mountain* hare, you fool!' cried Skelter, getting angry.

'So *you* say, but we've only got your word for that. And even mountain hares don't dig tunnels, I'm sure. They would be too ashamed to copy those manmade creatures who call themselves rabbits – the upstarts, the newcomers. Why would you want to copy them, when hares have always had the sky over their heads, the field for a bed?'

'Because mountain hares don't live in fields, and because there are golden *eagles* up in the highlands – massive birds with huge talons and a beak that can tear the heart out of deer.'

'So *you* say,' said Reacher, maddeningly, and to which there was no real answer.

'Yes,' snapped Skelter, 'you only have my word for that. If you had let me talk about where I come from and what kind of community I lived in, you would have heard all this before I dug the form, but you got bored and refused to listen, because you're an ignorant bunch of backward fools, who are so bigoted that you'll never learn anything new. No wonder you've never heard of mountain hare forms: you never listen to anything. I give up!' he finished in disgust.

140

They all turned their backs on him, a shocked look in their eyes, while Reacher mumbled, 'Best be on your way, before we do something we might regret later. That wasn't a very pretty speech and you're lucky we don't kick you where you stand. Go on, be off with you.'

'Gladly,' said Skelter. 'I'll go back to Jittie. At least she isn't living in the Dark Ages, like you lot. You deserve this flogre, whatever it is. You probably conjured it up, with those strange minds of yours . . . all right, all right, I'm going. No need for any more threats, I'm quite sure you're capable of carrying them out.'

He turned and left them, making his way back across the fields, his eyes hot with anger, and his heart too full of rage to feel despair. What nonsense. What utter nonsense. To accuse him of being a rabbit. Why, he'd rather be a rabbit than a field hare, if that's what they were like. He was ashamed to be called a cousin of such idiot creatures.

It was not easy finding his way back to Jittie in the darkness, with the owls sweeping the skies with their wings, and the stoats peering at him from the blackness of hedges. Once, he came across a couple of humans, a man and a woman, who startled him. They had been so quiet, the man leaning his back against an oak tree, while the woman pressed herself against him. As Skelter passed them they were whimpering softly to one another, as if the rest of the world had ears.

Skelter was glad when he had passed them, for the woman's aroma made him feel uneasy, and the whole scene was a little bizarre. What were two humans doing out at this time of night, in the middle of the fields? It was too unusual not to make a hare feel apprehensive. Skelter sensed something sinister about it, which made him worry.

He passed on by, and was soon concerned with his immediate troubles once more.

Shortly afterwards he heard a noise behind him, and whirled around to find he was being chased. He was about to bolt, when he scented his pursuer. It smelled like a jill, from that colony back there.

It was indeed a jill who came out of the darkness.

'It's no good you trying to persuade me to come back now,' said Skelter firmly. 'The damage has been done.'

'I wasn't going to,' said the jill, trying to talk and catch her breath at the same time, 'I just wanted to make sure you tell the hedgehog that you were *first* accepted, then *later* you were asked to leave. I mean, I did try to help. I got you in – it was your own stupid fault you got thrown out again. You be sure to tell the hedgehog that, won't you?'

'What's your name?' asked Skelter, angrily.

'Speedwell. Now, don't forget . . .'

With that, the jill was gone, back into the night.

Chapter Seventeen

'The reason field hares don't burrow like rabbits, nor use cover like the creatures of the woodland, is because their only real defence is their speed,' said Jittie. 'Next to the deer, they are probably the fastest animal in the countryside. Since they do rely on their speed, they don't like to be surprised by predators, and of course prefer a head start on any fox that comes creeping up towards their form. This is the reason,' she explained, 'why they live in shallow depressions in the middle of flat fields – so they can see what's coming from all directions.' Skelter was still feeling sorry for himself.

'That's all very well,' he said, 'but I'm not a field hare, am I?'

'No, but you want to live with them, and these hares, they haven't been to the mainland like I have. They're island born and bred. They're suspicious of anything new, any behaviour different from what they're used to. I'm not making excuses for them, mind – they're a narrow crowd of bigots – I'm just trying to explain to you why this has happened.'

'Well, I don't care,' said Skelter, 'I'll just stay here with you.'

Jittie went silent for a while.

Finally, she spoke again.

'Ahem – listen my fine hare friend, I'm not the world's most sociable creature. I don't want to sound like those hares back in Booker's Field, but I prefer my own company most of the time. You catch me in a particularly good frame of mind at the moment, but wait until autumn. I become bad-tempered and irritable. You won't want to know me. Then, when the winter comes around, I go to sleep.'

Skelter thought about this.

'Go to sleep? What do you mean?'

'I mean I go to sleep – for the whole winter.'

'You're making fun of me aren't you? How can you go to sleep for the winter? You've got to eat, haven't you? You mean you sleep a *lot* . . .'

'No,' snapped Jittie, sounding annoyed with him, 'I mean I go to sleep for the whole winter. I just find a warm nest of leaves and I don't need to eat when I'm in hibernation – my body slows almost to a stop.'

'Isn't that dangerous? I mean, what if your heart doesn't work?'

Jittie nodded.

'Of course it's dangerous, but that's the way hedgehogs do it. Anyway, if you die, you die. At least if it's during sleep you just drift away. What's to fear about death? Either there's something that comes after, which would be nice, or there's nothing, in which case I won't know about it. Nothing to worry about in either case. Better to die in your sleep than be strangled by a snare, or have your hindquarters blown off by a human with a gun, dying slowly in great pain. Or being caught and eaten by a fox. *That's* what's likely to happen to you. It's *life* that's to be feared, not death. Maybe death is wonderful?'

'Well, I realise all that, but I'm still scared of dying.'

'That's just a trick of life, to keep you trapped here. Life wants to keep you in its power for as long as possible – it hates to let anyone escape its clutches. So while it's in control, it gives you frightening thoughts about death. Life tells you that death is terrible, that you're much better where you are, when that's not necessarily the case. We struggle from one day to the next, avoiding something that we know absolutely nothing about. Life is a tyrant, my friend, and probably the real enemy. Death may be a field of carrots that goes on forever, into infinity, where foxes are toothless and hawks have had their claws and beaks clipped.'

'So, you don't want me to stay here with you?' said Skelter. 'You'd rather I went and looked for another hare colony?'

Jittie said, 'Oh, I don't mind for now, but I'm just warning you I get huffy and moody, quite often, and I shan't be here all the while. Look, let's face it Skelter, this is not a normal situation – a hare and a hedgehog? The other creatures will laugh at us and call us names. Not that I care about that, but you might. You're a sensitive animal. You like to be liked. I couldn't care less, I've got my fleas for company, but you . . . ?'

So Skelter was left wondering what to do, whether to move on or stay and take the consequences. Neither alternative really appealed to him. He decided to sleep on it. Sometimes things looked a whole lot different the next day. Sometimes a new day brought in things the old one wouldn't have sniffed at.

And this is exactly what happened.

The following morning brought about a whole new state of affairs, a complete reversal in fact. Halfway through the morning, Skelter was woken by Jittie.

'There's someone to see you.'

Skelter hopped outside his form, to find Reacher waiting to speak to him.

'Yes?' asked Skelter stiffly, 'what is it?'

Reacher gave a long sigh, then said, 'I've come to ask if you'll return with me to Booker's Field.'

'Why, so you can kick me out again?'

'No, we're sorry for the way we treated you. That wasn't right. We've decided to take you back in again.'

'Maybe I don't want to come now.'

Reacher looked pained.

'Well, we would *like* you to come.'

Jittie had been watching this exchange with interest and finally she butted in.

'Just a minute Reacher,' she said. 'You're not telling the whole truth are you?'

'What are you?' snapped the sunhare. 'A witch? You can read minds now?'

Jittie snarled. 'Don't take that tone with me, I'm not one of your hares. I'll bite your nose for you and put a hex on your back legs. Now you listen to me: you've got some ulterior motive for asking Skelter to join you. I can see no other reason why you would be back here so soon, practically begging him to rejoin the colony. It's as plain as that white piece of fluff you call a tail. Now, out with it, what's going on?'

Reacher looked a bit taken aback, then shuffled around in the dust. It was obvious to Skelter that Jittie was right, that there was a reason behind all this apart from any desire to put right a poor show of hospitality.

'Well?' he asked Reacher, 'what is it?'

145

Reacher looked trapped and then sighed.

'Fact is,' he said, 'we would like you to, ahem, to come and teach us, ahem, to come and teach us how to dig one of those forms you mountain hares use. If you wouldn't mind.'

'What?' cried Jittie. 'You send him packing because he digs a hole to sleep in, then you come chasing after him to show you how to do it? Doesn't make sense.'

'Nothing makes sense with the flogre around,' replied Reacher. 'That creature has got us all spinning where we stand. Anything that will help in outsmarting that monster is welcome, whether it's rabbity or not.'

Skelter saw a gleam appear in the spiny creature's eyes.

'Ah, so that's it?' she said.

'What? What's it?' asked Skelter.

Jittie shuffled forward to come nose to nose with Reacher.

'Tell him what happened at dawn this morning. The flogre came, didn't it? And, what, one of you escaped it by using Skelter's abandoned form?'

Reacher nodded, almost shamefacedly. 'That's about it. It was coming on dawn, the darkness beginning to slip away, when the flogre came. We didn't hear it of course, but Headinthemist caught a glimpse of something out of the corner of her eye, and she shrieked and jumped forward. She happened to land near your form, Skelter, and in her fright leapt into it. The flogre must have missed her by a fraction.'

'So no one was taken?' asked Jittie.

'Oh, yes, that monster came back a short while later and took one of the leverets, but don't you see, this is a major event. *Never before has a hare survived an attack by the flogre.* That's cause for great celebration. What was more, Headinthemist said she only had to poke her head out of the front of the short tunnel you made, and she could see right across the field. It's perfect – a little upside-down arch in the earth, just big enough to protect a hare's back, but open at both ends so that we don't panic. We are really sorry for our initial reaction, Skelter. Moonhare sent me to get you, and ask you to come back and help us each dig one mountain hare form, so that we can protect ourselves against this terrible persecution. What do you say? I won't blame you if you refuse – we treated you badly. But we need you, Skelter, to save us from extinction.'

Jittie interrupted. 'Well, I don't know, Reacher, the mountain hare and I were getting on very well together. We were just discussing how nice it would be if we were to stay near each other and look after each other's interests, weren't we, Skelter?'

'Were we?' said Skelter, feeling confused. Surely Jittie had just been telling him the reverse of that? Then he saw the hedgehog glaring at him from behind Reacher's shoulder, and he suddenly realised what Jittie was doing.

'Oh, yes, *us* you mean? That's right. I mean, we were getting on so well together – you said that, didn't you, Jittie. I don't know if I should just leave Jittie here now, after all our promises.'

Reacher looked astounded. 'You'd rather stay with a hedgehog than live with your own kind?'

'What's wrong with hedgehogs?' snapped Jittie.

'Well, nothing, but I mean, he's a *hare*.'

Skelter said, 'I'd rather stay with someone who *wants* me around than a bunch of hares that dislike my company.'

'Look,' said Reacher, 'I guarantee you'll be welcome. You have my word on that. And I will personally look to your welfare and make sure you're treated with the utmost respect. We need you, Skelter, and I am willing to put my own reputation on the line to assure you of a permanent home. If you get asked to leave again, I'll go with you. How's that?'

Jittie nodded at Skelter. Their little game had worked and he now felt he had all the guarantees he was going to get. Skelter turned to Jittie and said, 'Well, it sounds as if they really do mean to let me stay this time. Perhaps I'd better go with Reacher, after all?'

'Perhaps you'd better.'

'I appreciate all you've done for me, Jittie.'

'I know you do,' she replied, 'and so you should.'

Skelter nodded.

Then turning to Reacher, he said, 'Let's go. Thanks for the company, Jittie. I'll be back to see you from time to time.'

'Look after yourself, hare.'

The two hares then went racing over the fields, through the hedges, over the ditches, until they came to Booker's Field with its prominent totem. Some of the hares were asleep, but they were woken by Followme, the moonhare.

Fleetofoot cried, 'Ah, you brought him back!'

147

'He came back of his own accord,' snapped Reacher sharply, 'because he knew we needed help. I think we owe him an apology.'

Fleetofoot looked as if someone had kicked him in the face. 'What did I say?' he whispered to Headinthemist.

Moonhare drew herself up, after catching Reacher's eye. 'We're sorry for the way we treated you,' she said to Skelter. 'Our hospitality is appalling. It comes of a fearful time, when we distrust everything and everyone. Please find it in yourself to forgive us.'

It was a pretty speech and Skelter realised the moonhare had had to swallow a lot of pride to get it out. 'Don't mention it,' replied Skelter, 'I understand. These are difficult times. Now, let's set about digging a few mountain hare forms. These are *not* rabbit burrows, you understand, they're directly from our own culture. If anything, rabbits probably copied us, because we were here first. As you can see from the one I've already done, it's just large enough for a body length, with the tail just touching the air at the back, and the nose at the opening. Sometimes in the highlands we don't even dig, we find two rocks close together and build a form between them. It's simply for defence against eagles – or in your case, against the flogre . . .'

Thus Skelter was accepted by the colony as an intrepid and daring adventurer come from foreign lands, and his status rose amongst them as they sought his opinion on many aspects of life.

In the days that followed, Skelter came to accept his new life, and found the field hares a constant source of interest. He quickly learned that they were a superstitious lot who put great faith in lucky charms.

Harebells, thought to contain the spirits of dead hares, were never eaten because they were considered to be extremely lucky. And anyway, said Headinthemist, who would want two hare spirits in one body?

The forked twigs of wych elms were used to divine the future, according to the way they had fallen from the tree and the position in which they lay on the ground.

Honey fungus, which glows luminescent in the dark and was once used by humans to light pathways through the woods, was considered a holy plant, and treated with awe and reverence. Hares would gather round honey fungus and mutter orisons consisting mostly of asking for good fortune to come their way.

The religion (if it can be called such) of field hares is entirely selfish, in that they consider it right and proper to pray for good luck to befall them, *knowing* there is a natural balance in all things, and that if they have a fortunate season, their neighbour may very well have a devastating time of it.

'Someone's got to have good luck, so why not me?'

Then there were the four aspects of a *good life* which were considered to be the most important to field hares: fertility, longevity, health and happiness. There were at one time, Skelter was informed, only three, 'But three is such an untidy number, don't you think? So we added a fourth, to make it a nice neat square of a number.' No one seemed to know which of the four was the last to be included.

These four aspects of a *good life* were represented by certain symbols. Health and happiness used to be symbolised by the sun and moon, respectively, but that was in the olden times when man had not cultivated the land and everything was unkempt and disorderly. Since then, these two symbols had been changed.

The big barn at Major Farm now represented health. It was solid, hale and hearty, and its roof had never been known to sag, like that of the farmhouse. The farmhouse chimney often emitted dirty smoke, and its weak-eyed windows peered myopically out over the ploughed fields with dull uninterest. The big barn had no windows to weaken its body. Its steel frame was taller than the house, and its shoulders were those of a giant. It did not smoke, was not bulging or dropping in any place on its fine body, and its ruddy form glowed health. In the winter it had a heart of hay, and in the summer it was hollow, but always it stood foursquare and solid on the earth.

The tractor, which purred in contentment most of the time, represented happiness. The tractor, with its companion the tractor man, was never distressed. It went about its daily business, season-in, season-out, with unflinching felicity, purring and chugging. It had the enviable task of drawing straight lines on the fields, which it did with a precision and accuracy that filled *others* with great bliss. The tractor was the most contented thing on the earth.

Both these objects were red in colour and boxy in shape, having the neat square lines beloved of field hares, to remind them of straight squared hedgerows, sharp-cornered fields and orderly furrows.

Fertility was still symbolised by an ear of corn, which seemed to have no replacement available amongst the manmade objects, but long life had changed from the dishevelled oak tree, to the wonderful and most revered of all manmade things, the five-barred gate. The five-barred gate was considered by the field hares to be the most beautiful artefact in the world. It was a creation of the gods, the ultimate in combining art with science. Hares felt certain that man could not have invented it on his own, because nothing else that they made even came close to its exquisite form. The impeccable, perfect image of the five-barred gate had been given to the humans by a vision sent from hare heaven, originating from the great Kicker himself. Kicker knew that hares could never *make* things, so he had humans do it for them. The elegant flawless design of the five-barred gate was even worshipped by the humans themselves, who came for the Service of Renewal bearing hammers and nails, paint and oil, and proceeded to revitalise the gate with drumming and other religious rituals. The five-barred gate never died, or rotted away: it was indeed an appropriate symbol for long life.

150

Chapter Eighteen

In the corner of Poggrin Meadow was a gibbet on which hung the bodies of animals shot by the farm workers. Moles, crows, the occasional fox, weasels and stoats: all these were wired to the gibbet fence to hang in the weather, to rot away and become hard crusty pelts no longer recognisable as the creatures they had once been. There were no hares on the gibbet of course, for the same reason that there were no rabbits, partridges or pheasants, because these were taken to the farmhouse and baked into pies.

The gibbet was an endless source of fascination to the creatures of the wild, who thought the display grotesque but at the same time were strangely attracted to it. Some of them would even go out of their way on a moonlit night to stop by and stare at the lines of corpses waving in the wind, wondering if they could recognise any of the animals or birds as individuals they knew in life.

The mammals and birds on the gibbet were past caring about anything, having become a flap of hide for the wind to blow back and forth, or a husk of feathers for the maggots to investigate. Their eyes were stolen from them soon after they were strung up, and the empty sockets stared back at curious creatures who paused to inspect the gibbet for old friends.

Although it was the gamekeeper who put the gibbet in place first of all, the tractor-man used it too on certain occasions, though he never matched the keeper's fervour for death. The tractor-man really only used the gibbet on rare occasions, though he seemed to hate crows and rooks. In winter and autumn, he was especially busy, stringing up the executed, but in spring and summer he was too busy for killing much, which was why the incident surprised the hares so much.

The gibbet's occupants were seasonal too. In the summer there tended to be more moles than anything else, and in the winter, stoats in their ermine coats. Once, there was a badger, which shocked everyone, because the badger was supposed to be one of the toughest and wiliest creatures of the woodland.

Whatever time of year, and whoever hung upon the wire frame, the other creatures were bewitched by this macabre display of death, and would go out of their way to stop by the gallows and stare for long periods of time.

It was by the gibbet, visible through the gateway from Booker's Field, that the incident took place.

On moonlit nights during the spring the hares of Booker's Field had witnessed a regular rendezvous taking place in Poggrin Meadow, under the old oak and close to the gibbet. A man and a woman met there, held each other close, buzzed like insects. The scent of the woman, like the fragrance of wildflowers, would drift over the grasses and into the cornfield where the hares were clustered. The man, tall, and with a deep voice, stroked the woman's dark hair, and touched her lips with his own, frequently. Sometime later, the woman would cry, and the man would sigh, and then they would part, taking opposite directions across the meadow.

The hares themselves paid little attention to this human activity, simply noting the presence of these people, and wondering why they met in the darkness. It was not usual, for humans to meet in the corner of a meadow in the dead of night. However, the hares had more to worry about than the frivolous doings of two unknown people: they were more concerned with surviving each dusk and dawn.

One night, not long after Skelter had joined the colony, someone came and hid near the five-barred gate. He was carrying a shotgun, the smell of which brought him to the hares' attention, though they were not unduly alarmed. The reason for their unconcern was because they recognised the human as the tractor-man, who sat in their symbol for happiness, while it chugged around the fields. Tractor-men always carry shotguns, though they use them infrequently on hares, taking the odd pot shot at a pheasant or partridge, and oftener still, at rabbits.

Rabbits will frequently sit still to be shot, being most obliging in that respect. Hares are harder to hit, since they almost always run, fast. Since the tractor man was usually doing something else when they broke, and had to pick up the gun, aim and shoot, before the hare was out of range, it was often a worthless effort. The effective range of a twelve-bore shotgun is not great and a zig-zagging prey did not help him much, in his efforts to hit his quarry.

To cap it all, rabbits, partridges and pheasants made better eating than tough stringy hares, who needed hanging for a few days. They were barely worth the trouble of killing, except perhaps on an organised drive and shoot.

All in all, the hares were not too worried about tractor-men carrying shotguns, especially at night.

The tractor-man crouched down beside the hedge, peering through the beautiful five-barred gate, the hare symbol for longevity, until the couple appeared in the corner of the field. There was much urgent buzzing at first, more intense than usual, and they did not touch lips for a long time. The woman began crying, softly, quite early, but this night the two people did not part as they usually did at this point, but hugged each other really hard.

Before they were able to go their separate ways, the tractor-man stepped out from behind the hedge and opened the five-barred gate. He strode across Poggrin Meadow and confronted the two entwined people, who parted as suddenly as if triggered by steel springs. There followed much barking, mostly between the tractor-man and the woman. The other man stood stock still, the shotgun pointing at his belly, and the hares wondered what all the fuss was about.

Finally, the woman began screaming, striking the tractor-man about the head with her fist.

The hares saw the flash from the end of the barrels, and thunder hollowed out a hole in the night. The other man was thrown backwards by the force of the blast into some blackberry bushes, and lay hidden from the sight of the hares. The hares themselves dashed from their forms, tore around in circles, then back down into their forms again, hearts beating wildly.

Acrid smells began to drift over the fields. The screaming had stopped as suddenly as it began. The woman let out a strange whining, and began running across Poggrin Meadow, towards

153

the five-barred gate, while the tractor-man fumbled with his shotgun.

She ran through the colony of hares, not noticing any of them, and tripped in one of Skelter's newly-dug forms. Her longheeled shoe went flying and struck the white totem of the hare colony, bouncing out into Booker's Field. The woman scrambled to her feet, and started to run again, sobbing hysterically, but by this time the tractor-man had reached the five-barred gate and he aimed his shotgun and blasted another loud explosion into the moonlit air.

The noise made several hares bolt into the blackness, while others sat pop-eyed in their forms, frozen with fear.

The woman lay sprawled at the foot of the totem tree, her skirt around her head, her white legs visible to the night. A sweet odour of human blood filled the nostrils of the remaining hares, and they crouched deep in their forms, wishing they could worm down into the earth and stay there until this human activity was all over.

They could hear the tractor-man breathing heavily, and smell his sweat, and his fear. When he had been crouching by the gate, they had sensed nothing from him but a faint aroma of anger, but now that was gone. There was stark terror in his scent, and he seemed to be quite incapable of moving for a long while. Then he began sobbing, fell down beside the woman's corpse and clutched handfuls of her clothes, rubbing them in his face. He cradled her head for a while in his arms, but dropped it when blood smeared his cheek.

After a while he left the body to look for his gun, and finding it, he ran off into the darkness.

Once the tractor-man had gone the hares ventured out and those who had run away, came back again. They sniffed around the woman, twitching their noses at the strange scent of flowers combined with the smell of blood. A weasel came to the corpse and scattered the hares, who gave the slim little killer a wide berth. When she had gone the hares went back to their forms and settled down to talk about the incident.

'What was that all about?' said Speedwell.

'I've never seen human beings shoot each other before,' remarked sunhare, 'though I've heard it happens. It's not usual. Do you think he'll come and hang the bodies on the gibbet now?'

154

Skelter simply listened. He had nothing to add to what was being said and he was still a little shocked by the explosions, his ears ringing. The field hares were more used to the sound of the shotguns than he was. The farm workers were always taking pot shots at rooks, crows, pigeons and the rest of the wildlife that inhabited the farmlands. It was part of the scene. In the mountains, the shooters were few and far between.

Moonhare, lying on the roof of her form, said in a satisfied voice, 'Mating.'

'What?' said Reacher, probably wondering whether he was being asked to do something.

Followme lifted her head off her paws. 'Mating. That's what it was all about. Humans don't box or dance for their females, they fight over them with guns. The tractor-man and the other-man both wanted to mate with the female, so there was a fight.'

Longrunner said, 'Come on, moonhare, you're guessing. It doesn't make sense. I mean, if they went round killing each other in the mating season, there'd be dead people all over the place. This is the first time I've seen it happen.'

'All I'm saying is, that's what it looked like to me.' She sounded less sure of herself now that these points had been made to her.

Bittersweetinspring said, 'I must admit, it looked like some kind of ritual, they were all acting so . . . I don't know, *unnatural*. But to think they do it every human mating season – why, I don't even know when that is?'

'In the spring, like everyone else's of course,' snorted Followme.

'Not necessarily,' sniffed Bittersweetinspring, 'the foxes do it at other times.'

'The foxes,' growled the moonhare, 'may their souls grow damp and give them arthritic joints, are not the most natural creatures in the world.'

'Neither are humans,' retorted Bittersweetinspring, which everyone else had to agree with, by grunting softly, leaving Followme no choice but to cease arguing.

'Well, they weren't poachers, that's for sure,' said Reacher, 'because they didn't have guns and they weren't carrying traps or snares.'

'They might have been trespassers,' remarked Speedwell.

155

'The tractor-man doesn't shoot trespassers,' said Reacher, 'he only points the gun at them and takes them away.'

'That's true,' said Headinthemist.

Many other hares chorused their agreement.

So, they were at a loss as to what really caused the incident, and certainly Skelter had no idea. All he knew was that he didn't like it. When something unusual happened with humans, it almost always meant that more human activity would occur as a result.

Despite the fact that he took animal lives occasionally with his shotgun, the wildlife had a respect for the tractor-man. He was one of them, out in all climes, whether fine or inclement. His face was chiselled rock, his features weathered wood. In his eyes were the wind and water, the skies of the flatlands. He was solid, firm, predictable most of the time, the shooting of the two people being an exception.

The tractor-man smoked a dried herb in a stubby pipe that the animals and birds had got used to and associated only with him. It was a herbal burning aroma, similar to the smell of smouldering hickory chips used to smoke fish from the river, that was now comfortable in their nostrils.

There was no real malice in the tractor-man. If he caught you eating his crops he would shoot you, but not in any evident delight or bloodlust. He would shoot you because he thought it was the right thing to do to creatures who ate the produce of his hands. The tractor-man had planted the crops and he believed they were his once they had ripened. The wildlife understood the inevitability of this, if not the reasons behind it.

Sometimes, the tractor-man would feed the birds, while he ate his sandwiches under the shade of some oak tree, throwing crusts even to his hated enemies the seagulls and crows.

On most days, the tractor-man was where his God intended him to be, behind the wheel of his vehicle. He would sit for hours in the hare symbol for happiness, chugging up and down the fields, drawing plough or harrow, making those nice straight lines in the earth that hares so much admired. His leathery skin would darken under the summer sun, and the wrinkles and creases become more pronounced, and the hair exposed around his cap would become strawlike and acceptable. In the winter his chapped hands would be used to hammer posts into the ground, his great booted feet would kick at stones that had invaded his fields and threatened his honed ploughshares.

Later on that night, the tractor-man returned.

He brought with him a spade, and he began digging in the corner of the field, where the corn had missed being planted. It took him a long time and the hares could smell his sweat and hear him grunting, as the metal blade clinked on flints, and the scent of freshly turned soil drifted over the corn. When he had dug a huge hole, the tractor-man went into the Poggrin Meadow and took the dead man's body by the feet, dragging it back to the hole with its head bumping over the uneven ground.

When that was done, the tractor-man walked over to the female's corpse, and stared down at her face for a long while. He began crying, which shocked some of the hares, for they had never before this night seen a tractor-man in tears, and here was one doing it *twice*. Finally, he lifted her up tenderly in his arms, with her hair hanging long from her pale head, and carried her to the hole.

It seemed he was going to put her directly on top of the dead man, but he paused, then laid her down for a few minutes while he covered the other body with a layer of soil. Then he placed her inside and, wearily it seemed, shovelled earth into the hole. When it was almost done, he suddenly stopped, and stared at the woman's feet.

Then he looked around him, his eyes peering intently in the moonlight, looking bright and feverish. First he ran into Poggrin Meadow, and began searching the grasses around the gibbet. Then he retraced his steps to Booker's Field and looked all around the area where the totem stood. Light began to creep into the sky, and the tractor-man glanced at his wrist and hurried back to the hole, filled it up to the brim, patted it down, then threw stones and twigs on it until it looked reasonably undisturbed. It was beginning to drizzle.

There was some soil left over after the hole was full. The tractor man got rid of this by taking spadefuls and casting it wide, so that it showered into the ditches and became part of the landscape. The rain came down more heavily now and the ground was becoming muddy.

When he had done, the water was running from his hair down into his collar. His face looked drawn and grey and his eyes were now dull. The tractor-man then stared around the dawn fields, and was still lost in some kind of trance when the flogre came sweeping silently across the land. The big creature wheeled away on seeing the man and headed in another direction, swiftly but seemingly without perturbation.

Finally, the tractor-man left, trudging through the dense rain, towards the farmhouses.

The hares were glad to see him go. They had not felt comfortable with the night's proceedings, and his continued presence amongst them had been a trial. They hoped when he came back he would do so driving the tractor, which was where they expected him to be. Not walking around in the middle of the night, shooting people, then burying them in the corner of Booker's Field.

Once the day was on them, they ventured out of their forms and began looking for food. One of the leverets found the woman's shoe in the long grass at the base of the totem and started to use it in play, but the adults told her to leave it alone.

The shoe remained where it was, deep in the secret grasses.

Headinthemist read the signs from the wych elms twigs: the portents, she told everyone, were good, even though a leveret had mistakenly bitten the head off a harebell in the darkness the night before. This particular individual was waiting for the two souls to begin battling for his body, as everyone said they would, and his face was a picture of misery. There was a small pain in his gut for a whole day, but whether that was because he overate on a squirrel's cache of old acorns he had stumbled across, or because his soul was losing the fight, he was never quite sure. One thing though, he would never eat another flower in the darkness without smelling it first.

Chapter Nineteen

For two or three days after the human killings, there were men hallooing about the countryside, their voices bearing the foghorn tones of bitterns. The tractor-man was one of them, and his call sounded the most plaintive of all. Gradually, this unusual activity ceased and the hares were able to get some sleep during the day. The tractor-man returned to work as usual, driving the hare symbol for happiness.

Fleetofoot thought to help the tractor-man, and took the high-heeled shoe from the tall grasses, carried it in his mouth to the gibbet, and hooked it over the bottom strand of wire. The shoe was made of hide, after all, like the other tenants of the gibbet. It had been part of the woman, just as the strip of grey in the top right corner had been part of a water rat. It was the woman's husk, it had her smell, it was right that it should be amongst the other emblems on the tractor-man's homage to death. Because it hung downwards, by its heel, it gathered rainwater in the toe, from which drank a variety of small thirsty birds on their way from here to there, and back again.

There it hung in its colourful glory, between the carcass of a mole and a long streak of ginger hide which had once been a stoat. There it would weather and rot like the rest of the victims of the tractor-man's shotgun.

Except that when the tractor-man next went to the gibbet, with a rook he had blown out of its high nest, he dropped the dead bird with a startled cry and looked around him fearfully. The shoe-trophy was snatched from the gibbet and hastily thrown on a bonfire which was burning in the next field. For weeks afterwards, the tractor-man peered at the nearby thicket, as if he believed someone were hiding there, watching him . . .

*   *   *

Summer came, but by that time the hares had dispersed to their individual territories. These areas had no strict boundaries, were not defended in any way, and heavily overlapped in places. Visits between hares were not uncommon, and very few would argue if one hare grazed on another's land. This was the way it had always been done, and this was the way it remained.

When the hare colony began to break up, Skelter felt a flutter of panic. What would he do? No doubt moonhare would assign a piece of land to him, once he asked her to, but he had never lived completely alone before. The thought terrified him.

Finally, Skelter expressed his fears to moonhare.

'What am I supposed to do about it?' snapped Followme. 'Keep the colony together just because you're frightened of your own shadow?'

'Can't you suggest something?' he asked. 'Anything? I did help you protect yourselves against the flogre.'

The moonhare stood up on her hind legs and with her long ears straight up in the air she looked down her nose at Skelter from a great height.

'Oh, so you want a lifetime's gratitude and special favours, just for giving us a bit of information that we might have found out from anyone?'

'No, I just – I don't know . . .'

Followme was not the most understanding moonhare of all time, and had a tendency to eschew gratitude, believing it to be a sign of weakness in a great leader. Reacher was no better, being weak-willed and lazy, and he did nothing to moderate the moonhare's judgement in such things. Whatever she did was fine by him, so long as he need not be bothered with it.

However, a yearling jill called Eyebright came forward, and said that she would be willing to share her territory with Skelter if he so wished.

'There's plenty of room down by the meadow, and I'm sure we wouldn't get in each other's way,' she said. 'I think Skelter would like it, because the ground has a slight slope to it, as it falls down to the river. It's good bottomland, and though the soil's not the podzol you find fir trees and bracken growing in, nor heavy peat that mountain hares might be used to, neither is it that thin chalky rendzina like the soil on the mainland. It's a good rich loam.'

Skelter, who actually didn't care *what* kind of earth it was, was nevertheless impressed by her knowledge. Eyebright was obviously one of those hares who took great care in selecting her living area and knew what to look for when she did so. When he asked her about it, she told him that she had once had a long conversation with a gregarious mole, whose livelihood depended on a deep knowledge of these things.

Eyebright was a reserved and shy young jill, though not at all dewy, who had two large fields the northern border of which was the river. Mustard was grown in one of the fields and the other was Whinsled Lea, a meadowland of old grass covered with a multitude of wild flowers and herbs. A ditch ran between the two fields, and a hedge of blackthorn. There were seven trees along the ditch: a broad oak, a horse chestnut visited in the early autumn by hordes of human young, four field elms and an elderberry, all spread widely apart.

In the summer months the oak was surrounded by a rough circle of bare earth, pressed to a denseness geological time would be hard put to match. This phenomenon was caused by the feet of the same human young who visited the horse chestnut in the autumn, for they made rope swings in the oak and climbed up into its branches to fashion dens and lookout posts. They chattered like starlings, rarely saw the hares let alone bothered them, and were generally entertaining, especially when the farm workers saw them and chased them along the river bank.

The river itself was on a bend where it met the two fields, encircling them like a comforting arm. It was wide – too wide to swim across – and on fine days sailboats and dinghies could be observed drifting like moths over its shimmering surface.

The main enemy as usual apart from the flogre, were foxes who came along the riverbank and dropped down into the shallow basin holding Whinsled Lea. Their highways were well defined in the meadow, where animal paths were centuries old, but in the field of white mustard, whose mass of yellow flowers formed a mirror for the sun all summer long, their tracks were constantly being renewed and Eyebright suggested that she and Skelter dig their forms in some corner of the meadow where they could not be surprised.

There were two rabbit warrens in the meadow, but none in the mustard field. The rabbits never bothered Eyebright, and she had nothing to do with them. Grey herons came to the shallows of the river, which was partly tidal, and there was a great variety of waders and shore birds who made their homes along its banks, from godwits to curlews to sandpipers. There were no badgers, but there was an otters' holt in the bank of a stream that ran down between the meadow and a cottage. A solitary sparrowhawk, which disappeared for most of the summer months, was occasionally in residence. He could be seen drifting around on stiff wings, looking for prey much smaller than Eyebright or Skelter.

Skelter accepted the jill's offer immediately, though he knew nothing about her beyond the fact that she had been born and raised in the colony. She had been too quiet and serious to gain his attention before now and he did wonder what prompted her to ask him if he wished to join her. She told him that her reasons were the same as his: that she disliked being alone and would prefer company. That seemed fair enough.

She gave him a tour of the fields before she would let him accept her offer and he found them, for flatland country, more than adequate. Skelter especially liked the startlingly blue cornflowers, a plant he had never seen before. He asked moonhare if it was all right and she sniffed and said she supposed so. Thus it was all settled, and one hot still day when the insects were buzzing and clicking, and the ditchweeds were withering through lack of moisture, the two hares went off together and selected their spots to dig their forms. Skelter dug both of them, being more skilled at the work, while Eyebright watched and admired his technique, making him feel quite highland proud.

Skelter found the meadow especially good, almost as grand as the hillsides covered in heather that he missed so much, for there were so many grasses to choose between, as well as herbs, weeds and wild flowers.

At first there was an awkwardness between Skelter and Eyebright which was difficult to overcome, but once Skelter got the jill to talk about things she was familiar with and he was in ignorance of their relationship began to improve. He asked her to teach him more about the culture of the field hares so that he did not make any silly mistakes, and there is nothing like this sort of thing for overcoming shyness.

She told him about the signs hares used to pass messages to each other.

'A straight twig left in a furrow means food in the direction of the fat end. A crooked stick on a ridge means man has been here recently. A short paw scratch on the ground means that a small predator, such as a weasel, has passed by this place. A long paw scratch means a large predator, like a fox or badger. A U-shaped scratch is not really a signal, it's a method of turning mad spirits around to go back in the direction they came from.'

'Mad spirits?'

'Yes, you know the wind carries the spirits of mad, strange creatures called *idbitts*, which are unable to go to the Otherworld, or even Ifurin, because they actually never existed in real life. These are doomed to roam the earth, carried within the folds of the wind, and if they can they'll get into any living hare's head and send him or her mad too!'

Skelter was sceptical but tried not to show it.

'No,' he said, 'I didn't know that. We mountain hares have *bad* spirits, of the mountains, that hide in rocks and gullies, cracks in the peat, that sort of thing, but no *mad* ones.'

'Well there are plenty down here, on the flatlands, where the winds slice across the marshes and over the fields in sheets. If you draw a U scratch on the ground, any mad *idbitt* spirit has to follow that U and of course goes back in the direction from which it came.'

'Are there any other methods of getting rid of them? I noticed for instance that you placed a bird's skull you found right on the edge of the meadow.'

Eyebright sat up tall, her forepaws in the begging position.

'Ah, I'm glad you noticed that, Skelter: you're very observant. The reason I did that was because bird skulls often, that is usually, contain *immobile* mad spirits, called *iddabs*, which can't stop talking. If you put your ear to a bird's skull you can hear the *iddab* inside whispering away, and it's true, it never does stop. If you put one of these on the edge of your territory, any *idbitts* that try to pass will be engaged in conversation by the *iddab*, and in the end the idbitt is so distracted by the *iddab's*

163

incessant chatter it forgets to enter the field and goes on its way elsewhere.'

Skelter's mind was beginning to stretch at this point, so he said to Eyebright, 'That's most interesting. Most interesting. So any bird skulls I find I give to you to put on the periphery of our territory.'

'Except the land bordered by the river, because *idbitts* can't cross water anyway, so they won't come from that direction.'

'Of course not, how silly of me.'

Next, Eyebright told him about white pebbles, that the owner of one of these lucky finds would be protected against attack from dogs and foxes if the pebble was kept in the finder's form.

'They're very rare though,' she said.

Skelter had seen hundreds of them on the shoreline, with the crabs scuttling over them, but he did not say so.

'Then there's the fact that if you half-bury an ivy leaf near a form with leverets in it, this will help protect them from predators. A hawthorn or blackthorn twig buried near a path will deter humans from using that path . . . I think that's enough for now, don't you?'

Skelter agreed that he had taken on sufficient information to keep him happy for a while. He thanked his new companion profusely, while at the same time wondering whether there were even greater surprises to come from these superstitious creatures he had joined, and wished he were back in the highlands for about the hundredth time since he had left.

That evening, before the failing of the light, the pair of them went silly, and dashed backwards and forwards, rolling over, somersaulting, skimming around molehills and leaping over daisies in an overspill of exuberance, after the tensions that went with communal living. Despite her reserve and the intense nature of her personality, he felt he could share the territory with her without too many problems.

When dusk came they crept into their U-shaped forms and waited anxiously for the going of the grey. The flogre had taken a rabbit that very morning from one of the warrens on the edge of Whinsled Lea. The rabbits had overstayed their feeding period, too intent on getting food into them to watch the skies, and the dawn had come up on them unexpectedly. They had run for their burrows, but much too late, and the deadly giant predator came out of nowhere, grey out of grey, and snatched a fat doe just two body lengths away from the warren entrance. They heard her squeals fade into silence.

Moonhare had said to Skelter before they had dispersed that he must consider himself a marked hare and to watch himself more than ordinarily.

'News travels and no doubt the flogre has heard how the hares are managing to avoid capture these days, because a newcomer has taught them to dig a different kind of form. The flogre will be after that newcomer . . .'

There was no reason to suppose this were true, for who would it be that could talk to such a creature? Only another flogre, surely, and so far as everyone knew, this one was unique. Still, if it were a mythical creature, crossed over somehow from some twilight world, or out of Ifurin, then perhaps it had magical ways of finding things out? Maybe it could read minds at a distance, or was told secrets by the whispering grasses, the rustling leaves in the trees? Skelter imagined the flogre sitting on its nest, with an army of strange little insects all murmuring his name, 'Skelter, Skelter, Skelter, Skelter, Skelter, Skelter, Skelter . . .' and the flogre working itself up into a fury of hate, tearing blocks of stone to pieces with its claws, in its desire to get even with the hare from the highlands.

Skelter shuddered in his form.

'Are you all right?' called Eyebright.

He replied, 'Yes, why?'

'I heard you whimper.'

'Only a dream,' he said.

Chapter Twenty

The summer season was long and lazy, with visits from moonhare and sunhare, and nothing much to do but eat and watch the fields grow until harvest time. Butterflies, craneflies, damselflies, gnats and mayflies filled the air, bringing in the swifts and swallows. There were mice everywhere, hundreds and thousands of mice: field mice, wood mice, harvest mice. Voles and shrews too. They scrambled through the grasses, along the ditches, in a murmuring of frantic activity. Magpies glided like stringless kites from tree to ground, swaggered around, bullying even the squirrels when they had a mind to.

There were otters down by the river, sleak creatures who cut through the water like fish. Water rats and coypu lived around the banks and made a nuisance of themselves.

Children came and played on the oak, their constant chatter and shrieking becoming a familiar sound to Skelter's ears. He watched them build their dens, swing on their ropes, play their games amongst the hedgerows. If they ever saw him they merely pointed, their attention diverted for a few moments before they went back to their fantasy world again.

There were dangers, of course. Foxes came and had to be evaded: two of the colony's deaths were the result of foxes that summer, but luckily for Skelter and Eyebright there was easier prey along the banks of the river amongst the wading birds.

The flogre came, wheeling in at dusk and dawn, but had to take other meals because the hares had protected themselves with their mountain forms.

There were dogs too, sometimes walked by their owners across the meadow, but occasionally out on their own, looking for adventure. Dogs were not so dangerous as foxes. They were not out hunting through hunger, but for sport, and the hares knew that a sporting predator tires more easily than a hungry one.

Near to the meadow, just a short unmade lane away, was a small cottage where lived a man with hair on his face. There was a dog there too, a big St Bernard that often accompanied the man on his walks along the river and over the field. This pair turned out to be quite harmless, for the man seemed intent on observing wildlife, not on destroying it. There was always a pair of field glasses around his neck, and he often carried devices that were interesting but not harmful to the birds and beasts. Whenever hares or rabbits bolted he kept a rigid control of the dog, never letting it give chase. Sometimes the dog was out alone, but her discipline was such that she still allowed wild creatures to dash away from her without pursuing them. This was a novelty to Skelter, who had experience of sheepdogs with flocks, who would not chase hares, but this enormous hound had no such responsibilities and still kept herself in check.

One quiet morning in mid-season Eyebright and Skelter were feeding in the meadow, close to each other. Suddenly, a shrill sound hit the air, a high whistle. Instinctively, Skelter's ears went rigid, poking up out of the grasses, to ascertain what was going on. The next second a loud blast came from nearby, and the tops of grasses and wild flowers were mowed by a swathe of pellets from a shotgun.

Skelter was not hit by this first shot but bolted and made his unusual arcing run, towards the ditch. Another shot followed, this time much too high, and Skelter thanked his ghost-hare that the human was a poor shot. He stopped and hid in some tall grasses near the ditch, his heart pounding, hoping that Eyebright had managed to escape. Peering through the grasses he could see two humans, swarthy creatures dressed in bright scarves, tramping over the meadow looking for him. One of them lay down level with the tops of the grasses, while the other put two fingers to his lips and emitted another shrill whistle, but Skelter had learned his lesson: he kept his ears flattened against his skull.

The trick was an old one, played by humans on field hares since the invention of the gun. One would lie down at eye-level with the top of the grass while the other would whistle, and any unsuspecting hare in the vicinity would prick up its ears and reveal its position, either in grass or furrow.

Skelter had fallen for it first time because, being a mountain hare, he had never encountered this particular deception before, and no doubt in unwary moments in the future he would fall for it again. They had a cheek though, these two hunters, expecting him to respond immediately after doing it once. He might be a jack from the hills with little field experience, but he had not been born yesterday.

The two hunters, with their flat caps low over dark eyes, came walking towards the spot where he crouched. One of the pair was slashing the grasses with a stick. The other had a firm hand on the double-barrelled shotgun. It looked an old smooth-bore, small gauge weapon, with octagonal barrels and external strikers. The butt was worn to a stubby club-shape and the stock was shiny with constant polishing.

One of the men already had two rabbits joined by a piece of string slung over his right shoulder. By their lean hard faces and dark glinting eyes Skelter could tell they were *real* hunters, out to find a meal, rather than sporting types pandering to their boredom. These were men who knew the hunger of the fox, the empty winter belly that sharpens wits and will. They had fox-like features, expressions, intent. In a word, they were dangerous: this was no game to them, this was survival.

Skelter saw Eyebright bolt from somewhere about twenty lengths ahead of the men. The gun came up, but the man did not fire this time, and eventually lowered his weapon. Obviously the range was too great to waste a shot. The men came on, knowing there was a second hare not far away. Skelter kept absolutely still, flattened against the ground close to a cow pat.

The feet came on, until Skelter could smell the stink of the fired gun, and the smoke-breath of the two hunters. Feet came closer and closer, until Skelter was sure he would be trodden on by one of those boots. A foot finally passed within fractions of his head and squelched in the cow pat. It was retrieved hastily, with much growling and grunting from its owner, who proceeded to tear up handfuls of grass and wipe his boot just a body-length away from Skelter.

The two men tramped around, kicking at tufts of grass, staring into the middle distance. Finally, they walked to another part of the field, never seeing the hare that was right under their noses. There was a nightjar too, just a few lengths away from Skelter, sitting on her nest. She had been staring at Skelter with frightened eyes as the boots were treading all around her, threatening at any moment to land on her nest. He saw the relief in the face of the well-camouflaged bird, when the humans eventually left, and wished he could speak to her. They had shared a common experience between them. However, they did not share a common language, so Skelter said nothing.

Skelter found Eyebright not far from their forms.

'That was close,' he said, 'are you all right?'

'I'm fine,' she replied, 'but I hope they don't come back, now that they know we're here.'

'I doubt it. They probably thought we were rabbits and there's enough of those around.'

'No, they were gypsies, they knew what they were doing. If they come back, it'll be with a lurcher, to run us down. If they do, we'll really be in trouble. I hope those two rabbits they've got will satisfy them. I hate lurchers.'

'Lurchers?'

'Half greyhound, half whippet – all skin and bone, but fast as lightning. They're a devil to outrun, if you get one on your tail. Jaws full of sharp teeth.'

'Yes, I remember greyhounds.' He gave a shudder. 'These lurchers sound a formidable foe. What do we do?'

'Just be on our guard,' said Eyebright. 'If they come back, I suggest we dash down to the river. We can always jump in and swim if necessary.'

'Here? The river's too wide.'

'You don't have to go all the way across. You can let the current take you downstream, then struggle ashore on another part of the river. It's a drastic method of escape, but in an emergency you do what you can.'

'Of course,' agreed Skelter.

Later that day Skelter went down to that part of the river, to the point where a brook met the main body of water. While drinking from the stream he would have called a burn in his own highland country he was startled by something that broke the surface, almost under his nose. It was an otter. The creature came out onto the bank beside him, and its small bright eyes regarded him with interest.

169

'Good day, smallish hare,' said the otter, 'I have the understanding you are not of the local variety of *lepus*, is my comprehension accurate, would you say?'

'What?' said Skelter.

The otter shook himself.

'Ah, allow me to request a forgiveness of my abrupt intrusion on this salutary morning when the sun burnishes the landscape with its bronzing rays. I am simply desirous of introducing myself. My name is Stigand, of the local *Mustelidae*, and I am familiar with many of the different tongues of animals.'

'Oh, I see,' said Skelter. 'You mean you speak many languages – like a friend of mine, Jittie.'

The otter's eyes brightened to pinpoints of light.

'Ah, yes, the hog of the hedge, I know her well, an admirable creature of good standing. But still my initial question remains enravelled, which I would be delighted if you would distangle. Are you of the local tribe?'

'Tribe? Er, no, not of the local tribe. We call them *clans* where I come from. I'm a mountain hare.'

'Yes, yes, I see it now. Absence of black flash under tail, shorter ears, smaller stature. Yes indeed, the mountain hare in all its highland heatherfed glory. I am much pleased to make of your acquaintance, never having met such a hare before this very time, this very place.'

Skelter said, 'You seem to know a lot about mountain hares.'

'One listens, one talks with itinerant creatures, one learns. My own dear mate, Sona, the otter with whom I spend my seasons of joy, tells me that I waste my time on such entertainments as learning, but I am a lost case, my soul is captured by the very essence of knowledge, it makes a bonfire of my brain, it consumes me with interest. I must know all the secrets of the universe, or I pine. You are sympathising with this viewpoint, or are you of the Sona mind?'

'I think it's quite admirable, to wish to learn everything.'

The otter's jaw opened, revealing a mouthful of needles, reminding Skelter that he was passing the time of day with a fierce predator, albeit one whose diet was fish and things from the water.

'I am glad you envisage it so,' said Stigand with a sigh, 'too many

170

of our fellow creatures are intent only on filling the stomach with food. I am of the opinion that knowledge is superior to food.'

The comparison had never occurred to Skelter, he had to admit.

'Oh yes,' said Stigand, 'and I am not the only creature who has this persuasion, for the man in the cottage nearby is also of the same conviction. You may observe him going without victuals many a day in order that he not be interrupted in his study of wildlife. His great dog, the admirable Betsy, will not be harming you in any way. I tell you this, to stop any attacks of the heart, should she come near.'

'I had gathered the impression that the hound was not vicious, though I'm afraid I could *never* trust a dog, not in a million seasons.'

'I am of that understanding, for you hares suffer much in the jaws of such creatures, but Stigand tells you this great fluffy giant will not close her jaws on a gnat for fear of damaging its wings. She has truly the heart of a rabbit in the body of a dog. Now tell me about the highlands,' said the otter eagerly. 'What of the deer and the wildcat, and of the mighty golden eagle? Is the bird as magnificent as they say?'

Thus, Skelter met and befriended the otter who was famous around the land for his pursuit of knowledge and for his habit of encountering travellers passing through his territory, engaging them in conversation, and pestering them for information on anything and everything. When Skelter asked Stigand if he knew anything about the flogre, the otter shook his head sadly, and said that he had witnessed the flight of the creature occasionally, at either dusk or dawn, but the creature's camouflage was such that it melded with the twilight earth and sky, and was impossible to identify. Stigand added that the flight of the monster was swift and silent, quite unlike anything he had ever encountered before.

'I have to say, without shame, that I make myself secretive when the creature is about, for there is no proof it has eschewed a taste for otters, and I must therefore assume that my flesh is as delicious to it as any hare or rabbit.'

Skelter parted from the otter and went back to his form for a sleep in the afternoon sun.

When late afternoon came, moonhare visited.

Eyebright always fussed over Followme, but Skelter, who regarded no hare as above himself, greeted her politely but without obsequiousness. The moonhare seemed flattered by the attentions of Eyebright, but never favoured her above any of the other hares in the colony. Skelter wondered whether there was an incident in the past, which he had missed, involving the two jills.

Moonhare spoke about the coming harvest, when the harvesters would be in the cornfields and there would be general panic in the air. Harvest time came every year, when the corn ripened and was ready for cutting, but the creatures of the field were never prepared for it. Mice and birds had built nests amongst the wheat, barley and oats. There were new bolt holes from rabbit warrens, hidden by the corn. There were new animal highways across the tall fields.

Then came the combine harvester, changing the landscape within a day, revealing the rabbit bolt holes for the world to see, uncovering partridge nests, destroying mouse nests.

Naturally, the creatures of the field did not like this disruption to their lives, and regarded it as a time of terror. There was food in plenty at that time, with fruit, vegetables and grain, all ripening around the same time, but still late summer and autumn meant harvesting time, and harvesting time meant sleepless days for everyone.

'When harvest time is over,' said moonhare to Skelter, 'we must have a meeting. Since you taught us to fashion our forms like mountain hares, we have not been so bothered by the flogre, although we still need to be wary of course. By next mating time, when the hares gather again, we need to know what we are up against. We need to know exactly what the flogre is, whether mythical beast or real creature.'

'How do you propose to find out?' asked Skelter.

Followme looked directly at him.

'Headinthemist has studied the wych elm twigs and it's apparent that someone has to go to the church tower.'

Skelter shook his head.

'Why, no one would dare do that, would they? What would they do once they got there, anyway?'

Still the moonhare's eyes remained on his.

'They would have to climb the stone steps inside the tower, to

172

its top, and spy on the flogre. Headinthemist has discussed this aspect of the mission with harebell spirits, who suggested to her that it should be someone with a head for heights.'

Skelter knew now that the moonhare was talking about him – he was the one they wanted to go and spy on the flogre, find out what kind of creature it might be. He felt a flutter of panic in his breast at the thought, but he had been through so much recently it was difficult to feel the terror he should be experiencing.

'You want me to carry out the mission – isn't that right, moonhare?'

Moonhare nodded.

'None of us could do it. We are flatlanders, frightened of heights. We shake if we have to climb onto a fallen log. You, as a hare from the highlands, are used to such things. I imagine you could climb the steps to the top of the tower without any problems whatsoever?'

'Yes, I could do it easily, you know that. What are a few steps when you've lived on slopes of scree a thousand feet in the air? Heights mean nothing to me. However, you're not just asking me to climb to the top of a tower. You're asking me to spy on a monster – a monster that could rip the skin from my body in seconds.

'I really don't see why I should. I can tell you now, it's no mythical creature. Such things don't exist.'

'There are those of us who believe they do,' said moonhare. 'However, no one can force you to go, can they? Certainly none of us can do it, and I wouldn't trust another creature, even if we could persuade one to go, which I very much doubt. It must be your choice. However, when Headinthemist was under a honey fungus trance, she said she had a vision of you, Skelter, leaving the colony next spring. In this, er, vision, it seemed you were going away for good. I can't explain this, can you? Then again, I don't see how someone who has given valuable service to the colony, in return for being given a home, can be forced to leave it. Well, I'll be on my way. I want to get back before dusk, naturally.'

So the moonhare left them.

Skelter watched her go. He knew very well what she was saying: if he did not go on this mission he would be exiled. Moonhare would find some excuse to have him thrown out of the colony. He sighed deeply. He still had the choice, but if he said no to the mission, he would probably have to leave the colony. That would mean saying goodbye forever to Eyebright, who had become a good friend. It was a terrible decision to have to make.

He decided to say nothing to Eyebright, or anyone else, about moonhare's implied threat. It would do no good accusing her: she would only deny it. Instead, he told Eyebright that he did not believe in mythical beasts and might go on the mission to prove he was right.

Eyebright stared in disbelief at Skelter on hearing this news, and shook her head slowly.

'You're not seriously thinking of going?'

'Well, I have to at least consider it. After all, this business about mythical creatures is all rubbish. The flogre is obviously some kind of raptor, strayed into this area by accident, or brought here by men. There's no such thing as flying badgers . . .'

Eyebright looked around quickly, as if she suspected someone might be listening.

'Hush, don't say those things, the flogre might hear you! It may have asked the wind to carry secrets to its ear and want to prove its magical powers by appearing here this evening.'

Skelter shook his head sadly.

'You really are caught up in this thing, aren't you? Look, I realise the flogre is a formidable creature, but really this is all a bit silly . . .'

Her pained expression made him stop suddenly.

'Please,' she implored, 'don't talk like that.'

These field hares were superstitious beyond belief. Perhaps he should accept the mission from moonhare, get a quick sighting of the creature, and bring back a description which would satisfy these silly hares? Moonhare was right about one thing. The field hares had taken him in and he could show his gratitude for their kindness by ridding them of one of their fears at least. When it was proved to them that they were dealing with a normal creature with no magical properties they might be more willing to accept other methods of defending themselves, instead of viewing any new ideas as heresies.

'I think I might accept moonhare's mission,' he said grimly.

Eyebright gasped. 'No. What for? You realise *she* would not raise a paw to help you, if you were trapped in a snare, or a gin? She is entirely selfish.'

Skelter considered this to be true.

'Granted, I doubt she would help me, but I have to think of all of you, the whole colony. I'm not doing this just for her, I'm doing it – *if* I do it – for all the unborn leverets and those hares caught out at dusk. If we know what we're up against, we can prepare ourselves accordingly.'

'You must *want* to die.'

'No,' said Skelter truthfully, 'I don't want to die, but I have been extremely lucky so far and there's no reason to suppose I can't go on being lucky. This luck makes me a useful member of the colony. I want to help, to repay you all for taking me in.'

'You'll be killed,' replied Eyebright miserably. 'I know you will.'

Skelter could not understand why she was getting so upset. After all, it was him who was volunteering for the mission, not her. Why should she worry? She was just like Rushie used to be, going off into a sulk for no real reason whatsoever. Jills were creatures with hidden moods that were incomprehensible to the average jack.

Chapter Twenty One

Harvesting time came and the air was choked with tawny chaff and strawdust that dried the throat and blocked the nose. There were machines cutting, binding, threshing, gathering in the wheat, barley and oats, gathering in the very fibrous rays of the sun itself, splitting the shafts into golden wands, binding the sheaves with silver wire. Men worked with their collarless shirts stretched taut across their backs, their sleeves rolled to reveal pale muscles, their necks bared and reddening in the late-summer heat. The rain had been ordered to stay away, keep its wet fingers off the land until the harvest was in.

There was noise and confusion, but that was normal for the gathering of the harvest. Local women made corn dollies for visitors: little men-shapes, horse-shapes, hare-shapes. Gingerbread men with black-raisin eyes found their way into lunch boxes, surprising the harvesters. There were strange country rituals carried out by the young men and women, mystical rites the secrets of which were kept by mother earth. There was dancing on the village green, with leg bells and sticks and colourful knee ribbons. The spring-time fertility celebrations had reached fruition, and the pregnant fields were giving birth to riches: amber grain, ruby berries, emerald leaves.

When darkness began to descend, the harvesting machines were lit by lamps that swayed as the vehicle rumbled on, the men calling to each other across the shadows. Gnats came in clouds to pester the harvesters and these attracted first the martins, swifts and swallows, and then the bats.

Although the animals and birds were aware that this human activity was organised not against them, but in order to gather in the crops, the disruption to their lives caused them much anguish and anxiety. The shaven fields, exposed to the sky, were fine for the hares, but not for a thousand other creatures who depended upon cover for their survival. It was the rape of their homeland. They moved into hedges and ditches, into the woodland verges, and into fields that had remained as yet untouched by the reapers. Overcrowding caused squabbles and some serious fighting.

The worst was yet to come.

Some of the farmers set the stubble on fire, unleashing terrors upon the creatures of the countryside. Thick smoke enveloped the highways and byways, the hedgerows and trees, the hidey holes in the ground. Lines of flame swept over the landscape, deadly to those in their approach, and grass snakes, smooth snakes, mice, voles, hedgehogs, rats, toads, lizards, newts, shrews, and many other beasts of the field were burned to death. Innumerable insects, like rare delicate jewels, melted in the flames. Dusty-winged moths, butterflies, dragonflies, fragile lace-wings, bees and wasps, snakeflies and springtails, tiny red ticks and false scorpions, stoneflies, spiders complex as knitted wire, bullet-hard beetles, all incinerated. Not one, but many varieties of grasshopper and ladybird were amongst the victims. Wild flowers, herbs, fungi and grasses were destroyed with all the larvae and attendant parasites: the aphids, mealy bugs, thrips and mites.

Finally, it was over, the rhythm of the seasons having paused for a moment, but not halted.

Whinsled Lea, the meadow in which Skelter and Eyebright had their home, was not mowed that summer. Instead, some horses and cattle were put out to graze, every so often, which suited the two hares quite well. The big animals did not bother them in the least, and their presence deterred poachers and legal shooters from using the meadow as a hunting ground. So far as cows were concerned, the hares could often feed in and around their legs, without fear.

Skelter continued to consider whether or not to go on moon-hare's mission to the church, but he did not raise the subject again with Eyebright because it seemed to upset her so much. Moonhare did not press him for an answer either, probably guessing her implied threat would eventually have the right effect on his decision. Headinthemist had been to see him, and explained that a long exhaustive study of wych elm twigs after a recent storm had revealed that it was Skelter's destiny to attempt discovery of the flogre's identity. When he pressed Headinthemist for an idea of whether or not he would be successful however, he received the vague answer that 'the honey fungus was shining'. This only served to further entrench his belief that Headinthemist was no more an oracle than any other hare and merely pretended to be to give herself some status. She advised him to take a bird skull with him, so that the *iddabs* could protect him. Skelter thanked her politely for her advice. He had no intention of travelling around the countryside carrying a bird's skull in his mouth, though he did not say so.

'Anything more on that human shooting incident?' Skelter asked one day of sunhare when he came to visit. 'You remember, when the tractor-man hunted those two people, then buried them?'

Reacher said there was.

'The patch where the tractor-man buried the bodies seems to be especially fertile now, and the grass grows thick and lush on it. Of course, this means the animals all go there to feed, and this leaves the rectangle of ground plainly visible. The tractor-man doesn't seem to like this very much, and gets quite distressed. He keeps digging around at the edges of the rectangle, trying to change its shape. I think he wants to sort of merge it with the rest of the field.'

'How strange,' remarked Eyebright.

Sunhare shrugged. 'Well, there's no understanding human behaviour, is there? I mean, up at the church they spend all their time making sure such rectangles remain clear of weeds and stand out quite clearly from the grassed surrounds. One thing though, he does copy – he puts cut flowers on the patch some mornings. Little bunches of them. Then later he takes them away again. Most peculiar behaviour, even for a human.'

Skelter was fascinated by the strange antics of the tractor-man, who was the nearest thing among humans to a wild creature that he knew. Up in the highlands hares could get quite close to those without guns but Skelter had never been able to become familiar with a human. For one thing he had seldom seen the same human twice.

There had been shepherds he recognised, but they had been distant creatures, and the presence of their dogs made them inaccessible. Shepherds were intense, serious men, who were interested only in their flocks and their dogs. They lived apart from other men and were almost a race unto themselves. There were not so many of them now as there used to be, but they were still the same kind of creature. They had faces like weathered stone and hands to match, and they would sit on a piece of ground for a day long, content to stare at the hills and glens around them. If it weren't for their dogs, hares would quite like shepherds. Sheep dogs never attacked hares, or any other wild animal for that matter, for they were trained to work and not be distracted, but still they were canines, and so could never be trusted.

The tractor-man was something like a shepherd. He was seen at least once or twice a week, and sometimes every day for long periods. He had an animal earthy way about him. The arable smell of silage and kale clung to his clothes, and his grizzled hoary chin and unkempt hair full of wayward seedlings made him a less artificial creature than most men. His coat and trousers were stained with the produce of the land. His fingernails had much of the country's soil beneath them. Skelter felt that if the tractor-man stood still for more than a short period of time, grass would begin to grow in his seams.

He was not a noisy man, but silent, contemplative, though without any great show of philosophic observance that hares sensed in some of the lonely walkers in and around the region. He was a creature carved from the flatlands, so much a part of the landscape that hares considered him pure flint and alluvium, with a coating of human skin. They had seen him pick a bluebell and inspect it with pride. They had watched him dust the chalk from his hands in satisfaction at the end of a day. They had witnessed his delight at a strawberry sunset, and sensed his inner peace as he tramped over the fields on a frosty morning to carry out his ministry and mission on the land.

He was simply, the tractor-man.

'What a noble visage has the hare,' said Stigand one day, when the harvest was behind them all, and the land had settled once more into its gentle rhythms. 'Such a classical profile. We otters have not the presentation of hares: their chiselled appearance and regal bearing!'

179

'Oh, I don't know,' said Skelter, becoming embarrassed.

The hare and the other were on the bank of the stream, idling away a passive noon.

'You otters have such skill in the water. If you were my shape, you would probably be no good at swimming.'

'That's impeccably true,' said Stigand with a sigh, 'but those magnificent hind legs – you must be proud of them?'

Skelter glanced at his powerful legs.

'Well, that's true, but you have your ruddershaped tail, which is also very powerful.'

A head popped up from beneath the water and Sona, Stigand's mate, was there before them.

'*Fisc!*' she said.

Stigand glanced at Skelter. 'I think I have to go fishing,' he said.

'*Fisc!*' cried Sona.

'All right, all right,' Stigand wandered down to the water's edge, '*Ic cuman.*'

She disappeared beneath the surface, and immediately she was gone, Stigand wandered back to his spot in the sun.

'She is wanting me to fashion a new holt soon, but these sunny days – ahhh, how can one think of work? I am an ancient otter, too old for these employments. Now, you were telling me of the great quest you must be undertaking with valour and stoutish heart. A quest to find the identity of the flying monster, yes? This is a very brave thing you do.'

'Well, I'm not sure I'm going to do it yet.'

'Quite so, quite so. This is such a formidable endeavour, I would myself be full of quakings. But you! You are the noble beast of the field. There is no fear that touches your heart and mind. Such courage is a grand thing, smallish hare from the highlands.'

'Yes, grand,' replied Skelter, not altogether as convinced of his own bravery as Stigand seemed to be. It was very difficult to talk to the otter about the mission, without feeling one would be letting him down if he did not carry it out in the end.

He left the otter lying on his back, his belly warming in the sun, and went back to his form. Eyebright was out somewhere, feeding in one of her neighbour's fields. She had said she was tired of mustard plants and wanted something different. There

180

were lettuces to be had, and radishes, and onions – many other vegetables, more than enough for all.

Skelter decided he had to talk to Jittie. He had not seen the hedgehog since he left her in the early summer, and now he had a need of her advice. It was time for a visit. If need be, he could stay the night, in his old form if it was still there.

He set off over the fields at a reasonable pace, moving away from the river and travelling through territories of various hares, with whom he paused to pass a few words.

Longrunner greeted him with, 'I hear you're going to fight the flogre for us.'

'Fight it? No, no. Find out what it is, but not fight it. I'm only a hare, not a wildcat.'

Longrunner looked disappointed. 'Oh, misinformed again.'

'Well, these things get distorted, and anyway I haven't yet said I'm going to do it. I said I *might*.'

Longrunner seemed to lose interest.

'Oh, well, best of luck. You off to reconnoitre the church tower now?'

'No, I'm visiting a friend.'

'Oh.'

The same sort of conversation was had with Headinthemist and Fleetofoot, who were sitting together in a field of stubble that had not been fired. They were arguing over a white pebble that the harvester had upturned with one of its wheels when Skelter arrived, but they seemed animated by his presence and wanted to know all about the mission he was on to destroy the flogre.

By the time he left them Skelter had decided he did not want to run into any more hares. They disturbed him with their assumptions and he was feeling more than a little annoyed with moonhare and sunhare, who had obviously exaggerated what had passed between them and himself. He started to wonder what his old clan of Screesiders would say, if he told them he had volunteered to investigate the nest of a golden eagle. They would look at him as if he were mad.

'Maybe I am mad?' he asked himself, as he travelled alongside a ditch, to reach the five-barred gate. 'I keep thinking that perhaps my experiences have made me braver, but in fact they've probably affected my brain.'

181

As he was approaching the field in which Jittie's old rabbit hole was located, he glanced up into the sky. The evening was coming in like a purple curtain, trailing across the flatlands from the horizon. There was a smudge of redness on the bruised-fruit face of the heavens, and as he stared a silhouette crossed this fading blush. Although a long way in the distance, Skelter knew it was the flogre. It was huge in comparison to the birds who were returning to their nests. It was like a great upturned boat with wings.

Immediately Skelter began to shake with trepidation.

How could he even think of visiting the den of this monster, when he could not view it from a great distance without trembling? It was impossible. The whole idea was out of the question. Jittie would confirm his fears.

When he found Jittie's hole, the nest was empty. No doubt she had gone on one of her wanderings. Skelter was disappointed and settled down where he was for an hour or two, not wishing to venture out into the deadly twilight.

Chapter Twenty Two

Bubba was restless, shuffling through the bones of his victims that lay around the floor: femurs, skulls, mandibles, sternums, ribs, metatarsals. They rattled as he clawed through them, old and new bones, cluttering the floorboards of the ancient tower. There were probably more bones in the belfry than there were in the churchyard. Bubba was not happy. He always stirred the skeletons of former meals like this, when he was moody and depressed.

Men had been in his room lately, to inspect the remnants of the rope that dangled from the bell. Bubba had vacated the tower, when he heard them ascending the stone spiral staircase, but he could smell where their hands had been. It worried him, that odour.

What did these humans want in the nest of Bubba? Did they know he was there, or were they just carrying out some task of their own, which had nothing to do with him? Bubba decided that he must be wary of traps. Humans were strong on revenge, and if they suspected he had taken some of their pets – which of course he had – they might try to kill Bubba.

That was all right: let them try. Bubba was ready to defend himself. But it was better not to precipitate these confrontations. Let them take their course.

He shuffled around amongst the debris that covered the floor. The men *must* have seen *them*. What had they thought of the skeletons? It was obvious that the tower had not been visited for many years, that this was the first time those particular men had been in the belfry. It could be that they imagined the bones were old, the accumulation of many years of wild creatures using the tower as a home or refuge.

Bubba went to the sill and took off into the darkening purple. He cruised high above the map of the peninsula, away from the deadly telephone poles with their invisible wires.

The fields below him were the colour of wounds, darkening every moment. Night flowed from the ditches, down the winding lanes, out of the copses, spinneys and orchards. Bubba was leaving his tower later and later in the evening, until now he hunted when it was almost dark. This was not his preference but had been forced upon him by his prey, which had learned to make themselves scarce during twilight.

Of all the creatures he hunted Bubba was most unhappy with the hares: they had somehow managed to dig themselves fortifications, which he could not breach. The only way he could catch them was to linger after dark and swoop on the first hare to leave its form. This was a very rare happening, for Bubba needed moonlight to see by and he was becoming frustrated by the dark nights when no moon shone.

Bubba felt he should punish them. It was apparent to him that they had been taught unnatural ways by some creature they respected. It could not have been a rabbit, though that was the most logical choice, but Bubba had observed their doings from the tower, when he first moved in, and rabbits and hares went about their separate businesses without social contact with one another. They were not enemies, but they were not friends either.

No, some newcomer was amongst the hares, and had brought foreign ways to them. So far Bubba had not been able to detect this creature, but he kept his orange eyes open for sight or sound of an unusual animal. When he found this individual, Bubba was going to rip out its heart.

Bubba found a quirk of nature in himself. Now that he was being denied a kind of food that had previously been plentiful, even though at the time that food was not considered especially appetising, it had suddenly become a necessity of life. Bubba had not favoured the taste of hare over rabbit, duck, or even lamb, before those creatures had built their fortifications. Now however, he craved hare. Nothing seemed to match the flavour of hare. He could taste hare flesh in his dreams and woke with a longing on his tongue. It became increasingly obvious to him that hare flesh was essential to his diet, and that if he caught nothing else as the days passed he *had* to find hare.

As he was cruising over the fields, in the last dying rays of the sun, he spotted a hare by a ditch. Bubba continued in his flight, not deviating by even a fraction, in order that he avoided the hare's notice. Sudden moves attracted attention. It was Bubba's observation that hares rarely looked up into the sky: they studied the hedgerows and ditches for foxes creeping up on them, were wary of holes which might contain rogue badgers, but the sky was not an area they regularly scanned for signs of danger.

Of course, since Bubba had been on the scene, the hares were watching for him, but they were not trained observers of the skyscape. To the untrained eye of a hare, he would appear simply as a dark outline.

However, to Bubba's amazement and anger, *this* hare recognised who and what Bubba was almost as quickly as Bubba had seen the hare, for it had looked up and then immediately taken cover. It was as if the creature was habitually used to observing the skies, was vigilant, mindful of a need for intelligent examination of all overhead movement.

To make matters worse, the hare had immediately taken refuge in a rabbit hole, instead of bolting in fright (like he was supposed to). A *rabbit* hole. Surely this was no ordinary hare? Yet, though the time had been short, Bubba had not noticed any substantial differences between this creature and other hares in the vicinity. A little smaller perhaps, but maybe it was a young one? There was something his keen sight had caught but which evaded his brain for the moment. His instincts were often ahead of his conscious thought, and he knew if he left it alone, and did not worry it to death, it would filter through to his intelligence in the end.

He wheeled away, knowing that this strange hare who had the audacity to hide in rabbit holes – in itself very strange and disturbing behaviour and totally unharelike – was lost to him for the present. He would in future keep a sharp eye out for this creature.

For this night, he had to be satisfied with a rabbit who ventured out of its burrow a little too early, possibly eager to get at the fresh grass before its fellows. Its greed had been its downfall.

Bubba cruised towards the tower with his substitute prize for a longed-for hare, sliding silently down the black rays of night, to land on the sill of his tower. Once inside, he began to devour the still-warm creature, satisfying his hunger but not his craving.

As he tore at the skin of the rabbit, around its silly dandelion fluffball of a tail, Bubba's subliminal instincts suddenly connected with his conscious mind.

Of course! That hare he had seen. When it had retreated down the rabbit hole, its tail had been in full view.

There had been no black flash!

This was obviously a new type of hare in the district, one that Bubba had never seen before, and this creature was a keen observer of the skies, knew how to protect itself against flying predators.

Bubba brooded as he ripped at the rabbit and swallowed chunks of meat.

This small hare, without doubt, was the creature who had been transforming the habits of the local hares. He sensed a boldness and a confidence in this creature which was lacking from the local population.

This new hare would have to be dealt with. It would have to be hunted down without mercy and torn to pieces. The lord of the flatlands would not tolerate being thwarted, and his rule by the claw and hook was not to be questioned.

—Tower, I shall destroy this upstart.

—*Of course, Bubba, for the hare has upset the delicate balance of nature and taught the locals unnatural skills.*

—Am I right to be angry, tower?

—*You are Bubba, and can be anything you like.*

—I can't be a man.

—*In spirit you are a man.*

Bubba settled into the night, letting himself merge with the darkness of the tower, become one with the black stone.

PART FOUR

*

The Quest for the Flogre

The Quest for the Shark

Chapter Twenty Three

Autumn is a time which gives rise to hare unease, for it is the colour of foxes.

When the leaves turned to russet hues, and were a perfect match for the colony's main enemy in life, hares started at every turn, catching sight of their enemy out of the corner of their eyes, only to realise their mistake (or not, in certain cases) a moment later. It was not a happy state of affairs, to be constantly jittery, the heart jumping every few seconds into the throat.

Their nervousness during this period fed on itself, transmitting signals to other creatures until everyone was creeping around, continually on edge, irritable, moody, and not at all sociable. They constantly looked to the auguries for comfort, told their troubles to the luminous honey fungus, and spoke with the harebells and the spirits of their ancestors.

Not only was it a fox-coloured land, but hares regarded with disgust the untidiness of the season as it littered their beautifully clean fields with old leaves and dead blossoms, filling the nice straight furrows with mushy trash and clogging the ditches so that the water had no freedom of flow. They did not understand why the trees had to moult at all, especially just before winter. When other creatures were all growing thicker, longer coats, the trees got rid of theirs, ready to dance naked in the ice and snow and freezing winds. It just didn't make any sense.

Skelter was sitting in the corner of the meadow with Eyebright near him. There had been disturbing dreams, the day before, in which his ghost-hare had appeared to him. Skelter had decided these dreams were the result of autumn and the troubled times. When the air was thick with red and gold, the two colours of which he was most wary, was it any wonder he was fretting? Foxes and eagles. It was a good job that such creatures had not been painted brown and green, or hares would be nervous wrecks.

He had not been able to contact Jittie, but had made up his mind about the mission. He wanted to stay with the colony: they were his family now.

For some reason Eyebright was not pleased with him and again Skelter put it down to the fox-coloured land.

Eyebright said, 'So, you're determined to go through with it?'

'Yes, I'm afraid so.'

'How can you be "afraid so" when you've got a choice? Moonhare is just using you, you know. This information isn't vital to the colony. Why don't you reconsider? Stay here with me until the spring, *then* make a decision. What can a few months do?'

Once Skelter had made up his mind on something, it was very hard to dislodge him. He was a highlander. His kind did not go lightly into something, but spent long hours in thought before making a decision. Once that decision was made, however, it was in there, firm as a buried rock.

'It doesn't matter whether I go now or later, the danger will be the same. I prefer to get it over with. You believe the flogre is a supernatural creature, I don't, and I mean to prove I'm right. Once we find out what this creature really is we can work out more ways of defending ourselves from its attacks. I've seen a dark shape in the sky, but I mean to come back with a good description. It's probably some kind of giant owl or something.'

'Owl? That size? Don't be ridiculous Skelter. The rabbits have ancient stories about eagle owls, which they claim preyed on them when they lived in another land, but they say the flogre is twice as large . . . oh, you're *so* stubborn. Nothing I say is going to make any difference, is it?'

'Well, maybe not an owl then, but certainly not a supernatural creature either. Don't worry about me. It seems that I'm bound for a life of adventure, with many changes. I used to have the deer, the eagles and wildcats around me. Now I have field hares, hedgehogs, otters and flogres. Maybe tomorrow there'll be a whole new set of creatures. I'll survive.'

Eyebright sniffed. 'You'll have to settle down one day, so why not now. Let some other hare risk its skin.'

'No, I'm sorry Eyebright, it has to be me.'

She refused to talk to him after that and went to another part of the meadow. Skelter found this very odd behaviour but he had

190

ceased to try to fathom Eyebright. She was a strange hare, even for a brown. Instead, Skelter went to say goodbye to Stigand, the otter.

'Ah, it's fare you well, my confederate,' said the otter, 'and may we assemble again soon, eh? You must look out for your fleece. Stigand will hold the vigil and be ever watchful for your return – the coming of the hero.'

'Oh, I don't know about the hero bit,' said Skelter, 'but thanks anyway Stigand. Goodbye Sona,' he said to Stigand's mate, but she just rolled her eyes to heaven and muttered something in her own language. Females, they were all the same, always disapproving of something.

Skelter then set off to tell moonhare that he planned to visit the church tower this very day.

Before he left the meadow, however, Eyebright ran over to him. She looked distressed and he wondered if she had had an accident, but it seemed that she only wanted to speak to him one last time, before he went. If her expression was full of anxiety, her voice was full of aggression.

'Goodbye, and . . . take care of yourself,' she said fiercely.

'Why,' said Skelter, surprised, 'of course I will. I intend to take *very* good care.'

'Good,' she said, just as fiercely, and then ran away to crouch in her form.

Puzzled again by all this, Skelter left the territory he shared with this eccentric jill. He knew she was trying to tell him something, but he was not good at recognising unspoken signals. He liked his messages straight from the mouth, and in plain language, not hidden behind gestures. Highlanders were not good at playing subtle games.

When he reached the shaven Booker's Field, where moonhare had her territory, he found the venerable matron and told her of his decision. She seemed pleased, and called to sunhare in Poggrin Meadow, his territory abutting hers.

'The mountain hare is going on an expedition to discover the identity of the flogre.'

'Excellent, excellent!' cried sunhare.

Then the two field hares went back to eating, leaving Skelter standing around, wondering whether to say something else or

191

creep away and get the task over with. Clearly moonhare and sunhare had lost interest in him.

'Well, goodbye then,' he said.

Followme looked up.

'Oh, you still here?' she asked in a surprised tone. 'I thought you'd gone.'

'Just on my way.'

'Well, off you go then.'

She went back to her meal.

Skelter began the long journey to the church tower. He wanted to be there before dusk of course, before the flogre was up and around. If it caught him out in the open, he wouldn't stand a chance. The hedges tended to crowd in on the church, and there would be some cover for him.

He took one of the regular hare highways that cut across the landscape, travelling through other hare territories. Sometimes they acknowledged him, sometimes not, depending on whether they were busy at some task. Once or twice he crossed through the territories of hares from another colony, but word had spread that summer about a mountain hare taking up residence in one of the leas by the river, and though they stared at him curiously, and returned his greeting if they were close enough, they were not overly concerned at his presence.

Skelter kept a wary eye open for foxes, especially since there were piles of russet-coloured leaves collected in the corner of many fields and up against the drystone walls of some of the cottage gardens. Now and again, he had to cross a lane or man-path and sometimes there were people out strolling, or vehicles shooting along the tarmac, but Skelter was not shy of these.

Once though, he nearly shed his skin in fright as a hound threw itself, shouting and slavering, at a chain link fence. Fortunately, the dog remained trapped, inside the fence, while Skelter was able to skip away quickly before the noise brought a human with a gun.

The rise on which the church was perched was some way along a country lane from the village, hidden for the most part in some cedar trees, but the square greystone tower shouldered its way above these evergreens. Skelter had to cross a patch of marshland, where conspiratorial herons stabbed their silver victims secreted by the tall reeds, finding his way along tufted paths. Around him, the occasional tree was ablaze, the damp long grasses on the edges of the paths hung lank and dirty.

Because of the tall marsh weeds, he was unable to see more than a length in front of his face, and twice he became seriously lost. By the time he came to the open field which led to the church rise, it was getting very late. The day was dark and cloudy, and dusk came early.

Skelter wondered whether or not to spend the twilight hidden on the rim of the marshes. There was a danger of foxes there, however, because the red devils loved the cover tall reeds gave them and often went to hunt the plentiful birds. They would accept a hare as well as a plover. There were machinations on the marshlands that worried him, and he thought he would be much happier in the open.

He made his decision, and began to cross the bare furrowed field towards the church. He kept to a deep channel, padding across the layer of damp leaves, his sharp eyes ever watchful for movements in the sky. Once a sparrowhawk went zipping overhead and gave him heart tremors, but the raptor was there and gone, and his heart was soon back to normal. Not that he was in any danger from such a predator, but the presence of fast-moving fliers did nothing for his nerves.

When he was about halfway across, he smelled a fox, and froze. The direction of the wind was from his right flank, crosswise to the tower, so that if he moved he would be right in the fox's line of sight. Skelter knew that if he remained still he would be safer, for foxes lose their focus on immobile objects within a very short time. He knew that foxes rely mainly on their noses, and since Skelter was downwind, he was hopefully screened from this one.

The scent of the fox became stronger and Skelter formed a fairly accurate mental image of the creature's path, which would cross Skelter's furrow just behind him.

Skelter's eyes being situated on either side of his head, he had a very wide circle of vision, and was able to observe the fox crossing behind him, without actually moving his head. It was quite a youngster, probably born only that spring, and no doubt excited to be out hunting on its own. Immature and inexperienced, the young fox seemed intent on reaching the far side of the field.

Once he considered that the danger was past, the fox having disappeared through a hedge, Skelter considered his next move. He had to get out of the open and behind some cover now. He began to run along the furrow as rapidly as he could, towards the tower.

Evening was now closing in. The broad tower loomed out of the grey murk, its ancient pitted stones like faces watching for the coming of the night. There was a hawthorn hedge and a low wall protecting the graveyard beyond. Both these obstacles were tangled with ivy. Skelter could go through the hedge, but he would have to scramble over the thick drystone wall and the ivy would help him there.

When he was about seven lengths from the wall a great shape suddenly launched itself from the sill of the tower filling the twilight with its menacing form. Skelter had left it too late: the flogre was abroad. The evening air, swirling with sombre cloud, disassembled the flying monster so that its outline was fuzzy and indistinct. It cruised high above Skelter's head, as he crouched in his furrow, terror filling his breast.

Skelter hoped that the flogre would not consider hunting within the pale of the church, having exhausted that area when it first took up residence. It was likely that the creature would fly off into the murk, looking for its victims in known hunting grounds, where game was plentiful.

Just as he was about to move on, believing that the flogre was now somewhere over a woodland or river creek, Skelter saw the young fox again. It had retraced its path, caught his scent and was moving upwind, tracking the source. Although it had not sighted Skelter, the fox was moving through the field crosswise, sniffing the furrows as it went. When it reached the furrow down which Skelter was travelling, it stopped, and peered along it. Skelter remained as still as death. The fox began tracking the scent along the furrow. Soon Skelter would either have to bolt or face the consequences.

What should he do? Make a dash for the church? What if there were no cover there? He realised, for the first time, that he had no idea if he could actually enter the building. Would there be a door open, or a hole through which he could crawl? He cursed himself for not questioning these things before he had set out on this mission. He really was a most inexperienced spy.

Just as he was about to make a dash for the church wall, a shadow passed over him, frighteningly low. The flogre had come back, skimmed the hawthorn hedge and wheeled once around the tower. *This is it*, thought Skelter, *it's seen me. I've had it.*

The terrible form of the flogre went into its silent dive, swooping in from the direction of the tower, its shape lost in the dense greyness of the stones. Skelter could just make out the erectile crest, the bright eyes. He waited for the strike, wondering if he could stand the initial shock of those great claws snatching him from the ground. Would the impact of the strike kill him instantly? He hoped it would.

The giant creature swept down towards him, and then, miraculously, over him, missing him by no more than three hare lengths.

Skelter heard a sharp cry to his rear, and with his all-round vision, saw the flogre hit the furrow behind him, and come up with a struggling figure in its claws. The giant rose into the sky, a limp creature hanging from its talons, and disappeared into the gloom of the darkening upper reaches.

Skelter made his move, scrambling through the hawthorn hedge, then skipping over the ivy-covered wall. At first his heart was beating so fast he was dashing wildly around the churchyard, in and out of the crosses and gravestones, without any real aim in mind, looking for some cover. Then at last he spotted a triangular hole in the side of one of the oblong stone tombs, and squeezed inside.

There in the darkness, he let his heart pump out his anxiety, the sound thudding in his ears. The flogre had the young fox in its clutches, and the cycle had closed, the hunter becoming the prey. It would be tearing the creature to pieces now, all the training of its parents, all its gambolling and wrestling with its brothers and sisters, had come to nought. It had ended up as quarry for a creature that was terrorising the very animals that it terrorised itself.

Skelter's heart began to recover its regular beat, and he settled on the cold stone of the tomb, to await a time when he felt ready to go outside and face the next part of his ordeal. He had been lucky so far, but things had not exactly gone according to the very sparse plans he had laid for himself. It was time to assess his position, get himself back on track, and stop taking chances. He knew now that he should have taken his time and waited on the edge of the marshes for darkness to fall.

'I should have waited,' he admonished himself.

A hollow voice echoed out of the darkness of the far corner of the tomb.

'Of course you should.'

Chapter Twenty Four

'Who said that?' cried Skelter, staring into the darkness at the back of the tomb. 'Who's there?'

Skelter's eyes could not penetrate the murk within the blocks of stone and though he was sure he was being watched intently – by one whose eyes were obviously used to the dimness – he had no idea of who or even *what* it was. He felt helplessly insecure. He was trapped inside the tomb, for there was certain death outside, and had to face whatever the darkness held within its musty folds.

There was a snuffling sound and someone began to move towards Skelter. He backed up to the exit, ready to kick out if the creature turned out to be dangerous: his heart drummed in panic.

'I've got powerful hind legs,' he told the other occupant of the tomb, 'and I'm not afraid to use them.'

'I'm sure you're not, Skelter, but would you kick an old friend?'

The other animal came forward and nuzzled against his face, and Skelter felt a surge of joy go through him as he recognised the scent.

'Rushie?'

'The very same jill.'

'How did you . . . why . . . when did you . . . ?'

Rushie nuzzled him again, saying, 'Slowly, take it slowly. First you tell me what happened to you after I left that farm, and then I'll give my own story. Come on, how did you escape? Did they put you in the hare coursing?'

Skelter could hardly contain his feelings, but he could sense that Rushie did not want a lot of emotion poured over her, so he pulled himself together and tried to calm down.

'Yes, they did put me in the coursing, but I outran the

greyhounds. You should have seen me, Rushie, I was magnificent! The poor hare before me, a creature with a funny accent – he was torn to pieces by the dogs . . .'

So Skelter told the tale, of how he escaped from the coursing, and of everything that had happened to him since that time. Rushie listened patiently, interrupting him only when she wanted something clarified, and encouraging him to fill her in on the tiniest details. She was especially interested in the relationship he now had with Eyebright, and questioned him quite closely on this point.

'So, you share a field with this jill?'

Skelter said, 'More than a field, which can of course be of any size. We have two large fields actually: a meadow and a field of mustard. There's a river at the bottom, and a stream running alongside. I've made friends with an otter who has his holt in the stream.'

Rushie said, 'You seem to have made yourself quite comfortable.'

'Not bad. I owe a lot to the kindness of the creatures that I've met on the flatlands – Jittie the hedgehog, and one or two others. Moonhare and sunhare are a bit stuck up, but that's because they're leaders of the colony I expect. They've got a lot of responsibilities.'

'So what are you doing here, at the church?'

He told her that he had been asked to come and investigate the church tower, to see what kind of monster lived in the belfry. It was a mission, he explained to her proudly, that only a mountain hare could carry out with success, due to the fact that the field hares could not stand heights.

'It seems to me they're using you,' replied Rushie.

'No, no. I volunteered, I really did.'

'Well, more fool you, mountain hare. That *thing* up there will eat you alive. It's huge. I came in here to escape it, but once the darkness comes down, I'm off. That monster, whatever it is, has nearly had my pelt before.'

Skelter stared at the eyes that were shining through the darkness now that he had got used to the lack of light.

'It doesn't seem to be an eagle – at least, not the eagles we know. Its habits are nothing like a golden eagle's, and it's not the same colour. It's a kind of dirty grey, and you can't see it in the twilight, not properly.'

'I know,' said Rushie, 'it chased me into a wood the other day, and went from tree to tree, following me deep inside.'

'There you are!' cried Skelter, 'Eagles don't fly in forests, they'd get their wings caught on the branches. They're just not equipped for it, like hawks. This *can't* be an eagle if it goes into woodlands.'

Rushie wasn't so sure and said you couldn't make judgements on so little evidence. Skelter wasn't in the right frame of mind to argue with her, and anyway, he said, he was impatient to hear how she had escaped from the farm. Rushie then told him her own story.

'You remember the man who liked jugged hare and kept staring into my cage? Well, the night I disappeared he came to my cage, opened the door, and grabbed me around the throat. Before I knew it, I was in a sack. Instead of kicking like mad, which I felt like doing, I began to gnaw at the sackcloth. Fortunately, the man had a long way to walk before we reached his house. I had a reasonable sized hole going when I heard a gate squeak and knew we had arrived at his home. Frantically I ripped away at the hole, and he felt me doing it and held up the bag, barking something in my face.

'At that moment I was full of hatred for this human, and his nose was within distance of my teeth – so I bit him, sinking my teeth into that long piece of flesh.'

'You didn't?' cried Skelter, excited.

'Yes I did, very hard. So hard that he screamed and let go of the sack. I clung onto his nose for a minute or two, then dropped to the floor, ran out of the bag, and through the gate. I found a ditch and ran along it until I was exhausted, then fell asleep.'

It seemed that Rushie had missed being a jugged hare by a very small margin of time.

'Where did you go from there?'

'Well, I foraged around for a bit, keeping to the hedgerows, worried about the open fields because there was no cover from eagles.'

'Me too,' replied Skelter.

'Anyway, I came across a colony of hares on the mainland, and they told me there were no eagles in this part of the world, and that the only thing to beware of was foxes.'

'And the flogre.'

'The what?' asked Rushie.

'The flogre – the flying ogre – that creature we're in here to avoid.'

'Oh, no, not that. You have to remember, this was on the mainland. Your flying creature doesn't venture that far from his tower. I only encountered him when I came over here, to this island or whatever it is, looking for you. Our colony on the mainland isn't troubled by any flogre – only foxes and stoats really.'

'You're lucky, then.'

'Yes I know. The first time I saw that thing was when I crossed over from the mainland, along that causeway, and turned right once I reached the island.'

'You turned *right*? How sad. If you'd have turned left, you would have found me straight away.'

Rushie said, 'I realise that now. Anyway, there's a large area of woodland on the far side of the island, and I was travelling just to the east of that, during twilight, when I sensed something up above. I knew there were no golden eagles around, but my instincts took over, and I dashed into the trees.'

'Quite right too.'

'I ran deep into the wood, which was quite dense, through the thickets and between treetrunks, convinced that if there had been something in the sky, it could never follow me in there.

'I was wrong. I heard it coming through the trees. I couldn't hear its wingbeats, but every so often, it used a branch as a perch, as if it was cruising from tree to tree, using the boughs to launch itself deeper into the wood. I panicked a bit, of course, and looked up through the network of branches, trying to locate whatever it was that was following me, and I have to tell you my heart almost jumped out of my mouth when I saw it.

'I mean, I couldn't see it *properly*, not enough to get a clear view, but it was obviously huge, a giant creature, crashing through the small branches, unconcerned by the number of trees in the forest. It was *used* to woodland, it knew how to manipulate the trees, you could see that. Its wings were shorter than those of a golden eagle, and it knew its way around in the tangle of branches, though it was difficult to get a good look – mottled grey against the lacework of a dark wood doesn't provide the best of views.

'Quite frankly, I've never been so terrified in my life before – not in the same way. I mean, it was like a nightmare. There seemed to be no escaping this great bird. You get used to things, like with golden eagles, you know they don't fly when the light's bad, and certainly don't follow you into trees, and things like that. There seemed to be no stopping this creature, no obstacles that it couldn't surmount. It was as if man had invented a machine that would stop at nothing to get a hare in its talons.'

'I know, I know,' said Skelter, 'we live with it every dawn and dusk here. But you eventually escaped, obviously.'

'I found a space under an oak root and hid there. The creature flew around the trees for a while, but it was getting dark, and it left not long afterwards.

'I reached someone from your colony, a hare called Head-inthemist, earlier today. She said you'd been sent on a mission to the church tower. I didn't wait around for any more, but came straight here. Just as I arrived that monster left its nest and I ran into this tomb.'

'And here we are,' said Skelter, 'back together again.'

Rushie was silent for a while, then she nuzzled him and began speaking again. 'There's something I have to say to you, Skelter. I came looking for you after stories reached the mainland about a mountain hare that had taught a colony to dig blue hare forms, and thus protect themselves against a flying monster. I guessed it would be you, and I wanted to speak to you for the last time.'

Skelter was a little taken aback.

'Looking for me? For the *last* time?'

'I know how that sounds, but . . . look, you remember when we were younger, you didn't really understand why I got so upset about certain things?'

'Yes, I think so.'

'Well, the reason was that I was very fond of you. I hoped that one day, when we were in our first mating season, you would box for me, dance for me, and win me. You were pretty dense, you know. You didn't seem to be aware of me, in that way, though I practically threw myself at you.'

'Oh.'

'But the fact is, I've grown rather fond of another hare now. He's a fine field jack who took me into his colony, and looked after me, and he says he's going to box for me come spring. His name is Racer. I wanted to see you again, Skelter, to explain this.'

'Oh, yes.'

Skelter was thinking, how do you compete with a hare called *Racer*?

'You do understand, don't you?'

Skelter's heart was in his mouth. 'Yes, yes of course. Fact is, I've grown rather fond myself, of . . . of . . .'

'Of this jill called Eyebright?'

He grasped at this straw. 'Yes, yes that's the one. Eyebright.'

Rushie let out a sigh. 'Well, I'm glad you're not going to be too sad without me. But of course, you thought I was dead, didn't you, so you've had time to get over my being missing?'

'Yes, that's the reason,' said Skelter, 'otherwise I should be very sad that we could not be mates. I always thought we could be, but these things, they don't work out the way you think they will, do they? Never mind, you have your Racer . . .'

'And you have your Eyebright.'

'Exactly.'

He wanted to change the subject quickly.

'So what are you going to do now?'

'I shall get back to my colony, after it's dark of course, and that *thing* can't get me. I advise you to do the same. I can't think what has got into your moonhare, sending you out on such a dangerous errand. How on earth did you think you were going to get near it?'

Skelter shrugged. 'Well, I planned to play it by ear, you know, make it up as I went along.'

'Go home, Skelter.'

'I'll think about it.'

They continued chatting until they were sure it was dark outside, then Rushie said she would have to leave. She promised she would send a message by any itinerant animal going in the direction of Skelter's colony to keep in touch, and Skelter said he would do likewise, in the other direction.

Then Rushie went to the hole and peeked outside. Although it was quite dark inside the tomb, Skelter was aware that she had paused and turned, giving him one last long look, before she skipped outside and was gone.

Skelter settled down to wait a bit longer before trying to get inside the church. He felt a little melancholy. Seeing Rushie had brought back memories of his old life up in the highland country, where the heather overpowered everything with its fragrance and the scenery was rugged and powerful, with tough high shoulders and a strong arched back. He recalled the slopes, dips and gullies, the untidy rock projections and the peaks speartipped with ice; glens where the deer roamed in quiet herds; scree where the hare clans gathered when winter came. He remembered the woodlands, of pine, and the scent of the amber sap oozing from the trunks, the smell of the cones and the needles when the breezes were in the right direction. He thought about the burns, rushing down the zig-zagging rocky channels they had cut for themselves, waterfalling into lochs that mirrored colours of the sky.

He would never see it again. Rushie too, had given up hope of returning to her home country, for she had chosen a local hare for a mate and was preparing to settle down.

Rushie. Perhaps if they had remained highlanders the two of them would have been mates, producing litter after litter of leverets and gambolling away their lives in the mountains. Instead, they had been singled out for adventure, for a life of living amongst foreigners in a foreign land. The flatlands of the south. So be it. If that was the fate of a highland hare, then he would make the best of it.

He put his mind to other matters.

Chapter Twenty Five

When the darkness was heavy on the ground, Skelter crept from the tomb and stared up at the tower. In the dim light of the stars the great square oblong of stone, the tallest thing on the landscape, reached upwards to the heavens. It seemed to be supporting the night on its crenellations. Without the tower, the upper darkness might come crashing down, and flatten the rise on which the ancient church stood.

Thankfully the moon was a sliver in the sky, thinner than orange peel.

Skelter moved to the base of the tower, where the damp moss-covered stones with their crumbling mortar clung to some deep shadow. Around the churchyard the carved figures on the headstones: cherubim and seraphim, and fully-fledged angels with open wings, stood silent and watchful, studying the movements of this little mountain hare. So too the gargoyles on the gutters, their mouths open wide in surprise, kept their thoughts to themselves.

Skelter sensed a thousand winters of heavy idleness in those stones: of standing on the rise above the snaking river down which blond warriors once came in longships, their wild hair and wild eyes the terror of the local farmers. Eyebright had told him stories, passed down the generations from hares of the time, of men with iron in their hands, iron in their blood, iron in their souls. Of men who rampaged across the flatlands, killing and stealing, dragging females back to deckless ships rigged with square sails.

It was at that time the church was built, strong and sturdy, to withstand marauders from the seas. Its great blocks of stone had been brought by boats from the north and cemented together with local mortar. Living grey stone in those days, now weathered almost black, and dense, dead-looking. Within sight of its walls, witches had been dragged screaming from their isolated cottages, and burned or drowned. Cats, goats, rabbits and hares too, as accomplices of these human sorcerers. There were periods in the church's history, much of which had soaked into those granite blocks, when its tenants had lost their spiritual way and had worked unwittingly for the dark forces to which it was expected to be opposed. Now, it was a quiet place, visited only for service and prayer, having seen no invaders since those conquerers who brought with them the cousins of the hare. No gold of any worth lay within its walls, only the treasures of the soul.

Skelter moved along the blackness at the base of the tower, and round to the wooden portal. There, as expected, he found the great wooden doors closed against him. There was a light on inside the church though, which meant someone would eventually go in, or come out. He waited, hunched, by the door.

A long time later he heard footsteps crunching on gravel and saw a shape coming through the lychgate. A man was coming with some keys that clinked as he walked. Skelter kept absolutely still. A hand reached for the circle of iron by the lock, grasped and turned it, and the heavy door was opened with a creak. Skelter stayed right on the heels of the legs that went before and found himself on the cold stone floor of the church.

The man would have had to look down and behind him, to see the hare, which of course he did not, there being no reason to do so. Skelter skipped under a pew, and there he waited until candles were snuffed and the man had left the church, locking the door behind him. Skelter heard the iron-work clunk and knit together as the key was turned and withdrawn.

The church smelled faintly musty, of damp winters trapped inside, unable to escape. It smelled of an ancient time, mostly – time captured by the stones, locked inside when the church was built. The ambience within the church, had nothing to do with the world outside. It was a separate place, kept in the past by strong walls and roof.

Skelter ventured out from beneath the pew and skipped down the aisle. There was wood in there that had forgotten it had come from living things called trees, and had now metamorphosed into sacred objects that seemed to be ageless. Wood that had been polished deep brown by elbows, haunches, backs, until its shine seemed to come from deep within. In the dim light coming through the stained-glass windows, Skelter could see a brass plate on the floor, with a human figure etched into it. The man had scales, like a fish, and a bullet head. He held a pointed weapon in one hand, and a shield in the other. The brass plate proved to be very cold under Skelter's hairy pads.

What shocked Skelter more than any of the wonders around him was a cross which was fixed to the wall above an altar covered with gold-and-white cloth. Its position and the statement it made was, after a while, identified by the intelligent mountain hare. He recognised this thing as a gibbet like the one from which the tractor-man hung weasels and moles and rooks. On this cross-shaped gibbet hung a human form, a slim figure with outstretched arms. There appeared to be spikes through his palms and feet, holding him on to the gibbet. On his face, in the stained starlight, was an expression difficult to define, but Skelter decided it was a mixture of peace and pain.

Skelter studied this figure for a long time, wondering why men would take one of their own kind and hang him up on a gibbet. The animals on the field gibbet were there to warn other creatures, not to venture into the cultivated fields which were man's domain. The corpses were displayed to remind animals that men were the masters of the universe. Had this man been executed as a warning to other men? On whose ground had he been trespassing? Whose crops had he violated? Who had they been, his killers, who needed to show that they were the rulers of the world?

These mysteries left his head spinning, and Skelter finally turned away from the place of the gibbet and circled the room until he found the steps leading up to the top of the tower.

He decided he would not go up until daylight, for if he were to ascend in darkness, and reach the belfry, he would not be able to see the flogre anyway. It was best to wait until dawn, then while the flogre was out hunting he would make his way up to the tower and hide in some convenient corner waiting for the creature to return.

There was nothing to eat inside the church of course, and so throughout the night Skelter had only his hunger to keep him company. He ate, as usual, the soft pellets of his previous meal, but these were not enough to sustain a hungry hare. By the time morning came he was ravenous, but there was nothing for it but to go through with his mission.

After the first rays of the sun had penetrated the coloured glass windows, splashing hues all over the stone floor, Skelter began to climb the spiral staircase. It was not easy, jumping from one worn step to another, but the light coming through the arrowloops assisted his passage.

'I'm the only hare around here who can climb the tower,' he told himself, thinking of the flatlanders and their horror of heights. 'Except Rushie of course.'

His pride in his mountaineering ability kept him from thinking of his empty stomach, and from worrying about what he might find in the belfry when he arrived.

He hopped over the top stair, to find his way blocked. For a moment he was confused. Gradually, he realised his way was barred by a closed door. He knew he was not yet inside the room at the top of the tower. That had to lie behind this door. How was he going to get in? Had he come all this way for nothing: to be thwarted by a piece of wood?

He sniffed around the bottom of the door, investigating the strength of the wood with his teeth. There was one part of the door which touched the floor. This had caused dampness to seep upwards through the old beech panels and they had become soft and rotten.

He began to gnaw at the wood and discovered that it came away in small pieces. Working for quite a long time, he tried to make a hole wide enough to crawl through into the belfry itself. Damp chunks of sodden wood came away in his teeth, as he struggled to get into the room before the time came for the flogre to return. He did not want to be stuck halfway through the hole and come face to face with a monster that could rip him to shreds within seconds.

Finally, the hole was large enough for Skelter to squeeze himself through.

The belfry was empty of any living thing. Just inside the doorway was a sack, overflowing with bones, ready to be taken away. Some human had been up to the tower and cleared the flogre's leavings from the floorboards. There was other evidence of human intrusion in the flogre's nest: a new rope hung from the great bell.

The mountain hare settled down in a dark corner by the door, his heart knocking violently, as he waited for the flogre to come back from the dawn hunt. Now that he was here, inside the monster's den, his fear was at needle-point. He was determined to go through with it, although his legs wanted to take him down the spiral staircase, and away home.

The day was getting lighter outside. Down below, in the church, someone was moving around. A door slammed shut.

Wingbeats.

When the flogre attacked its prey, they never heard it coming, because he stooped on stiff wings.

Now, Skelter could hear its wingbeats as it came into land on the sill.

The belfry darkened.

A great shape hit the sill with a thud, wings closed, and the shape shuffled on the sill. Then it entered, landing on the wooden spar which supported the bell. It was an enormous bird with a topknot of feathers.

Skelter crouched low into the corner, wishing he could melt into the brickwork. His fear was a terrible thing in itself, holding his body in a grip like a steel gin trap. He studied the flogre in the dim light of the belfry.

The creature was gorging now, on some unnameable prey which had been ripped and torn out of all recognition. Its huge hooked bill was tearing at a red lump of flesh held by claws the size of a man's hand.

It was mottled grey in colour, with an erectile crest of feathers across its head. Its fanned tail was dark-banded, with broad stripes. Its talons and beak were those of an eagle, but it was like no eagle Skelter had ever seen. It was larger than those golden raptors that circled the highlands, and such a strange colour that it looked as if it had been made from woven shadows. Its eyes were deadly: cold and hard like gemstones. It was indeed a monster so formidable that it looked as if it could attack and kill a man should it ever be necessary.

The flogre continued to gorge on the meat, but when it was finished, and the bones and skin were tossed aside, it stared suspiciously round the room.

Skelter's heart stopped.

The bird knew something was wrong, and first pecked savagely at the new rope dangling from the bell. Then it hopped down to the floor and began a slow swaying walk, stopping every so often to cock its head on one side, as if listening. It moved away from Skelter, going first into the darkness of the two far corners, where it stayed for some time. Skelter could hear it knocking against wood with its bill.

What should he do? Make a dash for it and hope he could scramble through the hole before the raptor was able to skate across the floor? It seemed possible to escape, but actually attempting it needed great courage.

Before Skelter could move, the giant bird was back, this time on the sill again, staring into the room. It filled the space between sill and arch, preventing light from entering the belfry.

Skelter inched behind the sack of bones, squeezing himself between its bulk and the wall. There was barely enough space, and the bag was in danger of toppling over.

The flogre clacked its beak in a gesture which appeared to denote annoyance. The sound was loud in the silence of the tower, and made Skelter jump. The noise was repeated several times, and Skelter could imagine the creature's brain clicking over, trying to decide what was wrong.

It was restless, and flew back to the bell-perch again, this time its eyes towards the daylight. Skelter felt much happier when the flogre was looking in the opposite direction to his hideout.

Down below, there was activity. The sound of music floated up, as someone practised on the organ. Skelter recognised this as the seventh day, the day when the tractor-man and the gamekeeper stayed away from the fields, and people could be seen coming from their houses and going to the church. Later the singing would start.

There was a strange sound, coming from the flogre now, a sort of low rasping moan.

Skelter was stunned.

The flogre was singing along with the music, just like a human might do, only not in any known tongue. It was just making a kind of rhythmic noise, that came from somewhere in its belly, rather than from its throat.

Skelter decided that it was now or never. While the monster was distracted by the music, he would creep out and crawl through the hole in the door. He squeezed around the sack of bones.

Just at that moment, the music stopped.

Skelter tried to retreat, back into the corner, but the sack had been dislodged.

It went crashing to the floor.

Bones scattered across the floorboards, skulls bounced across the room, and Skelter found himself exposed to the incredulous gaze of the flogre. It let out a screech of anger and leapt onto the window sill, from which it could launch itself directly at Skelter.

It was just about to do so when the world came to an end.

DOOOOOOOOONNNNNG!

The belfry was a hell of blinding, numbing sound, which filled Skelter's brain and deprived him of all sensible thought. The whole room vibrated with appalling noise which threatened to knock Skelter's head from his shoulders. It was so ghastly he could not move, every muscle locked.

Then the great bell sounded again.

DOOOOOOOOOONNNNNG!

The flogre was gone, out into the world.

Skelter came to life, ran for the hole, scrambled through, and began to descend the spiral staircase. His progress was slow because a hare finds it much more difficult going down, than he does climbing such artificial slopes. Every second or so the tower vibrated with that awful sound, but Skelter was past caring. All he wanted to do was get down from the heights, and run out onto his beloved flatlands.

He was halfway down the staircase, when as he rounded a corner, he leapt straight into the arms of a man. There was obviously surprise on both sides, but Skelter felt the man instinctively grip him. Then he found himself kicking and struggling in mid-air, as he was held up by his long ears.

The man looked into his face and growled in delight.

Chapter Twenty Six

When the bell sounded, Bubba's head felt as if it had exploded. Instinctively, he fled from the noise, as he would from hunters with guns. He flew out of the tower, desperate to clear his head of that terrible sound. The hare was forgotten, a thing of much lesser account than saving his sanity. The tower had become something other than his nest: it was now the domain of a man-thing with a voice that instilled terror even into the terrible.

On leaving the tower, Bubba drew the immediate attention of several astonished churchgoers on the gravel path below. Then the trees masked his escape. This was the second time he had been seen in a week, for he had also been noticed by the gravediggers when he had left the tower because of the arrival of men at the belfry. It was time to vacate the area and look for a new, safer home. To live in the tower now would be impossible, since he would never know when that great metal voice would fill his head with its sound. In any case, humans now knew where he lived, and would set a trap for him.

—Goodbye, tower.

—*Goodbye, Bubba. May you quickly find another refuge from your enemies.*

Bubba circled once, then flew to the straits between the island and the mainland. Once he had crossed the island and reached the sea, he travelled southwards to a place he knew just down the coast. Below him the fields swept away, until there was green ocean, then land again. The journey took a long time, but finally he reached his destination, a place mother used to take him when mother was alive. The square tower was behind him, the round tower in front.

It was a ruined martello tower situated on a low cliff, which dropped directly into the sea. He liked to be high off the ground, and though this new nesting site was not as tall as the church,

212

it was visited infrequently, if ever at all. Difficult to reach from the landward side, it had the ocean to the east and the marshes on the west. Further security was provided by a peculiarity of defensive design: the only entrance to the tower was over three times the height of a man from the ground: halfway up the whole height of the structure. The main danger was from fishermen and birdwatchers, who would brave any natural hazard to reach an isolated spot. However, since Bubba planned to continue with the habit instilled in him by his mother, of leaving the nest to hunt at dusk and dawn, the danger of being seen was considerably reduced.

There were birds in the marsh area which would help supplement his diet of rabbits and hares. Ducks, oystercatchers, knots, dunlin, herons, gulls and many others. He preferred fat little mammals but he would settle for birds at a pinch. Winter was coming on and the place would soon be swarming with fat rhonking Brent geese, come down from the north to feed in the mud. Upwards of twenty thousand of them would be wheeling in, not expecting to find a predator the size and stature of Bubba lurking behind clouds, waiting to knock them out of the air. In the spring he could travel further inland for lambs and calves, though he knew this was especially hazardous.

One thing he promised himself was that he would eventually track down and kill that small hare. There was something very strange about that creature. It had come from nowhere and taught his favourite food how to avoid him. It was used to sky-watching and had seen him coming in on the back of the dusk that time and had avoided him by running down a rabbit hole. It had actually invaded his home, for reasons known to itself, as if it were some kind of warrior, a Bubba-killer, out to exact revenge for wrongs to its kind.

Bubba could not allow such audacity to go unpunished. He saw the hare as the creature who had chased him from his church tower home, its presence creating that terrible din which had sent Bubba's brain rattling back and forth in his skull. Not once had the sound attacked him, but several times, making the tower vibrate and tremble to its very roots. The dead, below in their narrow houses in the ground, must have started abruptly from their eternal rest at the awful sudden

213

clang, banging their heads on the lids of their boxes as they tried to rise.

This was more than just a hare though: it had to be something quite extraordinary. Bubba's mind went back a long way, to his birth, in that humid forested land from which mother had taken him. There were primitives there, who hunted with bow and arrow, blowpipe, and magic. Perhaps those primitive hunters had reached out for him. Perhaps a magical hare had been sent by Bubba's enemies to destroy him. It was a clever disguise, for if the creature had been a greater cat, or a fierce giant dog, Bubba would have immediately been on his guard. Instead it was a hare, smaller even than the local hares. It had abilities though, that were far in advance of its fellow creatures, and Bubba knew he would have to be as sly and cunning as this hare was courageous, in order to defeat it.

Bubba sighted the martello tower, and came in on the breeze to land on its battlements. There he found a hole in the ceiling of the room below, and entered, finding the near-darkness inside comforting and peaceful. He gathered some debris, of rags and sticks, and made himself a crude nest on the floor. Then he settled down to await evening.

—Hello new tower, I have come to stay.

—*You are welcome, Bubba.*

Bubba dozed. In his dream state the racial memories, vague and fuzzy, came through from the past of his ancestors. There were his kind, living in the green gloom of thick forest, their nests in trees high off the ground. Rarely did they venture out into the open sky, as Bubba was forced to do, but stayed beneath the canopy of the tall forest with its sweating leaves and murmurous insects. Life was thick on the ground, thick in the air, thick amongst the trees. There were dark rivers flowing through the undergrowth, spreading into great floodplains.

Bubba's ancestors were lords of the trees, ruling forests patrolled by a myriad of beasts and birds, few of which Bubba had names for. The food of his grandparents were man-shapes swinging through the branches, some fast, some very very slow: creatures whose athletic bodies were covered in hair. There were colourful exotic birds, with plumes and long hard beaks, to add to this diet of tree-men. Bubba had memory-smells of a dank sunless world in which he had never been cold, where the rain came down like a waterfall from the sky, making a thunderous noise on the waxy leaves. Here there had been snakes the thickness of a man's waist, and river creatures with long mouths full of teeth.

Bubba was taken from this world as a fledgling, by his mother, and carried through the air. He had indistinct memories of being hidden in a crate when he arrived at a new land, until mother could take him out and feed him on the chopped livers and kidneys of sheep.

On waking after such dreams, Bubba always felt disturbed, though not because he desired this exotic fantasy world. The disturbances were buried deeper in his brain than the place where wants were situated. He was not happy in his own world, but neither was he sad. There was food enough, and shelter, and a sky virtually to himself. Occasionally he could enter woodlands and small forests and find a kind of nostalgia there, in the green half-light of the place below the trees.

That dusk, Bubba left the martello tower and circled his new territory. It was some distance from his old island home, which he could still reach during the twilight, providing he kept his hunt there short. During the winter he expected to feast mostly on geese, because the twilight hours were shorter. On grey overcast days when the gloom was sufficient to give him a shadowy flight, he might go up and snatch a hare or a rabbit, just to let them know he was still around. Then, when the summer came around, he could make his trips more frequently, perhaps staying overnight in some woodland. The marshes were fine, but they did not have an abundance of rabbits and hares, his favourite food.

—New tower, do you think Bubba is powerful?

—*Bubba is the lord of the flatlands.*

—Yes, I am. This is good, this is right. Mother would be proud.

—*Mother is proud.*

Chapter Twenty Seven

After seven days, when Skelter did not return, the hares gathered in Booker's Field beneath the blanched totem whose single branch fractured the sky like white lightning. This meeting, in the middle of autumn, was not only unusual, it was unprecedented. The colony normally never came together before the spring. Those who were unaware of the nature of Skelter's mission were trying to gather information, and those who knew what it entailed had the burden of disseminating it.

There were even several rabbits on the periphery of the group, for Skelter's time in the warren on the mainland had been broadcast amongst the rabbit population. His history had been taken, expanded and embroidered, and passed on, and now his fate was of interest to many amongst them. His travels, his exploits, his fortitude and endurance, were considered by more than a few to have raised the consciousness of all hares. He had given them a pride in their order. He had scorned capture by men, outrun greyhounds, overcome distances and won his way into the hearts of the local rabbits and hares.

The fact that many hares had done the same, both in the past and in the present, did not diminish his stature amongst his following. It is a quirk of fate that some creatures are born to be lifted above their fellows, often encouraged by a natural attractive personality, to become great. The ordinary population is sometimes in desperate need of heroes and at certain periods in their history will look around for suitable candidates upon whom they might place this weight.

Skelter was not one of those *intensely* charismatic creatures, who lead their followers with fiery words and blazing eyes, but a likeable moderate sort of hare who had a reputation for taking on any task with a cool head. He was the elder brother looked up to. He was the father in control. He was the dependable mate. Skelter was dashing in a modest fashion, not a swashbuckler. Inventor of the anti-flogre shelter and a hare with sensible counsel, he was on his way to one day becoming a revered figure in lagomorph history: a legendary gentle lord, who had time for leverets as well as moonhares, and who took on monsters at dire risk to his own life because he saw it as his duty.

One of the essential ingredients of hero pie is that the potential idol be not of local stock, but close enough to identify with. Back home in the highlands, Skelter could have defeated half the world's winged shapes and would still have been forgotten by the next generation. Petty jealousies amongst those who had seen him grow to harehood would have besmirched his deeds. He would have been considered lucky, rather than intrepid. It is difficult to take seriously the hare you once saw being tripped by his own ears.

Here on the flatlands he was unusual enough to be noticeable, yet familiar enough to fit in. No one had seen him soil his form as a leveret. No one had seen him falling over his own feet during his first gambol beyond his mother's sight. No one had seen him run in fright at his first sight of a worm. He had appeared amongst them fully matured, giving an impression of being wise, worldly, knowledgeable. He was without stain on his character, with no visible mistakes scarring his past. He was a stranger bearing his own irrefutable reputation. He had been in political captivity, imprisoned *because* he was a hare. If he eventually achieved greatness, which seemed likely (especially if he had been martyred by the flogre) his time in jail would be said to have been his making: a period of meditation, and consultation with some Superior Being. His history as a leveret in the highlands would be re-invented, earlier deeds attributed to his younger years, and those who would say nay would be reviled as bearers of evil slanderous tales.

Skelter was good potential hero material.

Moonhare brought the meeting to order.

'Those of you who live on the edge of the community,' she began, 'may have heard that the highlander Skelter has not been with us for a few days. You may also have noticed that the flogre has not appeared amongst us for at least a week. These events, or rather non-events, are not coincidental.

217

'Just eight days ago Skelter approached me with the idea that he go on a mission – a mission to discover the exact identity of the flogre, so that we might know who and what it is that has been decimating our population. It was a brave and selfless decision, and the highlander set out on this mission shortly after we had spoken.

'Sadly, Skelter has not returned, and we must assume the worst. However, neither has flogre appeared in the skies at dusk and dawn, and here we must assume the best. It would seem that there has been a mighty battle, the flogre vanquished and the highlander so sorely wounded that he has not been able to return.'

A mixture of a general groan and a faint cheer went up amongst the hares, most of whom were not sure whether they were expected to mourn the highlander, or show joy at the defeat of the monster. It appeared that both were required.

'Our skies have been rid of a monster, but we have lost a friend. A sacrifice has been made, and we must mourn the departure of Skelter, one of the most courageous hares. You will all remember that peculiar curving run of his, that wide arc he described when escaping from a foe? It is the intention to hold a race, once a year, just before the colony breaks up for the summer-autumn-winter solitude, in which every runner will be obliged to describe that same arc when competing. In this way we hope to do honour to a valued and much missed highland hare, who sacrificed his life for the good of us all.'

Moonhare bowed her head slightly.

After a few moments she lifted it and said, 'That is all I have to say at the moment. You may return to fields which have been made flogre-safe for you by the leader you have chosen and her faithful errant mountain hare.'

Moonhare went and sat under the sun-bleached totem, watching her colony disperse. While she waited, Eyebright came up to her and accused her bitterly of lying. The jill could hardly speak through her anger.

'You put him up to it. He didn't volunteer.'

Moonhare was not in the least perturbed by this attack.

'Eyebright, isn't it better for his memory that he be remembered as being one of the most selfless creatures in our history? Why

218

should I take credit for some part of his act, when I can give *all* the credit to him?'

Eyebright stared at Followme suspiciously. 'Is that why you did it?'

Moonhare was adamant. 'Of course, why else?'

Eyebright could think of no other reason at that moment. She was upset and confused, and desperately missing her companion of the last season. A single season is a long time in a hare's life, and Eyebright had been looking forward to further more exciting times ahead, soft family times. Of course, Skelter had been a little dense, when it came to recognising that females found him attractive, but that would have changed in the mating season. Now all these dreams had been taken from her. She knew from the previous season that Longrunner wanted her, would try to frost-dance his way into her affections, but she wanted no one but her Skelter . . . and Skelter was gone. Skelter was gone and her unhappiness was increased ten-fold by the fact that she had not even given him a decent goodbye. She had been so incensed at his stupidity in taking up Followme's suggestion that she had let him go thinking she was angry with him. Of course she had been angry, and upset, and had wasted their last few precious moments together.

'It's a *humanly* world,' she said aloud, and with great sadness in her tone.

'Oh, I agree,' said moonhare, 'but one must go on, you know. One must go on.'

Eyebright, suddenly recalling that moonhare *had* claimed part of the honour of ridding the skies of the flogre, left Followme in disgust.

On her way back to the meadow, the miserable Eyebright met a hedgehog she vaguely knew. Jittie was vaguely-known by most of the animals in those parts, and many of them avoided her because of her uncertain temper. However, today she seemed disposed to stop and talk.

'What was the meeting about?' asked Jittie. 'I've never seen you hares gathering at this time of year before.'

'It concerned a hare, a mountain hare that joined us just after the mating this year.'

Eyebright could barely keep a catch out of her voice.

219

Jittie said, 'Not young Skelter?'

'Yes,' Eyebright said, 'you knew him?'

'Of course I knew him – *know* him. What's all this past tense? Is he dead?'

'We think so,' replied the jill.

She then proceeded to tell Jittie all about the mission that Skelter had been sent on, to the church tower, and how the flogre had not been seen since that time. Eyebright kept her account dispassionate, so as not to reveal her true feelings for Skelter. She spoke of him as if he were just another jack, not anything special to her at all.

When she had finished Jittie remarked, 'You're very fond of him, obviously.'

Eyebright was taken aback.

'Oh, I wouldn't say that.'

'I would. It underlines every word you say about him. I thought you hares weren't allowed to choose mates until the spring, when the jacks have to battle it out, or something barbaric like that. Mad practice, if you ask me. Isn't it true you're supposed to wait until then?'

'Yes, that's true to a certain extent, but a bit old-fashioned. We don't rely completely on the results of the boxing these days. Most couples have worked out who they want to pair up with before the boxing starts. I mean, there's not much point in going with a hare you can't stand, is there?'

'Well if you're asking me, I would've said that was pretty obvious, but who am I to interfere with the culture and customs of another species, however misguided they seem?'

'So, yes, everyone wakes up dancing in the frosts, and the jacks get themselves all worked up, boxing each other – and us too, though the jills don't go all out because we're bigger and stronger than they are and we might hurt them. If there are two jacks, or more, who like one jill, and the jill doesn't care which one she takes, then naturally they have to battle it out between themselves . . .'

'Naturally,' sniffed Jittie, seemingly unconvinced.

' . . . but where there's no rival, or the jill has definite preferences, the boxing is just for fun.'

'But what if another jack *did* insist on fighting for you, even though you had stated a preference?'

Eyebright shrugged.

'I suppose, strictly speaking, the fight would have to take place, but there would be no encouragement from me for Skelter's rival, and there's nothing like knowing your jill wants you to win, to egg you on to victory – so I'm told.'

'But what if this other jack *did* win? I mean, Skelter's not the biggest hare I've seen in my life, by any means. What if his rival did beat him?'

'If anyone beat Skelter I'd knock his block off,' growled Eyebright.

Jittie twisted her mouth wryly.

'Yes, that would do it. That might be the discouragement the other jack needed.'

'Anyway,' said Eyebright, 'all this is academic. Skelter's gone, and there's nothing that can bring him back.'

'Why do you say that?'

'What, that nothing can bring him back?'

'No, why do you assume that he's dead?'

Eyebright shuffled under the intense gaze of the hedgehog. 'Well, all the evidence points towards it, doesn't it?'

Jittie snorted. 'Evidence? What evidence. All we know is that he hasn't returned yet. Where's his carcass? Where's his empty pelt? I wouldn't cross his name off your list of admirers just yet, hare. That mountain jack has a way of bouncing right back into the arena, just when you thought he was finished. He's the toughest little hare that you're likely to meet. I'm ashamed of you, what's your name? Eyebright? You're supposed to be fond of this blue streak of obstinacy. Have a bit of faith in him.'

'But the flogre . . .'

'Just because the monster hasn't been seen, doesn't mean they both died locked in a death struggle. Can you honestly see Skelter battling it out with a giant bird, or bat, or whatever it is? A creature ten times his size, and covered in claws and hooks? He might be a brave hare, but he's not stupid. He'll run just like anyone else – anyone sensible that is.'

Hope sprang to Eyebright's breast and began glowing there. Did she dare let herself believe what she was hearing? This hedgehog seemed to know Skelter very well. Better than she did herself. Could it be that Jittie was right?

'But if the flogre hasn't killed him, where is he?'

'Don't ask such silly questions. How would I know? It may be that the monster *has* killed him, but I wouldn't stake my spines on it. More likely Skelter is hiding somewhere, while the monster is stamping up and down trying to get at him. I know that jack, I tell you, and he's a survivor. He's lived with golden eagles – not just one but probably half a dozen – hovering over him every day of his young life. He's had to contend with things called wildcats, as well as foxes. If there's a hare around here that can spit in the monster's face and get away with it, that hare is Skelter.

'Now, much as I'd like to spend the time of day with you, I'm busy looking for a place to sleep out the winter. It'll be coming on cold soon, and I want somewhere prepared, and out of sight of prying foxes and badgers, a curse be on their black souls for the nuisances they are, so if you don't mind . . . just think on, jill, just think on. There are two sides to any affair – the worst and the best. Before you get any hard evidence, expect either side to come out on top. Don't just assume the worst. There, I've said enough, good season to you.'

And with that the hedgehog waddled off, leaving Eyebright's feelings in a turmoil.

222

Chapter Twenty Eight

It is said amongst many animals and birds, probably originating with the geese and ducks, that if there is a Creator who once needed rest from his architectural labours, then the place he chose to lay his head was estuary country.

The flat world where two waters meet, the salt and the fresh, is a place of peace. Man is the spoiler, but like the mountain tops, estuary country is not easily accessible to him. The landscape is fractured by waterways often too shallow to navigate in boats, too deep in mud to traverse on foot, and man finds little business in marshes, maltings and saltings. Man lives on the fringes of such areas, and the heart of estuary country remains unspoiled. This place where rivers and seas mingle is where life comes together in myriad shapes and forms.

In an estuary the water is layered, with the fresh river water sliding over the heavier salt water, and between them a racial mix of the two, a brackish divider. These three layers move back and forth and change in quantity with the ebb and flow of the tides. All three types of water have their own forms of plant, fish, insect and bird life. Freshwater species live at the top of the estuary, saltwater at the bottom, and the unfussy between. There are shore crabs, grey mullet, gobies, soft squishy lugworms, multi-legged king ragworms, prawns and shrimps, sticklebacks, and many other creatures.

Where land barely rising to the surface becomes marsh, poa grass, seablite, sea aster and sea parslane grow. There is also rich alluvial soil around an estuary which attracts farmers with its fertility but which is too shifting to use as building land, limiting the presence of man and acting as a buffer zone, restricting visitors.

Unlike Skelter, Rushie appreciated the positive similarities of the estuary to her former mountain home. Skelter saw only the farmlands where nature had been landscaped by human hand: a direct contrast to the wildness of his birthplace in the highlands, where the only attempt at refashioning nature was the building of a cairn. Rushie felt the peace and tranquillity, the underwildness of the marshes, the secretiveness of the waterland with its cryptic creeks and mysterious mudways. The maze of channels left when the tide went out, were sometimes deeper than the height of a man, and spread at least to the horizon.

The sky was bigger: here it made a complete dome, the marshland captured some beautiful colours from the sunsets. Here, the air was as clean and as fresh as that of the highlands, with only pockets of marsh gas to make it interesting. Although there was a protected feeling brought about by natural walls in mountain country, here there was an unfettered world which to a hare who has the advantages of all-round panoramic vision is just as secure. When you can see behind your head, as well as you can in front, openness is appreciated. To Rushie, it was as if the door to creation had been left ajar.

There was an eerieness, a bleakness, which Rushie found worrying at times, but this dark side of the flatlands had its advantages as well as being disturbing. It told of a history of invaders, some of whom tried to settle in the place of mists and ghosts only to fall into a morose way of life that sucked them down to oblivion. There were old wrecks being swallowed by the mud belonging to travellers from distant lands, who had come periodically through history to conquer what would eventually conquer them. The loneliness, the solitude, the phantasmagorical aspect of the fevered waterland either drove them away with its morbid moods, or corroded their bodies and spirits until they wasted into shadows. There were iron weapons rusting in the bowels of the creeks and old bones shifting in the sludge with each turn of the tide.

What was hostile to man was friendly to beasts.

Rushie's mainland colony was on the edge of the marshes, and indeed spilled over into its creeks. They were wilder hares than those of Skelter's colony, their coats unkempt, their habits less neat. They ate plants and grasses that moonhare would have considered inedible, and drank from stagnant pools that would have offended sunhare's nose and taste.

One hare's good fortune is another hare's disaster, and though the flogre was now too distant to bother with Skelter's colony, Rushie's hares were well within reach. It began to hunt them down with a ferocity which sent a wave of panic across the marshes. Unlike the former colony, this one had not yet learned to make protective forms.

Rushie had returned from her meeting with Skelter in the tomb, and had imparted to her prospective mate, Racer, all that had passed between the two blue hares. This large brown hare was a little angry with Rushie, for going off without saying a word to him, and she detected a streak of jealousy in him when she spoke of her old friend.

'One of the reasons I went to see him, was to lay to rest my former life,' she explained to Racer. 'Now that's been done, we have no need to speak of it again – not unless *you* wish it. I've told you, I'm as happy here as I was in the mountains. I've accepted the changes in my life. You mustn't blame me for wanting to say goodbye to someone who thought I was dead.'

'You should have told me before you went,' was all he would say. 'I worry about you. You should have told me.'

She said she was sorry, that it wouldn't happen again.

Then word came to her, on the grapevine, that Skelter was missing, that there had been some sort of battle between the blue mountain hare and the flogre. She was distressed, and made up her mind to go to the church tower, to see if she could ascertain what had happened. She told Racer what she planned and he absolutely forbade her to go.

'When I said I would tell you before I did anything like it again, I didn't mean I was going to ask your permission,' she told him stiffly. 'I don't need it. You have no right to tell me what or what not to do. I shall go if I please.'

This upset Racer, who knew he had overstepped the mark, for he would never have dared to speak in that fashion to a brown field hare, or he would have got his ears boxed. It was just that Rushie was so small and delicate, and the protective instinct came out in him. He wanted to keep her from the world's harm. He was on the point of apologising to her when a dramatic change came about in the colony's circumstances.

The flogre appeared one dusk, and snatched a hare from a field next to the marshes.

It was back the next morning for another.

The elders of the colony, the seahare and the skyhare, called Rushie to account, saying that it was her kind that had forced a change in the flogre's residence, and that she – or rather her mountain friend, which was much the same thing – had chased the flogre to the martello tower.

'That's not true,' cried Rushie. 'How could Skelter make the flogre come here?'

'I don't know,' said seahare. 'You tell us.'

'This is absolutely ridiculous, can't you see that? A hare can't force a giant flying creature to leave its home and settle somewhere else.'

'Perhaps not,' skyhare said, 'but maybe this Skelter helped change the circumstances under which the flogre lived, and *men* forced it to abandon the church tower in favour of the martello tower? The responsibility still lies with the mountain jack, who should never have carried out his stupid mission in the first place.'

Rushie was angry now.

'He was told to, by his moonhare.'

'The way I heard it,' said seahare, 'he volunteered.'

Rushie continued to protest at this defamation of Skelter's name, saying that her friend would never rid his colony of a terror, at the expense of another. If the flogre was nesting in the martello tower, then that was by its own choice, and not because of any action by Skelter. It really did not make sense, she told them, that a hare had forced a flying monster to change its nesting ground.

While she was defending herself, she looked around for Racer, in order to gain his support, but the jack was nowhere to be seen. It appeared that he did not wish to become involved in her dispute with the elders. Instead another jack had something to say on her behalf, a hare called Creekcrosser, a rather disreputable creature who was often seen out on the mud, crossing from one dyke to another. Creekcrosser argued that what one individual did was not the responsibility of another, whether they were from the same place, colony, or even litter.

'If my brother does something wrong, that doesn't mean I'm

accountable for his actions,' said the jack to seahare, 'any more than you would be answerable to me if skyhare stole my food. To pick on this jill here, just because someone from her previous colony was indirectly responsible for sending the monster to us, is unfair, unjust and plain ridiculous.'

Unfortunately Creekcrosser was not well thought of in the colony. He made a habit of breaking rules and lacked deference. His insolence towards the elders had been a matter for censure more than once in the past. Although hares are not famous for their teamwork, many believed that Creekcrosser took individuality too far, and considered that the day he left the community, as he was always promising to do, would be a good day for them all. He was far too easy in his manner, too quick to prick the respectability of important members of the group, too ready with a joke when the situation called for seriousness.

'What you have to say on *any* subject is of no consequence to us,' remarked skyhare.

Seahare said to Rushie, 'Don't think because this rebellious individual is defending you that he cares what happens to you. He doesn't. He's just using the situation for his own amusement. In fact he has been heard to remark that he's never met such a snob as you and that your haughty attitude would be your downfall.'

Rushie looked at Creekcrosser, expecting him to deny the words. Instead he cocked his head to one side, in that indolent manner of his, and said, 'Sure she's stuck up, but that still doesn't make her guilty of something another hare has done. The trouble with you, seahare, is you're too rigid. You need a bit of flexibility. It would help you to see that you connect events and arguments that have nothing to do with each other and then congratulate yourself on being astute. I've said my piece: if you still can't see it you never will.'

With that, Creekcrosser went away, leaving Rushie on her own again.

Seahare reopened her argument. Rushie was told that dire events had come about as a result of Skelter's visit to the church, for it could hardly be co-incidental that the flogre left at the moment Skelter arrived to do whatever it was that he had done. Her kind had got them into a mess, and it was up to her to get them out of it.

The first thing she did of course, was to show them how to dig mountain hare forms, to protect themselves when they were in reach of their own homes. Some of the more traditional hares pompously refused to 'burrow in the ground like a rabbit', but they soon changed their minds after another victim was snatched from amongst them at dawn the following day. Creekcrosser, on the other side, said he found it fun.

'We should've dug these things ages ago. It'll be warmer and out of the rain. Got any more highland inventions up your nose, Rushie?'

But Rushie had not forgiven him for calling her a snob, and refused to answer.

Racer appeared on the scene again, saying he had been to check on his fields, and that they were in good order. The pair met by an old oak, and Rushie felt a little peeved with the jack who had promised to box for her in the spring.

'While you've been away,' said Rushie, 'I've been accused of all sorts of things.'

'Oh, I'm sorry, I didn't know.'

From the ditch came a high-pitched echo.

'*Oh, I'm sorry, I didn't know.*'

'Who's there?' cried Racer. 'Show yourself.'

Out of the ditch hopped Creekcrosser, bits of twig and mud stuck to his fur, as if he'd been rolling down drainage channels all morning.

'What's the meaning of this?' snapped Racer.

'The meaning of what?' yawned Creekcrosser.

'Why are you eavesdropping?'

'Look,' said Creekcrosser, 'I just happened to be in the ditch. If you two want to fight in public, that's up to you, but don't expect the rest of us to huddle in a corner with our ears blocked.'

Rushie said indignantly, 'We're not fighting.'

'Well you should be. The jack deserts you when you need him most, because he's worried about being censured by the elders for being a friend of yours? I'd fight the fur off him, if I were you.'

Racer said, 'We don't need your opinion here. It's not worth the breath used to express it.'

'Oh, a breath's worth quite a lot. In fact it's indispensable. Try doing without a couple.'

'If you don't leave us alone,' growled Racer, a much larger hare than the lean and loose-limbed Creekcrosser, 'I'll be forced to bite you.'

'Well, there's an offer I find difficult to refuse,' drawled Creekcrosser, scratching his ear with his hind leg. 'In that case, I'll be on my way, but should you need me highlander, I shall be at your beck and call. Watch that one. He's easy with his friendship when things are smooth, but a *little* unreliable over the rough bits.'

With that, Creekcrosser left them, lolloping through the hedge and over the pasture, heading towards the creek. Rushie watched him go with a mixture of indignation and gratitude in her breast. She was grateful that he had spoken on her behalf in front of the elders, but he had no right to attribute motives to Racer's absence. She accepted Racer's reasons for not being at her 'trial' and believed that he knew nothing about what she was going through before arriving back from his fields. He was a very handsome, fast-running hare, with a chiselled body that was a credit to nature. He was well-respected amongst other hares (unlike Creekcrosser) and seahare sought his opinion on many points of traditional custom.

Creekcrosser, however, was universally regarded as being a rogue and a roughie – universally that was, except for one or two jills with doubtful reputations – and his opinion, though often proffered, was sought by no one with any authority.

'I'm sorry about that, Racer,' she said.

Racer was staring after the retreating tail of Creekcrosser.

'Yes, so am I. One of these days I'm going to have to teach that jack a lesson. He's getting far too insolent for his own good. Every time he opens his mouth another questionable phrase comes out.'

'Well, he did stick up for me, when you weren't here.'

Racer's head turned and his eyes looked down on her. 'Yes, he did, didn't he. I wonder why?'

'Seahare said it was because he was amusing himself.' Racer nodded.

'That's it, of course. Creekcrosser does nothing for the good of the colony, or anyone else for that matter. He has only himself in mind.'

229

Rushie was sure he was right, but just the same, there was something about Creekcrosser that made her doubt he *always* had selfish motives when he brooked the elders and respectable hares like Racer. There was a kind of rough-hewn honesty behind his ill chosen words, as if he really did feel that there were some bubbles of pride to be pricked.

Well, she couldn't see herself calling on him to come to her aid again. Not while she had her Racer by her side. Now she had to consider her next move. What was she going to do to satisfy seahare and skyhare, regarding the flogre? Showing the colony how to dig mountain hare forms was one thing, but it did not get rid of the menace.

And what had happened to poor Skelter?

It really was a bad time for both of them.

Chapter Twenty Nine

Rushie set out after nightfall for the church on the island, concerned over the fate of her old friend. It was a restless night, with a strong wind coming in from the sea, roughing up the bushes. At one point a persistent squealing noise stopped her in her tracks, and she hunched on the ground, trying to ascertain the meaning of this sound. In the end she discovered it was only the branch of a tree, rubbing against a trunk, and with a sigh of relief she continued on her way.

In the swirling darkness she made her way out of the farmland surrounding the marshes and followed the road which led to the causeway. Occasionally cars came along the road and their light disturbed her, but she kept to the ditch in order to stay out of danger. She stumbled on a stoat once, but her greater speed left the predator standing. Stoats needed stealth to catch hares napping and this they are seldom able to achieve. She could hear it swearing to itself as she left it behind her.

The waves were breaking gently on the edge of the causeway, despite the high wind, for it was a leeward gale and was driving the waters onto the beach rather than along the channel. The swish and swirl of the ocean was comforting, rather than threatening, and she even paused halfway across to admire the light on the surface of the sea. It produced a dark green effect that looked valuable in some way.

Once over the causeway, she made for the church on the knoll. Its greyness loomed above the solid darkness of the surrounding trees with their thick evergreen foliage that kept the gravestones damp and the moss in happy perpetuity. Now that the flogre was not in residence, animals had resumed visiting the churchyard for the succulent fungi which the shady area produced in abundance.

The place was in darkness, the wind whistling around the stonework, causing the gargoyles to moan. Leaves and twigs danced among the gravestones and the sombre cedars heaved and pulled against their roots. Rushie went inside the same tomb where they had met a few days before, but there was no mountain hare to be seen inside the stone oblong. Outside again, she stared up at the tower, its walls dense with secrets. It revealed nothing, of course, and with the flogre no longer its resident it seemed lifeless and less menacing. No doubt the bats and mice were considering a return to their old home, though that would take time. It was difficult to get over a monster like the flogre in a lifetime.

Finding little to keep her there, Rushie continued her quest and crossed the fields to visit the leader of Skelter's colony. She had not yet spoken to Followme, though she had formed an opinion of her from hearsay, and that opinion was not a good one.

Followme was munching at turnips on land adjacent to Booker's Field, her fur rippling in the wind like a patch of still water. She looked up, startled, as Rushie approached, and then cried, 'Skelter?'

'No, it's not Skelter. My name's Rushie. I'm another blue hare, a jill. We come from the same highland clan. Are you the seahare here?'

Followme stared, then corrected her, saying, 'Moonhare. You came all the way from the mountains?'

'Well, originally, but not just now. Let me explain. You see, Skelter and I were captured together, but I escaped before the hare coursing took place. I've been living with the marsh colony on the mainland . . .'

'Oh, *them*,' said Followme.

'Well, yes,' said Rushie, bristling, 'but anyway, I managed to contact Skelter before he went to spy on the flogre. Now I understand he's gone.'

The moonhare sighed. 'Gone to the Otherworld I'm afraid.'

'Do you have proof that he's dead?'

Moonhare shook her head. 'No proof, but as the big red barn is my judge, we've searched high and low for him. He's nowhere to be found. Either his body is lying on the floor of the belfry, next to that of the flogre . . .'

'The flogre's still alive,' interrupted Rushie. 'It's moved its nest to the martello tower on the edge of the marshes.'

Moonhare blinked a couple of times. 'In that case,' she said, 'he's definitely dead – a meal for the monster. Out in the marshes, you say?'

'It's terrorising my colony every dusk and dawn.'

'Oh well, at least it's gone away from here, that's one thing to be thankful for. We thought Skelter had died locked in a death battle with the flogre, but it seems he's only chased the creature away. That's something I suppose. I expect we can still allow him to retain the status of hero.'

Rushie could hardly believe her ears but since she was visiting another colony wisely decided to keep her thoughts to herself. 'So, you really have no idea what happened?'

Followme said, 'None at all. We can only assume that Skelter did his duty and was caught and eaten. Hares die every day. It's a sad but true fact. Skelter was our friend and we grieve for him, but life must go on.'

The moonhare went back to munching turnips.

Rushie went to her side. 'Look, supposing he did escape the flogre – is there anywhere he might go? Is there someone who might give him shelter? He may be wounded, and lying sick somewhere. We have to explore all possibilities.'

'Do we?' said moonhare, clearly implying that she herself did not have to do anything of the sort.

'Well, I do,' said Rushie.

Followme deigned to stop eating for a moment and applied her mighty political brain to the subject.

'There are two possibilities,' she said at last. 'There's a hedgehog by the name of Jittie that he was very friendly with and I'll tell you how to reach her nest. Also, when he first escaped from the greyhounds, after the coursing, he stayed with some rabbits in a warren inside a wood. It was when he showed us how to make mountain hare forms that we thought some of their rabbity ways had rubbed off on him. I don't know exactly where the warren is located, but it's near the causeway on the mainland. Shouldn't be too hard to find. Now the way you get to Jittie's place, only be careful, because the hedgehog has a reputation for bad temper . . .'

Rushie listened to the directions in silence, thanked the moonhare politely, and left the field thinking that moonhares and seahares were much of a muchness. They were both extremely selfish, lacking in tact and thought a great deal of themselves. Perhaps politics did that to you? Maybe they had been decent hares before they took up leadership responsibilities? Or maybe you had to have a certain type of personality in order to *want* leadership? It certainly wasn't worth a great deal of thought, however, and Rushie quickly put it out of her mind.

She followed moonhare's instructions for reaching Jittie's home and eventually found the empty rabbit hole, but not the hedgehog. Boughs were cracking ominously in the big tree overhead. After sniffing around inside the nest Rushie came to the conclusion that the hole hadn't been used for some time and that the hedgehog had gone away.

'So much for that,' she said to herself. 'I'd better see if I can find the rabbits.'

She went back past the church, reached the causeway and crossed it, then went in search of a wood. In the darkness she came across a hare from another colony.

'I'm looking for a warren in a wood around here,' she said. 'Can you help me at all?'

The jill stopped nibbling the cabbage she was eating.

'Rabbits? You don't look like a rabbit. At least, not much.'

'I'm not a rabbit, I'm a blue hare from the highland mountains. I'm searching for a friend, called Skelter, who stayed with some rabbits around here last season . . .'

'Oh, Skelter. I hear he's dead.'

'Well, he may be, but I want to make sure.'

'Died killing the flogre, so they say.'

Rushie didn't want to go into all that again and repeated her first request.

Eventually the jill said, 'There's a wood just two pastures north of here with a rabbit warren inside it run by a creature called L'herbe. It's said that Skelter once stayed with them for a while, which to my mind does him no credit. You can pick up some awful habits from those manmade creatures. I wouldn't go near a warren myself. You can't trust creatures put together like rabbits, can you? And the lies they tell! My advice would be to stay away from them, if you don't wish to be corrupted. I've never actually been inside a warren of course, because they say there's some

234

terrible rituals go on inside – I've heard it said that at some dark magic ceremonies they sacrifice their own kittens . . . they're a lazy bunch of layabouts, is what my mother used to tell me, and I see no reason to doubt her . . . they steal, even from their own kind . . . not really *animals* of course, but some kind of lower life, a thing fashioned by men . . .'

Rushie left the hare muttering to herself about the idleness of rabbits, their peculiar habits, and the advisability of never going near them – because of what she had heard.

When Rushie reached the wood it seemed to be enraged, the tops of the trees lashing against each other as if they were having a battle. Inside, the wood was very black and there was a smell of foxes and badgers. The damp odour of rotting leaves and fungi added a sinister aspect to the environment and it took all Rushie's strength of will not to turn and run for the open land. She had to keep reminding herself that she was a mountain hare, used to living amongst the rocks, and if she could just imagine that the wood was an outcrop, and the trees thin stone tors and monoliths, she might stop her heart from banging against her ribs.

She hopped and ran through briars and bracken, sniffing for the scent of rabbits. She found a run, with fresh droppings on it, and followed it to find the holes she had been looking for. Around her the wood was going wild. Just as she was about to go down a hole, a large shape ambled out of a nearby bush and made for another hole. The strong smell of badger hit her nostrils and she stopped to let the creature pass. She knew she could outrun it, so she could stay, but it meant keeping an eye on the beast until it was safe to go down the hole. She remained perfectly still under an oak, knowing that the smell of rabbits was so powerful the badger would not scent her. She could hear the creature muttering in that strange dark tongue of ancient origin which badgers, stubborn inflexible creatures that they were, still used as their only means of communication.

As Rushie watched the badger snuffling and snorting its rubbery nose, she became aware that it was going down the very hole near to where she stood. She moved away quickly and hid behind a bush, leaving the large animal free passage. It went down inside. This was obviously a badger's sett. There would be more of the creatures around somewhere, gruffing away to themselves. What was going on here? She tried to recall her conversation with Skelter about his time with the rabbits. Had he mentioned badgers being close by, or was this a raid on the warren? She inspected the hole down which the badger had gone. It was too large for a rabbit.

A badger's sett? Why the strong odour of rabbits then? She was in a dilemma now. What to do? There was no way she was going down that hole now, with the place probably full of badgers, who would take a hare if available and within distance of its mighty jaws.

Just as she had reached a pitch of indecision a rabbit came hopping through the trees and skipped down one of the holes leading to the sett – or perhaps it was a warren? Maybe the badger was a stranger come to kill all the rabbits below. Perhaps Rushie should warn the inhabitants?

'What are you doing here?' said a voice from behind her, startling her.

She turned quickly, to see a large doe rabbit eyeing her with suspicion.

'Spying?' said the doe.

Rushie said, 'No, no. Not spying, I was looking for a warren run by a rabbit called L'herbe. Am I at the right place?'

'Why were you lurking in the bushes?'

'I wasn't *lurking*. I was hiding. I just saw a very large badger go down one of those holes and if I were you, I'd warn the rest of your clan . . . colony . . . warren.'

'Badger? We share our warren with badgers. They keep the foxes and stoats away. Oh, I know what you're thinking, but they don't touch us. They might kill rabbits from another warren, but not the one where they live.'

'Isn't that a bit like living with the enemy?'

'Look,' said the doe impatiently, 'if they didn't live with us, they'd live somewhere else, so what difference does it make?'

Rushie had no answer for that one.

The doe asked, 'What did you come here for?'

'Ah, yes, my name is Rushie, I'm a blue hare from the highlands of the north. I'm a friend of Skelter and I understand he stayed with you once.'

The doe's expression changed from suspicion to friendliness in an instant. 'Come on down, out of the wind. My, it's a blustery night tonight. You have to be careful of branches falling and being carried along. You can get a nasty knock from a bough if it catches you on the head. My name's La framboise. I knew Skelter very well. We were well-acquainted, as they say. Come on, come on, let's get out of this wind . . .'

La framboise led the way down the hole, which, after a moment's hesitation when recalling the size of the badger that had gone before, Rushie followed.

'What does "well-acquainted" mean?' asked Rushie as they went deeper into the middle-earth, the smell of underground soil strong, and the feeling of being squeezed, trapped in a long tube of earth, causing her breast to constrict in panic making it difficult to breathe. 'Were you – more than friendly?'

The tail on the rump before her twitched and the voice of its owner came back, muffled. 'I don't know what you mean. Skelter and I talked a lot together. He spoke to me more than he did to other rabbits. Does that answer your question? I liked him because he had no side, you know what I mean? He wasn't prejudiced about us. He had an open mind.'

'Oh,' replied Rushie, still fighting the terrible feeling that the tunnel was getting narrower and that her body was too big for it, and any moment would jam fast so that she would not be able to go either backwards or forwards. Would the rabbits dig her out? Maybe they would not be able to before she ran out of air, and died of asphyxiation? The earth was like the throat of some giant beast, swallowing her. She could feel it, a consistency like a tongue, rubbing against her fur. Many rabbit bodies had smoothed the walls, but to Rushie, unused to the touch of anything on her body, they felt rough. She did not know how long she would be able to fight the growing hysteria.

'Is it much further?' she gasped.

Almost as she spoke the words, the tunnel opened up into a gallery, and the fear subsided enough for her to breathe freely again. At least when she was on her way out, she would be heading towards *fresh* air. She found she had to visualise her environment with organs other than her eyes, as she did on moonless nights above, sensing and smelling her surroundings.

Down here the air was stinking, stale and used, and the odour of earth was overpowering. There was a thick root like a dark-grey snake just above her head, running flush with the ceiling, and knobbled chalk-covered flints stuck out of the walls as if they had been placed purposely for their decorative effect, though they were too big to have been handled by rabbits, and must have just been exposed during the digging.

This underground world was a fascinating, terrifying place, full of ancient memories. The memories were like odours in her brain, triggering scenes that remained misty, on the edge of recognition. Unable to grasp these dream-like racial recollections, she wondered whether perhaps hares had once tunnelled like rabbits, digging deep into the earth to protect themselves from the savage monsters of prehistory. She could smell iron and bronze things buried in the walls, and old bones and old rotting birchwood twigs laid like a path running just above their heads. The earth was full of heavy stones, some as large as her highland crags, suspended by the dense material that held them there.

Rushie was in the belly of a monster.

Chapter Thirty

Rushie heard La framboise say to her, 'Well, so you're a friend of Skelter's, from his old country? Have you travelled all that way to seek him out?'

Rushie explained to La framboise that she had been among the same batch of hares carried south for the purpose of hare coursing, as Skelter. She said that she herself had managed to escape before the coursing and had made her home among a hare colony on the edge of the marshes.

'I know the one,' said La framboise.

'Now,' Rushie explained, 'I'm trying to find out what has happened to Skelter. It may be that he's dead – killed by the flogre. But it's also possible that he's lying wounded somewhere and needs help. I came to see if you rabbits had any ideas which would help me in my search.'

At that moment another large rabbit arrived in the chamber.

Rushie could sense the newcomer close by when a voice, undoubtedly that of a buck, asked, 'What have we here? A scent I don't recognise.' There was authority in the tone, yet it was not unfriendly.

'Ah, L'herbe, we have a visitor. An old friend of Skelter, from the mountains that he talked about so much.'

'Hello,' said L'herbe. 'You've come looking for him, I suppose? I heard he went missing.'

'Yes, I was just asking La framboise here, if she had any ideas where I might start searching?'

'Well, I'm sorry to say,' replied L'herbe, 'that he hasn't been here. No one has seen him since he left the warren, though we hear of him from time to time. News travels fast amongst rabbits – we cover the territory. I'd like to be of help – Skelter is a favourite of ours – but we've nothing to offer.'

Disappointed, Rushie thanked the buck. 'You were my last

chance, I don't know what to do now. Accept the fact that he's gone I suppose, and get on with my own life,' she said, stoically.

La framboise was sympathetic. 'Were you mates?' she asked.

'No, not really. Just friends – good friends. Skelter and I grew up together: he was my link with the old life, with the mountains. I shall miss him very much, even though we have only spoken once in the past few months. He was always there, close by, if I needed him.'

'Nothing for it, I'm afraid,' confirmed L'herbe, 'but to accept the inevitable. Hares and rabbits get killed every day. It's a fact of life. Nature has marked us down as the prey, and predators need meat to live.'

'Yes, but we don't have to like them for it, do we?' said La framboise.

'No, but we must *accept* it.'

Finding she could do nothing further there, and feeling the oppressiveness of the warren weighing her down, Rushie decided to leave. She wondered how Skelter had managed to keep his sanity down here in the hot fetid air of the warren for the length of time that he had been with the rabbits. She mentioned this to the two rabbits.

'Oh,' said L'herbe, 'he didn't stay down here. This is one of the deepest galleries. We put him up near the badgers, close to the surface. He could see a bit of light from where he was.'

'Near the *badgers*?' gasped Rushie.

'Yes, that was *his* reaction too, at the time, but we get on all right with them, actually. And though they complained about Skelter's noisy habits – I suppose he got restless down here with us rabbits on occasion – they thought he was all right – for a hare, that is. Badgers complain about anything and everything.'

Rushie tried to imagine Skelter with badgers for near neighbours and the image was one which sent shivers down her spine. She thanked La framboise and L'herbe for their hospitality, then went back up the tunnel which had caused her so much concern on the downward trip. It was not half so bad going up, but she was pleased to reach the surface anyway.

The trees were still tossing their crests. The light was beginning to filter in from the east. She wondered whether it might not be wiser to stay in the wood until dawn had passed into day, but she hated the denseness of the woodland and the solid lumps of darkness it trapped beneath it. She knew that trees did not stop the flogre in any case, and she would have to go underground again to protect herself. That was definitely out. There was no way she was going back down that hole.

It was best to make for open country, where she might find a place to nestle until the daylight came.

On the edge of the wood there was someone waiting for her. It was Creekcrosser, as scruffy as ever, but she was pleased to see him nonetheless. He shuffled his feet awkwardly when he noticed her gaze was on him.

'What are you doing here?' she asked.

'Came looking for you. I saw you come back across the causeway, so I followed you.'

'Whatever for?'

Creekcrosser shrugged. 'Thought you might need help.'

Rushie said, 'I can look after myself.'

'I know that, but two's company, isn't it? Anyway, I've got something to say to you. I've decided I'm going to box for you, when the frost dancing comes round.' He stuck out his jaw belligerently. 'What do you say to that then?'

'You? Box for me? I – I don't know what to say. I think you're making a mistake, Creekcrosser. You know I've promised Racer.'

'I know that, but I'll fight him anyway. That's if you have no objection.'

She was concerned.

'I can't withdraw my promise to him. It's been made, for better or for worse. It would be wrong of me to support you, you know that.'

'I don't know anything of the sort,' he retorted. 'You put too fine a point on what's expected of you. Customs were made to be broken when you get hares like Racer. He would kick you out of the way if it suited his purpose, quicker than that.'

Rushie shrugged.

'I don't know about that, I think you're being too hard on him. He's very sensitive about his image, that's all. You can't blame him totally, it's partly the colony's fault – it expects perfection. I think I understand Racer and I know that deep down he's a fine creature.'

'Well I've known him longer than you and forgive me if I snort in disgust.'

Rushie said, 'You're rivals. You're bound to think badly of him.'

'Can we drop it now?' asked Creekcrosser. 'He's not my favourite subject. I've told you what I intend to do and if you're not dead set against me I'm giving it a try. Maybe I'll lose – there's a strong possibility of that – but I would regret it for the rest of my life if I let the opportunity go by. I don't want any of the other jills – they're all too insipid for me . . .'

'Oh, I think you're being too hard on them, too.'

'That's one thing I don't like about you, you think well of *everyone*. I expect if the flogre came swooping down and snatched your leverets you'd forgive him, wouldn't you?'

His reminder made Rushie look up at the sky, and she saw that it was a murky grey.

'We'd better be getting on,' she said.

They headed for a ditch that they could travel along until they reached a point where they would have to break across open country. Two fields away, there was an overhanging drystone wall, at the bottom of which they could crouch until the sun was fully up. There were hollows beneath the stones that would hold a hare safe.

The two hares travelled along the ditch, a haunt of stoats, hoping they would not come across another predator in their efforts to avoid the creature in the sky. Rushie guessed they were barely on the periphery of the flogre's hunting ground but it was an unpredictable creature and on occasions extended its territory beyond its normal boundaries.

At the end of the ditch they came up into a meadow of short grass where cattle had been grazing recently. They launched themselves over this, racing for the distant wall, knowing that once they reached this point, they could use the stonework to protect themselves.

Creekcrosser was about three lengths behind Rushie when she saw the shadow on the ground, moving in rapidly from the east. Without looking up she knew it was a huge bird, the bizarre shape unmistakable to her, with its short wingspan and fan tail. It was the flogre, larger than a golden eagle, more athletic, and possessing a more developed manoeuvrability. The situation was desperate, though Creekcrosser was in a worse position than she, and was more likely to be the chosen victim.

It was a matter of survival, she could do nothing to help the jack behind her, and she increased her speed. The adrenalin coursed through her body, driving her to a swiftness she had never before attained. Creekcrosser was somewhere further back, still in the open field, when she was almost at the wall. She allowed her companion a brief compassionate thought, before diving for the cover of the stonework.

Then came the hit.

Rushie's breath left her body as she felt the cruel claws snatch her from the turf and carry her through the whistling air, into the sky. In an instant the world was a patchwork below her, as if she were standing on the highest peak of the northern mountains, looking over a sheer edge. It was a sickening, dizzying experience, and her body went rigid with fear. There was nothing below her but rushing air and flatlands. She could see the ocean, the creeks in their crazy patterns, the fields and their borders. The talons of the flogre were piercing her skin, causing her great pain, but terror overruled the hurt, dominating her heart and her head.

She struggled a little, trying to ignore the pain, attempting to make the flogre drop her to a swift death. But its cruel ridged claws had muscles and tendons that would need a machine to open. Certainly no hare could do it.

Chapter Thirty One

Bubba was very pleased with himself. At last he had caught the hare that had been giving him so much trouble over the past season. It had even crossed from the island to the marshes to teach the hares in that district how to avoid Bubba by digging little holes in the ground. Well now he had the magical hare he was going to make it suffer. Since this was no ordinary hare, it would suffer no ordinary death. Only those creatures with whom Bubba was pleased were given the honour of being torn to pieces and eaten. This one was the first animal that had ever made Bubba angry, and for that it was going to agonise in some way yet to be thought of by Bubba.

He swept down to the martello tower through the hole in the roof, and dropped the hare on the floor. It lay there, stupefied and still, in the dust and grime of the dim room. Bubba's bone collection had begun to build up again, though he had nowhere near the same number he had gathered in the old tower. The creature on the floor stared at these bones with fixed glazed eyes, as if they represented some kind of hope for it. There was no hope. Once a creature came into Bubba's possession, it never escaped.

—Tower, what shall I do with this strange hare?

—*Give it to me, Bubba. You have enough to eat. Let me torture this one to death.*

—You mean starve it?

—*Yes. Leave it here, inside my stone belly. It can't escape. There is only one way out for creatures who can't fly, and that involves a drop long enough to break a hare's back. All it can do is run around in here, looking for a way out, when there is no exit.*

Bubba considered this very carefully. The exit to the room was halfway up the tower, which itself was six or seven times the height of a man. The hare could not escape through the hole in

244

the ceiling because it couldn't fly. Hares hated heights. Bubba knew that because they screamed when he took them aloft, and their teeth chattered in fear.

Bubba reminded himself that he had previously believed this was a magical hare. It was true that it had managed to climb the steps to the old tower. But then the old tower was easy to climb from the inside. This new tower had no steps, and if the hare was a good sorcerer, it would have made itself vanish, or would have destroyed Bubba, even before Bubba had climbed up to the clouds with it in his claws.

Bubba came to the conclusion that this hare did not have the kind of magic that allowed it to do supernatural things, but rather the kind that allowed it to foresee events. It could invent things to protect other hares and it knew when Bubba was in the sky, but it could not do enchantments. It could not save itself from an impossible situation. This was a satisfactory discovery.

The hare moved in the dust at his feet. He pecked its back, but not hard enough to cause it great harm, just enough to make it cower in fright.

It was probably wondering when Bubba was going to begin eating it.

Bubba flew up to the hole in the ceiling and stood on the broken edge, looking down. The hare squirmed below him, making for the shadows on the periphery of the circular room. That was all right. Let it search. Let it seek a way out. There was no way out.

Bubba unfolded his wings and took to the airways. He searched the immediate area, finding nothing of interest. Then he noticed a formation of large birds on the horizon. A skein of geese was coming in from the north. This looked promising. Bubba preferred the meat of mammals but birds would do in a pinch. He was not confident enough to take one on the wing – that was not his way – but once the geese landed it would be a different matter.

He circled the sky, watching the flock looking for a landing space. The geese were exhausted, obviously having flown a long way. Bubba was aware that birds came and went, flying long distances to reach warmer climates, or arriving from colder ones, and he thought the whole business unnecessary. What was wrong with these creatures, that they could not stand a little cold? He, Bubba, was not a native cold-climate creature. There were in his hazy egg-memories, remembrances of a hot humid place where the air was heavy and lethargic. He had been born in a land whose inhabitants moved slowly through the day, the heat causing drowsiness and languor among the creatures of its green waxy bosom.

Yet Bubba had adapted to the cold, and scorned those who migrated to escape a little frost and ice.

The geese landed, winding in their necks, padding about on the mud of the estuary with their great ungainly feet. Bubba chose his victim, a large goose that was obviously very tired from its flight across the ocean. The creature was completely unsuspecting of the danger from above since it was in a country where there were no flying predators that would bother a bird the size of a goose.

Bubba landed with a thud on the back of the goose and silenced its rhonking within seconds. The rest of the flock scattered, running for take-off, their exhausted wings beating frantically. There was much noise and excitement. Once they were up off the ground they formed a ragged flight pattern, and went rippling over the landscape to find another area in which to rest, away from monsters that fell out of nowhere and killed you where you stood.

The day was coming in fast now but Bubba decided to eat his food on the spot. The large goose was a dead weight and rather than carry the whole of it back to the tower it was best to eat his fill first and then take back the remains.

Bubba gorged, tearing and ripping away at the corpse, scattering feathers and pieces of skin. Later the kill would be blamed on foxes by man and beast.

When his hunger had been satisfied, Bubba grasped the shapeless piece of flesh in his talons and took to the air again, heading directly for the tower. Once there, he dropped the carcass through the hole in the roof and then landed on its edge to peer down into the gloom.

For a moment, his heart skipped, thinking that despite all his calculations the little hare had escaped. But no, there it was, tight against the wall, clinging to the shadows. Bubba was happy with his prisoner. Bubba dropped down inside the room, his hard claws scraping on brickwork. There he played with the carcass for a while, tearing off small strips and forcing them down his throat.

The hare watched him from the darkness.

Bubba ignored the creature, aware that it was suffering. It was enough to know that the hare was terrified, and would remain so, as it slowly starved to death.

A little later, Bubba fell asleep.

PART FIVE

*

The Magical Hare

Chapter Thirty Two

Since hares have always been herbivores and quarry for the predators their history is somewhat placid. They have no great wars of which to boast, no legendary warriors to revere, no conquering heroes to hail. Only the great Kicker, who is regarded as more of a god than a hero, has any prominence in their history. It is true that their one great claim to fame can be found in their feet: hares are swift runners and proud of their speed. However, this quickness in their legs has been employed mainly in the art of escape, not for any positive action against an enemy.

The ghost-hares of those deified only two thousand winters before today were not the only hares to have been worshipped as gods, only the most recent. They were aware of ancient ghost-hares on the landscape, beings faded almost to nothingness, creatures who had been venerated by the early men when the bipeds first emerged from their caves. These wisps of half-light were evident only in the most remote places and took no part in watching over living hares, for their time had long since gone. They were snatches of mist from another world, another epoch, and had no relevance to today. There were paintings of them on cave walls, their likenesses caught in the ochres and charcoals of the history of man, rather than that of hares.

The ghost-hare that watched over Rushie however, was a strong spirit and came to her in dreams to give her strength in her time of adversity. This ghost-hare was aware of the greatness of hare history and legend, reaching back some fifty million winters, but had only been deified herself at the time of Boudicca and the Iceni.

Rushie dreamed that she was told that her imprisonment showed not that she was a pathetic creature, but that her captor was himself a miserable wretch, full of fear and unhappiness. Hers was a prison which dignified the prisoner, and demeaned the jailer. Even were she to die in the claws of her captor, she need have no worry, for she was destined for the Otherworld of hares where there was no fear.

'You must see that since the First Hare, Kicker, known to men as *Palaeolagus* or *Eurymulus*, countless hares have come and gone from the world. Yet they still cover the whole face of the earth, in the hottest and coldest of climates, and no man is their master. They are a proud species, wild and free, never tamed by anyone except another hare at mating time.

'Yet that pride is not an arrogant pride, born out of might, but a humble pride, the pride of never having capitulated, never having become man's pet, even though the species itself is not a savage one. Only towards rabbits does the charity of hares fail, in myths perpetuated by the ignorant and bigoted, the prejudiced few. The shame of this failing causes much pain to Kicker's ghost, that weak ray of sunlight that flits over hill and valley on a winter's day, for Kicker was both rabbit and hare in one, and father-mother of the whole lagomorph race.'

These words carried comfort to the morose jill as she twitched her way through the dreams brought on by starvation. She lay in the shadows of the wall, away from the now blinding light of the shaft of sun which joined floor to ceiling where sat the hook-billed monster, watching her with bright, feverish eyes, greedy for the sight of suffering in others.

Rushie felt she was going to die, but she wanted the great bird to have none of the satisfaction of watching her waste away, and determined to throw herself out of the doorway, to dash herself on the stones below the tower. This she planned to do when the flogre left its nest that coming dusk.

'Have no fear,' said her ghost-hare, 'for while I cannot help you to live, I can certainly help you when you die. You will not be alone along the dark passage to the Otherworld, for there are hares like me every step of the way, and they will show you where to tread, and the precipices of the nethermost regions of the land between the quick and the dead will be of no consequence to you.

'Remember those who have gone before, keep a cool head and a cool heart, and it will not be so hard. Think of Kicker, the first of those to travel that path, with no others to show the way. Think of the daunting prospect of travelling through the dark craggy

252

regions of the underworld, where there are pits with no bottom, and ridges guarded by fierce creatures without names, without recognisable shape.

'Though these are all illusion, they are terrifying enough, and are there not to tear you, for you will have no body to destroy being only a spirit, but to rob you of your reason. Kicker did not know of the insubstantiality of these phantoms of the nether regions, yet the First Hare ran bravely through the swirling darkness, scattering their forms like mist.

'You at least will have friendly guides, whose advice will comfort you, and keep you sane.

'And what will you find in the Otherworld, that place of boundless meadows and green mountains, where all hares harmonise with its perfection? What besides a million hare spirits racing through the dawns of eternity? Why, toothless foxes and clawless eagles! They will be there too, in that place of many names. Even humans. Yes, you will find man there, stripped of his weapons, without clothes on his back, without brick or mortar, or metal machines. You will find the naked spirits of men wandering the fields of the hare, a new gentleness in them, a new knowledge to guide them.

'Once there, you too will become aware of the whole, as well as the essence, of hare history. You will learn that hares were once giants – huge lagomorphs that pounded the earth flat with their great hind legs. However, because they were large they were easy to see, and monsters of the landscape, all teeth and claws, chased them into a state of exhaustion.

'So it was, because hares are not savage predators, with a large array of weapons at their disposal, they had to turn to other defences. And what they turned to was *magic*. They studied the stars, the moon and sun, the earth and the waters thereon, and learned the art and science of magic. They became the magical hares which fascinated men, who made totems of Kicker and his progeny. Hares were venerated by the early men, who wore hare masks and carved hare symbols.

'The first thing that hares did with their magic, was to make themselves smaller, altering their size until they found the perfect length and height. Now they could hide in the fields, in the rocks, or be still on an open piece of ground, yet not be seen. They were masters of disguise, and could become a clod of earth, or log of tree, in a moment. They had noble countenances, tall ears, powerful back legs.

'There were some hares of course, for there are always unbelievers, who had not the strength of mind to go through with the magical change, and these creatures were caught in a storm of enchantment. Because of their scepticism, instead of changing size they were turned into stone, magicked into frozen forms of granite and gneiss, that many men took to be natural rocks, moraine and such, appearing to have animal shape by mere accident of formation.

'Over the course of millennia most of these statues have been covered by silt and earth, by peat and turf, until now only the ears remain above the surface of the landscape. Those wandering over moor, mountains, or wasteland, will often come across these weathered stone ears, sticking out of the earth as monoliths and tors, sometimes a single one where its twin has fallen or eroded, sometimes in a group where more than one hare was caught in the blast of sorcery that blew across the land.

'Oh, the magical hares that have raced over the landscape of time are too numerous to count, too wonderful to measure, and you are part of all this, Rushie: you are part of legend and myth, mystery and wizardry. Now you are caught, trapped in the den of the monster, but you will escape to a place he can never follow, and you will laugh down the long tunnel of darkness at him, and the sounds will ring in his head, maddeningly, until he will know that you have defeated him.'

On waking from these dreams in her fevered state of hunger Rushie could remember little of substance, but retained a feeling of wellbeing and peace.

One evening while the flogre was out hunting Rushie went to the edge of the bright blinding opening and looked downwards at the rocks below. It seemed to her that there were small ledges on the sheer wall, which she as a mountain hare, might use to climb down. She stepped out onto the first of these and managed to hunch against the stone. On the next step a giddiness overcame her. She managed to get one paw in a crease between two stones, but then lost her footing. She slipped sideways, out into open space, and felt herself falling. In her almost weightless state, having grown so thin that she was nothing but skin over a framework of bones, she seemed to float rather than hurtle towards the earth.

The marshy ground in the shadow of the tower was softer than it looked. The fall knocked all the wind out of her frail body, but did not kill her, though she knew she was close to death. She began to stagger over the rocks, into the tall marsh grasses, towards her home. The journey was a long one, and she could never hope to make it, but someone had come to meet her.

Creekcrosser came out of a frosted field and found her lying on a patch of frozen turf, breathing out the last few wisps of life. 'Creekcrosser,' she said, seeing his misty shape above her, 'I should have chosen you first.'

'Last is best,' he said, then, 'are you dying, Rushie?'

'I am dying, but there's no need to be sad because I know where I'm going, and it's a *good* place, Creekcrosser.'

Creekcrosser could not promise such a thing, but hares do not weep for the dead: they remember.

'I shall box for you at the frost dancing,' said Creekcrosser, 'and I'm sure you'll know.'

'I shall be watching you,' she replied, and then her eyes glazed over, and the thin breast was finally stilled. Creekcrosser left the place where the spirit of Rushie was struggling through the passages of darkness, her ghost-hares to guide her, towards the Otherworld of hares and rabbits and all things gone from the place of the living.

That evening, the flogre arrived back at his home to find the hare gone. He was enraged and immediately flew out into the darkness, searching for the creature he hated so much. He never found her body, though the tower told him over and over again that she *must* have died, for she had been so close to death when he had left for the hunt. He wished now that he had stayed to watch her, but that was in the past and he had lost his chance.

* * *

The following day, a gamekeeper from one of the nearby farms came across the frozen carcass and seeing that it was fresh he picked it up. He was amazed at its leanness, and saw that the hare had starved to death, and would be no good for the table.

However, gamekeepers are much the same as tractor-men, who like to keep the world tidy, so he took the skinny carcass of the mountain hare, and hung it on the gibbet which he kept on his own land. It was displayed there, along with two weasels, a stoat, five moles and three rooks. The weasels and stoat were there because they were suspected of killing game birds. The moles were there because they made untidy humps in flat fields. The rooks were there because they were rooks, who built their nests high in the elms shouting insults at men who walked beneath and blackened the sky as if officiating at the funeral of the sun at the end of each day.

For a while, until time and its helpers had ravaged the face of the mountain hare, animals and birds would often pause to study the strange expression on its features. Some of them thought they knew what they saw, some of them gave up on it, lost in ambiguities.

Chapter Thirty Three

The hands that held Skelter on the spiral staircase to the tower were strong and powerful: a farm worker's hands. They were calloused and creased by the outdoors, by the handling of leather harnesses, tools, farm implements. They were hands that had broken the necks of chickens and rabbits. They were marred by scars from the bites of ferrets. They had gripped hemp ropes, hammered in posts, and torn down fences. They were not the kind of hands to allow a hare any consideration of escape.

Holding him out at arm's length with his right hand, the man removed his jacket from his left side, then transferred Skelter to the other hand and took off the whole coat. Skelter was wrapped and bound in this nasty smelling garment so tightly that he ground his teeth in anger and would have whistled shrilly if his chest had not been constricted.

In the darkness of the folds of the coat Skelter was carried somewhere, through a muttering of people, away from the deepthroated sound of the church's musical voice. All he could remember of the journey was the smell of that dried weed that men burned in their mouths, stale sweat, and many other old, old scents, buried deep in the cloth that had seen many summers, many winters, yet had never been immersed in water for the purpose of cleansing it. There was some paper in the inside pocket near to his teeth which he bit into savagely venting his frustration.

When he was unrolled from the coat, he found himself in a run: a wooden frame with chicken wire covering it, forming a cage some six lengths long and three lengths wide. The floor of the run was concrete, so there was no possibility of tunnelling his way out. In fact, his initial reaction was to race backwards and forwards, within the confines of the wire, in a kind of controlled panic. When his hysteria began to subside, and he entered a kind of calmness, he found he had been wearing down his claws on the rough concrete. If he continued to dash backwards and forwards, much as he wanted to, he would have no nails to dig with once he finally *did* get out. He decided to crouch in a corner for a while, and only jumped away when some human came near to the wire, either peering in too closely, or poking something through the holes.

There were young humans there, pushing cabbage stalks through the chicken wire every so often, trying to get him to eat. He ignored the gestures, partly out of fear, and partly out of sheer cussedness. The stalks had been handled so much they smelled of humans, and in any case he was too miserable and terrified to satisfy his hunger. If he could have bitten his own head off and ended it right there, he probably would have done so. This was the second time he had been in a cage, and he liked this time the least. There was a sense of permanence about this cage, and this time there were no companions to keep him company.

It was a long while before he could bring his eyes to see beyond the wire, into the yard itself, not because his vision was blocked, but because his mind would not allow him to concentrate on studying anything that was not immediately related to his situation inside the run.

When the young humans finally tired of him and went to a different part of the yard to play he was at last able to ascertain his geographical position. He seemed to be on a kind of rough concrete square that had perhaps at one time been the floor of a shed but was now open to the elements. Behind the run was a house, with a back door and an outhouse protruding into the yard.

Next to the back door was an archaic water pump, rusted and obviously no longer in use. The curved S-shaped handle looked as if it had seized long ago, and the snout of the pump, jutting over Skelter's cage, was blocked with soil.

Skelter could smell the liquid below the device: a deep well that still held sweet fresh water above the rock table. This natural spring water was no longer used by the humans, only by the creatures who lived in the hole that the humans had dug, and then covered over a few decades ago.

There were toads trapped down there, who had been immured

since the humans had stopped using buckets on a rope in the well and had installed a then modern device, a water pump. Skelter's sharp ears could hear them murmuring to one another in the deep dreamful language of spiritual eremites.

Toads are long-living creatures, and sometimes all that time may be spent in the hollow below a stone. Such an existence produces surrealist minds which bend thoughts into strange shapes, and weird philosophies, odd concepts and eccentric theories emerge. Even were Skelter able to understand what the toads were saying it was doubtful he would comprehend the notions which they passed to one another in their vacuous ootheca world with its opiate atmosphere. What did he know about the different musical qualities of light or the material textures of darkness? Or the mystic poetry of still waters, sought and found by the roots of distant trees? Or the whispered history of stone, pressed from creatures and plants beyond his ken?

The toads of the closed well could speak with water, stone and wood, could feel the earth turning, could smell the leaves of the cycad fossils from forests of a former sun, could hear the screams of dinosaurs coming from deep at the bottom of time. The toads of the well had reached an enlightenment unknown to any other creature on the earth, their souls bound for the lap of God when the final darkness came upon them. The vertical abyss in which they existed, wetwalled and smooth, was the hollow core of the universe, and around this shaft of fetid air the macrocosm moved as on a frictionless spindle. They were the inner sanctum of the cosmos and their concentrated minds dreamed of things that were yet unknown to ordinary life.

Above this dark oubliette the pump was a kind of obelisk, indicating the place where the toad generations might continue until the end of time, producing perhaps brilliant though bizarre insights to the mindscape, parodying the artistic achievements of men, thinking in symbols and images that would stun the greatest of philosophers – beast, bird, fish or man, that the world has ever known – yet lost to any useful contact by the very nature of their situation. They may have had the answers to death and war, disease and famine, life and peace, and all the mysteries of the struggles going on outside the well, but if so these solutions were locked in with them in their vault, never to be opened again.

Skelter shook his mind free of the mumble of monastic toads.

Around the yard itself was junk-fence made of pieces of chicken wire, linear wire, bits of boxwood, the top of a kitchen stove, rusty corrugated iron – anything that filled a hole. In the far corner was a small vegetable patch in amongst which the chickens scratched a living when they were out of their coop, which was during the day. At night they were locked inside their protective house, away from foxes and stoats.

Chained to the coop, night and day, was a bedraggled mongrel with a black, matted curly-haired coat. He was a savage beast, growling even at the master of the house, though softly in the back of his throat. Most of the time the dog would lie in the dirt, watching the world with morose and dangerous eyes that turned to pebbles at the slightest infringement of his territory. The only creatures he ignored were the chickens and the smallest member of the human household. Skelter was glad the dog was well away from his run, for it studied the small hare with dark interest. Skelter knew a killer when he saw one.

The rest of the yard was hardpacked earth, with broken toys of young humans scattered here and there. A boxwood cart, which the youngsters had made out of pram wheels, was tied to the fence as if it were a horse and likely to bolt if left unattended.

From one end of the yard to the other ran a washing line on two poles, which was continually in use, there being seven youngsters in the house to keep clean. The earth below this line was sodden and marked with chickensfeet tracks. Wild birds would drink from the puddles there when water was scarce elsewhere.

In a small potting shed by the vegetable patch were other animals whom Skelter occasionally glimpsed when the door was left open. A hamster, some gerbils and a dwarf rabbit shared a shelf amongst a clutter of garden tools, pots, boxes and dried bulbs (some of which were decades old). Spiders were rife, weaving and interweaving webs until all the corners of the shed, and most of its darkened ceiling, were covered in their flimsy flytraps. So thick and layered were these webs that sometimes the catching of a single fly in the strong silken threads of one would jangle the alarms of all the arachnid occupants of the place and they would come dashing out in their dozens only to find that the victim was not theirs at all, but belonged to a far-flung neighbour on the other side of the world.

Skelter could see all this activity, but hares do not have strong enough voices to reach any distance so he was not able to converse with any of these creatures, even the rabbit. They seemed a poor motley bunch in their smelly cages, either staring into space or playing with some human toy, like the hamster's wheel, or the cardboard rolls in the gerbils' cage.

This then, was Skelter's new environment and one he came to hate with a venom unmatched by any feeling he had experienced before his incarceration. It was the concrete that was mostly responsible for this enmity. The unnatural feel of the substance beneath his feet, and its ability to retain the stale smell of his urine and faeces, made him regard it with great loathing. There was no way he could punish it, either, for it resisted his most savage bites. Instead, he had to content himself with gnawing the wooden framework to his run.

Once the children got used to him, and ceased to tease him, he came to regard them as something of a diversion from the terrible boredom that overcomes animals kept in cages. He knew that if he sank into apathy he would become like the animals in the potting shed, all hope having gone from their eyes. Skelter was made of sterner stuff and dreamed of escape. It was possible, he reminded himself, that he was being fattened for the pot – jugged hare – but he did not think so, for the man who had caught him would be paying more attention to him if he were. His food was adequate, nothing more, and if he were being fattened he would be receiving mounds of the stuff.

There was a third possibility: that he was destined for another run against the greyhounds, but that too seemed unlikely. The people who held the hare coursing meets were not the working men, with the soil engrained in their features, but the owners of the farms. This man who had him in his clutches was clearly a fellow like the tractor-man, closer to the earth than those who had captured him before.

Besides the children, who ran and jumped and squealed and cried and laughed, sometimes all at once, causing Skelter much bewilderment at first, there were the chickens. Most of these were hens of course, who spent much of their time pecking at ground that had been pecked to a barrenness unknown outside bare rockfaces by centuries of hens. It would be difficult to find another patch of earth that had less living matter amongst its hardpacked grains of dust. The arid deserts of the world were abundantly fertile compared with the yard in which the chickens pecked. Yet they continued to peck, perhaps out of habit, perhaps for something to do, perhaps from sheer obstinacy.

The chief of the chickens, for it was an hierarchical society, was the cockerel. This mean-looking rooster drove the hens insane with his complete disregard for any mating season. He chased them, pinned them down, and had his way with them no matter what the weather, the colour of the light, before a solstice or after an equinox. Nothing mattered to the cockerel except the satisfaction of his own lust. The only thing that saved the hens from constant abuse was their numbers, which were sufficient to space the rooster's attacks on their person to an almost tolerable degree.

One or two of the hens liked his attention of course, and would parade up and down before the strutting male bird, showing their dirty brown feathers to the best advantage. Such is the contrariness of life however, that the behaviour of cockerels is no different from any other creature, and those which desired notice were the ones that received it the least. The rooster bypassed these hotblooded females for the shy or haughty ones who spent their time trying to avoid his rushes.

The hens ignored the new hare, not even looking up when he tried to make contact with them. Skelter felt he did not exist in the eyes of chickens. He was like everything else: not being a grain of wheat or yardworm he was nothing to them. They clucked and grumbled away, pecking round his concrete domain, without showing the least bit of interest in his being there.

Occasionally one of the hens would be grabbed by the man and its neck would be wrung for all to witness. The first of these acts so shocked Skelter with its suddenness, that he did not stop trembling for an hour. The man simply came out of the house, looked around the yard, selected his victim, stalked over to the unsuspecting hen, grabbed it, held its body under his arm and twisted its neck. All over.

Skelter looked around wildly, expecting to be next.

After two or three of these executions, Skelter came to realise how the victims were chosen, and was glad he did not lay eggs. It was the bad layers that went to the pot. He could see the desperate amongst them, as their egg-laying abilities dwindled, trying to force out ovoids that were not there. Despite what the rest of the world believed, hens were not stupid but as intelligent as any other creature. They knew when their time was approaching. The rooster too knew who was next for the chop and began to give the hen a wide berth, possibly considering it bad form, or unlucky, to expend his precious seed on those marked out by death. That member of the harem would be ostracised by the rest of the concubines too, making her last days the most miserable of a miserable life on earth.

The only other members of the human household that paid any attention to the hens was the female, who fed them and collected the eggs, and the smallest barely-walking youngster, who loved to see them scatter, and walked amongst them like a giant trying to tweak their tails. This fearless little creature, who would poke at Skelter through the cage wire and burble strange noises at him, could sit on the dog's back and pull its ears and tail without the slightest indication of annoyance from that proud savage beast whose heart had been turned to stone by those that had chained him in the dust – for life.

Chapter Thirty Four

Skelter did not manage to escape in the first few days, nor the first month and then finally winter massed over the land like slow-gathering iron, taking possession of the outdoors and resenting the resistance of indoors. It took the sky in its firm grip and gave it enough body to crush the three seasons that had gone before, hardpacking them down into the earth, until all traces of them were out of sight. It was as if there had never been a blossom on a tree, or a bird singing, or a delicate insect flying, just this ponderous mottled sky that pressed down like a great metal weight on the land below.

The hedges, shorn of their leaves, were networks of black twigs, and the trees on the skyline were stark and discomforting as gallows. Old birds' nests were embarrassingly exposed. The nakedness of the land was disconcerting.

Skelter found himself the object of much attention from the household, and was bemused by the reasons for this. Even the man, who once he had caught Skelter and put him in the run, came out to stare at him and shake his head. It was all very strange. They stood over him and barked and growled in the way humans do when they are excited by something, and pointed to Skelter not once, but many times. Friends of the youngsters were brought round and Skelter was displayed for their benefit. They seemed sufficiently amazed by him.

Eventually, the novelty of his presence wore off and things went back to normal. He was ignored by most of the humans most of the time. The adult female fed and watered him without fail, and the young one still poked twigs and things through the wire at him, but that too was usual.

Skelter had ceased, like most of the animals about the place, to resent the attentions of the youngster. The small human had nothing but joy in its heart and its attentions were the result of an insatiable curiosity. It wanted to know what fur felt like, tasted like, ruffled like. It needed to grab ears to see what happened when it did so. It needed to chase, with the noise of water swilling down a drain, anything that was prepared to run. This was simply the effervescence of life bubbling up in the youngster and not the malevolence it seemed to be.

After the first hard frost the man came and slipped a wooden box with a hole in it under the run, and some straw followed. Skelter guessed they were worried about him being exposed to weather with nothing but concrete under him. He sheltered in the box occasionally, but ignored the straw. He was not a hamster or a gerbil: he was a wild mountain hare.

A light fall of snow came one evening, settling like white peace over the land.

The dog stayed most of the time in his kennel and Skelter could hear the creature coughing in the night. Foxes sometimes drifted near the coop, but the dog let rip with some foul language if ever they came too close, and they caught his battle scent as well as his words and drifted away again. Skelter wondered why the dog did his duty when he was clearly neglected and misused, never given a walk let alone a run, and treated like a pariah by all, even those he guarded. The chickens were the worst of all, scornful of him, knowing they were safe from attack. They knew they were more valuable than the dog and he would be punished, perhaps by death, if he assaulted one of them.

Why then, did this bitter morose animal carry out diligently his task of protecting the birds? It seemed he had spent his life on the end of a chain, despised by the domestic creatures of the household and neglected by the humans. It was a mystery Skelter never solved.

After the snow, savage winds came and tore into the landscape, trying to rip it apart.

It became much colder and the water they put out for Skelter turned to ice very quickly. Sparrows came to drink it, squeezing through a hole in the wire. Skelter did not mind that. He knew they were dying in their hundreds, trying to find what little unfrozen water they could. The woman threw out crumbs, but the chickens ate them and she seldom remembered the water for the wild birds. Her washing was dried somewhere inside the house, for if she put it on the line it would go as stiff as boards within a short time.

One cold night Skelter was in his box, shivering and trying to keep warm, when there were some sounds by the run. Skelter could smell a familiar creature and when he recognised the scent, he poked his head out of the hole to look. There in the moonlight, just a few inches away and staring in at him, was the dog. At the other end of the yard was a broken leather collar on the end of a chain. Snow was settling all around and gradually covering the manacles of his slavery.

The dog had finally got loose.

Skelter was alarmed. What was the beast going to do? It stared in at him with bright feverish eyes and said something in its own language. The words were soft, no doubt to prevent being heard by the sleeping household, but there was something in the tone that gave Skelter the idea that the dog meant him no harm, that he was commiserating with the hare. The mongrel stared at him a little while longer, gave the house a hard uncompromising look, then slipped away into the night.

Good for you, thought Skelter, *get away from this place as fast as you can.*

It began to snow very heavily. The escapee had judged his time right, knowing his footprints would be covered and his route unknown. How long he had been planning this deliverance could only be guessed at by Skelter, but the collar must have been ready for snapping for a while for the dog to be able to choose his time so carefully.

When the household woke the next morning, there was no hue and cry, for no one noticed the dog had gone. They put his dish full of food outside his kennel, and did not even bother to look inside. The chickens ate the potatoes and scraps of meat, and still no one missed the guardian.

The youngsters came out into the yard, and there was much excitement for a while. They played snowballs, throwing the missiles at each other, built a snowman, and gave each other rides on a sledge. None of them thought to look inside the kennel for the faithful family guard. When they were exhausted and wet they went indoors, and Skelter did not see them again that day.

Two whole days had passed, by which time the mongrel was

probably halfway across the world, before someone thought to peer within the kennel, and found him missing. They dug under the snow and found his chain and the broken collar and there was much barking amongst them. They went off in different directions, letting out yelps, seemingly distraught that their captive slave had taken it into his head to be so ungrateful as to run away from their kindness.

The dog never reappeared and Skelter hoped that he was alive and well and had either found a new home, one that treated him with respect and consideration, or was wild and free, and living off the land.

A clear day some time later, before the new dog came, Skelter had cause to be concerned. At dawn he sighted a shape in the sky and knew it to be the flogre. He remained inside the protective box, watching the terrible creature glide across the heavens in search of a victim. Skelter knew he was quite safe inside the run but this did not help his nerves in any way. He still found himself trembling at the sight of the grey form moving over the world.

He did not come out of his box the whole day.

There were dangers everywhere, even in captivity.

Presumably the family were still hoping to find the mongrel and return him to his chain, for they left the post of guard dog empty for some time before getting a new mongrel.

Skelter was resting inside his box as usual one moonlit night, keeping out of the wind, when a scent came to him that made his heart start pounding in his chest. There was a fox in the yard. He saw the dark shape slip through a hole in the makeshift fence and stand there moving its head slowly, looking from Skelter's run to the chicken coop.

The chickens smelled his scent too and began to get restless, clucking away within their wooden walls. The house itself was mostly asleep, with only the various tribes of mice active. Certainly the humans were not stirring.

The fox, a young vixen, came over to his run and stared in at him with amber eyes. Her mouth was parted slightly and Skelter found himself looking down a channel lined with sharp white teeth. He began to whistle, which made the vixen narrow her eyes, and she said something. Skelter stopped whistling and ground his teeth, looking around wildly for some avenue of escape, knowing that he was trapped.

Skelter knew the run was not strong enough to keep out the vixen. Formidable as it was to a hare, it was a flimsy piece of wood and wire to an animal the size of a fox. She could drag the frame from the concrete onto the yard and upturn it with only a little effort.

Her eyes glittered as she stared at him, knowing she was terrible, the manifestation of a nightmare.

Then she turned abruptly and headed towards the chicken coop. She worried and fussed around the wooden structure for a while, then eventually found a rotten plank, which she pulled away with her teeth. Then she was inside amongst them and there was bedlam. The noise was such that it woke every creature in the vicinity, including the metaphysical toads, who joined in the cacophony.

The smell of death was in the air. One of the hens squeezed through the hole in the side of the coop and escaped, but inside the wooden walls many were dying. Skelter dashed backwards and forwards in his run, wondering whether the world was coming to an end. There were sounds from within the house, and lights went on throwing swathes of brilliance over the snowy ground.

Just as the vixen emerged from the hole in the coop with a dead chicken in its mouth the door to the house flew open and a half-dressed man came tumbling out. There was a short pause and the fox slipped into the darkness: a liquefaction of its form, becoming darkness itself.

The night roared sound and a flame reached out over Skelter's run. The hare's heart stopped in mid-beat and his eyes popped. There followed the unmistakable odour of fired gun, and Skelter pressed himself down into the cold concrete.

There was much activity after that, with several of the humans coming out to inspect the henhouse, counting the dead bodies, and many barked curses were flung in the direction the fox had taken. The man with the gun went off into the night, but returned without the carcass of a fox.

Finally, the household went again to bed.

Skelter realised he had had a lucky escape and that if the henhouse had been difficult to breach he might have become prey to the vixen. It seemed she had gone mad once inside the coop and had slaughtered the hens, even though she could only take one of them away with her. There was something about foxes, Skelter knew, that made them into machines once they were amongst several prey: if the henhouse had not confined the creatures, most of them would have escaped.

The following morning, there was blood on the snow. Skelter watched the clean-up operation, noting the mood of the woman and man, which was extremely dour. The cockerel's body appeared amongst the dead, but whether he had died bravely in defending his harem or whether he had panicked with the rest of them and died in the same hysterical struggle to find an escape was never known.

The man came and stared at Skelter for a long time, his eyes dark and heavy and his face long. Skelter wondered whether he was now destined for the pot, since the family had lost many hens and eggs and chicken would be scarce for a while.

Instead, later that day another man came to inspect Skelter the way he had been examined at the beginning of the winter season by the rest of the household. Skelter recognised this new human: it was the man from the cottage in the field next to Whinsled Lea, Eyebright's field. His black bushy beard and dark eyes had not been so closely observed before, but Skelter recognised his shape and scent and knew him to be the man so highly regarded by Stigand the otter. To confirm his suspicions, a hound appeared shortly afterwards by the man's side, and it was the St Bernard, Bess.

Amazingly the dog spoke to him.

'Hello hare, you look a little frightened, but I wouldn't worry. My master has come to buy you from the other man.'

'You speak my language?'

'I speak many languages because my master collects animals from time to time, so there is ample opportunity to learn.'

Skelter considered this, but of course wondered why the man should *want* to collect other creatures.

'Am I going to be eaten?' he asked.

'No, we're saving you from that. You're very lucky that you're not a brown hare, or my master would not be so interested in you, but since you're obviously a blue hare . . .'

269

'From the highlands.'

'. . . from the highlands, yes, then you interest him. He must have heard about you from one of his contacts, and now he wants to take you away to study you.'

'And when he's done that, what happens to me then?'

'You'll probably be sent to a zoo or something.'

Skelter blinked. 'What's a zoo?'

'It's a place where they keep wild animals so that they can be studied. It'll be a nice zoo, if you go at all, because my master doesn't believe in keeping animals caged. If you were a brown hare he would have let you go, but it's doubtful he will travel all the way up to the highlands.'

'But I have made my home down here on the flatlands now. You can ask Stigand the otter – he says he knows you well.'

Bess looked down on him with soulful eyes. 'Oh, I remember, I've heard of you. You're Skelter, aren't you? I don't know what I can do to help though. I can't speak to humans, even the intelligent ones, because they only bark and growl, as you know. I can get *some* things across with sign language, but the fact that you're a blue hare come to settle in the south is too complicated.'

'Please *try*. I don't want to go to one of those zoo places. They sound just as bad as what I've got now.'

Skelter had heard vaguely of places like zoos. He was appalled at the thought of spending the rest of his life in captivity. While he was under the hare run they had made for him there was always the chance of escape. The humans would eventually do something careless, or leave the run until it rotted enough for Skelter to gnaw his way out.

Chapter Thirty Five

Bubba was angry that the hare had escaped but he soothed himself with the knowledge that it had been close to death and must have died on its journey back to its colony. A creature as starved as that hare had been would have needed a miracle to survive and recover and Bubba knew that miracles were so scarce as to be virtually non-existent. Nevertheless, he brooded on it because he had not planned it to end this way. In his dreams he had satisfied his revenge by finally tossing the carcass out of the doorway himself, as unfit for his consumption. The act of deliberately not devouring his enemy was one which he felt was symbolic of his utter contempt for magical hares. He called to the tower for sympathy.

—It escaped from me, tower.

—*Perhaps that was your intention, Bubba, to let the creature escape? So that it suffered the more. So that hope died gradually in its breast as it crawled away from here believing it would live?*

—Yes, yes, tower, you are always so comforting.

—*I merely speak the truth from the depths of my stone heart, as my brother did before me.*

So Bubba was mollified, the tower having come to his rescue once again. Stone was something he could rely on to confirm his opinion and set his mind at ease. He and the stones were so close in spirit as to be almost one.

Winter came upon the land, cruel as the claws of a mythical beast, sharp as the beak of a legendary bird. It left frost on the hair of the marshes, the reeds and grasses, turning it white and hoary as if with age. Creatures that lived on and around this land grew scarce, some finding holes in which to sleep, others migrating to warmer climates.

The backwaters of the brackish rivers froze over, leaving sticks like signposts jutting from the ice. There were many geese to eat, but men also came to hunt these fat foreign birds and Bubba had to be careful not to be seen. The rabbits were still there of course, and the now difficult to get at hares. With both of these creatures Bubba had to be patient and wait for mistakes, for he could not be assured of sweeping down and taking one when he felt like it. They had quickly learned ways to avoid him.

Bubba hated the winter with its cold hard nights and its wet frozen-fog days. Winds came across the flatlands, over the sea from the continent, with savage intent. Days were dark however, allowing Bubba a much wider hunting circle, so that he was able again to reach the hare colony on the island. In the murk of the winter light he was able to hide his flights from the people below and extend the distance. In any case, humans were not attentive during the winter. They moved between their houses quickly, wrapped to the eyes, and seldom stared around or above them, as they might do in the other seasons.

Bubba hated the winter though, because the cold seeped through his feathers, and chilled him. In his nest in the tower, he would dream himself back to being a chick, to a place where there were no winters, only hot sultry summer, never ending. In that place, green-dark and overgrown, he had never been cold. But mother had brought him here, where there were few trees and where the land froze over white for almost half the year.

Bubba cruised over this blinding landscape, looking for food in the gloom and found the white backdrop helpful in spotting quarry which still wore summer camouflage. He had taught himself a trick too, on the hard ground. He could land near a hare's form, and even if it had dug a short tunnel and was hiding in the U-bend, Bubba would peck its rump savagely, forcing it out head first. Then Bubba would snatch it up and carry it away, to feast on its entrails and gorge on its liver.

One day he landed near a wire gibbet in a field and found the carcass of a hare pinned to it. On inspecting its pelage, Bubba was certain that this was the hare he had incarcerated in his tower and was triumphant. Not only had the creature died in great distress, its starved figure had been humiliatingly displayed for all to see, a sort of testimony to Bubba's ruthlessness when dealing with his enemies. Even the magical hare had succumbed to his power.

Bubba cruised above the winding rivers and streams, watching for creatures crossing the ice, for he could snatch them more easily from the flat surface and when they tried to run they skidded and fell in their desperation. Once, over a bridge, Bubba almost stooped on a human baby in a carriage, but checked himself, knowing that once he had killed mother's kind he would be hunted down and destroyed. On that day he was unhappy, because it reminded him that he was not like mother, who had had no feathers, no claws, no beak.

—Tower, what am I?

—*You are Bubba.*

—Yes, Bubba is my name, given me by mother, but what am I? Bird, beast or man?

—*You are the dark lord of the flatlands, bird, beast and man in one. You are all that is strong in a beast, you have the power of flight, you have man's strength of will and ruthlessness. You are your mother's son.*

—But I look like nothing on this earth nothing on *this* landscape.

—*What are features, outward appearances? Does the mountain question its shape? Does the torrent ask why it is raging? You have been given gifts of talons and hook, of a sharp brain, of a completely cold heart. Are these not enough? It is what you can do that's important, not what you look like.*

—Yes, what I can do. And I have no match here, no peer, no rival. I am the ruler of all, the red slayer that has no equal, the assassin of the skies. They see my shape and tremble. They watch for my shadow on the pale earth, and they die of fright when they see it. I am what I am.

—*Precisely.*

Bubba never stopped asking the tower these kind of questions, for there was always that weak spot within himself which questioned his uniqueness. Bubba wanted a history, like all creatures. He wanted a lineage, a past, a time to look back on and dream of. He wanted ancestors to revere, to call his own, to ponder with pride.

He had mother of course, but was mother enough?

It seemed not, for the questions were always there, nagging at him, pricking him like the little hooks of teasels when they got under his feathers. They were parasites, these questions, feeding

273

on his uncertainty, his insecurity, his misery. He wanted to be happy. He desperately needed to feel complete, and he could never do that while he had no history beyond his own awakening in the world.

The tower never became impatient with these repeated requests for a past, and always treated such enquiries with seriousness. The martello tower (like his brother church tower) was Bubba's guardian, his surrogate parent, who had his welfare at heart and would protect him from his own fears, as well as from intruders and enemies.

Bubba was grateful to the tower, and if he had never been capable of affection, he at least thought of the tower with respect. They were like each other, wrought from the landscape, unique in their small world.

Chapter Thirty Six

Skelter left the yard the same day the new dog arrived. Perhaps the man of the house had planned it that way so that attention was taken away from Skelter, who had become a favourite of the little human which could make so much noise when it was displeased. A new arrival was always more interesting than an old pet and the youngster got caught up in the excitement of his siblings, capering around the yard, causing the new dog to become overexcited and yell foolish nonsensical things.

Anyway, the new dog was a mongrel, similar to the previous one, though of different colouring. She had a sort of dirty sandy coat. She was certainly very frisky and Skelter hoped they would not keep her chained up like the last one, to break her spirit. Her big brown liquid eyes might be her saving grace, however, and keep her from permanent shackles.

And when he came to think of the old guard dog it seemed to Skelter that his spirit must have been quite strong still for him to have planned his escape so well. Where was he now? In some kinder human household, or roaming free? Skelter would prefer the latter, but then he was not a dog. Dogs, he knew, liked a roof over their heads and a hand to feed them. They related much more to humans than to wild creatures, and those that were roaming free, were pretty weird creatures, it had to be said.

Immediately the new dog arrived the youngsters took her out for a walk.

The bearded human came on a bicycle, without his giant dog, to collect Skelter, whose cage was placed on the back of the machine, on a small rack. This was better than being in a vehicle, which Skelter had been dreading, and the man obviously had an idea that animals did not like being enclosed.

When they set off, at a gentle pace, Skelter was able to observe the countryside slipping by. Trees went running past them, going in the opposite direction, and the roadway flowed like a black river beneath. Everything was on the move, rushing back to where Skelter had come from, as if some great event was taking place precisely on the spot where he had been for the past few weeks.

He stared out over the leisurely moving fields. It was a cold world out there. The snow had gone but conditions were still icy and the hoar frost clung to the stark hedgerows as if it owned them. Everything crackled with frozen stiffness, even old leaves which the man rode over on his bicycle. It was a clear crystal day though and very fragile: a touch might shatter it into a million shards of light. Skelter could see for miles across the flatlands since he was higher than the hedgerow and he enjoyed the sensation.

At one point, he noticed a great deal of activity going on in a huge area a short distance away. A tall chainlink fence had been erected and there were diggers and tractors and all sorts of machinery at work laying a large concrete strip the size of several fields. There were buildings going up too, one taller than the rest: a sort of stubby tower with a glassed-around second storey. By the concrete strip were meadows of trimmed grass and Skelter could see one or two hares on this, eating mushrooms and seemingly oblivious of the workmen and the building. They obviously felt quite safe there.

The bearded man stopped his pedalling and stood for a while, scowling at the activity. It seemed he did not approve of what was going on, though it was difficult to tell how angry he was behind that black facial hair.

Eventually, the man climbed on his bicycle again and set off, glancing and muttering, until the building activity was out of sight.

Finally, they arrived at the cottage and Skelter got very excited, because he could see Whinsled Lea from his position on the back of the bicycle and knew that somewhere in that frosty field was a hare called Eyebright. It was almost too much to bear, being so close yet so far away. Freedom! He could smell it in the air.

Bess was there to greet her master with as much fuss as if he had been gone for several winters, and then she gave some attention to Skelter.

'He's got a run for you, out on the back lawn. The ground is like concrete though, so you won't be able to dig yourself out.'

'Thanks for telling me,' said Skelter, sourly.

'Oh, you'll be all right. I shan't be able to help you to escape – that would be more than my life's worth – but I'm sure he'll let you go in the end.'

'To a zoo place.'

Betsy shrugged and looked suitably sympathetic.

Once Skelter had been installed in the new run and the female of the house had cooed over him like a dove for a few minutes he did feel more secure. Even if he were transported away to a zoo it was better than being stuck on that piece of concrete outside the farm worker's house for the rest of his life. Even a zoo must be better than that. Furthermore, there might be a quick thaw before then: one or two hot days which would get rid of the top layer of frost in the soil. In which case Skelter could dig himself to freedom.

Skelter spoke to Betsy about the building activity he had seen out on the road.

'Yes, my master doesn't like that place, or what they're doing to it, but I have no idea why. Jittie the hedgehog has been inside . . .'

'But there's a tall chainlink fence all around the area,' protested Skelter.

'Oh, hedgehogs are good climbers. They'll scale a chainlink fence or an ivy-covered wall quicker than a hare can dig a form. Didn't you know that?'

'Well, in the highlands I didn't get much chance to talk to hedgehogs. I mean, I had my own family up there, anyway, so I didn't bother a great deal with other creatures.'

He looked at Betsy's enquiring features, feeling a little shame-faced that he had been such an elitist in the old days. It was true though, that when you had your own kind around you, you didn't bother too much with outsiders. In fact you treated them with contempt, only tolerating their presence, and sometimes even chasing them away. His cousins, brothers and sisters, aunts and uncles, nephews and nieces had surrounded him, cushioned him against the outside world. It was almost fortunate, from his spiritual standpoint, that he had been captured and given a look at the wider world.

'So no, I didn't know hedgehogs could climb.

Betsy nodded. 'They've got powerful little legs, each with a strong claw, and anything they can grip, like wire or ivy, they'll use to climb an object in their path. They can't climb trees of course, unless they're covered in ivy, but then why should they? Anyway, Jittie has been inside the area you're talking about, and she says she can't see what all the fuss is about. They're just putting up a few buildings and laying some flat roads.'

'They didn't look like roads to me. They were far too wide. And they stopped at both ends and the fields started again.'

'Well, I can only repeat what I've been told. I haven't been inside myself, though my master has taken me for a run and walked around the outside of the fence. Some other men came and barked at him, pointing back the way we had come, and my master retraced his steps. He was in a foul mood though and kept looking back at the people that had chased him away as if he wanted to punch their noses. Humans do that sometimes you know – punch noses. It means something in their culture.'

The run in the back garden of the cottage was infinitely more pleasant than the concrete slab which had been his previous home, but it was still not freedom. Skelter wondered whether Stigand would come to visit the garden as he said he often did so that Skelter could get word to Eyebright that he was alive and well and in need of assistance.

The man with the beard came out to look at him quite a lot, and the woman too. It was disconcerting to be stared at for hours on end as if he were a freak. The other thing that happened was that the man kept pointing a black box at him and making clicking sounds. At first Skelter had been afraid of this box because it was used like a gun, but when there were no loud explosions, and no missiles came his way he realised it was a harmless piece of equipment.

278

There were activities of interest in the garden. For instance, the man had many humane traps, in which he captured mammals and birds. These creatures were only retained for a short period of study before being released.

One trap was near to Skelter's cage. It was a net even flimsier than the one in which he had been captured himself during that hare-gathering in the highlands. This net, so fine that it was barely visible, was strung across the garden. In it the man caught small birds, which he ringed around their legs, then let go again. The birds suffered no real physical injury in the net, and the man or the woman was almost always on hand to rescue them quickly from its folds. Skelter could not even imagine what reason the man had for putting silver rings around birds' legs, and Betsy was no help either. If it made him happy, said the dog, where was the harm? Skelter was inclined to think that the harm was to the dignity of the creatures who suffered the humiliation and terror of being caught in a human spider's web, but he didn't argue with the dog, for she always came hotly to the defence of her master.

As it happened, the bearded man did not keep him long in captivity. One frosty morning the run was lifted suddenly and Skelter was grabbed and bundled into the bicycle box. Then he was taken for a longish ride.

Obviously the man had decided not to send him to a zoo but to let him go in the wild. Skelter was taken down to the marshes, presumably where the man felt he would be more at home when he was released, and there the cage was opened. It would have been better if the man had just lifted the run and let him out in the garden, but freedom was freedom. The man watched him walk off into the tall marsh grasses, where he stayed until he heard the bicycle leave.

'Free!' shouted Skelter, almost delirious with happiness.

He could hardly believe it.

He ran out of the marshes and into farmland. Once the short grasses were under his feet, he did something which hares reserve for very special occasions, for times like this, and which has rarely been observed by humans.

Skelter did a dancer's whirligig.

Standing on his hind legs, his ears flat against his head, Skelter spun like a top in the frosty grass, sending droplets of water spraying up from his hind paws. His front legs were held out straight and to the side, as he twirled on the spot, balancing his perfectly vertical stance. Faster and faster he went, the wind rushing in his ears, his hind paws tripping nimbly on the spot: a true dancer's feet. To any astonished onlookers it might seem as if he was attempting to drill through the earth's crust to its molten centre.

For him, it was a heady glorious experience: it was a dance to mark his moment of freedom.

The witnesses, animal and bird, to this extraordinary sight were amazed by it. A hare doing a vertical whirl was something they saw once in a lifetime if they were fortunate. It was a dance that was the morning's secret, something seen and gone like a passing dream, yet caught forever between the folds of light and shadow. His eyes held that look in them of formal ritual, full of pride in himself and his species. The excitement in him was evident in his rapid movement. He was the hare, the wild-headed madfooted breathless hare, who had danced on the lawns of God since the First Creation.

When he had finished, he fell forward on his forepaws, and lay still, resting for a few moments. The world waited with him. Then he was on his feet and bounding across the meadowland, scattering some rooks who happened to be sitting around a fence post plotting the humiliation of scarecrows.

When he came to the river he ran along its banks, looking for a narrow place to cross. The river was coursing through the countryside in a gentle winterly manner. The water looked as heavy as quicksilver, its currents like the rippling muscles of some giant serpent. By the time Skelter found a suitable crossing point, a bright light-yellow sun was on the world, causing the frost and ice to glitter. He entered the freezing water and swam the short stretch, most of his body above the surface. On the other side he stopped to shake himself free of the droplets before they froze in his fur.

He lay in the weak sun for a while, letting it warm him through before he continued his journey. In the direction in which he was heading the first hare he would encounter would be Followme, the moonhare. It might be best to see her in any case, since she was head of the colony and liked these marks of respect for her position.

Skelter set off for Booker's Field, where the hare totem tree, blanched whiter than the whitest snow by the hard sun of a thousand summers, its wood almost become stone, stood waiting for the return of its lost son. He and the totem had something in common now which had not been there before.

Chapter Thirty Seven

When Skelter reached Booker's Field there was a husk of hares around the totem. Followme and Reacher were there, and Hindwalker, and one or two others. The discussion they were having seemed to be intense, and Skelter approached slowly to surprise them with his presence. He could not see Eyebright amongst them though, which was disappointing.

Here and there on the ground had been flung patches of snow like cast-off pelts, mostly in the shadows of the hedgerow and trees and in the shallow ditch. Skelter was hot from his long run and decided to rest a while on one of these cold patches, waiting for a suitable time to interrupt the meeting.

'There's nothing we can do,' Reacher was saying. 'It's not Skelter's fault that things have turned out this way. The forms did protect us for a long while, remember.'

Skelter's ears pricked up at the mention of his name.

Moonhare said, 'What I can't understand is how the flogre manages to undermine everything we do. It must have some source of magic.'

'Let's face it,' said Hindwalker, 'the flogre *is* magic. We've come to accept its presence over the land, but when you think back, why, there's no other creature like it, is there? Where did it come from? Who are its parents? It just *appeared*, didn't it? I say it's been sent from the Otherworld, to rule over us. We should offer it sacrifices to appease it rather than running away and hiding from it. Maybe it would come less often then?'

Skelter couldn't believe his ears, but he remained quietly in the shadow of the tree.

Headinthemist said, 'What do you mean, *sacrifice*? Are you suggesting we should draw lots or something, and the loser just stand out there in the open, waiting to be snatched?'

'No, no,' Hindwalker replied, 'not us. But each set of parents should put up one of their leverets in turn. The older hares are established members of the colony but the young ones, well, some of them will die anyway. Why not give the weak ones to the flogre so the strong amongst us will live?'

Headinthemist let out a startled cry. 'That's a *terrible* thing to say. It's easy to see you haven't had any litters yet. I'm not giving up any of my leverets to save *you*.'

'Not to save *me*, to save us all. If the older hares are all killed, the young will die anyway, because there'll be no one to look after them. We have a duty to ourselves and the stronger leverets to survive the best way we can. It's the colony that's important here, not individuals. We can't afford to be sentimental.'

Sunhare said, 'I wish Skelter were here . . .'

'Skelter, Skelter, what good would it do us if he *was* here. If he hadn't taught us to make those mountain hare forms maybe the flogre wouldn't pick on us so much, maybe we made it so mad with us, it wants to wipe us out? There are plenty of other victims to be had – lambs, geese, rabbits. Why does it always come here? Skelter was probably the worst thing that ever happened to us. He left us with a curse.'

Moonhare said, 'Hindwalker may have a point.'

'No, no, I can't accept that,' said sunhare. 'Skelter did the best he could for us.'

'He came out of nowhere,' said moonhare.

'And taught us tricks that made the flogre furious with us,' cried Hindwalker.

Headinthemist said quietly, 'Well, he's gone now, and it's always easier to blame someone who's not here and can't defend himself, but I must admit he was a strange creature . . .'

Skelter could stand no more of this.

'What a lot of hypocrites!' he exclaimed. 'Not so long ago you were singing my praises. Now the first thing that goes wrong, you're blaming me for it. Blame *yourselves*, or better still, get your heads together and find a way out of your troubles. The flogre is the flogre. It's going to kill where the killing is easiest. What you must do is make it a little harder for him to get you, rather than other victims, and you, Hindwalker, you should be ashamed! To advocate sacrificing the young, so that the old may live. I never heard of such a selfish thing . . .'

After this speech, during which the other hares were standing, transfixed, staring at the patch of snow on which he stood, Skelter moved out onto the brown earth of the field.

Immediately, several piercing whistles went up from the husk of hares and most of them scattered, running over the fields.

Hindwalker alone was left frozen to the spot, trembling from head to toe. The fear in his face was terrible to see. Skelter looked around quickly for a fox or badger and seeing none, stared at the sky. There was nothing on the land or in the heavens.

'The totem will protect me!' shrieked Hindwalker, in quavering accents. 'You can't touch me while I'm by the totem.'

Skelter realised that the jack was talking to him.

'I wouldn't touch you with someone else's foot,' replied Skelter in disgust, 'let alone my own. What's the matter with you? What's the matter with *them*?'

He walked forward a few more paces.

At this movement, Hindwalker thawed and took flight. His fore and hind legs criss-crossed each other so rapidly in his panic to get away from Skelter that he tripped himself up twice and went tumbling over. He took the low hedge in one leap, sailing over it as easily as a hunter chasing a fox.

Skelter was mystified. What on earth was the matter with them all? Surely he wasn't such a formidable character as to frighten the wits out of them with his presence. Yes, he was angry with them, but most of them were big hares, larger than he was himself, and could box his ears for him. As a group, why they would have pummelled him into the ground with no bother at all. Had his legendary exploits grown so much out of proportion, that he now seemed invincible?

It was certainly very mysterious.

There was nothing for it but to go and find Eyebright, and find out from her what was going on.

He travelled across the fields again, occasionally sighting a hare he knew, only to have it go shrieking away, running as if a wildcat was after it.

When he reached Whinsled Lea he searched for Eyebright and found her down by the river. He approached her from behind, softly called her name. She turned, stared wide-eyed at him, then half-jumped, half-fell into the river. The current was fast and strong and it carried her some yards down the bank, where she scrambled out and took off over the grasslands.

Skelter had had enough.

'This is ridiculous,' he muttered, and raced after her.

He ran her to ground at the foot of a giant oak and as she cowered breathlessly, protected on all sides by the exposed roots of the tree, Skelter approached.

'Don't come any closer, ghost-hare,' she said. 'If my time has come, so be it. I'll accompany you to the Otherworld.'

'Ghost-hare?' cried Skelter. 'I'm not dead. It's me. Skelter.'

Eyebright stared at him, looking unconvinced.

Skelter said, 'Oh, I understand. You thought I'd been killed by the flogre, right? Well, I wasn't. A man captured me and I've been a prisoner for all this time, but I'm free now.'

'You may have been Skelter once,' whispered Eyebright, 'but you're definitely a ghost now. Don't you understand? This man, this place where you've been a prisoner, it must have been in the Otherworld.'

Skelter thought back over his experiences, wondering if perhaps she was right, since they were all so convinced he was dead. The more he thought about it, however, the more he knew they were wrong. He didn't *feel* dead, for a start. Then there was the bearded man and Betsy the dog: they weren't dead too were they? If they were it was a remarkable coincidence that all three of them died together.

'Why are you so sure I'm a ghost?' he finally asked her.

'You *look* like a ghost.'

He stared down at his white fur.

'I'm just *me*,' he replied, puzzled.

'Just your voice, but inside a white hare,' she said.

Skelter then remembered back to when the young humans had shown such an interest in him, at the beginning of winter, and how he had been the centre of attention for a while, until they got used to his new coat. *Now* he understood. It was that old monster raising its head again: ignorance. It was a question of winter whiteness.

'Listen,' he said, gently, 'there's no need to be frightened of me. I'm quite normal.'

'You don't look normal.'

285

'Maybe not to you, but I would to a mountain hare like myself. We *all* turn white in the winter, just like stoats, or ptarmigan. I don't suppose you've ever seen ptarmigan, but you've seen ermine, haven't you?'

'Yes.'

'Well then, you know that in the spring, summer and autumn, an ermine is a stoat, with a rusty coat – yet in the winter that coat turns white. I don't see the need to change my name like the stoat does, but my coat changes, just like his.'

Eyebright leaned forward.

'You're *not* a ghost-hare?'

'How could I be? I haven't been deified.'

'But you fought the flogre. Maybe that entitled you to become one of the elite?'

Skelter shook his head.

'I didn't fight the creature. I did what I set out to do, and got a good look at it, for all the help that's going to give us, but I have to say if it had come to a confrontation, it would have snapped me in two with one peck of its beak. It's a monster of a bird.'

She hopped forward.

'So you're just Skelter, with a winter coat?'

'What do I have to do, to convince you of that?'

She came forward, bravely, and sniffed his fur, wrinkling her nose.

'You smell like Skelter.'

'Good clean mountain smell, I hope, of heather and sedge, with a whiff of glen grass thrown in.'

'You sound like Skelter, too.'

'Good highland timbre, proud and simply magnificent.'

'Something like that.'

They stood for a while, together, sniffing each other and feeling the warmth from each other's fur. Skelter began to get embarrassed by her attention after a while, but remained where he was, allowing her time to get used to his strange coat. Now he knew the problem it was not difficult to see why he had frightened the other hares. If they had never seen a hare with a white pelage before naturally they would be startled and confused – just as he would have been perplexed if he had come back to find them all with pink eyes and yellow tails. The unusual caused alarm first, and curiosity followed quite a long while afterwards.

It took some time for Eyebright to relax but when she finally did so she demanded to know of his adventures. He began by describing the flogre: how it was a giant bird with talons the size of a man's hand and a terrible hooked beak as big as a hare's head; how its crown had a horizontal crest of feathers running from ear to ear; how its eyes were as cold and hard as quartz.

'It's impossible to imagine anything that could defeat such a creature,' said Skelter. 'I think it could kill even a fully-grown fox with ease.'

He then went on to describe his adventures from the point of meeting with his old friend Rushie in the tomb, to his capture by the man on the spiral staircase, the yard with the concrete run, then his eventual transfer to the cottage nearby, and freedom.

Eyebright nodded, at each turn of the events, not interrupting. When it was over, however, she expressed her happiness at finding him alive and well, and added, 'This, er, *Rushie*. Were you close friends?'

'Very close. We grew up in the highlands together. No doubt we would have been mates if we had stayed together.'

'I see,' said Eyebright, quietly.

'What? What's the matter?' asked Skelter.

Eyebright looked at the river as if it were a source of courage, and then told him.

'I'm afraid Rushie is dead. She was taken by the flogre, who for some unknown reason did not eat her. He let her starve in his tower. She escaped and made her way back to the marsh hares and was met on the journey by Creekcrosser – he's one of her old colony. She died right in front of him. I'm sorry.'

It took a few moments for the information to sink in.

Then Skelter said, 'She *starved* to death?'

'Yes.'

Skelter ground his teeth, and he too looked out over the swirling waters of the river. He was quiet for a long while. There was in his eye a faraway look, as if he were not on the flatlands at all but in some other place beyond normal vision. Owls had that look sometimes, when the world was bleak and bare in winter, and food was scarce. They sat on a post and gazed into the middle

287

distance with undisturbable firmness, and it was as if they were staring across infinity and wondering how long it would take to fly to the far side. Skelter's look was that of a wintering owl.

Finally he turned to Eyebright and said, 'You say it was a hare called Creekcrosser that went out to find her? Not one named Racer?'

'Racer was interested in her as a mate, but it was Creekcrosser who went after her. I don't know what it was all about.'

'Thanks for telling me, Eyebright. Nothing we can do now, is there? Now, how are we going to go about telling the colony about *me* . . . ?'

Chapter Thirty Eight

It was not surprising that the colony was concerned over the change in Skelter's pelage, for the legends told of many magical hares with different coloured coats: experiments of Kicker when that first great hare began producing various species of *lagomorphs* to cover the earth. Perhaps the colony believed Skelter to be one of these ancients, returned to a period of time not its own, to disturb the living.

Among the first of the primal *lagomorphs* were the midnight hares, or jewelled hares, that crowd the heavens. This was long before the humans came out of their caves in the ground according to the hares, out of the sea-of-chaos according to the canids. This was in the time when there were giants on the earth, and when rocks and minerals were living things, before they had been frightened into immobility and their present inanimate state by the coming of men.

Once God had created the hermaphrodite Kicker, the great hare was left to get on with populating the earth with its own kind, in competition with the other original giants, like A-O the first fox, and Sen-Sen, the first wolf. In the beginning there was the shaping of the world to carry out, which each original giant did to their own specifications. This often resulted in several reshapings. For example, Oomaroo the first otter wanted the world to be mostly rivers, and used sharp incisors to cut thousands of canals through every piece of landmass. Then Riff, the first deer, who liked huge plains to roam, followed behind and filled most of them in again, leaving just enough to provide waterholes for those deer he-she would create to cover the land.

Kicker made the flatlands for the brown hares, and the mountains for the blue hares. However, when it came to the actual creation, Kicker was as inexperienced as any other artistic beginner, and his-her initial impulse was to go for the gaudy, the showy, the flamboyant. Kicker wanted something to match the parrot for colours, the lion fish for style, the anaconda for sleekness.

The first of these experiments was the crystal hares of the snow country to the north, which Kicker made from the finest desert sand fired in the furnace of the sun. These creatures were as clear and fragile as thin freshwater ice and roamed the cold zones of the earth for a short time. But their feet were too slippery and they kept falling off cliffs and shattering on the rocks below. Soon they were so few in number they could not find each other to propagate and quickly died out.

Then came the painted wooden hares of the forested lowlands, but these creatures with live sap in their veins instead of blood, were lazy and spent most of their time in their forms. Consequently in the rainy season they took root and grew into other things, such as trees and bushes.

Next came the stone hares of the mountains, who lasted a great deal longer than the crystal or wooden hares, though eventually they too disappeared under the onslaught of the inclement weather, worn down by wind and rain, cracked by the hot sun, they eroded to become the mere pebbles and rocks that now lie helpless on the hillsides.

Kicker's most wonderful achievement of these times of experimentation, before he-she perfected the art and produced the brown, the blue, the Irish, the jackrabbit, the snowshoe and all the other species of blood, flesh and bone hare that roam the earth today, was the beautiful jewelled hares. Kicker was determined that this creation would neither take root nor wear away with the weather, nor shatter when they fell over. So he made them of the hardest materials he could find.

These marvellous hares, though a worthy artistic accomplishment, were caused to depart the earth, they were not doomed like the others to extinction. During the daylight hours these dazzling creatures were fashioned of lapis lazuli, with aquamarine eyes, but at night their bodies changed to dark sapphire, and their eyes turned to diamonds. They fed on precious and semi-precious minerals like opals, garnets, moonstones and bluejohn. They were placid timid creatures, despite the hardness of their bodies, and bothered no other being, since they were not competition for grasslands or bushes and trees, nor did they attack and kill other animals and birds for food. They wanted no water to sustain them and their feeding grounds were the mines they created in the barren hillsides and mountains avoided by other lifeforms.

However, these exquisite hares were still around when men entered the world and were immediately coveted by the bipeds because of their innate beauty. Men began to trap them and use them in their trading with one another, sometimes prising out the eyes to put into settings on their finger rings and pendants. Naturally the jewelled hares went into a panic whenever they saw a man, and great migrations began as herds moved from one part of the earth to another, swarming in husks over continents, sometimes falling into the ocean where their weight caused them to sink immediately to its depths.

Finally, in desperation, they fled to the skies, the last sanctuary from man, where they still crowd to this day. They are so thick in numbers that only occasionally does the old sky – a bright scarlet-coloured heaven – show through their blueness during the twilight hours, when the sun is on the move and its heat causes the hares to shuffle aside and clear a path for the fiery disc. At night, when they change to dark sapphire, only their glittering diamond eyes are visible from below.

Men tried to get their giant Groff to stand on the highest mountains of the earth and pluck the hares from the sky, but even though Groff is the tallest giant the world has ever known he could not reach high enough to grasp the bounty of the sky. The tips of his fingers could barely brush the smooth rump of the lowest jewelled hare, and these treasures remained out of his clutches until man stopped believing in him and he faded away to mist.

The flesh-and-blood hares that inhabit the earth today often witness men staring up at the Kicker's jewelled hares, no doubt still coveting the opulent rewards of Kicker's fertile creativeness and hoping one will lose its grip and drop down to earth.

Occasionally, amongst the more elderly of the midnight hares, an eye works loose and its owner cannot prevent the precious stone from falling down the face of the sky to land somewhere in the deserts and barren places of the world. This gives rise to expeditions of men who go out into the wilderness to look for these gems, often to die of thirst and hunger, disease and injury, in their plaintive search for wealth. In this way the jewelled hares obtain their slow revenge on man, through the latter's foolish regard for shiny stones and metals.

Every once in a while, Kicker visits his-her hares in the sky, coming in the guise of a great storm, the dark pelage crackling with electric fire, and the great teeth grinding in fury. In the occasional flashes of anger at the way hares have been treated by men, and it has to be said, foxes and wolves and other carnivores, Kicker often slams down a hind leg on a storm cloud, creating a thunderous sound in the heavens.

On summer days though, when the air is clear through to the lapis lazuli, embedded with aquamarines that melt into the bluer colour of the jewelled hares' diurnal coats, most creatures of the world are thankful that these precious mammals retreated to the heavens. For who would want to laze under a blood-drenched sky, reddening the bushes and grasses with its scarlet hues, menacing the hills with its crimson backdrop? Red is not a colour which inspires calmness. It is a dangerous tint, causing restlessness and unease. Whereas skies of cornflower blue are quiescent and full of tranquillity.

So say the hares of hill and lowland, anyway.

PART SIX

*

Frost Dancers

Chapter Thirty Nine

Eyebright went away for some time, then returned and asked Skelter to accompany her to Booker's Field, where the whole colony was gathered under the totem tree. When Skelter arrived at the traditional meeting place, he found the hares waiting for him. Eyebright joined them and for a while they simply stared at Skelter, one or two of them obviously nervous. The young ones were at the back, peering over the shoulders of the adults, as if Skelter were some kind of monster.

Finally, moonhare walked forward.

'Eyebright tells us you are alive and that the reason for your white pelage is that all mountain hares turn white in the winter.'

Skelter nodded. 'This is true. In the same way that stoats change into ermine. This is not an uncommon winter change.'

'Yet,' said Followme, 'you don't think to change your name, the way stoats do?'

'It's nothing to do with me,' replied Skelter, becoming a little annoyed with all the fuss. 'I don't have any control over what colour my coat is. It changes on its own. So far as I know, we're hares in the summer and hares in the winter, whatever the colour of our fur.'

Moonhare stared back at the still quiet husk of hares behind her, and finally she turned and said, 'Welcome home, Skelter.'

With that the hares began creeping forward, all murmuring, 'welcome home', but still cautious. Skelter thought them a silly bunch but had to remind himself that they were not worldly, like him, and had never been beyond the island. In fact many of them had not been outside the fields owned by the colony. They came forward and sniffed him, and stared in wonder at his white pelage.

Moonhare was giving a speech at the same time.

'May the tractor bestow happiness on you, Skelter, for your efforts so far in helping us defend ourselves against the flogre. May the five-barred gate grant long life to you and may that life, by the power of the big red barn, be a healthy one.'

'And may the many-eared corn grant you fertility,' murmured someone in his ear, and when Skelter turned to see who it was he found himself looking into the eyes of Eyebright.

'Thank you very much,' he murmured back, a little confused, then loudly, 'Thank you, moonhare, for your welcome. Thank you all.'

Once they had got over the white coat they seemed genuinely pleased to see him and asked about his adventures concerning his quest for the flogre. He repeated what he had told Eyebright, and the hares looked suitably horrified when he told them about the bell tower, though his description of the monster he had seen was news to them no longer, since the flogre was now landing on the ground, and had been observed from close quarters by many of the hares.

'There is no way to defeat such a creature,' he told them, 'so we must learn to counter it. We have to invent new ways of thwarting its rapacious ways. We're not *dim*. We're *hares*, clever as they come. Let's do something about this new development instead of moaning about it. We don't have to live with it.'

Reacher, the sunhare, said, 'Or *die* with it.'

'Tell me about the trouble you've been having,' said Skelter, 'so I can form a better picture of the problem.'

Followme, the moonhare, said, 'I don't want to influence this meeting, but I have something to say.'

She walked away from the group and sat on a half-exposed root of the dead totem tree, which was her seat when she was holding counsel. She stared out over the hares until they took the hint and gathered around her, awaiting her words. It always amazed Skelter what power she seemed to have over them, though she did very little for them, so far as he could see.

Moonhare spoke.

'As you are all – except Skelter – aware, we are experiencing greater losses this winter than we have ever known before. The flogre has a new trick,' she stared at Skelter as she said these words, 'of landing near the forms and pecking at a hare's rump to

296

force it to leave its tunnel. Then the unfortunate hare is snatched up and taken away to be eaten. If things go on as they have been doing we shall soon be in danger of extinction. I should like to hear what Skelter has to say about this.'

Skelter cleared his head before he spoke.

'Fact is,' he replied, 'the forms we make in the mountains are to protect us against golden eagles. We either use a space between two or three rocks, of which there are none suitable on the flatlands, or dig the short tunnel I have shown you. Golden eagles do not land on the ground and force the hare from its form.

'Now, perhaps the answer to this new trick it has is to dig deeper forms, but I'm sure you've already thought of that. Can I just say that though the season is barely two months old, spring will be with us one day, and the flogre will then have to be more careful. The dark days of winter won't be with us forever, and the flogre needs the half-light as camouflage. It knows that if men see it and report it there will be a hue and cry, and they'll hunt it down.

'We must hope for this to happen. At the moment the flogre has to fly a long way from the martello tower to reach our colony, and as spring and the possibility of lighter days approach it may decide that such flights are too dangerous. It will then have to hunt in the vicinity of its nest. This is a strong possibility.

'Of course, it's not the answer, because we have *next* winter to worry about, when the flogre will no doubt be back again on regular forays. As for protection until then, all I can suggest is that during dull days, especially dusk and dawn, you seek out hiding places, under walls and tree roots. I know this is not our way, but these are unusual times, *difficult* times, and we have to protect ourselves as best as we can.

'I have heard that you're considering sacrificing the weak leverets to this monster. Can I say that apart from being barbaric and unharelike, this would not achieve anything. The flogre is a monster – we can only guess at the amount of meat it needs to sustain it – but I think we can say quite positively that the runts of our litters will not satisfy its voracious hunger.

'Now, I think this is the longest talk I've ever had to give in my life, and I'll shut up.'

Moonhare was obviously not happy with Skelter's answer and had no doubt been expecting a more positive reply recommending action against the monster, but she accepted his ideas. At least he had offered hope with the coming of the spring, and hope was important. The meeting broke up and hares went their various ways, to seek new hiding places.

Skelter and Eyebright returned to Whinsled Lea and searched the area for a protective place out of the open. In the corner of the field was an old marble horse trough, no longer used but probably too heavy to bother removing. One end of the supporting structure had collapsed, so that the trough was at an angle, like a ramp. The two hares dug themselves shallow forms under the collapsed end, until they had a marble roof. The stone supports were still there, though they had slipped to either side and jutted like wings from the corners of the trough. These provided protection on either side of the forms.

In this way the two hares had solid stonework fortifications on three sides of them, and above, and the entrances were in a very tight space below the sloping bottom of the trough. There was no way a rook could squeeze in the space to get at them, let alone the flogre. So long as they were not caught out in the open they would be safe. A fox or badger could dig them out of course, but then if they smelled a four-footed predator coming, they could dash out into the open, where their legs could save them, as they always had done.

The winter moved on through snow and ice, wind and rain, with occasional clear sharp days. The flatlands were even flatter in the cold seasons. The weight of the snow and the driving rain flattened the grasses and winter crops. The marshland reeds bowed under the press from above. There was no foliage to block the view. It was a time the hares enjoyed, for there is nothing better to a field hare than being able to see across the world, from one side to the other.

On the stark trees and hedges the ivy had remained in blossom a little longer than usual, and drone bees, driven from their hives by the workers, still clustered on the pale yellowish-green blossoms to eat the intoxicating nectar. Winter moths too drifted dusty and dim between bunches of flowers, weaving drunkenly, watching other insects fall buzzing to the ground in their inebriated state.

Closer to the ground, beneath an overhang of bracket fungi on an elm near the trough, a troop of snails had sealed themselves into their shells with their own slime, not to emerge until warmer weather.

Men had been busy while Skelter was in prison. In the field over the river stood a haystack, covered by a tarpaulin sheet. In the early part of the winter, while the jack was behind the wire, the farm workers had threshed the ricks of corn, and got rid of the shucks and chaff and built themselves a straw copy of their houses.

In the season when the grasses are beaten down the backwater meers are dominated by the brown bolts of the bulrushes through which the white-nosed coots swim. The marshlands are populated by many forms of birdlife, some of them immigrants like the Brent geese, just for the winter. The redpolls, siskins, fieldfares and redwings escape a harsher whirlwind ice in the north by making the same journey as the geese.

Shortly after Skelter arrived home the marsh hares sent a messenger to Moonhare to ask if they could join with her colony. Their numbers had been depleted so much by the flogre that they were on the edge of extinction. Seahare and skyhare had both been taken and only seven hares remained including Racer and Creekcrosser.

Moonhare granted the request. Skelter believed this was because moonhare felt it would increase her prestige to have another colony under her control, but he had to admit she was under that haughty exterior basically a kind hare. So seven unfamiliar hares were allowed into the vicinity.

The new hares were put into the fields of the hares which had been taken by the flogre, and fitted comfortably. There is basically no difference between a hare that lives on the edge of the marshes and a hare that lives in the field, apart from some slight nuances of culture. They are the same species, right up to the black tips on their ears, a distinguishing feature shared by Skelter and his blue mountain hares, but not by the common rabbits that made such a mess of the crops. Few creatures will live with rabbits for neighbours because of this habit of leaving their feeding grounds in such a terrible state, and the black tips helped hares to separate themselves from the slatterns of the animal world. These markings were mentioned in almost every hare song and verse and story since the seasons began their gentle rhythms.

The season grew harder and ghostly delicate skeletons, the haulms of cow-parsnip and red campion, framed the ditches. Laurel leaves, crushed by the car wheels on the lane to the church, let out a pungent almond odour which Skelter found quite pleasant. The winds from the east became sharper and colder, savaging everything in their path. The flogre came and went, less successful now because of Skelter's advice to find protection. Many of the hares discovered holes at the foot of drystone walls and used these for shelter, though they felt uncomfortable and less secure from other predators.

There were occasional meetings at night under the white totem in Booker's Field, but nothing new came of these. Most of the hares were resigned to sit out the winter, hoping that Skelter was right and that when the spring came the flogre would not be able to venture far from his martello tower and would seek out new hunting ground to the east.

Skelter's relationship with Eyebright grew stronger, though he often thought of Rushie in a sentimental way, which left him sighing and unhappy. At first Eyebright used to ask him what was the matter, but when he declined to answer she left him alone, thinking perhaps that he was yearning for his highlands, a place she would never know nor understand, a place of dreams as far as she was concerned.

She was sometimes right, for he would stare at a Scots pine, the needles of which the ants used to build their nests, and his heart turned to amber sap, and his eyes saw the rugged hills and mountains of his birthplace.

Yet, he was contented enough, most of the time. Eyebright was an exceptional jill and he was determined to make her his own when the frost dancing came around.

He had to keep reminding himself that she had yet to be won, despite her obvious preference for him.

Chapter Forty

One hoary morning about fifty days after Skelter had rejoined the colony he woke with the blood singing in his ears. His head felt hot and his whole body was electric with excitement. There were bees, swarms of bees, buzzing in his loins. His breath was coming out short and sharp. He felt *alive*. He felt in prime condition. His white fur was crackling with static and his eyes were as hot as two tiny suns. At that moment if the flogre had flown over him he would have leapt a thousand feet in the air, and bitten off its head. Nothing was beyond his capability. He was immortal, invincible, hare of extraordinary powers. He was Skelter.

Around him the world was sparkling, the sun glinting from a clear sky of thrush egg blue. Everything was bright and new and full of zest. He loved it. He loved the world. It was effervescent and he was king of the mountain, prince of the field.

Up he went on his hind legs, chest puffed out, and walked around in a circle, staring across fields powdered with cold dust. He whistled, the sound going out like an arrow, towards the place where a husk of hares was gathering. There was a returning whistle.

It was the frost dancing time.

Eyebright was gone from her bed under the marble trough, and Skelter was a little hurt that she hadn't waited for him. He set off after her, the frost flying in clouds under his feet, determined to catch up with her. He took a low hedge with the ease of a riderless hunter, sailing over it and landing in a shower of frost on the other side. Eyebright was just ahead.

'Hey, wait for me!' he cried in excitement.

'Can't!' she called back. 'Bad form.'

He hardly heard her, his mind was alive with insects like jewels and there were birds in his feet.

When he reached the totem, Eyebright was just gathering her

breath. She stared at him, her eyes flashing messages and he could hardly contain his excitement. He raced around in a circle, went up on his hind legs and did a little jig to try and work off some of the excess exhilaration.

The other hares too were in the same state of enthusiasm, even moonhare. Normally stately, dignified and reserved, moonhare was leaping and rolling, cavorting in front of Reacher, who seemed mesmerised by her behaviour. Other hares were on their hind legs, some already boxing each other, though not at all seriously yet, just warming up.

Longrunner dashed at Eyebright and nipped her rump, and she batted him on his nose with her paw. She did not appear to be in the least bit offended by this attention from Longrunner. In fact she seemed flattered and excited by it, and for a moment Skelter faltered, realising he had a serious rival. Eyebright was fond of him, Skelter, but like all the hares, her blood was singing and all her reserve was gone. She was out of her head with the excitement of the time. She had made no promises to Skelter, nor to anyone, for that was not good form. She was still to be won, no matter how much preference she had shown for him in the past.

This would have sobered any other creature but a hare at frost dancing time. Instead of being shocked and stunned by her behaviour, Skelter was thrilled by it. She was not just any jill, she was *desired* by other hares, by such strong and handsome hares as Longrunner. She was magnificent, beautiful, charged with delightful attractions. Skelter would have danced through fire for her at that moment.

Instead, he skipped over to her on his hind legs, displaying his lean mountain hare's body for her benefit, shouldering Longrunner out of the way as he did so.

Her eyes sparkled, watching him sway before her.

From her shadow world Skelter's ghost-hare watched her charge, willing for his victory over any jacks that might battle with him for the favours of Eyebright. Skelter had always been a favourite with her, even though she had other hares to look after: she found him earthly-attractive and wistfully wondered what it would be like to have flesh around her spirit and hot blood in her veins once again. He was such an appealing jack, especially when he was on his hind legs like that, with his eyes full of fire. Such a noble visage, such muscled flanks and strong hind legs. Her body was dust, but her carnal desires remained.

Now Longrunner knew that he was not going to get a walkover. He would have to fight the small but tough highlander, who had braved flogres in church towers, travelled on great journeys across the world, escaped a hare coursing, knew of wildcats and golden eagles, and was still alive to tell the tale. Skelter was a formidable opponent, despite his stature: a muscled little hare with the spirit of a wolf.

Longrunner went up on his hind legs and batted Skelter lightly round the head, letting him know that the challenge had been accepted, though the fight would come in order of precedence, after the older jacks had settled their affairs and ensured their jills.

Suddenly, all movement stopped. The hares went quiet and still, and only their steamy breath moved in the morning air. It came out in plumes from every mouth and filtered into the blueness. The frosted fields stretched away on all sides, flat and cold, a brown rise and furrow showing just here and there. The hedgerows had crystallised, the trees had petrified.

Across Booker's Field came a figure, a man, bearing something in his hand.

The hares remained as still as death as the man approached, passing near the five-barred gate. His breath was coming out as sprigs of steam. It was the tractor-man and in his hand he had a small bunch of crocuses, white and yellow. He did not see the hares, though there were many around him, for his eyes were wet and his attention was on another world. He went to the foot of the tree, where the two bodies were buried, and laid the flowers on the patch of earth. Then he stood for a long time, staring down at the place, making mewling noises like a kitten with his mouth.

Finally, he took off his flat cap, ran his fingers over his head, then turned and walked away.

303

The hares waited until he was on the far side of the field, then sprang to life again, dancing and cavorting.

The first to make a claim for Followme was of course Reacher. The sunhare went up on his strong hind legs and danced in front of moonhare, his feet spraying onlookers with frost dust and his fur scattering drops of moisture gathered from rolling on the ground.

Fleetofoot went up to meet him after first doing a preliminary dance in front of the jill in question, as required by etiquette. Not that he wanted the matronly moonhare especially, though he would probably like to be sunhare, but more because no jill should go unchallenged. It was not very flattering to have only one hare stand up for you, and Fleetofoot was ever one for correctness and courtesy. Just because he was ready to box Reacher for his jill, did not mean he could not box again, for another female, if he lost.

Reacher, who was the largest jack in the colony, flattened his opponent with several short sharp jabs, and then a push in the chest with both front paws. Fleetofoot went over on his back and signalled that it was all over, he accepted defeat. It was not much of a match, but then it was not expected to be, for the two jacks were just going through the motions for the benefit of moonhare, who sat looking imperious and grand as the short fight took place.

Two more sets of hares boxed for females, then something interesting happened.

One of the new jacks, from the marsh colony, stood up for Bittersweetinspring. Immediately, another newcomer stood up with him. They did their dances in front of the jill and then a savage battle took place. What it was all about, the tree totem hares had no idea, but obviously there were some old scores being settled here.

The jack that had watched and waited for Racer to place his claim was called Creekcrosser, and two more different hares were not likely to be found in any community.

Racer was long, finely-muscled and one of the most handsome jacks ever to walk on four legs. In viewing him, Skelter had to admit a pang of envy, mixed with some other feelings concerning his old friend Rushie. He could understand however, why she had fallen for the jack, whose body was so perfect it verged on the insipid. Skelter could tell he was a total conformist, without asking any of his former colony. He looked like a hare that rarely put a paw wrong, was deferential to the colony's elders, cared for his appearance, and ran and walked to a fine degree of excellence. Skelter found him boring, thinking that just an iota of wickedness would improve the jack no end.

Creekcrosser, on the other side, was a rangy-looking beast, smaller in stature than Racer, but with a tough stringiness about him. His fur was slightly unkempt, as if he scorned the idea of preening himself and he had a rebellious air about him, in his face, in his demeanour. He was often close to insolent with the elders, when he believed something stupid was being said or done, and his behaviour caused much gossip among the matronly jills. He had many times been in danger of being ostracised from his old colony, though he had been a little more conservative in his ways under moonhare, who would have thrown him out much more rapidly than his old seahare.

So these were the two combatants who were battling for Bittersweetinspring, herself a creature that jacks from her own colony were wary of standing up for. They knew her hidden ways, for though she was a very beautiful hare she was also sulky and petulant, wanting attention, yet when it was given, rejecting it with disdain.

Creekcrosser boxed well, but his stamina was his worst enemy. He was no real match for the larger Racer and took several unnecessarily vicious blows to the face which left bloody claw marks. It was obvious to the spectators that he was likely to lose an eye or something if he continued, but he refused to give in. It seemed that nothing would make him step down, and in the end Racer began to tire a little and Creekcrosser managed to get in one or two well-placed punches himself, making his opponent's eyes water with the sting of them.

The eventual outcome of the match was in no doubt however, and missing several pieces of facial fur, Creekcrosser finally conceded victory, though you could tell it almost broke his heart. He limped away, having damaged his right foreleg, to the periphery of the field, to nurse his wounds. When Skelter went across to him, he found the jack almost beside himself with frustration, grinding his teeth and slamming his hind leg down on the hard frozen ground.

'I wouldn't worry too much about losing that one,' said Skelter, trying to cheer him up. 'She's not worth it. Bittersweetinspring would have given you a terrible time, with her moods . . .'

'Who asked for your opinion?' snapped Creekcrosser, glaring at him.

Skelter was a little taken aback. 'Well, no one, I just thought . . . ?'

'That's just the trouble with you jacks, you think too much, and where did you get that stupid white coat?'

Skelter could see what was happening now.

'It's no good picking a fight with me at the moment,' he said. 'I've got to box for my jill so I'm not going to get into any battle with you. If you think that bashing me will help rid you of your frustrations over losing to Racer, well fine, I'll come back later and let you have a go.'

Creekcrosser stared at him, then sighed. 'I'm sorry, it's just that . . . look, you knew Rushie, didn't you? You were her friend. How can you stand to see that obscenity on four legs walking around, getting any jill he pleases, and not feel angry? He should have protected Rushie, stood by her, instead he turned his back on her when she needed him the most. I could tear his head off and stamp it flat.'

'I have no idea what went on between him and Rushie, but I'll tell you this, Rushie was no fool. She might have fallen for his looks in the beginning, but once she found out what a shallow creature he is, she would have scorned him.'

Skelter let this sink in before going on.

'So,' he continued, 'you boxed Racer because of what he had done to Rushie? You didn't actually want Bittersweetinspring – you just didn't want *him* to have her? Well, my friend, I think you'll be glad you lost, because he's going to get a bit of a shock, that one. No doubt he's after her because she's beautiful, but she didn't earn her name by being a predictable loving creature. I've been told she's hell to mate with, because she encourages you

306

one minute and rejects you right on the point of . . . well, to be fair to her, she's probably getting her own back on us jacks for something that's happened earlier in her life. I just wouldn't want to be the scapegoat for someone else's crimes. I tell you brother, she has moods on her that make the flogre look like a baby sparrow in comparison, and Racer is one jack that's going to *suffer*. Serve him right for going for looks instead of soul, eh?'

Creekcrosser was quiet for a minute, then wiped away a trickle of blood from his nose with his paw.

'Aw,' he said, 'you're all right, Skelter. I'm . . . I'm sorry I – you know.'

'Don't worry about it.'

'You better get back to the frost dancing – looks like Longrunner is standing up for Eyebright, if I'm not mistaken.'

'What?' Skelter whirled round, and indeed there was Long-runner, up on his hind legs, dancing before Eyebright. Skelter cursed. *He* should have been the first one up, calling for challengers, not Longrunner. Now he was already starting off at a disadvantage and Eyebright would think he was simply making a challenge for her because he was expected to, not because he wanted to. It would look to her that he had deliberately vacated his place at the dancing to get out of being the one to stand up for her first.

He raced back to the dancing area, thinking that life was a stoat's orphan, and somehow he always managed to get himself into trouble without really trying. Now he had to make a good showing, or spend the mating season counting the leaves appearing on the branches. Not just a good showing: he had to win. By the time he reached the circle, his heart was pounding.

He skidded to a halt and went up on his hind legs.

'Let's go,' he said to Longrunner, hoping to make up for his errors so far by showing Eyebright how eager he was to box for her favours.

Then he remembered he hadn't first danced in front of his hoped-for mate – another *faux pas* – she would feel insulted by his casual attitude towards her.

I'm doing really well, he told himself as he noticed the

307

fierceness in Eyebright's expression when she caught his eye, *really* well.

Even if he won she was going to tear him limb from limb, and throw the carcass to the crows.

Life was really a stoat's orphan.

Chapter Forty One

Longrunner was quite tall when he stood on his hind legs, but he was not as stocky as Skelter. Skelter was perhaps half-a-head shorter, with shoulders thicker and stronger. His bullet head was more firmly fixed on those shoulders, too.

Longrunner was an older jack with more experience, and had already gone through one frost dancing. Skelter had heard no ill of him though, and his character was known to be dependable, if leaning towards the stolid. The jill Longrunner had won last year had been taken by the flogre and only one of his leverets was still alive, now a yearling.

They considered each other worthy adversaries.

The two hares went into each other straight away, without any preliminary jigging around. Their paws flew, and though he had to reach up a little, Skelter got one or two blows into Longrunner's face.

Unfortunately for the highlander, his head was just the right height for Longrunner's punches and no matter how many blows he got in, Longrunner gave him three in return. It was going to be a test of stamina, for Skelter was only going to give up when his heart gave out, and mountain hare hearts are made of good stout stuff, strengthened by highland pride.

During the fight, Skelter's mind kept returning to his heather-covered hills: the stone-and-turf crofts with the peat smoke curling from their chests; the golden eagles gliding through the glens, with gemstone eyes and wicked beaks; the wildcats with their array of pointed weapons; the deer with their elaborate signals and visible pattering hearts; the purple saxifrage and heather forming the mountain's skirt. This was what he was fighting for, as much as his potential mate. The homeland that he would never see again. The Screesiders amongst the rugged tumbledown rocks, dancing *now* on the springy turf between the boulders. All this, which he missed to the bottom of his heart, was part of his reason for needing to win.

Once or twice both boxers glanced towards the jill they were fighting for to gauge what effect their success would have on her. It was obvious to both of them, for every time Skelter took a blow, Eyebright winced. And every time he gave a blow in return, an eager look sprang to her face.

Longrunner redoubled his attacks on Skelter's head, the blows stinging the highlander, driving him backwards. The two hares frequently dropped onto all fours, then came back up again onto their hind legs to renew their efforts. The fight would be over when one of them stayed down on all paws, while the other went back up. It was a furious match, with blinding blows flashing against the sparkling frost, and back legs dancing to keep the boxer's balance.

Skelter was forced backwards to the edge of the ring of hares, and there he dug in, held on and traded punch for punch, knowing that when he did hit, it hurt his opponent. His short legs were thick and stubby with all the strength of a climber's shoulders behind them. His was not a clean body made for swift running on the flat – not lean and lithe – his were limbs and shoulders that were needed to power an uphill climbing run. They were not made for top speeds, but for traction and endurance, surefootedness, grip. His legs did not *carry* him forward, they *drove* him, usually onward and upward. Had he been in a race against Longrunner he would have lost, but in a boxing match he could take the blows and deal them out twice as hard.

Gradually he began to wear the field hare down, gaining in authority after every short four-cornered rest, actually feeling his potency increase as Longrunner's energy diminished. His was a body used to circumnavigating tors on steep slopes, and his hind legs could bear his weight all day. His stamina was unmatched by any amongst these brown hares. He was the rugged hillsider, the fell runner, whose chunky form was made for durability. Longrunner might as well have been thumping away at a geological mass. If Longrunner had been the wind and rain, the field hare might have eroded the highlander in ten thousand years but that was the only way he was going to win.

Longrunner began to lose heart.

Poor Longrunner. By all reckoning, taking into account his length, his reach, and his experience, he should have won without too much of a problem, but how could he win against a hare with the whole of the highland country behind him, with the jill in question urging him to victory with looks if not with words? The flatlander jack fought with great vigour, with skill and determination, but eventually the tough little highlander wore him out. Longrunner came to a point where his blows seemed to have no further effect, and Skelter appeared like a half-buried boulder, impossible to knock over.

In the end Longrunner's spirit finally gave out when he saw how futile was his task. He fell away, conceding victory.

At that point in time Skelter had almost had enough, and was going on blind persistence only. He was so grateful for Longrunner giving in, he almost fell on him sobbing with relief, but fortunately retained his dignity. Going over to the other jack he said, 'A good match. You almost had me there. I think my joints must have locked, otherwise I would have fallen over.'

Longrunner, fighting to get his breath back, shook his head.

'You would *never* have fallen over. It was like fighting stone – all I was doing was scratching the surface.'

The other hares, apart from Eyebright, and perhaps Creekcrosser, were not so happy with the result. Skelter was an outsider, a small blue hare come down from the highlands, and in the first round of frost dancing he had beaten one of their best boxers. It was not something that would have had them prancing among the buttercups in delight. They stared at him sourly and exchanged dour looks as he cleaned up his wounds.

Moonhare was even suggesting that the fight had not been legitimate and that it should be fought again at some time in the future.

'Skelter should have first observed the formalities and performed the courtesy dance before Eyebright. There's been a breach of protocol here. I'm not sure we should let the result stand . . .'

Fortunately, Skelter did not need to protest, for Longrunner jumped to his defence straight away.

'What a load of rubbish. I've never heard of such a thing, moonhare. Dancing in front of the jill is just a question of

311

manners, an old-time tradition, with nothing at all to do with the actual fight, and of *course* a newcomer doesn't know all the nuances of our traditions. Why should he? This is his first frost dancing on the flatlands.

'No, I'm sorry, but as his opponent I have to say the fight was fought fair and square. He's a good boxer. You can't take that away from him. *Next* year I'll give him a better battle, because I've got his measure now . . .' he narrowed his eyes at Skelter and nodded '. . . but this fight stands.'

Moonhare was not used to being put down so firmly.

'Well, I'm still not so sure . . .' she began, but Creekcrosser said, 'You can't make them fight again, if neither of them wants to, moonhare.'

After that she was quiet – sulky – but quiet.

Skelter went over to Longrunner and thanked him for his intervention.

'I have to tell you,' he said, 'that we actually do the courtesy dance ourselves, up in the highlands, so I *should* have remembered.'

'Listen my white-coated intruder,' replied Longrunner, 'I'm not too happy with you at the moment. You come into the colony as smooth as you please, and proceed to steal away the jill I have had my sights on for the last season – don't expect me to like you for it. It may be we can be friends at some time, but not now. As for the fight, I meant what I said – it was fought fair and square and the result stands. Don't ask me for anything more.'

With that the flatlander jack turned his tail on Skelter.

Skelter shrugged and went over to Creekcrosser, who gave him the praise he deserved.

'Well done, you showed that jack where his back was. I wish I'd done the same thing in my fight . . .'

Skelter's ghost-hare, from her shadow world, was highly satisfied with her little champion. Throughout the fight she had been encouraging him with whistles and grindings of teeth, none of which the living could hear, but which helped her own excitement. She was convinced that Skelter had won because of her enthusiasm for him, believing that she had put heart into him with her support for him.

She wished, as she always did at the frost dancing time, that she was still flesh and blood, so that some fine jacks would once again stand up and box for her.

A flatlander herself, she recalled with nostalgia the king-hares of her Celtic past, vying for her favours. How they had danced on those far-off bronzed mornings, when the frost-fire was blazoned across the flatlands, and how they had battled for her affection in the ruts left by chariot wheels. What wild redhaired days they had been. That was before her capture, before she became a stately matron, with amulets around her ankles, and a slim copper chain about her neck. Those were cloaked days, and horse days, and spear and fire days, all gone, all gone.

She left the scene of the frost dancing and made her way along the shadowy paths which led to the Otherworld.

During the rest of the boxing, Skelter studiously avoided meeting Eyebright's eyes. He had won her, she was his and he hers, but now things had been settled according to the rules of society, they had to be settled between them, and he wasn't too anxious to get to that part. Now that they were to be mates he found himself agonisingly shy with her, and this was silly, for they had been close friends and field-sharers for quite some time. He couldn't even meet her eye, while he watched and encouraged other boxers. There was something inside him which wanted to put off that first important meeting with her, during which he knew he was going to be awkward, probably say all the wrong things, and be unable to find the real Skelter.

In the afternoon the day greyed to near darkness and the hares had to scatter and hide in various places, as the flogre came gliding over looking for meat. Skelter watched it circling the fields and finally it dropped, coming up with a domestic cat that had wandered too far from its safe home. The cat was screeching, '*Au secours!*', over and over again, until the sound faded into the dull heavens.

'Well, that's that for the day,' said Skelter to Eyebright, as they both emerged from under a log. 'It won't be back until dawn tomorrow.'

'Hopefully,' she said.

'I don't suppose there'll be any more frost dancing, so we might as well dig our forms under this log. It's as good a place as any. Now that the season is here, officially, we'll all be moving back together, won't we?'

'Yes, we will.'

They dug their forms under the log, in positions which would make it very difficult for the flogre to force them out with his beak, even if he found them. When that was over, Skelter suggested they go down to the river, to bid farewell to their summer-autumn-winter home. Eyebright thought that was a good idea.

Neither of them talked very much on the journey, though Skelter kept sneaking glances at his mate, and wondering how he had been so lucky as to win such a beautiful jill. Once or twice he caught her looking at him, and they both turned away quickly, in confusion, as their eyes met.

On their way to the lea, they passed through a wood. Heavy rain had begun to fall, for the third day running, and many of the low-lying fields in the broad shallow valley down to the river were becoming flooded and difficult to cross. Gulls were circling and landing, picking up the drowning worms and insects that floated on the floodwater.

Both hares were soaked through, their fur sleeked back, making them look much leaner and larger-eyed. The rain was thrashing the wood's leafless canopy, passing through the bare branches to the ground. Around them, on mossy banks, were blooming crocuses and yellow aconites, and in other places the snowdrops hung their heads. A gorse bush, forever in bloom, had crept in below the edge of the woodland. The season of the black frost had gone, and the world was now in bud again.

Wet through, they lay side by side in a patch of crocuses, and it was now that Eyebright took him to task.

'You should have danced for me.'

'I know, I know. I'm sorry. I was so eager to get it over with, I forgot.'

She sniffed.

314

'Oh, so you haven't even got the excuse that mountain hares don't follow the same custom?'

He was honest.

'No, we observe the same courtesies, I just forgot. I was excited, and scared. Not that he was going to hurt me, but that I would lose to him – and lose *you*. I know that's no real excuse. Can you forgive me?'

'I don't know. Let me look into your eyes.'

He turned to face her, their noses touching.

'Yes,' she said in a soft voice, 'oh, yes.'

They tumbled then, in a fever of excitement, flattening the crocuses like two wanton vandals. The sky turned upside down, the earth slid away from under them, until they didn't know which was which. The moss was soft and springy under their feet, their flanks, their rolling backs. They forgot how sharp their claws were sometimes, and when they stood on their hind legs, it was Eyebright that boxed *him* around the head, sometimes harder than she intended, sometimes just hard enough to pay him back for forgetting to dance for her. He tried to bat her back, but she was a strong jill, and his playful efforts were easily parried.

Often they stopped, for breath, and a serious look would come into their eyes, and she would turn, and he would rise to her, while the rain was beating the twigs into submission, and guttering from branches onto their backs, splashing the splattered crocuses into the moss. This was their time, and no other would match it again. They were the progenitors of future hares and hare futures, and leverets would stream into infinity from their meeting on the moss.

When it was over, she said to him, 'You look like a drowned rat.'

'You don't look much like a hare yourself,' he said.

They could say such things to each other now, safe in the knowledge they were mates, together for at least a season, perhaps longer, perhaps until the death of one of them.

They crossed the drowned meadows, sometimes having to swim in the freezing water, and finally reached the lea. There they found Stigand, down by the river.

'Ah,' he cried, 'it is the grand hares, my excellent neighbours from the horse drinking trough. How is it with you on this glorious day?'

'It's raining heavily,' Skelter pointed out.

'Yes, yes, and how wonderful is this natural water from the sky. Now I can wander away from the stream without my beautiful coat drying coarse and uncomforting to me. Such is the supreme bounty from the heavens, that it is like a river from the cumulus, and falls upon my waiting body in torrents of ecstasy.'

'We've already tasted of ecstasy once today,' said Eyebright, 'so we know what you mean.'

Stigand's eyes gleamed with delight.

'So, already you have been rained upon by these cascading waterfalls from the welkin? Such a transcendental experience, wouldn't you say hare? Such marvellous silvery happenings when days like this let you slide through them, almost to swim through the air to the ether above, and dance on the clouds.'

'We know about dancing too,' said Skelter.

'Or at least, one of us does,' Eyebright added.

'Then you know of my talkings,' cried Stigand, his eyes closing in bliss, as the heavens opened again and the rain gushed down from above, and all but flattened the two dripping hares by his side. 'You know of the beautiful nature of *rain*.'

They left him there with his poetry, enjoying the watering of the land. Finding their forms under the horse trough, they went to sleep, side by side, touching. Both were as content as they could be at such a time.

Chapter Forty Two

As the season moved into the month of scattered winds, the totem came more into its own. During the winter the petrified tree, being of a whiteness similar to frost and snow, could hardly be distinguished from its background. It melded with the landscape, like a ghostly cloud against a pale sky. Now the brown earth was showing through the frost, it became once more an imposing symbol of protectiveness. Lightning had been responsible for its death and deification, and lightning had left its mark in the split trunk. It was like frozen lightning itself, against a clear blue sky: a forked crack on the glaze of the universe. Headinthemist, the priestess of the colony, said that if you looked at the trunk of the totem for long enough, you could see into the Otherworld, but it made you lightheaded for a while afterwards.

During the mating season couples frequently consulted Head-inthemist about their futures and she spent much time in divining wych elm twigs and searching for luminescent honey fungus. Harebells were not yet in bloom, but once they were, she and other hares would begin talking to their ancestors, whose spirits inhabited the pale mauve flowers.

Eyebright, whom Skelter considered was normally a sensible sort of jill, insisted on setting her *iddab* bird skulls to trap the mad *idbitt* spirits that wandered over the landscape. The whole colony was steeped in superstition and mysticism, a dark age that had never quite gone away, and Skelter found it difficult to come to terms with. When Speedwell told him that sycamore seeds were really the dried droppings of horseshoe spirit-bats, he openly scorned her.

'Oh, come on,' he said, 'I'm willing to accept certain things, but this is going too far.'

This ridicule of the colony's 'religious' beliefs brought him the condemnation of moonhare, who barely made a move in her life without consulting her oracle, Headinthemist, and obtaining a few handy prophecies. Moonhare told him he must respect what he did not understand, or leave the colony. When he complained to Eyebright, she sided with moonhare.

'There are some things you blue hares are very backward about,' she said to him, 'and one of them is the mystery of the future.'

'It's the brown hares that are backward,' he retorted. 'Highlanders got rid of all this dark magic stuff ages ago. It's a load of nonsense, and I'm surprised at an intelligent jill like you believing in it.'

She lifted her chin in a haughty fashion.

'Why do you think I'm pregnant?' she said.

Skelter snorted, and said, 'Well, if you want me to tell you *that*, I think we're in a bit of trouble.'

'It's because,' she cried triumphantly, 'I buried a few corn ears under that star moss where we first . . . you know. I put them there in the late summer then led you to the spot so that we would have the best chance.'

Skelter was astonished.

'And you think they made you pregnant.'

'Well, not *made* me pregnant, we both know that, but made me more fertile.'

The mountain hare went quiet for a while and munched at the grasses round the log. Finally he looked up and said, 'I followed you that day you buried the corn ears. It wasn't in the spot where we first tumbled, but in another place altogether, on the far side of the wood.'

Eyebright looked terribly unhappy at this news, and her nose twitched.

'Was it really?' she said at last. 'Perhaps our leverets won't be healthy then? Oh dear, I wish my memory was better. I so wanted to give us the best chance of a healthy litter.'

Skelter, who had not followed her at all and had told a blatant untruth because he was annoyed with her was suddenly awash with guilt. She had believed him implicitly rather than trust her own memory, and he felt terrible. He couldn't very well say now that he had been making it up, she might not believe him, and when she did, there would be an element of distrust between them. It was a foolish thing he had done, and after all, what harm was there in these superstitions? Did it really matter that she had planned their first union so far in advance? It was flattering really.

'I could be mistaken,' he said, staring across the manicured fields, 'my memory's not what it used to be either.'

'Oh, no, you're just trying to be kind now. You know what a scatterbrain I am.'

'No, really,' he said desperately, 'I could be wrong. That was the day – yes, that was the day I got a knock on the head, from a falling branch. I think I was dizzy at the time. I could very well be wrong. In fact I'm sure now, that I got my east and west mixed up a bit. You're probably right, you did bury the corn ears below the star moss in that exact place.'

'I don't remember you being hit by a branch.'

This was of course another lie he had so casually spun out, and he was getting into a tangle.

'Well, you wouldn't, if you were interested in ensuring that our first union place was fertile, would you?'

Eyebright stared at him.

'But I would. I remember how I was at the time, completely besotted with you, and I couldn't take my eyes off you. You didn't know it of course, and I've got over all that nonsense now . . .'

'I don't know,' he said, 'it's not *really* nonsense.'

'I know my memory isn't to be entirely trusted, but I don't think I would have forgotten if you had been bashed on the head with a log.'

Skelter savagely tore at the grass with his teeth.

'Well,' he said through a mouthful of green, 'not a log, exactly, more a sort of heavy twig – from a great height. I didn't make a big fuss about it because I didn't want to upset anyone. I just remember feeling quite dizzy, especially when I followed you across the fields to the wood. I was particularly giddy at that time.'

'So, you think you may be wrong about the place, and I'm probably right.'

Skelter spat out a stringy piece of weed. 'Yes, to be quite frank, I think you're the one who's right, and I'm wrong after all.'

'Well, I must say I'm very relieved.'

Skelter munched away on some toadstools. 'It's nice that

319

you thought so far ahead,' he said, 'and prepared the place for us.'

She nodded and joined with him in the toadstools. 'Well, not so much *us* as me and whoever,' she remarked.

'You and *who*?' he said, his head jerking up.

'Precisely,' Eyebright said lightly, 'I mean, I didn't know which jack I would end up with at the time, did I? It could have been Longrunner.'

'Oh,' said Skelter coldly, 'I thought you were dead set on having *me*?'

'I was, but I had to make contingency plans, didn't I? In case you lost the boxing. I mean, I wanted *you*, but if I didn't get you, well, I needed *some* or other jack to father my leverets.'

Skelter sighed, trying to make light of the hurt he felt, when he thought of her with some other jack. It was a very unpleasant image, and not one he liked to think she had considered very seriously.

'You would have been upset if I hadn't boxed for you though, wouldn't you?'

'Oh yes – but Longrunner's not such a bad type. He's very upright, honest and courteous and we would have got on quite well I think.'

'A bit boring though, eh? Longrunner?'

'Depends what you want in a jack. A good provider and father, or a partner that's dashing and exciting. Some of these things wear off, after a while, especially when the young come along.'

'Oh, I'm sure, but I can be a good provider and father too.'

Eyebright said sweetly, 'We'll have to wait and see, won't we? I mean, you haven't had a chance to prove yourself yet, have you?'

Skelter felt very cast down at these words.

They ate in silence together for a long while, before Eyebright said, 'I'm off out into the fields, to look for some vegetables. You're the best jack I could ever wish for, but next time you want to play subtle games with me make sure you know the rules, and *do* brush up your skills a little.'

With that, she walked away through a hole in the long straight hedge. Skelter stared after her, then narrowed his eyes, taking in the combed furrows and ridges of the neat field, and the arrow-straight ditch. Somewhere along the line he had been fooled, but precisely when and how, he was still not sure. He knew one thing: there wouldn't be a *next time*. He wasn't going to get himself into a mess like that again.

Much to the annoyance of moonhare and her colony, a warren of rabbits arrived to take possession of the corner of the field, under the big tree where the human bodies were buried. The rabbits had been chased away from their old home, which had been on the edge of the village, when a new house was built right on the spot where their previous warren was located.

There was very little discourse between the rabbits and the hares, for the two do not make good neighbours, and most of the colony thoroughly resented the encroachment. No real trouble ensued, for hares and rabbits do not make war on each other, but the hares remarked that the atmosphere was less pleasant than it used to be. Hares, and it has to be said, other mammals with fussy ideas about straight lines and tidy surrounds, maintain that rabbits have unsociable habits, and leave the feeding grounds in such an unsavoury condition that those who follow have to wade through mess in search of a clear eating place.

The rabbits affected an air of indifference to the snobbishness of the hares, and went about their task of burrowing their new home with no apology on their lips, nor any attempt at conciliation. They sent no envoys to the hares, saying, 'Do you mind if we . . . ?' The rabbits simply arrived with all the mayhem created by a motley murder of crows, chattering excitedly, the younger ones dashing out into Booker's Field to play on the roots of the hare totem (an act which horrified Headinthemist), the does getting on with digging the holes, while the bucks wandered around looking important and pointing out the advantages of the spot to one another. One of them ate the day-old bouquet of crocuses that lay on the patch around which their females were hard at work.

During their digging the does found bits of cloth and leather, which they dragged out with irritation, and left to litter the field.

The hares were disgusted by this disregard for the environment, but they certainly were not going to clear up behind a bunch of manmade mammals that lived in dark underground passages and gave each other feline-sounding names.

So, the rabbits installed themselves, and there was little the hares could do about it except grumble.

Skelter, who was not as concerned by tidiness as the brown hares, tried to establish contact with the warren, but they were not interested in forming any sort of relationship with a hare, especially a blue one from the mountains. They kept themselves to themselves (they said) and bothered no one.

Unfortunately for the rabbits, though the hares had quite the opposite opinion, their untidy habits caused them to be moved on yet again, to the wood where Eyebright and Skelter's leverets were conceived. Skelter witnessed the whole incident.

A passerby, a harmless elderly human who walked with a stick and was often seen strolling across the fields, came through the area the evening after the rabbits had settled themselves. Normally the walker would not pass that place, for it was not a footpath, but many of the fields were still covered in shallow water and in order to avoid the flooded areas the man came through the five-barred gate and along the edge of the ditch. When he reached the place where the rabbits had scattered bits of cloth and leather over the furrows, he stopped and looked about him, and finally with a little effort reached down and picked up an oblong leather pouch that the rabbits had kicked out.

The white-haired man began investigating this leather pouch, taking out soggy pieces of paper and staring at them. The hares were willing him to stay around until after dusk, for the flogre would not attack them while a human was so close at hand, but as the light was fading the old man hurried away.

The following morning six or seven men dressed in blue uniforms arrived with the old man, all barking at one another excitedly. The old man was pointing to the bits of cloth on the ground, but when he tried to pick one up, a man in blue yelped at him, and he left it alone. Some workmen then arrived and began digging with spades. It was at this point that the rabbits began filing out of their bolt hole in Poggrin Meadow on the other side of the hedge and running for the far wood. Some of them no doubt thought the hares were responsible for this terrible invasion of their privacy, but were at a loss as to explain how.

During the morning the two decomposed bodies of the couple shot by the tractor-man were uncovered, and a foul stink polluted the air around the colony. None of the humans were worried about the presence of the hares, and while there were no guns or dogs in evidence, the hares were not too concerned about the humans. The hares kept their distance of course, most of them moving into Poggrin Meadow, and continuing the frost dancing under a crack willow out of sight of the activity, but there was no great alarm. The hares knew that the humans would only be around for a short while, for there were no houses to keep them out in the fields.

More humans arrived, until there was a huge crowd. The farmer began barking at the men in blue, and soon most of the people were sent away, tramping over the farmer's field and causing him to suffer a mild bout of apoplexy. On the edge of the crowd, the hares noticed, stood the tractor-man looking edgy and anxious, peering over the shoulders of those who went forward to view the corpses, only to reel back clutching their noses and mouths when they got too close. The hares wondered what the tractor-man was doing in that awful mêlée, instead of sitting in the chugging symbol for happiness, a place of blissful contentment.

After a while, they saw him leave the crowd, pale and clearly nervous, to lean on their symbol for long life, the five-barred gate, and stare at their dances in Poggrin Meadow. Now that the winter was over they knew he would be by soon with a saw and timber, hammer and nails, paint brush and green paint, to carry out the tri-annual ceremony of renewal which ensured the immortality of the five-barred gate. They looked forward to this, for hares love the smell of recently cut timber, and the odour of fresh paint. And of course they delighted in witnessing the rejuvenation of their great symbol for longevity at the hands of their respected tractor-man.

Happiness and long life – these were the two important aspects of existence entrusted to the tractor-man, who had never been known to fail the hares yet.

The remains of the dead humans were carried away, and life returned to normal in Booker's Field, and of course, the rabbits had gone for good and all.

Chapter Forty Three

Bubba knew that the magical hare was back, to torment him again, to thwart his desired feeding. It had taught the other hares how to use logs and rocks to avoid Bubba's deadly beak and claws.

There were dark forces at work here which were moving against Bubba, for he was certain the hare had died. How could it have lived, so close to starvation? Some magic had surely revived the creature, had rescued it from the grave and brought it back to plague the flier born of man, who needed meat in vast amounts. Certainly it had not been with the other hares during the winter months.

—Tower, what am I to do?

—*What has been deprived of life before, can be killed again, Bubba.*

—But it will return to haunt me.

—*Not if this time you devour it.*

How wise the tower was. Bubba shuffled on his shelf in the martello tower, thinking that next time he caught the hare, and he *would* catch it again, he would eat it on the spot, fur, bones and all. There would be nothing left of the creature to bring back to life. Perhaps when he had eaten it, Bubba too would be magic, as well as physically powerful?

Winter was on its way northwards, forced upwards by the springtime that had spent months gathering strength in the south and was now putting its shoulders against the ice and snow, pushing it back towards the pole where it rightly belonged. Bubba was glad of this in one way, but not in another.

The days were becoming lighter, and brighter, and it was getting dangerous to venture far from the tower. The greyness was no longer there to mask his movements. His hunting was now confined to the marshland around him, at dusk and dawn, except on stormy days. The hare population had been depleted, and he was no longer able to find the creatures. He was surprised how much his craving for hare meat had increased, now that he was no longer able to get it.

There was plenty of other wildlife to be had of course, from stubborn grey herons to stupid rabbits, but Bubba did not just want food, he wanted the food he wanted. It was not right that a small creature like a hare should dictate to Bubba what he could or could not have for his diet.

Bubba went up in the dusks and dawns, patrolling the marshlands, dropping, snatching, feeding, gradually depleting the area of all mammals and birds. The other predators starved because of his voracious appetite and moved into other areas, causing a rolling effect amongst their kind.

Life for Bubba was like a slow dream of drifting in dark grey skies, the marshes sliding away beneath him, racing towards the far horizons. In the skies he was lord, his eyes unmatched for keenness, his size frightening the other birds. Flocks would wheel away from him, heading out to sea, hoping he would not follow. Sometimes he would, just for the sport, fly over the restless waves with their sprigs of white that flourished and died within the moment. Life was like a dream, a drifting dream, that held him aloft and bore him on its soft shoulders.

In the tower he had much time to think, and sometimes he lost himself within himself, and only the fading or the rising sun was able to rescue him from drowning in himself. Surrounded by the old stones, he was like the live grey centre of the world: a savage core that sprouted talons and beak enough to rip the heart out of a man.

Chapter Forty Four

Before the birth of Eyebright's leverets a high wind came to devastate the countryside. It began as a sharp but fairly gentle breeze from the east, and swiftly grew to hurricane proportions. The east was the birthplace of many of the worst winds to hit the island, there being nothing to stop them from sweeping across the sea and attacking the flatlands.

Skelter had been out to the north, foraging, and when he returned he had to cross a road to reach the meadowland that led to Booker's Field. The wind was already gusting and racing in circles, stirring up the twigs and grasses and scattering rubbish over the hedgerows. It was throwing rooks around as if they were single feathers and tossing their nests from the high elms, out into the fields. Other birds had vacated the skies, having found themselves niches in the landscape, to wait out the anger of the air.

Skelter hated crossing roads, even though traffic on the island was fairly light, for many cars were so fast you couldn't see them coming. It was best to stop and listen for a while, until you were sure that a quick dash was safe, then sprint over the tarmac. Even this method was not foolproof.

Coming out of a ditch into the long grasses at the edge of the lane Skelter approached the edge of the asphalt. Then, as he paused for a moment, he looked along the roadway and saw something on its surface that gave him a jolt. He hare-walked along the periphery, about seven lengths, before making his dash. On his way across, he confirmed what he thought he had seen. It was a squashed Jittie, flattened onto the tarmac. He recognised her little snout, and her protective bristles.

Filled with sadness, he stared back at the sight from the other side of the road, wondering how she had managed to get herself killed. She had been quite fast on her feet when she wanted to

327

be, and could sprint as quickly as most mammals. No doubt she had come out of her winter sleep, from a hidey hole filled with old leaves, and had been groggy and disorientated. Maybe she staggered around for a while, before absently crossing the road, having lost all concentration. It was she who had told Skelter how dangerous it was to hibernate, for she had to slow her heart rate down almost to a stop. Such a state must need some considerable recovery time.

Well, she was gone now, and no goodbyes had been said. He owed a lot to Jittie and would liked to have told her so.

Skelter continued his journey with a heavy heart. Eyebright would sympathise of course, but she would not understand how close the two of them had been, for to her Jittie had just been another grumpy neighbour. He would have to bear this hurt by himself.

It was now mid-day and the gusts increased in force, until Skelter realised this was no ordinary wind. It began tearing cabbages from the ground and rolling them like balls across the fields. Some of the thinner branches of the trees were beginning to crack and go spinning away. The old leaves left by autumn took on a new lease of movement, and became animated travellers, filling the air with their brown corpses.

The blue hare sheltered behind a log for a while, to catch his breath. Each time he went out in the wind, he was robbed of air, and he did not like the way the wind rushed up his nose. It made him snort involuntarily. The sensible thing to do, he supposed, was to stay where he was, but Eyebright was in a delicate condition and he wanted to be with her, to offer her company, assistance and comfort if it was required. Her belly was now round with the little ones, and she was very protective of herself for that reason. He ought to be with her.

While he was behind the log, someone got blown off their feet and went rolling by. Then the creature recovered its legs and managed to scramble behind the log at the far end.

Skelter's fur stood on end. The animal was an adult male stoat, the largest of his kind, halfway through moulting its winter coat. Rusty brown patches showed through the arching white of its back.

The hare was still out of breath, and though his back legs were primed for the bolt, he remained where he was, alert and watchful. The stoat stared back at him intensely, with eyes as red as glowing berries. Neither animal moved a muscle, as they both recovered their breath.

Stoats were lithe dancers, like hares, only their swaying performances were dances of death. They went up on their hind legs, tall and willow-wandy, and swayed back and forth, mesmerising their victims. Their hypnotic eyes would hold the eyes of the prey as they danced forward slowly until they were within striking distance. Then they would leap for the head and sink those needle-like incisors into the back of the neck, and blood would flow. Usually the stoat's victims were rabbits or other smaller mammals, but Skelter knew that they would take on a hare if they felt they could get away with it.

'*Hwit hara!*' said the stoat in its harsh tongue.

Skelter said nothing, not understanding the archaic language of badgers, weasels and stoats.

It was repeated, several times.

'*Hwit hara. Hwit hara.*'

The stoat looked down at its own coat, and then stared at Skelter's pelage, before saying it one last time.

Then Skelter understood. He still had the vestiges of his white coat himself. The stoat had obviously never seen a hare whose fur changed in the winter. The stoat nodded slowly and put his head on one side in an unusual gesture.

Skelter had the strange feeling, as the wind raged round him and this other ancient creature of the landscape, that they were caught in a kind of brotherhood: winter souls meeting on the windy plains of the flatlands. There was a rare truce between them for the moment, allowable by the unusual circumstances of the weather, in which they could study one another closely.

For Skelter, the atmosphere was sinister yet exciting, and his feelings were at needle-point. This was the second time he had encountered a stoat in the flatlands. The first had been that stoat in the rabbit warren, chased away by the badgers. There he had felt nothing but terror. This unique time there was the fear, but it was a calm terror, which could be examined minutely with fascination. It was a strange glittering thing, a dreadful jewel that one possessed

329

and wanted to cast off, but whose deadly beauty forbade such action.

And the stoat itself was a small fearsome thing, cold as an icicle, hot as fire. When it opened its jaws, there was that small pink-red patch with pure white points. From its small shining eyes to the tip of tar on the end of its tail it was demon. It was dark of tongue and dark of soul. Yet in the same instant it was ordinary life, a creature of the woods and fields, a carnivore fashioned to prey on herbivores.

The wind raged around them as they studied each other, each lost in his own thoughts.

Suddenly, the stoat made a slight movement towards Skelter, perhaps not even threatening, perhaps just easing an uncomfortable cramped position, and the hare's instincts took over. His hair-trigger hind legs were sprung, and he was off, punching holes in the air with his bullet head, running breathless into the brunt of the wind. In his breast the excitement remained of having shared space with a deadly enemy, and almost touched his brother-beast's fur.

Skelter kept to the open fields now, away from the ditches where the trees were planted, for huge branches were being wrenched from their sockets and cast to the ground. The air was full of flying objects: pieces of slate from distant rooftops, cans, wooden planks, all manner of loose implements. The mighty trees themselves were crashing to the ground, and all along the lanes the telephone poles were coming down.

It was a terrible wind, and worthy of respect. It would *have* respect from those in its path. Along the shoreline, it enraged the ocean, causing monstrous waves to thunder inland further than they had ever been before, sweeping aside formidable obstacles with the sheer weight of water. Domestic creatures were suffering, especially the birds. Some of the objects being blown along were chickens, whose unfirm grip on ground and whose feathery bulk made them vulnerable to the wind's force.

Skelter kept low to the ground, several times losing his footing and being blown head-over-heels across the flattened grasses. Eventually he came to Booker's Field, and made his way to the log under which, thankfully, Eyebright was resting.

'I'm back,' he said, snuggling beside her, 'are you all right?'

'Yes,' she replied. 'Oh, I'm glad you've come. I was worried about you. This looks as if it's going to be a bad one.'

'I think we'll be all right,' he said. 'There's not much can happen to us under here. Even if the tree comes down and falls across us, the log will protect us.'

'I'm sure you're right.'

The next few hours were hell for the creatures of the island, as the wind came screaming in with a force never seen or heard of before. It was truly awesome in its might, and even stone walls came tumbling down, scattering themselves over fields and roads. Gulls not on the water were torn from their perches and carried away to God only knew where. A tenacious owl became a bat for a while, when it refused to let go of a branch, was blown half-circle round it, and found itself upside down, staring at a world of different shape. Fieldmice went through the air like bullets, some meeting an unpleasant end.

Eyebright and Skelter waited out the fury, relatively safe under their protective log.

'I'm not sure what the food situation will be like once this wind has died down,' said Skelter.

'Oh, we'll manage,' Eyebright said with the placidness of an expectant mother. She was content to just *be* most of the time and had grown round and soft and liquid-eyed. Skelter fussed over her a lot of the time, as did Longrunner and many others, and she got together with the pregnant jills to talk about the coming leverets and the hope for their future. She seemed, to Skelter, to be happy.

The colony badly needed a new generation, for the flogre had decimated them several times. One in ten hares had been taken at intervals separated by one or two months. That was the flogre's way, to attack at every dusk and dawn for a few days, then leave them alone for a while, before returning to do the same again. He knew the value of periods of intense terror, when his attacks were relentless, followed by a period of calm when the hares sometimes came to believe they were rid of him for good. It was worse than being attacked at close regular intervals, for the respites allowed hope to flourish, which was crushed by the next series of devastating raids. It ensured that they never got the measure of their oppressor.

When the wind had finally died, the hares emerged from their hiding places. Thankfully the totem had survived intact, its single ironhard bough having no foliage on it, to form a barrier for the wind. It would have either stood unyieldingly, or been torn down completely. As it was, it had remained, its white roots locked around a large rock below the topsoil, anchoring it firmly to the land.

Several oak boughs were lying on the ground and the hedgerow was torn in places. The whole scene was very distressing to the brown hares who liked their world neat and tidy with no debris and the straight lines of the hedges travelling uninterrupted into infinity. They wandered about, looking a little bewildered, walking between the heavy branches and picking up the smaller ones in their teeth, only to drop them again a bit further on. Although they had tidiness in their veins, the hares would not dream of doing anything about the mess themselves. That was for others to do, and for them to appreciate. They were not activists, they were admirers of the art of neatness, they were the critics of the agricultural scene. Hares could tell you when it was not right, and even make suggestions for improvement, but they could not do it themselves. They wouldn't know where to start, and if they did try, they would certainly never finish the task.

They were quite pretentious at times, about what was artistically *good*, and what was unacceptable. They would view a set of fields, and hedgerows, and ditches, and trees, and tell at a glance whether the arrangement was superior, or definitely lacking. They could run their discerning eye down a furrow, along a line of seedlings, and judge its straightness according to the rules they had made themselves.

They were true critics, in that they had none of the skills themselves, they decided what was good and bad according to their own ideas of taste, and the language they used to describe *good* and *bad* neatness was entirely composed of airy phrases that when examined closely made little sense to anyone outside their circle. A farmer who appeared to take little heed of the views of hares, in designing and sheering his hedges, was not necessarily dismissed as a cretin, but worse, his work would be completely ignored and if anyone raised the question of his efforts, cold looks of uninterest lasting about two frozen seconds would be the only response.

So, after the hurricane, the sensitive hares had to feed and run amongst debris that offended their very souls. It was a time which, when recalled, would invoke shudders of distaste. Their world had never been in a worse state, not since the chariots in the century of ghost-hares had thundered over the landscape, making wiggly ruts over the combed and manicured country, and weapons and dead humans were strewn from here to there, spoiling the careful lines ploughed into the earth by yeomen and villein.

Chapter Forty Five

The morning after the hurricane, when the world was still in chaos, Skelter again wandered far from home. Though the wind had died, the weather was still unsettled and simmering with anger, likely to show its petulance in some other way. Skelter was in an open field, feeding on beet leaves, when the clear sky suddenly clouded over and a storm lowered itself over the land.

Now, hares are normally unconcerned by thunder and lightning and when the dark clouds threaten they shrug their shoulders and say, 'Oh, here comes a storm,' and continue with whatever it is that they're doing.

This is exactly what Skelter did, forgetting that there was a menace abroad, who came in on the backs of the storms. In the highlands a black sky like this one would rid the heavens of predators. Here on the flatlands it served to camouflage the most deadly of local terrors.

Thus the world darkened and as Skelter ate steadily the thunder crashed through the sky and the lightning crackled with brilliant displays. Skelter munched away, looking up at the sky occasionally, and thinking how magnificent it all was, when he suddenly realised what he was doing. He was out in the open in conditions which the flogre could use to get a long distance from its martello tower and over the colony's feeding grounds. He had to get back to warn Eyebright of the danger.

He swallowed his last mouthful and headed for a drystone wall, along the foot of which he intended to run, to use as a shield. No sooner had he reached the wall, when he heard the beat of wings and instinctively jumped for a hole between the stones. He felt the talons rake his back, just skimming the fur, but not penetrating his hide. There was a swiftly-passing odour of musty feathers, which made him wrinkle his nose.

Skelter squeezed himself, with a little bout of panic, into a small

334

space between some stones. There he remained, his heart beating fast against a rock, hoping he was well protected. He looked up into the skies, though his field of vision was seriously impaired by the wall in which he was hiding.

There was a rolling darkness above, illuminated every so often by a flash. Kicker was up there somewhere, displaying his anger with the humans. Unwittingly, the First Ancestor had brought with him-her an enemy of the hares. As if realising this the dry storm was beginning to move on towards the sea. Skelter could not see the flogre, though he was sure it was there. He dared not stick his head out to get a wider view of the sky in case a sudden bolt of claw-and-feather dropped on him.

Then he saw it, high above, descending in circles. The lightning seemed to arc from its very back and illuminate its silhouette against the heavens. The forks of electric sprang like jagged weapons from its form, and static crackled along its shape, from wingtip to wingtip. It was indeed a mythical creature, a thunder-and-lightning bird. It had come from Ifurin, the hell of hares, to fracture the skies above the flatlands.

Skelter smalled himself as much as possible so that not a whisker was visible from above. Yet the giant kept his wide slow circle above, peering downwards, ready to drop. If it was to be a waiting game, Skelter knew he could win, but he wasn't sure the flogre would allow that.

He was proved right a short time later, for the great bird landed on the grass and stalked up to the wall. Again, the size of the flogre was astounding, and the highlander almost swooned from absolute terror. Its eyes were cold stones in its face, and its savage-looking hook could surely tear a deer's head from its body. The crest on its head, running from side to side, gave it an even more terrifying appearance, as if it had deliberately arranged itself that way in order to paralyse its prey with fright. Skelter knew that it was going to peck wounds in his body if he did not move and he dropped to the ground on the other side of the wall. He began running, his heart pattering faintly, along the foot of the wall.

Instantly, the flogre flew to the top of the wall, and hopped awkwardly along it, keeping pace with Skelter below. Skelter's brain went into its hysterical mode, and in this state he couldn't think properly. Foolishly he broke for the field, thinking he saw a rabbit hole, but when he reached it found it to be a mole hill. Now he was out in the open, the debris of the previous day's wind hampering his movements.

The flogre took to the air again, slowly and deliberately as if it knew it had its quarry where it wanted it and was now playing with his food.

Skelter dashed for the edge of the field, leaping fallen branches, hoping to find holes along the ditch, but when he reached it there was no trench, only a wooden two-bar fence to keep domestic animals from straying onto the road beyond. He slipped under the fence, and out into the road.

Still there was little cover, except for a fallen telephone pole. The top of the pole had struck a milestone, and there was a gap between it and the ground large enough for Skelter to squeeze under.

This he did, just as the flogre was dropping, lazily to the earth, like an autumn leaf.

It was here that Skelter had his first stroke of luck, for keen though the flogre's eyesight was it did not detect the thin wires stretched tautly between the two standing poles and running down to the top of the fallen pole's head. The wires were like the strings of a cat's cradle, a dozen or so, running parallel to each other.

The flogre suddenly found itself caught up in these, its winged shape cumbersome now that it was on the ground and the more it struggled in the wires, the more it became entangled. It shrieked with frustration, the piercing cry making Skelter's frayed nerves stand on end. The hare could see the thin steel wires caught amongst the wing and tail feathers, and the legs were hampered in their movements.

Skelter felt it was time to dart away, to get out of the area as fast as he could manage, and leave the flogre to its fate. Perhaps a vehicle would be along the lane soon, and be unable to stop, thus running into the giant? It was a scenario he could not wait around to witness.

But the flogre was not so easily trapped. As Skelter stared at the enormous creature it dipped its head and clacked its beak. There was a immediate *twang*. Skelter was trying to puzzle this out and identify the strange sound, when the same thing happened again – the head dipped, the beak closed, and a second *twang* was followed by a flash of a steel strand. *Twang, twang, twang.* One by one the wires were snipped with that strong sharp beak. Skelter took to his hind legs, dashing along the country lane.

When he looked back, the flogre had escaped from the web of wires and had taken to the air again. It came hurtling along the lane, just above the ground. There were cottages on the side of the lane, and a man was sawing logs in his garden. His mouth dropped open as the great bird flashed by his gate. The man rushed into the house, either to fetch someone to see this extraordinary sight, or to get his shotgun.

The flogre had obviously thrown all caution away, and was determined to have Skelter, or die. This was a bad situation for the hare, who was beginning to wonder why he had been singled out for this victimisation. What had he done to be persecuted in this fashion, except climb to the belfry of the old church tower and confront the flogre in its nest?

Skelter broke away from the edge of the roadway to enter a wood not far from Whisled Lea. It was a neglected tangled place, more thicket in its centre than sturdy forest, and was there for no other reason than it was more trouble to clear than leave alone. Skelter searched in vain for a rabbit warren, down which he would have gone in an instant, but he found nothing but a fox's earth. He even considered going down this, but the entrance smelled strongly of recent fox and to enter the hole would be to face a similar death to the one which threatened him from above. Skelter ran on.

The flogre entered the wood as if it belonged in such places. Skelter remembered what Rushie had told him of her experiences and realised that far from hampering the creature, the trees were of use to it. They were the apparatus of an acrobat and the great bird used them to swing itself around the tight spaces, its short wingspan fashioned for just such activity. It might have been born in the tangle of such an ivy-vined network of branches. It dipped and weaved beneath boughs, around the boles of the trees, through the loops of parasitic creepers, instinctively knowing which patch of foliage was easily brushed aside by its wingtips, and which was to be avoided. The tightest spaces were no obstacle and snaking tunnels of sharp thorns were traversed with ease. If it was lord of the flatlands, it was king of the forest. Brambles, briars, bracken – nothing presented any kind of barrier to the flogre as it curved and banked, looped and dived, and harassed the hare this way and that, causing it to run in circles in its effort to shake off the flier.

Skelter was beginning to feel despair. Was there nothing which could stop the creature? It seemed to have an answer to all his tricks. He was beginning to lose energy rapidly and would soon have to stop. Once he halted, he knew he would be unable to regain his feet, having run himself to a state of complete collapse.

He broke out of the wood again and took the ditch along the road to Whinsled Lea. Eyebright would be in the totem field and nowhere near this place, so Skelter did not need to worry that he would run into her and involve her in the chase.

The flogre zipped along the top of the hedgerow, keeping its quarry in sight, waiting for the end of the ditch to arrive.

Skelter cut across the corner of the field, down towards the river. He thought vaguely that if he jumped into the river and began to swim, the flogre would not be able to get at him. It was not a sea eagle after all and perhaps the idea of water below it would be sufficient to put it off the hunt. Skelter hadn't much hope for such a plan, but it was the only idea left to him.

Then, as Skelter ran towards the river's edge, he saw a pair of otters sitting on the bank. It was Stigand and Sona, unaware of the drama until they looked back and up at his approach. He saw the surprise and horror in their expressions and knew he could not lead the monster to them, for it might easily take one of them in passing. They were frozen in their attitudes – sitting targets.

Instead, Skelter headed for some cattle that crowded the corner of the field. They at least were a match for the flogre, which came hurtling through the air. Skelter found himself dashing in and around the legs of the restless beasts as they bellowed their annoyance and began skittishly to stamp around, ready to stampede at any moment. Skelter was in danger of being crushed under a stray hoof, if not snatched from the ground by the enormous raptor.

The flogre could do nothing while Skelter was amongst the cattle. Once or twice it swooped down between the beasts and tried to scoop its prey from the turf, but each time Skelter dashed under the belly of a bullock and avoided the talons. Finally, the bullocks broke and thundered away towards the far side of the field, leaving Skelter exposed.

The hare was almost on his last legs now, his heart banging against his ribs and his lungs harsh and painful. He skipped across the stream which was the home of the otters and towards the cottage, hoping that perhaps Bess was around and her size and bark would frighten the flogre away.

Skelter took the garden wall in one leap, worthy of a deer in flight, and found to his disappointment that the garden itself was empty. He dashed to the following side, to reach the potting shed, and this is where his energy gave out. Several lengths from the protection of the raised shed, he flopped onto his side and lay panting and helpless.

The flogre came in low and fast, missing the top of the wall by the thickness of a slate. Its talons were outstretched and there was a cry in its throat, which could be nothing but triumph. Skelter lay on his side, panting rapidly, watching the dark shape hurtle down, swift and merciless, and waited for the sharp sting of its claws piercing his skin, the rush of air as he was snatched aloft.

Suddenly the monster was transformed into a ball and hit the ground, rolling across the lawn to within a length of where Skelter lay.

The highlander watched amazed as the flogre struggled, screeching fiercely, as it tried to escape the fine film that wrapped around its form. Then Skelter realised that the conscientious owner of Bess, the trapper of small birds, had put his invisible nets back up immediately the high wind was over. The flogre had flown straight into one of these nets, draped between poles across the garden, having a gap beneath their curtain-like folds under which grounded creatures could run.

There would be many species of bird carried out of their usual territory during the hurricane, blown in from an ocean flight on their way from one distant land to another, but the naturalist had caught a creature which would astound him, so far out of its normal habitat as to be nothing short of remarkable. A wide ocean separated the flogre from its true hunting grounds, where the hardwood forests were thick and the rivers flowed long and wide through half a continent.

However, the danger was not yet over for Skelter, as the flogre ripped a hole in the fine netting for its beak to emerge, and began shuffling towards the exhausted hare. The wicked claws, though tangled in the mesh, were able to pierce it and grip the turf, pulling Bubba closer to his prey. His hook clacked and snapped, so close to the highlander's nose he could smell the old meat on the breath of the monstrous bird.

Skelter struggled to get to his feet, but his run had made him uselessly weak, for a hare will race to the point of exhaustion, when every ounce of his energy has been drained and he has nothing left.

The flogre shrieked, almost deafening the mountain hare, whose ears sprang up at the startling sound. At last the flogre's beak snapped on flesh, gripping a dark-tipped ear. Bubba began to pull, dragging the hare towards him, in order to get it close enough to administer a few swift jabs at Skelter's eyes. Thus he could pierce the hare's brain, and immobilise it permanently.

Skelter was vaguely aware of a distant shouting, as if from behind some barrier or wall.

The mountain hare dug in his paws, resisting the flogre's attempts to get him within striking distance, but was unable to get a grip on the slippery grass. His claws left tracks on the top of the lawn, as he slid gradually towards the monster. The death strokes were an instant away, when the sharp beak finally severed the eartip and released him.

Skelter rolled away, and at that moment a greater shape flung itself on the flogre, and held it fast. It was the bearded man from the cottage, and he quickly taped up the flogre's beak, and its claws, rendering it helpless, as it struggled inside the netting, its eyes blazing with indignation and naked fury.

The huge bird was taken from the lawn, to the cottage, and the man disappeared inside with his prize.

Bess came out to join Skelter on the lawn.

'Are you all right?' she asked.

Skelter looked up at the great hound. 'I think so. Lost a bit of an ear, but under the circumstances . . .'

Bess said, 'What on earth is it? I saw it from the window when I heard the commotion, and yelled for my master. He was doing something in the kitchen, but when he saw that monster he went berserk. I've never seen him so excited.'

'He was excited – I was terrified.'

'I'm not surprised. Do you know what it is?'

Skelter replied, 'The wild creatures call it the flogre, but what it really is, or where it comes from, no one knows. Apparently it just appeared in the flatlands some time last year, and it's been terrorising the countryside ever since. It needs a lot of meat to sustain it: another season or so and it would have wiped us out. Will – will your master let it go, once he's ringed its foot?'

Bess snorted.

'I very much doubt it. I should think the only place that creature is going is to the zoo. It's out of its habitat, and there's all sorts of things to consider, like the balance of nature and such. I'm sure he won't let it go. He only releases creatures that live around here. You were an exception.'

'Well, thank goodness you were around Bess, to raise the alarm. You saved my life. I'm so weary I can hardly move a paw. How can I thank you?'

'Pooh, think nothing of it. I'd do the same if you were a St Bernard.'

It was a little while after Bess had left him that Skelter realised she had made a joke.

It took several minutes to recover, but then he was able to stand and totter down to the stream, where Stigand and Sona were waiting patiently to hear his story.

PART SEVEN

＊

The Greater Birds

Chapter Forty Six

Skelter was limp with relief at having escaped what should have been his death. Crossing the garden his legs would hardly hold him up, having been weakened not only by tremendous physical punishment, but as a result of his mental state too. Many wild creatures would have keeled over and given up on life – had he been a mouse, or a sparrow, his heart would have stopped long before now. But he was a hare, a highland hare, and he would not surrender his life without good reason. Such an experience, however, left him fatigued in brain as well as body, and it was going to take some time to recover fully.

As Skelter scrambled under the garden gate and made his way down to the stream where Sona and Stigand were standing and wondering, a shadow passed over the land. Skelter instinctively cringed and looked for shelter, for the shadow was of a great bird, high in the heavens. For one moment the mountain hare thought that the flogre had escaped the clutches of the man, was looking for its final revenge, but as he crouched there looking up at the shape in the sky, Skelter could see this was not so.

The bird which flew overhead, casting a stiff shadow on the ground, was too inflexible to be the flogre. It did not wheel, or circle, or do anything except fly in a straight line across the sky. Its wings stuck out rigidly from its body, and the longer Skelter stared at it, the less like a bird it actually seemed. It appeared to be a stupid creature, with little will of its own and from its throat came a growling sound that never varied in pitch or tone.

The great bird then began to descend, still in that fixed flight pattern, towards the fields beyond the island. Skelter wondered whether they were going to be plagued by another predator so soon after getting rid of the one that had been menacing them for so long.

He continued down the slope, until he reached Stigand and Sona.

'Did you see that?' he asked them.

Stigand asked, 'Are you all together all right, youngish hare? Sona and I were in great trepidation.'

Skelter realised the otters had not looked up when the great bird went overhead: they were still concerned about the flogre, not having witnessed its capture. He decided to forget about the new menace for a while and set their mind at rest on the old one.

'Yes, I think so. I'm feeling a bit washed out at the moment, but I'll be fine later. The man's got it now, you know. He captured the flogre before it could bite off my head. It was close enough for that, I can tell you.'

Sona, staring at Skelter's head, asked a question of Stigand in their own language. Stigand acted as interpreter.

'My mate of the female sex asks if you were wounded in body, and what must happen to the monster?'

'No, no wounds of any kind, except for this little clip out of my ear, which will soon heal. The blood's already started to clot. As for the flogre, Bess says the man will send it to a zoo. We shan't be seeing that one again. But there is . . .'

Stigand rattled away to Sona, and then turned to Skelter with a look of relief. 'This is good happenings. Everyone can breathe with less difficulty nowadays, with the flogre being incarcerated by mankind. I must remark that when we viewed the creature in its ascension, we were replete with apprehension, wondering if it would kill us all and every one. Then you, the bravish hare, led the creature to the hands of the man. This is legends in the making! This is heroes for breakfast stories!'

Skelter said, 'Now don't you go making me out to be some kind of selfless champion. All I was doing was running away from that thing, and mighty glad I was to get rid of it. I didn't save anyone, I was just trying to save myself.'

'Still, you decoyed yourself and Sona and I are brimmed with gratitude. We have our most obliged feelings to place at your feet. Please accept our thanksgivings.'

'Now, Stigand . . .'

346

'No, no more explanatories. You must get back to your female mate, and tell her of your great conquer.'

Skelter was going to do nothing of the sort, but he took his leave of the two otters and told them he would be returning with Eyebright to Whinsled Lea in the summer, probably with a few leverets in tow.

He travelled over the fields, reaching the colony about dusk. The twilight shadows had begun to creep across the land, transforming it into that nightmarish time of grey shapes which caused inanimate objects to move as if they were live creatures. Headinthemist was chanting one of her ritual songs, about wych elm twigs, totems, and other protective items.

Skelter sat out in the open, scratching at his wounded ear.

Moonhare cried from her hidey-hole in some stones.

'Skelter, if you stay out there any longer, you will die. The flogre . . .'

He decided to be a little flippant.

'Let the flogre come! I'll scratch its eyes out.'

There was a gasp from the rest of the hares, and everyone started muttering at once. Eyebright crawled out from beneath their log.

'Have you gone mad? You'll be killed.'

Skelter did a somersault, stood up on his hind legs, and shadow boxed the air.

'I'm ready for the monster. Bring it on!'

Another series of gasps and groans from the other hares.

Eyebright started to panic, rushing backwards and forwards, crying that he had gone mad and someone must help her get him under cover. Skelter realised he had gone too far at that point. His mate was in a delicate condition and he could harm the leverets by his silly play acting.

'It's all right,' he told her, 'I'm only joking. The flogre has gone. It's been captured by the man in the cottage and it's on its way to a zoo, somewhere far away from here. If not today, then tomorrow.'

He then told them all the story of his experiences, and how he had escaped death by the merest fraction, offering his clipped ear as proof of his claim. They were all suitably impressed, though Eyebright was upset, because she said the black tip had gone from his ear completely and she had admired it so much when it was there.

347

Few of the hares would emerge from their protective places however, and it would be many days, weeks, before they would feel safe in the open – especially since a number of them had seen the same stiff birdform in the sky that Skelter had witnessed, and they too wondered if they were in for a fresh bout of persecutions.

Creekcrosser came out though, and so did Bittersweetinspring, and with Eyebright the four of them remained exposed until the darkness came, hoping to try to get back to a normal existence once again, now that their deadly enemy had gone. The new rigid creature had not proved aggressive, and until it did, Creekcrosser maintained he was not going to cower in a hole any more, but use the world as it was meant to be used, as a flat open space for hares to run in.

Bittersweetinspring was showing a marked preference for Creekcrosser at this time, but then it was usually her way to turn from the mate who had won her at the frost dancing, and to indulge in illicit activity with another jack. It was something to do with her dislike of being attached – 'snared' she called it – to one jack. She liked to be 'free' and though she got into all sorts of trouble for it, for the colony was pretty conservative and conventional in its general outlook, she cocked a snook at the gossips and did as she pleased. Skelter admired her courage and though he could see she was to be avoided if at all possible by hotblooded jacks – for once she had them on the hook, she discarded them with disdain – she was an individual in a world of mad conformists and you could not help but view that with some admiration. Creekcrosser seemed to have got her measure, however, and somehow managed to retain her interest even when he had clearly committed himself. It was something to do with his own individualistic personality: his unkempt appearance, his contempt for society, his devil-may-care attitude. They made a good, if unconforming, pair. They were either at odds with one another, yelling or not speaking, or they were off somewhere together sneaking furtively under the curtains of willow down by the river. Racer, poor jack, left out in the cold, was the only one (apart from the morally inflexible moonhare) who did not view the relationship with a certain amount of amusement.

The other hares, jacks and jills, were engaged in producing

348

families and had little time for anyone else but each other. Spring was on its way: there was promise in the air and so the buds opened and the blossoms swelled and became overblown. The lean belly of winter was now behind them, and the fullness of summer stretched ahead. More of the stiff birds appeared in the skies overhead, growling steadily, coming and going from the mainland. None of them ever deviated from their steady courses and soon the hares became used to them. Few even bothered to look up any more. The flogre was gone for good and they could all relax and spend their time usefully worrying about foxes.

Creekcrosser and Bittersweetinspring left Booker's Field to found a new marsh hare colony and one or two other misfits went with them. It seemed an exciting venture to some, and there was still enough of the leveret in Skelter to arouse his enthusiasm for new schemes. Skelter talked to Eyebright but she reminded him that they had been allocated prime bottom land down by the river. They would be foolish to give up Whinsled Lea and the accompanying agricultural land, for unknown ground bordering marshes. Then there were neighbours to consider, for they got on well with the otters and might find an earth of foxes in the new area.

Skelter, who fancied a new adventure, reluctantly agreed that they would be silly to leave the lea.

The Brent geese flew northwards in their tight formations, wave on wave of the dark creatures clouding the sunset, rippling over the treetops, disappearing over the sea towards an horizon the hares could not even contemplate.

One evening when a vermilion sunset was creeping through the clouds and the tractor-man was opening the five-barred gate to drive the tractor through and park it in the big red barn, two men in blue were seen coming from the direction of the village, crossing the fields.

The tractor-man stared at these figures and when he saw them coming towards him the hares smelled the fear-sweat on him. The two men in blue began running, but the tractor-man ignored their shouts and went back to the chugging symbol for hare happiness, and took his shotgun from behind the seat.

The hares all froze, thinking he was going to shoot something for his supper, and it might be one of them.

Instead, he turned the weapon around the wrong way, to look down the barrels, and then the gun went off.

The sound shocked the hares, many of whom jumped and ran for the hedgerow. By the time the two men in blue arrived, puffing and panting, to switch off the tractor's engine, the tractor-man was dead. They took his body away that very evening and the tractor stayed out in the fields all night, allowing the hares to jump on the bits closest to the ground and thoroughly enjoy a familiarity with their favourite machine.

There was much speculation amongst the hares as to what the tractor-man had really intended to do with the gun. Longrunner maintained he had intended to shoot the two men in blue, but had made a mistake with the weapon, turning it the wrong way around. Reacher said that was ridiculous, because the tractor-man had used a shotgun all his life, and certainly knew one end from another. Headinthemist was convinced he was either mad or possessed by some evil spirit, which had made him *believe* the gun was the right way round, when of course it was not. Moonhare thought he was checking that no mud was in the barrels, and had pulled the trigger by accident.

It was indeed a great mystery, and one which would be the subject of many debates for generations to come.

The new-tractor-man was a young fellow, with a ready smile, and he never carried a shotgun. He had an intelligent face, and barked at the hares and other creatures good-naturedly, sometimes pretending to chase them across the field. Often he went off into a dream, for there was a faraway look in his eyes, as he ploughed the fields. A young female human used to come sometimes at mid-day, to bring him something to eat, and they would laugh and yap together, sharing the food and drink. When they parted they would touch lips, like the couple who were shot by the old-tractor-man used to do. But unlike the earlier pair, this couple did it with a sparkle in their eyes, and they waved and yelped to one another as they parted, she going over the fields to the village, and he humming along with the chugging of the hare symbol for happiness.

One or two hares remarked that their greatgrandfathers had told them stories of when the old-tractor-man had laughed and been fed and watered by a young female under the noonday sun, just as the new one was doing, but this was merely hearsay, and not taken seriously by anyone but the leverets.

Life was very good for the hares, now that the flogre had gone, and they lived it to the full. It was a world of cabbages, and carrots, rich grass and beets, swedes and turnips, and a host of other vegetables. The jills grew fat, while the jacks waited anxiously for the days to pass. Sunsets came and sunsets went, and the earth grew warm and sweet.

Chapter Forty Seven

Bubba had suffered the indignity of capture and he was mortified. Now he was in a cage, out in the garden where the nets had caught him, next to an aviary full of twittering balls of feather that others might call birds, but were like mites to him. Bubba had now resigned himself to spending the rest of his life behind wire netting.

He wondered how the tower was faring without him. And what would he do now that the tower's advice was not available? Nothing, for there was nothing *to* do, except watch and wait, and shuffle along an inadequate perch.

Bubba didn't mind the man. The man was like mother had been, gentle with him. The man had soon realised that Bubba was a special creature, an almost-man himself, had let Bubba sit on his gloved wrist, and fed him tidbits of meat. It brought back memories that had Bubba swaying on his perch and crooning to himself. He wondered if he was going to be able to stay with the man for the rest of his life, or whether he would be sent away to another place.

There were many other creatures in the house, all manner of juicy rabbits and succulent ducks, and little morsels of guinea pigs and gerbils which would go down in one swallow. Bubba eyed these creatures with some attention, wondering if he would be given any of them by the man.

There was one creature Bubba did not like, and that was the dog. The dog was big, larger even than Bubba, and it had a special place beside the man. It followed the man around as if it owned him. The dog tried to talk to Bubba, spending a long time in front of his cage, but since Bubba knew no languages he could neither understand nor answer. He wondered if the dog were threatening him, in a kind of soft silky way, telling him that if he tried to escape he would leap on him and tear him to pieces? Bubba decided this must be so, for why else would the creature bother to talk to him? Bubba did not like the dog. The dog had a flabby look about it, while Bubba was fit and lean, and Bubba was convinced that in a fight between the two of them, the dog would lose. If he ever got the chance, Bubba was going to kill the dog.

Besides the man there was another human in the house, a female of the species. Bubba had not had anything to do with women before, and only knew that when his mother had brought one home once, he was locked in the woodshed for a few hours. When he had been allowed back into the house, the woman was gone, and there was a funny smell left behind.

This woman smelled of rich orchids, the kind of scents that were locked in Bubba's memory from the land of his birth. She was soft and delicate, with skyblue eyes, and wore colourful clothes. Bubba did not like the woman. She touched the man too often, putting her arm around his shoulder as he worked, touching his hair, his cheek. Bubba did not like her caressing the man, it made him feel angry inside. If Bubba got the chance, he was going to kill the woman.

Out in the garden cage, Bubba was able to observe all life, and he noticed the new things coming over the sky, the dark shapes that looked like stiff replicas of Bubba. Bubba knew men better than hares knew men, and he knew almost immediately that these were machines fashioned by humans. They were like the machines that ran on wheels, along the black highways, except that these flew through the air. There was nothing to fear from such things, for they were only carriers of people. You could shriek threateningly at these machines, challenging them to fight, and they would do nothing but maintain a motionless silence. They were big, and looked menacing, but they would do nothing but obey the whims of men.

Bubba knew this, for lodged in his brain was a faint memory of being carried by such a thing, from there to here. He did not recall where *there* had been, but it was different from *here*, having heat and jungle and wide rivers and mountains.

Bubba's cage was high enough off the ground for him to be able to stare out over the narrow river that wound its way through the meadows at the bottom of the slope. He enjoyed just resting on his perch, with the breeze ruffling his feathers, and taking in all the small movements out in the fields, along the river, down by the stream. There was a family of narrow, sleek mammals that lived in the stream, which would have made tasty eating, had Bubba been free to indulge himself.

Besides himself there were one or two other raptors in the garden, though they were all kept well apart. There was a large owl, a hawk of some kind, and two harriers. These birds all stood, inert figures on their perches, as if they were carved from granite. Motionless, timeless as fossilised lifeforms, they regarded some unfathomable point deep in the universe with glittering eyes. Behind those eyes was a cryptic knowledge of something terribly swift, and sharp, and deadly. They shared, with Bubba, a secret knowledge of weightlessness, of swift flight, of lightning movements and meteor-fast falls from incredible heights, of rapid lancing kills. Theirs was a world of either dark brooding stillness, or bright blinding speed.

Bubba did not like these creatures with their prehensile claws and fatal eyes, and had decided he would kill one or all of them, if he got the chance.

Chapter Forty Eight

There was spawn of frogs, toads and natterjacks in the ponds, the frogspawn in clouds and that of the toads and natterjacks in strings, like the discarded black pinpoint-eyes of small birds. The sticklebacks would eat a few before they grew tails and hatched, and then carnivores like the waterboatman would sting and feast on many more. Only a very few would live to grow into adults, become giants, and take their revenge on their former persecutors.

To the hares the appearance of the spawn was just one of the numerous signs of seasonal change: nature is a clock with ten thousand hands. Eyebright was thirty-three days into her pregnancy and had only between seven and twelve days to go before the birth. She was fit and healthy, and all seemed well. Several other jills were in the same condition.

Skelter felt a deep sense of satisfaction at how things were finally turning out. Then Reacher's ghost-hare appeared to him one morning in a dream, and the sunhare knew that something momentous was about to happen. He discussed this with the other hares, that night, under the totem.

'This morning,' he explained to the others, 'I dreamed I saw my ghost-hare, running alongside a hedge. Has anyone else dreamed of their ghost-hare recently?'

There were one or two murmurs of assent: about as many as Skelter expected, for few hares were sensitive enough to *see* their guardians, even in their dreams. Many said they had *felt* the presence of something from the Otherworld while they slept.

'It's possible,' said Reacher, 'that something is about to happen to *all* of us, not just an individual. Now, we know that when our ghost-hares appear to us while we sleep, it can be a good or a bad sign. How do you all feel about this?'

Moonhare remarked, 'The flogre has gone. I expect that's what it is.'

Reacher argued, 'But that's not something that's *about* to happen. It's over and done with.'

The next to speak was Headinthemist. 'I have been consulting the wych elm twigs, and the patterns of white pebbles turned over by the plough, and everything augurs well. My own judgement is that the ghost-hares are pleased with our progress as a colony. We are about to have a birthing, of several jills and to increase our number. We are fertile. We are strong. We are increasing. Surely, this must please our ancestors?'

This was something that had not crossed Reacher's mind and he had to admit that things were going very well for them all. Perhaps the ghost-hares were giving them a sign that they were on the path to contentment, and to remain that way? After all, they had been persecuted for so long now, and at times in danger of being wiped out completely, so a peaceful future was indeed something quite momentous.

For once, Skelter agreed with Headinthemist, at least with her point about recent changes being for the good. Although he did not believe in her magic he felt she had intuitively grasped at the truth.

'I think there may be something in what Headinthemist is saying. We all dream of ghost-hares from time to time, and while I personally don't think we can interpret these dreams into anything real, I do think they come at times of change. I think that the recent changes have been to our advantage, but the concerns of the past are still lingering and causing us to dream. I wish there was someone more knowledgeable than me who could convince you of this.'

'Why don't you ask your pal the hedgehog?' said a jack sarcastically. 'I thought she was a great friend of yours, and she's supposed to know everything.'

Skelter stared at the jack before saying, 'That's a very cruel thing to say, especially since I told everyone I saw Jittie squashed on the highway.'

'Well, there's a funny thing,' said the jack, 'someone must have pumped her up again, because I saw her this morning looking like a balloon covered in pine needles.'

The jack glanced around the circle of hares, seeking approval of his witticisms, but no one commented. They were all watching Skelter, who was looking dangerous.

'You'd better be right, friend,' said the highlander slowly, 'because if you're not, we're going to have a confrontation, you and I.'

'Suits me,' said the jack, and shrugged, before going off with one of his pals to the corner of the field.

Skelter told Eyebright where he was going, made sure she was settled for the night on a good feeding ground, and set off for Jittie's old rabbit hole, fully convinced that he was going to have to return and fight the jack in the morning. As he had guessed, the rabbit hole was empty, and he set his jaw and prepared his powerful hind legs for the coming battle.

Just as he was about to take off for home, there was a rustling in the hedge, and a snout appeared. Then the rest of the creature, and it was indeed Jittie, struggled through a hole until she stood before the jack.

'Jittie!' cried Skelter. 'I thought you were dead!'

The hedgehog looked at him with an annoyed expression. 'Why should you think that? Who are you anyway?'

'Why, it's me, Skelter, the highland hare.'

Jittie snorted, blowing up dust with her rubbery nose. 'I can't be expected to remember *every* creature in the neighbourhood.'

Skelter took this blow philosophically. 'I thought we were friends. I saw your body, squashed on the highway, and believed you dead. I came to make sure.'

With these words the hedgehog's expression softened a little, and she waddled to the entrance to her nest. For a moment she busied herself with the leaves and straw inside, then turned and faced the hare. 'All right, yes, of course I know you. But I don't want to be bothered with other creatures all the time. I told you when I first met you, Skelter, that I wasn't a sociable animal. I keep myself to myself.' She stared at him fixedly for a minute, before continuing with, 'Squashed on the highway? That was Blik, an old friend of mine. I saw him too, poor old devil. He was on his last legs anyway. We all look alike to you, us hedgehogs, don't we? I expect he did it on purpose.'

'Did what on purpose?'

'Stayed out in the road, until he was run over. It's the hedgehog way of avoiding the ailments that old age brings. A road death is quick and clean, not slow and lingering, like illness.'

'Hardly *clean*.'

'Well, quick and painless then. Now what is it you want, highlander, before my patience runs out.'

Skelter explained to her about the ghost-hares, and asked if she had any ideas.

'You want me to tell you if your colony is going to be subject to any disasters?'

'Yes,' said Skelter, 'and more specifically, the kind of disasters we're likely to get.'

She shook her head. 'You're an impossible creature. There must be a list as long as this field, of potential disasters. My advice to you is wait until it comes, *if* it comes, then act on impulse. If the urge is to run, then run, if not, then freeze. What else is there to do anyway?'

'I suppose you're right, when you put it that way. The hares are not likely to vacate their territory because of a feeling. They'll need proof, which isn't available, and the omen need not be bad anyway. Maybe it is a *good* happening coming?'

At that moment there was a roar from above, and Skelter instinctively cringed as a rigid bird went overhead. It was considerably lower, here over Jittie's field, than it had been in either Whinsled Lea or Booker's Field.

When the thing had gone, he straightened up, feeling a little abashed at his behaviour. Jittie was looking at him as if he were a worm.

'Don't tell me you're frightened of aircraft?' said Jittie.

'Aircraft?'

'That's the general name for them amongst the animals. I was talking to a seagull the other day, and she was telling me that these aerial machines are quite common in other parts of the country. Humans use them like cars apparently, to get around in the sky. No end to their deviousness, is there? Human hawks. Anyway, there's a piece of land that's been flattened and concreted just west of the island, on the mainland . . .'

'I know it,' cried Skelter, 'I passed it on a bike.'

Jittie frowned and looked aggravated. 'You're not going to tell me you can ride a bicycle? I don't expect you know what a bicycle is, either.'

'No, no,' cried Skelter, 'don't be foolish. I was captured by a human in the church tower, and another human . . . well anyway, the *man* rode the bicycle, while I was perched up behind, in a cage. I saw the machines at work on the land, and a fence going up. Listen, someone told me that hedgehogs often climb those chainlink fences. You haven't been inside that place, have you?'

'Of course I have. Do you think I'm going to let something get built around here without having a good look at it? There's nothing of interest there. Just some buildings and a concrete strip where the aircraft run up and down to get enough speed to take off and come down – a bit like swans using the surface of the water. There's the fence, all the way round though, and only a few humans seem to be allowed there. I saw quite a few hares in there, on the flat grassy area surrounding the concrete.'

'Weren't the hares worried, about these *aircraft*?'

'Why should they be? They're only *things* after all, and they never leave the concrete. As long as you stay on the grass, you're safe. A bit like fields and roads. Not only that, the place is so neat and tidy your moonhare would go into ecstasies if she saw it. Straight lines, trimmed grasses, neat fences, flat as an iced-over pond, and hardly a human in sight.'

Skelter immediately began pining for his mountains at the mention of flatness and said, 'I don't see the point of going to a place like that.'

'Neither do I, that's why I didn't stay. Some of the hares seem to like the noise of the aircraft – I expect that's why they stay. Hares are peculiar creatures, you must admit.'

'Some of them,' said Skelter stiffly.

'Yes, *most* of them.'

'Matter of opinion.'

'Quite, and that's mine.'

They lapsed into silence for a while, before returning to more acceptable subjects, until Skelter finally took his leave of the hedgehog to whom he owed his life, and set off over the fields, back to the place of the totem.

When he got back to Booker's Field, Eyebright was anxiously waiting for his return.

'Was she there?'

'Yes,' replied Skelter, his mind still full of the tumbledown mountainsides, 'yes, she was there. Couldn't help us though. She said to forget all these signs and symbols, and to take things as they come. I think she's probably right. We can get as obsessive as a rabbit over such things.'

'What were you talking about all this time?' asked Eyebright, a little piqued by his long absence.

'Oh, this and that. Mainly about the aircraft – those are the rigid birds that fly overhead all the time. They're manmade things apparently. I suppose we guessed that. They carry people and things from place to place. Jittie said the area where they take off and land is fenced in – an orderly sort of place. Sounded pretty boring.'

'Has Jittie been there then?'

'Oh yes, once. She thought it was awful.'

When Skelter had satisfied her curiosity, he went and had a word with moonhare and sunhare, who were actually less concerned by the ghost-hare dreams than Skelter himself, so they needed little convincing to let things take their course. Jittie was right in any case: what could anyone do before the event? When it happened, *that* was the time to make decisions. Run or freeze. The only two hare options. Normally, it was run, and when you did so, it was blindly. That was the way of the hare.

Chapter Forty Nine

They were all sleeping in the early morning sun when it happened. One or two hares bolted immediately, without thinking or waiting to see what others were going to do. The urge to run was instinctive and there were those whose legs were moving even before they were fully conscious. Others froze for an instant, then they too began running. Skelter and Eyebright were among the last to scramble through the hedge and dash over Poggrin Meadow, past the gibbet replete with the hollow stares of eyeless moles and crows.

The reason for the panic was a terrible din to the east of Booker's Field, and it was moving towards the colony as they had been resting around the totem. There was shouting and clashing sounds and whistles and the beating of undergrowth with sticks. It sounded as if the whole human race were moving across the landscape, intent on rousing some sleeping monster buried deep in the earth.

Skelter, though hysterical, kept Eyebright in view the whole time, and stuck to her heels. Some of the pregnant jills were slow, and their jacks were having to make the agonising decision of whether to abandon them and save themselves, or remain with them despite being helpless to aid them in their flight. Skelter stayed just behind Eyebright, slowing when she slowed, and increasing his speed when she did likewise. In his head was a kind of *déjà vu* feeling which the fear would not allow him to identify. It was like a fly, buzzing around in his brain, worrying the memory-shadows there.

They ran across two more fields and past a stagnant pond surrounded by alders, before it suddenly hit him. He *had* been in this position before when he was a younger hare, and it had resulted in his exile to the flatlands. The sounds, the situation, it was a repeated pattern from the time when he had been resting on the side of a mountain and had been chased down into nets.

'Eyebright!' he yelled. 'Stop running. All of you, everyone stop running.'

His voice had such power of command at that moment that seven hares actually halted, paused for breath and stared at him with large wild eyes, the pupils dancing with hysteria. Behind them the clashing, yelling, whistling sounds continued, getting closer, but *slowly*, as if at walking pace. The nervous hares, with their twitching legs, would not wait around long to hear Skelter's speech.

'Listen everyone, I've been through this before,' said Skelter. 'We're running *into* danger, not away from it. I know what they're doing. They're chasing us into some nets. They're gathering hares for a hare coursing. If we keep on running, we'll end up in their hands.'

Just at that moment, the sound of many guns came from in front of them: *blam, blam blam, blam, blam blam blam*, sometimes a single shot, sometimes in bunches. The odour of spent cartridges wafted to them, over the shrubs, and there was a smell of blood in the air. Warning whistles came from wounded hares, and there were shrieks from others, who lay dying.

The group that had stopped listened in silence, the fear spiralling within them again.

It was Reacher who said, 'Skelter's right, but it's not a netting, it's a *shoot*, a hare shoot. My grandfather told me about hare shoots. There'll be dozens of guns out on the line. The first of the hares to bolt are going down now, under a storm of shot. They must be slaughtering us out there. This is terrible.'

Moonhare said, 'Well, never mind what's happening ahead of us, we're being pressed from behind, so what are we going to do about it?'

Eyebright snapped, 'You're the leader, *you* tell us.'

No one moved.

Eyebright said anxiously, 'They're getting closer. Look, if the beaters are to the east and the guns to the west, we only have two other options. To run south or north. Which is it to be?'

'North,' cried Reacher, and immediately took off, heading south.

The other hares followed automatically, Skelter realising at the last moment that they were going in the opposite direction to the command, but thinking *what does it matter*, so long as it was down the gap between beaters and guns.

The beaters were formed up in a crescent, and the hares ran into the tail end of the left flank of that crescent, but the men were not prepared for hares running towards them, and though there were one or two guns there, they were taken by surprise. The hares dashed between their legs, leaping high over shrubs, zig-zagging, curving, weaving, until they were all through. It was a glorious move and the hares might have appreciated it if they had not been so terrified.

There was a dog amongst the beaters who gave chase for a couple of fields, but the hares shook him off quite easily. He was a fat retriever, allowed to eat himself to a flabby state, and though he might have been good in the water, he was absolutely useless on the land. The eight hares left him far behind, his chest heaving and his eyes misty.

Fatigued, they all stopped in the corner of a foreign field, asking each other what they should do. They could hear another shoot going on further south and guessed that the marshland hares were having the same problems as themselves. Some keen hare sportsman had organised the humans this year and had them out in force. The danger was still acute, and there would be single guns wandering around on the fringes, waiting to pick off the stragglers.

'We have to get out of here,' said Longrunner, another of the escapees. 'Which way do we go?'

Moonhare visibly pulled herself together, and did what she normally did best, which was to offer leadership. She had many faults, but she did have authority, and she was not one to avoid responsibility.

'Skelter,' she said, 'what was it we were talking about two days ago? The place of the rigid birds?'

'The *aircraft*,' corrected Skelter. 'The airfield is on the mainland. I know the way. You think we ought to go there?'

'I seem to recall you mentioning the fact that it's got a fence around it, and that humans from the outside do not appear to be welcome *inside*.'

Reacher said, 'What are we waiting for . . . ?'

Even as he spoke, dust kicked up not a paw's length away from where he sat, and then the blast of a shotgun followed. Three young humans with guns were running towards them, from the far corner of the field. They had large round coloured heads, with transparent face-pieces through which their eyes glared.

The hares took off, with Skelter in the lead, and Eyebright staying close to his heels. They would have outrun the youths very quickly, except that the creatures with the guns ran back to the corner of the field, and there they climbed on motorcycles, and kicked them into life.

The machines were track bikes, and they roared across the ploughed fields as if they were merely bumpy roadways.

Skelter led his group over ditches, and through hedges, under gates, and still the motorbikes followed, jumping the ditches, crashing through the hedges. The youths seemed to be enjoying the pursuit, for they yipped and yelped, and let out raucous noises. The hares suppressed the desire to separate, and run several different ways, knowing they had to stay together to reach the new airfield.

Finally, one of the three riders was taken off by the lowhanging branch of a rather strong hawthorn, and Skelter glanced back to see him somersaulting through the air.

'Break your neck,' he whispered breathlessly.

The young man crashed to the ground in a nettle bed, and he lay still. Even before the wheel of his crashed bike had stopped spinning, he sat up and removed his helmet. The two remaining motorcyclists halted for long enough to see that their companion was not badly injured, before taking up the chase once again.

Now that the hares knew their enemy, and were no longer confronted by a hellish noise that had no shape or form, they were less terrified. The nameless dread had gone, to be replaced by a genuinely frightening but identifiable situation, and though they wished themselves elsewhere, they at least had something to bend their minds around.

They reached the causeway, and began dashing along a wet road to the mainland. The ocean was in a frenzy, on both sides of the causeway, and waves crashed around them, washing and churning through the great rocks that formed the hardcore base of the causeway. The wind was high, running through the narrow channel between the two pieces of land, and the sea was being lashed into a state of anarchy. It sent up tall nebulous growths, which fell slapping onto the roadway, spraying the hares as they ran. Their coats sparkled with salt water, and their eyes stung them, but not a hare paused in flight. They had to run the gauntlet of the white arcing waves, if they were to reach safety.

Now that the motorbikes were on a flat smooth surface, they were more easily handled and could be driven much faster, but the riders needed to keep both hands on their grips in order to steer their machines, due to the state of the sea. They could not afford to ride one-handed and use their guns.

Suddenly one of the hares was swept away by a larger than normal wave thundering over the causeway. It was the jack Fleetofoot. He was dragged by the wash of the giant wave, into the booming ocean. The last the other hares saw of him, he was attempting to swim through mountainous seas towards the beach.

A motorbike too, came to grief, when its front wheel skidded on a wet patch of road, and the bike went from under the rider. Both machine and man went spinning crazily through the running hares, the metal showering sparks, and actually ending up some distance in front of them, but the rider was too shaken to take advantage of the situation. He sat up and dazedly inspected his leathers, worn to the skin at the elbows and knees, the waves breaking over the roadside rocks and drenching him with spray.

The hares zig-zagged around him as he finally looked around for his gun which had gone spinning on ahead. Skelter leapt over the weapon, as it lay gleaming wetly from the spray of the spume that leapt and danced around the causeway. The second rider paused for his friend, and helped him onto his machine, which gave the hares time to reach the mainland. Then the chase was on again, over the fields, through the woods.

The hares weaved between the trees. The motorcycles weaved between the trees. Rabbits out for feeding scrambled for their burrows, yelling at each other that they were under attack from hares and humans. The bikes roared and coughed, throwing divots at the trees, churning the moss and grass with their thickly treaded tyres, their slewing acrobatics. For a time, as the hares and rabbits mingled, everyone was confused – then the rabbits were gone, down their holes, and the hares would liked to have followed but the instinct was to keep running on the flat, and in any case the rabbit holes were full of retreating rabbits.

The motorcyclists barked at the hares, as they chased them over the fields, not in anger or frustration, but with the sheer exuberance of the chase. It seemed the shotguns had been forgotten, and it was now a case of the bikers trying to run down the hares. The hares had less speed, but more acceleration and manoeuvrability. The smaller creatures could turn on a blade of grass, while the bikes took a much larger turning circle. The hares bucked, leapt, telemarked, rotated, skidded, jumped and somersaulted in their efforts to avoid the machines, and the meadow was churned to mire.

Finally the hares broke away and continued their journey towards the airfield, managing to traverse a wide ditch near a pond. Their destination was now in sight, for they could see a windsock flying in the distance. Soon a tall green-glassed building came into view.

One of the motorcyclists took a run at the ditch, to get his machine to leap across, but failed. His front wheel struck the far bank of the channel, and sent him flying through the air to land in the pond. Scum and spray showered the hares as they scampered past the pond, out into a field of cabbages, neither amazed or concerned by the flight of the human, for they were too intent on escape. A green chickweed monster crawled coughing and spluttering from the slime-covered pond.

The third and last rider, having seen his two friends come to grief, seemed determined to get at least one of the hares. He took the ditch slowly, rolling his machine down and up while out of the saddle. When he mounted on the far side, the hares were some two hundred yards from the airfield fence, and tiring rapidly. The creatures had had a long run, and they were exhausted, and close to dropping.

The final machine and rider went hurtling across the field, sending cabbages like severed green heads splattering this way and that, fountains of mud arcing from the rear wheel. He stopped and jumped off his bike just thirty yards from the fence, and unslung his weapon from his back. The youth was now between the hares and the chainlink fence. They veered away from him, some of them stumbling in their fatigue.

His shotgun was an old .410 with a three-penny bit single barrel, and an external hammer which he cocked with his thumb. It was a short range weapon, nowhere near as powerful as the mighty 12-bore the tractor-man had owned, and the youth had enough sense to wait until the hares were almost in line with him, to the east of his position. He aimed the shotgun at the hares, but probably made the mistake of the amateur hunter, in not picking a specific target. No doubt he was excited, and the several hares presented a confusing group, and so he fired into the middle of running prey.

An innocent bystanding cabbage was blasted to smithereens, wet bits of green showering the area, some pieces landing on the backs of the fleeing hares.

The youth broke the smoking weapon, ejected the spent shell, and fumbled in his pocket for another cartridge.

Skelter began running alongside the fence, away from the danger area, looking for a suitable place to dig. His lungs were almost bursting, and his legs felt as if they belonged to someone else.

Finally, he found a patch where the earth was soft and began frantically to scrape out the soil. Almost at once he had a tunnel big enough to scramble underneath.

One by one the hares bolted down the hole he had dug, until all of them were on the other side of the fence. The youth came running alongside the fence, inserting his second cartridge, his face a mask of determination. They could see he wanted to shoot a hare, even if it meant that he would have to leave it to die on the far side of the barrier.

The shotgun was fired again, and this time many pellets struck the wire fence, pinging off in all directions. Several hares, including Followme and Reacher, felt sharp stings as small round pieces of lead penetrated rumps and thighs. With their energy flagging, the hares made one last effort, and dashed across the neatly trimmed airfield, to where a man was riding a sit-on mower across the perfectly flat grasslands.

When the hares scampered past the mower, the man stopped his noisy machine, and turned to see the dome-headed youth with the gun. He shook his fist in the boy's direction, and the would-be hunter was soon on his bike, and roaring across the field of cabbages, sending the roundheads flying again.

The mower-man stood by his bright green machine, as it idled and chuntered, his hands on his hips. He watched the youth disappear into the ditch on the far side of the cabbage field, and then he shrugged, and climbed back onto his mower.

The hares were resting not far off, some of them licking their superficial wounds. The man regarded them for a while, and then showed his teeth the way humans did when they felt good, and started his mower rolling again. The hares watched as needles of grass filled the air in clouds, and the smell of newly-mown meadowland mingled with other pleasant odours of the morning.

The hares had their new symbol of happiness, a green machine that chuntered and chattered.

The tractor-man was dead, long live the mower-man!

Late in the evening another bedraggled hare arrived at the airfield. It was an exhausted Fleetofoot. He had been washed up on the beach, half-drowned, and had crawled to the dunes. There he had lain, all the rest of the day, recovering from his ordeal. He still felt sick and dizzy, and it was doubtful if he would feel better for days.

'I swallowed so much of that stuff, I never want another drink. It tasted *awful*. My mouth is terrible, even now. I ran out of energy, but a big wave took me and threw me up the beach, where I lay in the wash for a while, until I could summon the strength to crawl. I thought I was dying. If a fox had come along, well, that would have been it, but the sound of the guns must have kept them in their earths today. Anyway, here I am, what's left of me.'

His coat looked awful, covered in dry salt, and he could hardly see through his stinging eyes.

But he was alive, which was more than could be said of the rest of the colony, back on the island.

Skelter fussed over Eyebright, hoping against hope that the terror of the day, and the subsequent flight, had not hurt the leverets in her womb. Eyebright was resting now, but she told him not to expect too much, for she knew the leverets were not in good condition. Some of them, she was sure, had not survived the run, but they had to wait to discover whether any at all would be born alive.

Skelter, never a good waiter, wore out large patches of the airfield with his nervous energy, before the birth.

Chapter Fifty

Only one of Eyebright's leverets was born alive. This hybrid, a jill, she named Scootie. Skelter thought she was the most beautiful leveret that had ever entered the world, and hardly stopped talking about her for a minute during the first few days of her life on earth. Eyebright had to tell him that he was boring all the other hares in the end, and that though she agreed with him, they had better just talk about Scootie between the two of them for a while.

Skelter was surprised and said he couldn't see how anyone could possibly be bored with the subject of his leveret. However he quietly accepted Eyebright's advice. She was usually right about the field hares, though Skelter considered them a strange bunch of lagomorphs, and certainly poor judges of beauty in the young. If he were one of them, he told Eyebright, he would find Scootie just as attractive as he did, and would want to know everything about her. She was after all an extraordinary creature. Eyebright nodded and said of course he would.

Life on the airfield was noisy but safe, with humans going about their business, not bothering the hares in the slightest. They worked in, on and around the aircraft, though they occasionally pointed out the hares to one another, for there were over a hundred of them, and more coming each day.

The hares gathered on the short grass of the land on either side of the runways and watched the mighty aircraft taking off and landing, until they were used to them and lost interest. The roaring of these great metal birds lost its excitement after a while, though the hares never failed to enjoy the man-made thunder.

For the brown hares, the scenery was perfect. Straight lines everywhere, cultivated fields just beyond the perimeter fence, manicured grasslands mowed in dark and light stripes. It was Otherworld on earth. The tractor-man had indeed been replaced by the mower-man, his green machine becoming the symbol for hare happiness. The great hangar of hangars, the largest structure in the universe, became the hare symbol for health, taking over from the big red barn. They mourned the loss of the five-barred gate, and chose instead for the symbol of longevity the glass tower, about and within which the humans buzzed and bustled in frantic activity, yet the green-tinted glass remained unruffled, all-seeing, unaffected. It just *was*, and always would be, which was right for a symbol of longevity. As for the symbol of fertility, nothing was able to replace the many-eared corn, and this remained as it was, for fortunately the airfield was surrounded by fields of wheat, barley and oats.

To Skelter, the flatlands were much the same as those he had left behind on the island. Nothing would ever be able to touch his rugged mountains for beauty and splendour, and even if he had to live in a sanitised society of brown hares, he did not have to accept their cultural ideas of harmony. He dreamed, as always, of his heather-cloaked hills and glens, of the glint of moonstones and garnets in the burns, of the shining lochs, of the crofts wafting peat smoke from their turved roofs, of the sedge, the ptarmigan, the red deer in all its highland glory, the distant stone castles on impossible peaks, the gnarled and bearded shepherds with their archaic staves, of ancient rusting claymores and dirks beneath hillside stones, of the cairns, of the wildcat and the eagle. Eyebright, suckling Scootie, would listen patiently as he tried to explain to her what his homeland was like, and her eyes grew hazy and sad when she realised how much he missed it. She wanted to replace that void in him with something else, but of course, that was impossible. Once a highlander, never anything else, and though the flatlands surrounded his body, his soul would always be in the mountains, drifting with the mist amongst the heather.

Three days after the hares had established themselves on the airfield, Jittie came to visit Skelter and Eyebright. She admired Scootie for as long as was hedgehog possible, which was for at least two seconds, before going on to describe the events that occurred on the island after the hares had departed. There had indeed been a slaughter, though the hares were not wiped out by any means, and even some of moonhare's colony had survived and still gathered under the totem in Booker's field.

371

'It was a noisy day, that's for sure,' said Jittie, 'and a bloody one for the lagomorphs. They brought in terriers afterwards, for the rabbits, and a lot of them lost their lives. Later, Bess's man came and barked at the hunters, especially when the badgers were being disturbed by the terriers.'

'But you got away all right?' said Skelter.

'Pooh, who wants to kill a hedgehog? The only way they get us, is with their infernal cars, on the highway, and that's not on purpose, I'm positive of that.'

'I've heard that gypsies cook hedgehogs in clay, so that when they're baked and peeled, the bristles come out embedded in the hard clay,' said Eyebright, shifting her position for the restless Scootie.

'Might have been true in the old days,' said Jittie, 'but not now. Gypsies want to eat the same food as all the humans. They'll take a chicken, pheasant, hare or rabbit, but I've not heard of them eating hedgehogs, not lately.'

'Anyway,' said Skelter, 'we're fairly safe here, behind the fence. Of course, we have to stay off the concrete strips, or we'd get flattened like . . . like hedgehogs on a highway. It didn't take long to learn that. No reason to go on them anyway, really, except to get to the other side.'

'Yes, you seem to have come out of it all pretty well. I don't suppose your moonhare is very pleased, having her colony stripped down to seven or eight members?'

'She's getting old anyway,' Eyebright said. 'I think she'll be ready to step down soon. I don't want to take over myself, but I have hopes for this little one, someday. She'll make a good moonhare . . .'

Skelter exchanged a look with Jittie. Both of them knew that the brown hares would never accept a hybrid as a leader, but there was no need to say anything to Eyebright. Skelter was sure that once the newness of the recent birth wore off any great ambitions Eyebright had for Scootie could be modified, and compromises sought. As far as he was concerned, his leveret was better off just being an ordinary member of the colony, and letting others take the responsibility of leadership, whenever it was necessary.

Jittie left them once the morning came and set out for her home.

372

That night a spring storm swept across the airfield, and drove rain into the ground like nails. Now that the flogre was no longer a threat, the brown hares did not dig blue hare forms, but had gone back to their old method of a scraping on the surface. The only one who still dug a U-shaped hole was Skelter himself and as he watched the others being hammered by the hard raindrops from under his little roof of turf, he felt a little superior.

Bubba guessed they were going to move him somewhere, because the man kept coming out to his cage and staring at him. He was glad, because he hated the cage. Mother had never kept him behind wire or bars. It was the first time in his life that he had been imprisoned in anything smaller than a house, and he loathed it to the core of his being. He would rather die than remain in such a place.

When the two new men came with another cage, Bubba was sure. Still, he did not see why he should be compliant, even if it meant that he was being moved, so when they put the cages together, and opened both doors, he remained firmly gripping his perch. The men spent a long time trying to persuade him to go from one cage to another, and the more they tried, the more he resisted. When they gave up and went for a drink, then he calmly climbed from his perch and transferred his great bulk from one cage to the other. Bubba enjoyed the way they barked at each other when they returned.

The door to the new cage was closed and locked by one of the two new men. This second cage was a lot lighter and flimsier than the one the hairy-faced man had kept him in. It was a cage for transporting things by air. Bubba had been in one of these cages a long time ago, when mother took him from the dark steamy forests and brought him to this land of rabbits and hares.

Was he going to travel again by air?

How strange that had been, to fly without the use of his wings. Although he had been in a drugged state at the time, he had been aware that he was flying. A bird knows when he is in the sky, above the turning globe: he feels it in his every nerve and fibre. The sensation of flying is an experience of the soul, as well as the body.

He hoped they were going to take him back to the place of huge trees and great rivers. That would be fine. He had eaten everything around here. The forest would be well stocked, with those hairy creatures that looked like men, but had tails and swung from the trees. Of late his dreams of this far off land were becoming clearer, less distant.

His cage went up on the back of a truck, and then they were off, travelling on the road, the harsh sound of the engine in his ears. He watched the countryside sweep past, the hedges and fields flowing the other way, faster than they did when he was aloft and cruising on the thermals. Soon the cottage was far behind him, and he had left the silky dog, the sleek creatures by the stream, the hawks and harriers without having had the opportunity to kill just one of them. This was his only regret, that he had not left them all for dead.

Skelter had slept in the sun for two hours after a night of feeding on the new shoots of corn. He felt dissipated. When the sun became too hot to remain in his form, he came out and checked on Eyebright and Scootie. They were fast asleep, curled up together in the scraped out form that his mate preferred, and he left them there, a warm feeling in his stomach.

There were other hares, other insomniacs, walking around the place, nibbling at this and that. Skelter was not in a nibbling mood, and hare-walked to the edge of the runway to feel the down-draft of the aircraft running through his fur as they took off. It was probably a dangerous occupation, but all the hares did it. It was then he noticed something on the far side of the concrete strip, and his fur prickled. He wondered whether to cross and get a closer look, but that was *definitely* too dangerous and he was not into foolishness, having barely escaped death in various forms during his time.

What he had seen were some bags of white crystals, one of which had broken open and was spilling onto the ground. Skelter knew this to be man-food, for the female human at the cottage had once given him a cube of that stuff, one of which she also put in her hot drink. It had been a delicious experience. Skelter had never tasted anything so sweet in all his life. He would really like to taste that stuff again!

In the end, he resisted the urge, knowing that the aircraft were taking off and landing all the time, and those giant wheels were large enough to squash a pig, let alone a hare. The sweet white crystals would have to remain where they were, and Skelter would make do with a certain kind of beet, which had a faint taste of the same substance. Should he go out into the fields and look for some? In truth, he told himself, he couldn't be bothered going anywhere. He was in one of those apathetic moods, whereby he wanted to do nothing except sit and scratch his clipped ear.

The fields drifted by Bubba, as the vehicle rumbled on towards the airfield. Bubba could see the great metal birds lifting off the distant concrete, and knew how the people inside were feeling. Some would be afraid, but most would be feeling exhilaration, the wonderful sensation of flight. How terrible it would be if Bubba were ever robbed of this ability to fly. He suddenly had a terrible thought. What if he were not being sent to the place of hot jungles? What if they were taking him somewhere else, to put him in another cage? When mother had been alive he had shown Bubba to other humans and had witnessed their amazement. Humans were intrigued by Bubba, found him fascinating. What if these two men with the truck were taking him to some place where men would put him in a cage, not knowing he was part man himself, and leave him there for the rest of his life, to be stared at by a passing line of people?

He shuddered. The thought was too horrible to contemplate. Of course he would rather die.

But why was he thinking this way? He was going to be taken in a metal bird, and the metal birds flew between the jungles and the flatlands. The journey had already been made once, by Bubba himself, so he knew this to be fact. He surely did not need to punish himself with these horrible nightmares.

Up in the sky, above a field, a kestrel hovered. Bubba watched it drop like a red star from the heavens and hit something in the grasses, some small creature that wriggled for an instant, and then went limp and still in its talons, terror having stopped its heart. The kestrel lifted itself on its powerful wings, rising up into the vast blueness of the world of birds, into cloudland, and the seas

375

of high winds. Bubba envied the kestrel, wanting to be out there himself. Bubba could have done to the kestrel what the kestrel had done to the small mammal.

Skelter did not even feel like passing the time of day with the other hares, and went to the far end of the runway where the vehicles were rumbling along, pulling flat carts of leather boxes, sacks and other paraphernalia around, to load into the belly of the aircraft. It was interesting, but not *that* interesting, so he lay with his head on his paws and watched the activity with only half an eye.

Bubba felt the truck pull to a halt. There were a lot of humans around this place. They were hurrying here and there, carrying things, most of them in their finery. Vehicles of all kinds were being parked, driven away, unloaded, loaded. Bubba knew that it was time to be taken off the truck himself. He felt the excitement surge through his breast. He was going to fly, without using his wings!

The cage was lifted off the back of the truck and put on a flat cart to be taken out to a metal bird. Bubba studied the landscape with sharp eyes, noting that there were lots of hares out on the short grass. If he were free now, they would not be gambolling around in such a carefree fashion.

A vehicle was hooked up to the cart and began to pull it along, making the cage sway, and Bubba rocked inside it. He was not afraid, he told himself, just a little excited. He was going on a long journey, to another land . . .

At that moment he saw the hare, the *magical* hare, lying by the side of the concrete strip, staring right at him. His mood changed instantly. No longer was he the passive creature, ready to be flown away in one of man's metal birds. He was incensed, outraged, infuriated.

Something snapped inside his head. This was humiliating beyond all words. This was impossible to endure. The hare that had caused him so much trouble, had been starved to death, yet had risen again to torment the lord of the flatlands, was here to gloat over Bubba's incarceration, over his deportation. It was monstrous.

The anger flared inside the great bird, until it was a raging fire, and he knew that if it was the last thing he ever did, he had to tear that hare asunder. Let it come back from the dead then, to show its smug features to the world! Let it piece itself together, when its bones lay in regurgitated fragments! Let it reincarnate itself, from inside Bubba's belly!

Bubba flung himself at the door of the cage, smashing his body against the network of metal. He went berserk, throwing himself this way and that, rocking the cage back and forth.

The man on the vehicle began to get alarmed, but instead of stopping, he speeded up, probably hoping to get the cage off his hands that much sooner.

Skelter was suddenly wide awake as his brain sent jangling messages to his feet, *run, run, run*. The flogre was *here*, on their safe airfield. Not only was it here, it was going mad inside its cage, and seemed determined to get out. Skelter knew he had been seen by the creature. Their eyes had locked, and the recognition on both sides had been simultaneous.

Nevertheless, he did not run, for there was nowhere to hide. The airfield was as flat and open as an iced-over lake. He just had to hope that the terrible raptor did not burst out of the cage.

He remained frozen by the sight of the creature that seemed to hate him so much. It was some while since he had seen the great bird last, and it seemed to have grown since then. Its bulk covered half the cart that was carrying it. Skelter could see it smashing its heavy beak against the door of the cage, using it like a claw-hammer to break out of its temporary prison. Surely it would succeed soon? The bird of prey was immensely strong. Skelter had seen it snip telephone wires with its beak.

The cart began to go faster, and the cage swayed and rocked with the motion, until the inevitable happened. Bird and cage toppled from the speeding cart to crash on the concrete. The door to the cage broke open on impact with the peritrack, and the great flogre struggled through the hole, and was free.

*　　*　　*

Bubba shrieked in triumph as he took to the air, the wind rushing through his feathers.

Now was the time of the raptor! *Now* was the time of the hunter! *Now* was the final end of the magical hare.

High he flew at first, to feel the force of the sky in his bones. It had been so long. The power flooded into his wings, into his body, into his legs. His talons were hooks of iron: his beak was a curve of steel. In the spiral of his eye was the hare, far below, frozen in fear. Bubba would fall on that hare like the sun dropping out of the heavens.

Nothing on the earth could withstand the force of Bubba, the greatest bird of prey in the world, the largest raptor on the face of the sky, anywhere. He was the king of death, the mightiest flier, the terrible vengeance of the sky upon the earth. His was the heart of stone that dropped upon the running kind, and scooped them helplessly up in gin-trap claws. He was the scourge of the mammal caught in flight, its own heart beating fear into its brain.

He screamed again in triumph, and the wind screamed with him as he stooped to kill.

Skelter could not move. His heart had all but died. His brain was alive, but with nothing but terror. That he was about to be killed was certain, for there was no hiding place. His only hope was that the flogre would choose some other hare, some other poor creature, on which to descend. That would not happen, for he knew he was the goal, the target of the flogre's hatred.

He watched the bird climb on its short but powerful wings, a great mottled creature that was king of the dome. It became a speck against the clouds and for a moment the highland hare lost it against the backdrop of blue, then it appeared again, growing rapidly larger by the second.

It was then he found enough vitality in his body to run, and run he did, out onto the concrete strip, careless of any wheels that might descend and crush him to paste.

*　*　*

Bubba saw the hare start to life, dash out onto the runway, and knew that he had him. There was nowhere for the creature to go. It was a stark target on the flatness of the concrete, and could be whisked away in an instant. The talons itched to tear flesh. The beak was primed to pierce pelt. The landscape was a whirlpool, of which the hare was the centre, and red-eyed Bubba was the descending slayer. All else was a fog, a mist, scarlet before the eyes. There was only the hunter and the prey, and this spiralling madness of a lust to kill.

There was a noise, a roar, and unexpectedly another great bird stooped to kill, snatching Bubba out of the sky like a hawk on the wind takes a sparrow. The hunter had become the quarry, the circle fused, the cycle complete.

Bubba, intent on the hare, never saw the giant bird.

Then he was gone, a fluff of feathers on the wind.

At the last instant, Skelter looked up, saw the two shadows merge, the one swallowing the other. A great bird had come, a bird a thousand times bigger than the flogre, and had taken it in a single mouthful. The flogre had been there one moment, a menace with death in its eyes, and the next second it was nothing. There was a kind of muted *phuuut* sound, as the metal bird sucked the predator into one of its four mouths. Then down began falling like flakes of light snow.

Skelter stood and shivered as he watched the aircraft that had eaten the flogre land further down the runway. Then he heard someone calling his name, and realised that Eyebright was there, on the grass verge. She was telling him to get off the runway, or he would be squashed. It's dangerous out there, she called, what on earth was he doing?

Skelter ran from that place, onto the trimmed grasslands, knowing that Eyebright and all the other hares were unaware of the drama that had been taking place on the runway. Skelter followed Eyebright back to her form, where she had left Scootie unattended. He found his leveret waiting for them, her large eyes brimming with concern.

Eyebright was angry that she had had to go looking for Skelter, who asked in the end, quite reasonably, 'Why did you?'

She stopped complaining then, and stared at him for a moment, before saying, 'I don't know.'

'I go off all the time,' said Skelter, 'and so do you. I might have been out in the fields, feeding. What made you so anxious this time?'

She shook her head vigorously.

'I don't know. I don't know. I just ... something made me worry, about us, as a family. It doesn't matter now. The feeling's gone. We're safe – aren't we?'

'As safe as we'll ever be. There are always the foxes, but then, there always have been.'

'Yes,' she said, 'as safe as we'll ever be.'

Skelter, like some fathers and mates, sensed this without really understanding it. So he said nothing about the flogre, not wishing to raise terrors in the young, who knew nothing of such things. So far as Eyebright was concerned, the flogre had gone some time ago, and was almost forgotten. Why cause the air to buzz with it anew, creating nightmares for his leveret? Why fashion a ghoul out of a handful of feathers floating on the breeze? Let them fall to the ground, be swallowed by the dust, become part of the earth.

The flogre was dead, long live the hares.

Afterword

This short afterword is for those readers curious as to the identity and origins of Bubba. He is in fact a harpy eagle with a metre-long body: the largest eagle in the world. His natural home is tropical South America. His normal diet, in the rain forests, would include monkeys, sloths, opossums and parrots. Harpy eagles usually live beneath the rain forest canopy, rarely venturing above, but Bubba had to adapt himself to the environment to which he was brought by the man who captured him as a chick.